THE ALPHA EXPEDITION

PROJECT SIRIUS
BOOK 2

Jon Wasik

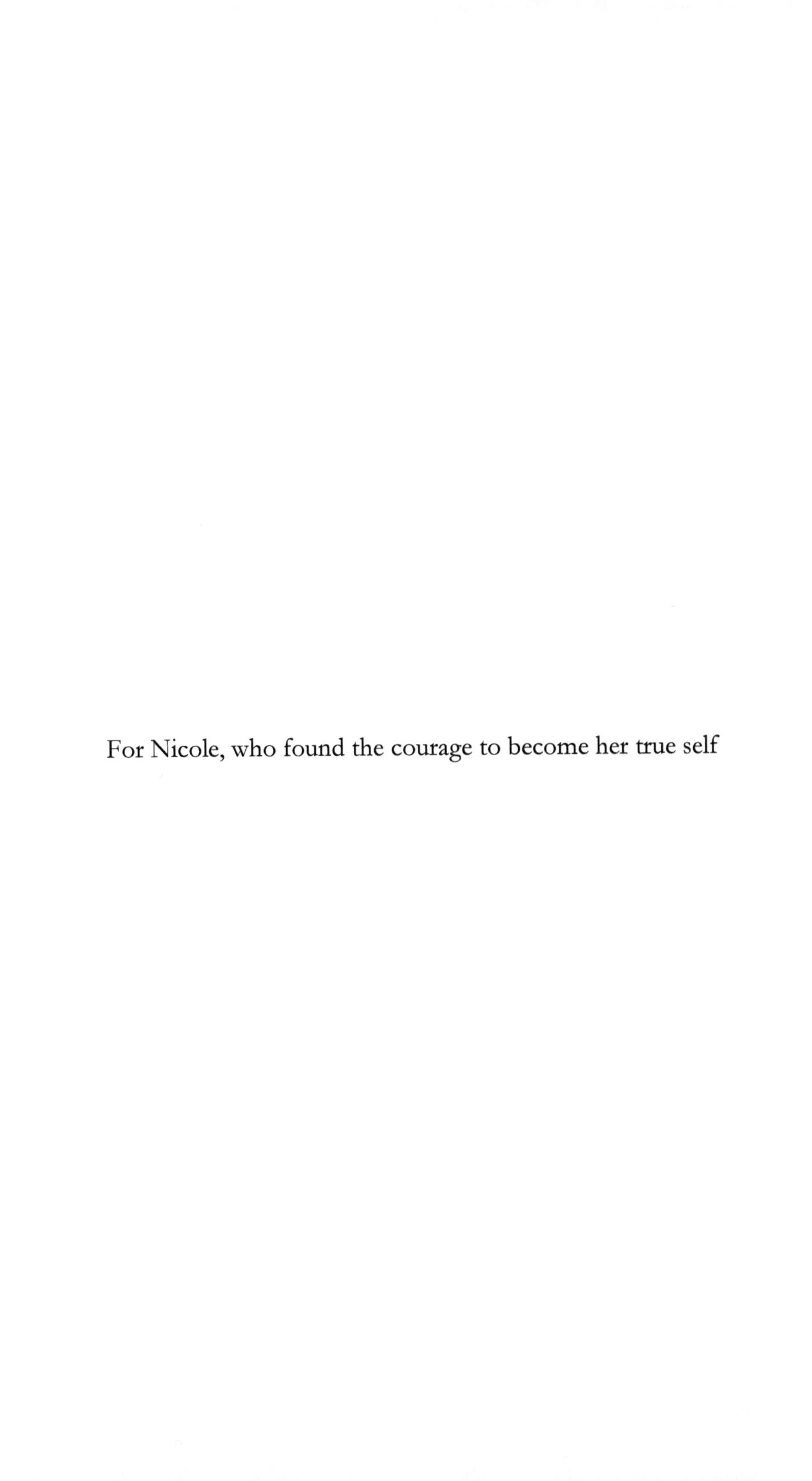

For Nicole, who found the courage to become her true self

Also by Jon Wasik

The Sword of Dragons *(Reading Order)*
1. *Rise of the Forgotten*
1.5. *The Orc War Campaigns*
2. *Burning Skies*
3. *Secrets of the Cronal*
4. *Advent Darkness*

Chronicles of the Sentinels Trilogy
1. *Legacy*
2. *Retribution*
3. *Champions*

Project Sirius
1. *The Awakening*
2. *The Alpha Expedition*

ACKNOWLEDGMENTS

Project Sirius has been a passion project for so many years, and *The Alpha Expedition* owes its existence to far more than just my imagination.

As always, the first credit must go to Beck, my Starshine, my muse. Even when I wanted to give up on myself, they never gave up on me, and they pushed and nudged and encouraged me to write a story that was true to my heart.

Thank you also to all of my beta readers, Nicole, Natalie, Wayne, and Caroline!

Thank you to all of my Facebook, Instagram, and blog followers for enduring my social media ineptness! I struggle with it to this day, but for those who have stayed with me, I appreciate your dedication!

And though I have already mentioned her more than once, I must once again say thank you to my oldest and dearest friend, Nicole. She has always been there for me to bounce ideas off of, to work plot holes out with, and to keep me sane while I invent whole new worlds.

THE ALPHA EXPEDITION

My name is Mika Kai, and I'm the smartest person in Rhea.

I know, bold claim, isn't it? But trust me, in a town of five thousand people living in a medieval-style fantasy world, no one else knows as much as I do. It helps that a few days before this story begins, a neural-networked A.I. controlling a starship 8 kilometers long uploaded a bunch of information into my brain.

Knowledge of engineering, physics, chemistry, basic human physiology, and so much more, was forcefully shoved into my head so that I could fix the ship and, consequently, save Rhea. Which, by the way, was built inside of a dome aboard that massive starship.

When magic failed, when the Oracle fell silent, and winter didn't end, our king sent me and five others out into the wilderness, betraying the Oracle's highest law of 'no one leaves Rhea, ever.'

What we found was the truth.

What we found was the starship *Sirius*, battered and broken, and an alien intruder in an exosuit stalking the halls, destroying or rerouting power sources so it could signal its friends.

We stopped it. We saved the ship, and all of Rhea.

But at considerable cost.

You might think the journey ended there, but oh no, dear readers. Believe me, we've barely scratched the surface. Life certainly didn't get easier for us. It *certainly* didn't get easier for me.

The adventure has just begun.

– PART 1 –
CONSEQUENCES

ONE

For the third day in a row, I woke up in one of the *Sirius's* observation lounges, spread out across a bunch of couch cushions that Karina and I had laid out on the floor in front of the window. *The* window. The same one we came across five days ago when we first stumbled into the corridors of the *Sirius*. A huge, single piece of glass, over two hundred feet in width, and giving off almost no reflection.

It provided me with the most incredible, starry view in all the Universe. I opened my dark eyes and smiled, drinking it all in. Billions of tiny pinpricks, mixed into a band of blues and whites and purples and oranges and so *many* colors.

The Milky Way Galaxy. *Our* galaxy. I'd learned about it, what it was and where we were in it, when I checked our position in our current star system three days ago. Normally, when the *Sirius* jumped into a new system, she came in on the edge and would drift at a relatively high speed on a course to pass near to the star. As we traveled closer, temperatures in the dome, in Rhea, would go up, starting Spring and leading into Summer.

But we'd drifted into winter longer than normal, and with people nearly frozen to death in Rhea, I'd known that we didn't have time to be subtle. I'd asked the ship's Neural-Networked Artificial Intelligence Apparatus, Naia, to change course to bring us in closer, to warm up the dome faster. She'd complied.

Since then, after a short two-day visit back to Rhea, my girl Karina and I had roamed the ship, repairing damaged systems and restoring damaged service repair units known as S.A.R.U.'s.

And every morning, we woke up to the rising of the *galaxy!*

Except…Karina wasn't there this morning.

We slept next to one another. I know, how *outrageous*. Especially considering same-sex relationships are outlawed in Rhea. I was used to waking up and either finding her baby-blue eyes gazing into mine, or a mess of tangled carrot-red hair in my face.

I sat up, pushing the covers off (taken from the medical bay, and sooooo much softer and nicer than wool!), and I looked around. "Karina?" I croaked through a dry throat.

My black hair fell around my face like stringy drapes, and I tried to blow some of it away before I grumpily shoved loose strands behind my ears. I couldn't see her anywhere, but considering we had all but the emergency lights shut off for sleeping, that was no surprise. "Naia, lights up, please."

Every light in the ceiling came alive. I winced and narrowed my eyes, waiting impatiently for them to adjust. I stumbled off the assembled cushions and stood up, stretching out.

It was nice not to have to worry about others seeing me – with heating and general life support aboard the *Sirius* restored, we usually slept in our underwear and shirts.

Scandalous! Is that what you're thinking? Well when we came back from Rhea, I'd not thought to pack warm-weather clothes, and neither had Karina, and the *only* clothes that seemed to be lying around the ship were maintenance coveralls.

There was some sheepishness about it that first night, a lot of flushed cheeks and nervous giggles, but it'd been a long day, and we practically passed out minutes after going to bed.

No, nothing heated happened.

Unfortunately.

When my eyes finally stopped hurting and I'd rubbed the crusties out, I looked around again and called out, "Karina?"

A voice from everywhere replied, "Karina Ticho is in the nearest restroom." Naia, ever-helpful, ever-watchful. I shuddered, but I didn't bother to cover up, despite the creepy sensation I got every time I realized she could literally see us anywhere we went. Well, almost anywhere.

It was the only reason Karina and I hadn't, um…explored being together more. We didn't feel comfortable under Naia's watchful cameras.

That was why I was anxious to get to the front of the ship sooner rather than later. There were crew quarters at the bow, and they didn't have cameras in them, or so Naia had helpfully explained to us. Something about privacy laws, a rather novel concept for us.

The bathrooms, or 'restrooms' as Naia called them, didn't have cameras either, but that wasn't exactly the most romantic place in the world. So we waited.

I hated waiting for this.

Hellfire, I hated *waiting,* period.

I glanced again at the galactic arm and smiled. Even without Karina, it was still a gorgeous sight to behold. I stepped closer to the window, stretching again as I went and letting out all sorts of bizarre, inhuman noises.

The dome in Rhea simulated atmosphere, which turned our sky blue during the day, and at night, it occluded some stars and made the visible ones twinkle. Here, with virtually nothing between me and the vacuum of space, those infinitely tiny points of light shone steady and true, and somehow I found comfort in that.

And then I heard that gorgeous voice. "Hey, you," Karina spoke softly.

I jumped and eeped, not having heard her approach, and I spun around to see her only a few feet behind me. A broad smile stretched across my face, and I swooped into her arms and lifted her up in a hug, twirling around halfway before I set her down and planted a kiss on her mouth. She giggled through the kiss before kissing me back.

"Good morning, gorgeous," I whispered, setting my forehead against hers.

Karina had already dressed for the day, and it was a bitter reminder of what was in store for us. Since we'd left Rhea, we'd mostly worn navy-blue clothing I now knew to be called maintenance jumpsuits or overalls, with vests and harnesses over them to carry tools and other necessary implements around the aft end of the ship. There was always too much I needed, so Karina helpfully carried half the load, and even though she didn't have a clue how to fix anything technological, she had been so incredibly helpful to me.

Today, however, we were going to have to put our Rhea-made clothes back on. For Karina, that meant hand-made boots made from the leather of cows, grey wooly trousers, and a tan wooly shirt, not to mention she would later don her thick jacket and cloak, since we weren't sure how warm it'd grown in the dome. I had similar clothes

I'd be putting on today.

We had promised everyone that we would return to Rhea after only a few days. Not just to see friends and family again, but to also attend to a somber duty.

Thelon's funeral.

The guardsman who had joined us on our expedition to save the town. Who had sacrificed himself to protect me.

Who was dead because I panicked and shot his shield, disabling it and giving that monster a clean shot at him.

I blinked away the memories as best I could, but my face must have betrayed my thoughts. Karina drew me in closer, wrapped her arms around me, and held on tight. I blinked through tears and stared back out into the infinite abyss.

I wasn't one to wallow in self-pity for long. Or at least that's what I told myself. So I tried to think of something to get my mind off of the impending gloomy day. I didn't have to look far, relatively speaking. Something caught my attention through the window, and after sniffing back some tears, I frowned. "What's that?"

Karina's shoulders deflated, and she pulled back to try to look into my eyes. "Mika," she started to lecture – she had brought up Thelon every day since we'd come out here, insisting that I needed to talk about it.

I looked past her, though, and tried to get her to look out the window with me. She gave me a skeptical look, but complied, and followed my finger as I pointed out to the far, far right.

Barely visible from our line of sight was a star, except…it wasn't a star. It was a lot larger, and a lot *brighter* than the surrounding stars.

"Woh!" she exclaimed and drew me to the window, where we plastered our faces against it to get a better look. "Naia, what is that?"

"I am sorry, Karina Ticho," Naia replied, relatively dispassionately. "You will have to be more precise in your inquiry."

"Uh, port-side," I helpfully said, thinking about where we were on the ship. We were at the far left, or port side of the ship, and this part I knew looked out at a bearing of about 2-1-0, so not perfectly left but looking back from left. "Not sure on the exact bearing, but definitely not on our bow. A bright sphere that I swear I don't remember seeing yesterday morning."

There was a momentary pause, and I wondered if her pauses were a programmed response for dramatic effect, or if some of her quantum processor nodes were damaged. Finally, she said, "I believe you are seeing a planet that we are approaching."

I blinked and looked up at the ceiling, a habit I just couldn't seem to break when speaking to Naia. "A planet? I don't remember ever reading in our records about approaching planets before, or anything like this being recorded in Rhea's chronicles." I looked again at the bright sphere. "Nothing this big or bright." Somehow that fact alone made me feel uncomfortable. Nothing changed in Rhea, ever, not until very recently. So this was something new, and I had no idea if it was a good new or a bad new.

"Correct," Naia said. "We will pass within one million kilometers of this star system's innermost gas giant, which is much closer than we have ever approached a planet since launch."

Thousands of questions teemed on the edge of my consciousness, and it was hard not to ask them all in rapid series. Where did we launch from? Why were we launched? Why were we lied to? Those were just a few of the more important ones.

But Naia had been evasive when I asked, and she prompted Karina and I at every turn to hurry up with the repairs. We'd restored several key systems, and we'd restored multiple sarus, all of which were continuing the repair efforts even as we gawked out the window.

Nevertheless, we had barely scratched the surface of what needed fixing. For one thing, I hadn't yet repaired the tram system that circumnavigated the dome between the fore and aft sections. That was my next priority after Thelon's funeral.

Naia continued to explain, "If we had entered this system at the place, time, and speed I had originally calculated, we never would have approached any of this system's planets. Our course change will avoid all of the other planets, and take us out of the orbital ecliptic of the asteroid belt, but the only way to accomplish all of our needs was to have us pass near this planet. I have been scanning and charting all of its moons to ensure we do not risk a collision."

I gulped at that thought. I hadn't yet restored the *Sirius's* shields. Maybe *that* would be my next priority, not the tram system. It certainly explained why Naia insisted on prioritizing the shields.

Maybe I should have trusted her judgement more.

Except, her judgement had kept us trapped in a lie for two-hundred forty years. So I still couldn't trust her entirely.

Not until she started answering my perfectly reasonable questions.

In any case, my body insisted I give it some more attention after sleeping in this morning. Sighing, I turned to Karina and smiled. "Well, I guess it's my turn in the restroom."

She smiled back at me, but…something was off. It wasn't a full-faced smile.

I quirked my head to the side. "Something wrong?"

Letting out a shuddering sigh, she shook her head. "No. Not exactly. I just…"

My body *really* wanted me to find that bathroom now, but I felt like she needed to say something, so I waited patiently. Or maybe not so patiently, you know how it is when you gotta pee.

"It's my parents," she finally said, and then looked up into my eyes. I tried not to swoon over her baby-blue eyes. This was serious talk. *Focus, Mika!* "I, uh…didn't tell them I was coming with you." I gaped at her, and she quickly amended, "Not in person. I left them a note. And I don't think they're gonna be too happy with me when we get home today."

I coughed to cover up my surprise. "Um. Yeah, no, probably not."

Karina shrugged one shoulder and averted her eyes. "I'm sure I'll endure a very long lecture before…" She trailed off and shook her head, clenching her jaw. She whispered, "Well, before."

I nodded, searching for something to say. Finally, I reached out and grasped her cheeks with both hands, forcing her to look at me. I still couldn't think of anything to say, or rather, nothing that didn't involve sarcasm. So I did the only other thing I could think of – I drew her close and kissed her forehead. "It'll be okay," I said, looking into her eyes again. "And if you want, I'll face them with you."

Instead of smiling like I thought she would, she grimaced. "No. Um," she reached one hand up to grasp mine. "No, that's okay Mika. I…I need to face them alone. You and I…it would only make them angrier."

I felt my stomach drop. She was right.

And we needed to talk about this more. Talk about how we would present ourselves in Rhea. *Together,* or just together.

I knew what I wanted. But I also knew that the people of Rhea might not be so accepting of it. It was, after all, one of those highest laws. You married only whom the Oracle told you to. Once you had an arranged marriage, there was no more dating other people, that was a thing for teens only.

Plus there was another 'high law' – every single couple was to have two children. No more, no less, and only when the Oracle said it was okay to have children. The only time there was ever an exception was if someone died unexpectedly. Now I knew why – Naia needed to maintain our population, both due to limited resources and to ensure genetic diversity.

Naturally, that meant there were no same-sex unions of any kind, and it had become a societal taboo.

I wanted to tear the whole system down. Unfortunately, I knew that Karina wasn't yet ready to join me on such a crusade. At least, I didn't think she was.

It might be time for that hard conversation. This really wasn't how I wanted the morning to start.

TWO

By that point, my body was urgent about taking care of business, so I left Karina in the lounge and hustled for the bathroom. After I finished up, I was able to do something I had enjoyed every single day since we'd come here – I took a hot shower!

There is *nothing* like it in Rhea, and I never knew that having streaming, steaming-hot water flowing over your body could feel so *good!* So I was determined to keep up the ritual, even with an uncomfortable conversation ahead. In fact, I think it was necessary to help brace me for it.

I spent several minutes in the shower just soaking up the warmth, pressing my forehead against the sidewall and letting my muscles relax. It wasn't just talking to Karina that had bunched them all up, my muscles were tense from long hours of repair work.

The damage done to the *Sirius* was extensive, far more than I had thought. Given how large the ship was, that meant a *lot* of ground to cover. A lot of what we'd done was find and repair sarus, knowing that there wasn't a chance in hell I could do it all alone, and so far we'd reactivated nearly a half-dozen of them. Unfortunately, those were the salvageable ones. We found a lot more that were beyond repair. And we still had only found a small fraction of them.

All the while I tried to teach Karina the basics of mechanical engineering. I thought it was going to be a losing proposition, but I remembered how useless she'd felt when all of this started. I didn't want her to feel that way anymore.

Still, Karina's experience learning carpentry didn't really prepare her for working on fusion reactors.

Right, fusion reactors, I thought, deflating. We still had to rebuild all the ones the alien had demolished. It turned out that *Sirius's* reactors had special parts embedded within them that allowed an almost lossless energy conversion to occur from the fusion reactor to our energy grid. I hadn't yet examined the alien's power converter for its ship, but Naia and I believed that was why the alien had destroyed so many.

So, rebuild reactors, rebuild sarus, find and restore more sarus, and then identify any damaged power conduits and repair and replace them. That would be the bare-minimum of getting the *Sirius* back up to peak performance, and necessary to get those shields up and running again.

Not to mention we still had to do something about the big ass alien ship wedged into our ventral hull. How in the hellfire were we going to remove that thing and rebuild the breached hull and decks?

Stop it, Mika! I lectured myself. *Keep your focus on one thing at a time.*

Groaning, I grudgingly shut off the water and dried off with one of the towels we'd found in the restroom. The showers were part of a larger area, and they were weirdly communal, slotted next to one another with nothing but a curtain keeping others from prying in. Next to those showers were multiple lockers and benches to sit on as needed. It seemed *strange* that people would shower together like that, but it brought up only one of innumerable questions about the people who had built this ship and put my ancestors on it.

Questions that Naia liked to avoid answering.

I found the locker I'd stuffed my Rhea winter clothing into and pulled it out – it *stank!* Grimacing, I looked up and asked, "Naia, is there any sort of…I don't know, automated laundry devices on this ship? Was that ever invented?"

My mind swirled as I searched for the answer to that question myself – it had been less than a week since my Intellectus Apparatus download, and as Naia had pointed out, it had been a larger download than was normally recommended. As such, my brain was still trying to sort things out, and sometimes knowledge came and went seemingly of its own accord.

The headaches didn't help. One came on right then, too.

The moment she said, "Affirmative, there are laundry facilities both fore and aft," my brain clicked the info into place, and I knew where it was in the aft section. Two decks up, and about a kilometer starboard-side from the security office Karina and I had visited during our escape from the alien.

There wasn't time now, but I resolved to properly wash my Rhea clothes after we returned.

For now, I put the stinky, soiled clothing on. At least I could change into something fresh at my parents' house.

I looked into the locker to see if I'd forgotten anything, and felt my chest constrict. Hanging from a hook at the back, I found the thigh holster I'd donned in that security office, and the particle weapon.

The one I'd used to fight the creature.

The one that, by my hand, had killed Thelon's shield.

I'd left it here and forgotten about it. Now, seeing it, I felt this horrific feeling well up inside of me, and when I closed my eyes, I saw the rust-red shot lance out, hitting Thelon's shield and draining its power cells.

I saw the alien's golden beam crater Thelon's chest.

I saw his body lying on the ground...

I gasped in air, barely holding back a sob, and looked away. I couldn't pick it up again. I couldn't risk missing and hurting someone else.

So I slammed the locker shut and left it behind.

I met Karina back at the lounge. She was sitting sideways on one of the fancy, cushioned chairs, her legs hanging over one arm, while she stared out into space.

Not willing to show how shaken I felt, I conjured up as much courage as I could and said nonchalantly, "Ready to go?"

She smiled weakly and stood up. Together we put our backpacks on, and then our satchels. While my satchel contained two thick books and one of the town chronicles, which I had dutifully updated during our first night, Karina's satchel contained a dozen arrows sticking out of one corner. I'd given her the ones that I had, knowing that if we needed weapons, I could always...

Well, maybe I couldn't always use my pistol. But it didn't matter now, the alien was dead, and we'd seen no evidence of a second intruder on the *Sirius*.

She grabbed her unstrung bow, and I grabbed mine, and then we headed for the hole in the Rhea dome.

We walked silently at first. I didn't know how to bring up the topic. Unfortunately, I knew that we didn't have a lot of time to spare – we were less than a mile away from the breach, and with most of the bulkhead doors open, it'd be more of a straight shot than when we had first arrived.

So I drew in a deep breath, held it, and then asked the question, "What are we going to tell the others?"

I looked at Karina and saw her jaw set tightly, while she stared ahead. "You mean about us," she said. I nodded. Looking down, Karina shrugged uneasily. "I don't know. Maybe…nothing?"

Her baby blues turned to me, searching my face for a response. I set my own jaw for a second, a rushing sensation coursing through my chest. It wasn't a good feeling.

I felt my voice threatening to tremble when I asked, "Why nothing?"

"Well," she motioned towards our destination, even though it wasn't in sight yet. "Because it's Rhea. Because of the law."

"Yeah, the law a certain Naia invented," I looked up at the ceiling, squinting at the light panel we passed beneath. "One she could easily lift."

"I am afraid I cannot do that," Naia replied.

My temper flashed, and that rushing sensation turned into something stronger. "Why the hells not?" I growled.

"Nothing has changed, Mika Kai," Naia stated, her voice matter-of-fact. "Once you complete repairs to the *Sirius*, the breach will be sealed and Rhea will continue as it has."

"Fuck that," I spat out, "I won't let it stay the same!"

"Mika," Karina implored, resting a hand on my shoulder, "don't."

"Don't what?" I shrugged out of her grip. "You expect me to do that?" I again turned upwards. "You expect me to go back to my life, just because *you* say so? After everything I've seen, everything I've done? Naia, you've lied to us for two-hundred forty *years!* And for what? Why?"

Silence followed. I glanced at Karina, hoping for her support, but she didn't give it. Instead, she looked forlornly ahead. Towards our destination.

Towards Rhea.

"You know why," Naia replied. "The people of Rhea have already endured hardship beyond what they should have, and it will have disrupted their lives. Our transit across this star system will already be shorter by nearly a year, Mika Kai, which means a much shorter growing season. We may encounter food shortages as a direct result of this disruption. Any additional disruptions could prove to be fatal or catastrophic to the equilibrium required to maintain the status quo…"

"To hell with the status quo!" I snapped. "If the system is that fragile, maybe it deserves to be dismantled."

"And then what?" Karina asked. Her tone was calm, soothing, and it derailed my hot-headed rant. "What happens when the system is torn down, Mika? What happens to our families? To our people? To *us?*"

I didn't have an answer to that. Nothing logical nor sane, anyway. I started and stopped talking three times before I clamped my mouth shut, and fumed, not meeting Karina's look.

So she pressed on. "I get it. I do. I have loved being here with you, Mika. I *love you.*" That drew my gaze back to her. "But we can't just destroy everything and hope for the best. We have to think about it. We have to plan."

I swallowed my pride. Or at least I tried to.

"I just," I started, and then clenched my teeth and took a moment to breathe. I'd balled up my fists at some point, and I wanted to hit *something,* though I didn't know what. "It's so *frustrating,*" I grumbled.

"I know it is," she nodded, her hand returning to my shoulder. This time, I didn't shrug it off. "Just try to be patient, Mika."

"Not really my strong suit," I murmured.

That elicited a snorted chuckle from her, and I flashed her a grin.

"No," she said through laughter. "But that's why you've got me, right?"

My anger deflated with her touch, her laugh, her smile, and her words.

Dammit. I wanted to stay mad, but how the hellfire could I with all that leveled against me?

Besides which, we still had the *Sirius* to be together in.

I slid my arm around Karina's waist and drew her in, and together, we walked on. A few minutes later, we rounded the corner and beheld the familiar sight of a hole in the corridor wall, and a natural-looking landscape beyond.

In three days, the ice-packed snow had softened and melted considerably, but it was still a wintery landscape. It was cold, but not frigid, and the ship's warmer air flowed through the hole as a gentle breeze.

The moment we stepped through, I looked up to the blue sky and planted my hands on my hips, shaking my head. Somewhere up in my scattered brain, there was a clue as to how that technology worked, how the dome projected a blue sky when there wasn't nearly enough atmosphere in the dome to create it.

"Wuff!"

I turned back to the hole, and was pleasantly surprised to see Saru, the first service unit we'd come across when we ventured into the corridors of the ship. He looked at us with static eyes, the cones of his ears motionless, but his bone-like metallic tail whipped back and forth excitedly. His torso and six legs were a mix of metallic grey and matte black, patterned like a dog's fur.

"Saru!" I surged back through the hole and dropped to my knees, throwing my arms around him. He wiggled excitedly and wuffed at me again. "Come to see us off, boy?"

I pulled back and looked at him. He didn't have a mouth as far as I could see, just a little speaker on the tip of his snout, but I still imagined him with a lolling tongue. We had dogs in Rhea, but they were few and far between, mostly used by the sheep herders to move the herds around where they were needed.

Saru was weird, even for a Service and Repair Unit. All the others that we had reactivated spoke, and they acted like the robots they were, albeit highly advanced ones. My Saru was the only one to act like a dog, and I had no idea why. I'd so far avoided asking Naia why, out of an irrational fear that she would realize the programming mistake and would correct it, turning Saru into just another repair unit.

"Wuff!" he barked and nuzzled my cheek. I pictured that same imaginary tongue licking my face excitedly, and I burst out laughing.

"Well, as much as I wish you could go with," I said between giggles, "I don't think the people of Rhea are ready for you yet. But you'll keep an eye on the ship while I'm gone?"

He backed out of my embrace so that he could bounce around excitedly, and he wuffed again.

"That's a good boy!" I stood up. "Go on, now!"

His tail wagging stopped for a moment, the skeletal appendage lowering between his legs. I was sad to see him so sad, but there was no way he'd be accepted.

Not yet.

"Awwwww!" Karina lamented, stepping up next to me to watch Saru mournfully trudging back into the ship. "He looks so sad!"

"It is because he wished to attend Thelon's funeral," Naia explained.

I frowned up at the ceiling. "He did?"

"Yes," she said. "Because of how playful Thelon was with Saru, or so he perceived."

I gaped upwards, and then looked back at Saru just as he disappeared around the corner. Thelon had never played with Saru, but he *had* chased him through the ship. I remembered Saru acting like it was a game, and now realized the unit's artificial intelligence really *did* think it had been playtime.

"Huh," I shook my head. I almost asked the question about Saru.

But I looked forward to seeing how happy he would be when we returned.

So instead, I smiled at Karina and held out my free arm. She intertwined her arm with mine, and together, we trudged into the slushy snow. I closed my eyes for a moment and looked towards the sun, letting the warmth wash across my face.

I'd missed that feeling, even if it was tainted by the knowledge that it was filtered artificially. But the damp smell and the hint of the coming Spring helped mask that knowledge, and for a moment, arm linked with my girl's, I felt content to be home.

We made it to the tree line in short order, and weaved our way between them, a renewed lightness having sprung up between us. For a moment, I was able to forget the solemn duty we were about to perform today.

Until we emerged from the trees and saw the fields of Rhea, and beyond that, the densely-packed town.

The outer edges of the domed landscape were covered in trees, which were normally harvested very carefully, and always replanted. Naia had kept tight control over how many trees our lumberjacks took down every year, ensuring that we never ran out. Except that I noticed multiple new trees cut down in this section, which wasn't yet due for harvesting – no doubt cut down in a panic to start fires during the crisis.

I wondered what the long-term fallout from that would be.

Inside the ring of trees was a ring of farms, ranging from crops like corn, cabbage, and potatoes, to livestock like cows, sheep, pigs, and so much more. The farmland encompassed a circumference of almost fourteen miles all-told, encircling the entire town – it was amazing how efficiently space was used in the dome.

Inside of that ring were the houses, all of which were at least two stories, containing workspaces and shops on the bottom, and bedrooms up top. Again, very efficient, and densely packed.

At the center of it all was the castle, though it was a castle in name only – it was really just a fancy, stone-brick mansion. Nothing like the fortresses described in some of the books in my library.

My library... Would it still be my library if I told everyone in town the truth? If we broke tradition and stopped following Naia's laws? Would I still be a chronicler?

Karina drew close to me and leaned her head on my shoulder, and I felt her tense up. *This is it,* I realized. We had to part ways here. And, since we were in sight of one of the farmers tending to his pigs, I knew that I couldn't even give her a kiss goodbye.

So she pulled away, and looked one last time into my eyes. "See you in a few hours?" she asked.

I nodded solemnly. "Yeah," I whispered.

She squeezed my hand one last time, and then headed off to the left, to go between a corn farm and a pig farm, nearest to her house.

I turned right and looked to where there was a sheep farm next to a potato farm. The path between them was my destination, and I could already see my house beyond the sheep farm.

Somehow, I wasn't sure how to feel about seeing home again after only three days. I missed my brother and I was looking forward to seeing him. But how had my parents' perception of me changed? Would they still sing my praises to all the neighbors? Or did they not understand everything that had happened?

Did they think of me, with my newfound intellect, as a freak?

I clenched my jaw and tried not to think about it. I really tried.

But I failed.

Because maybe they'd be right to think of me as a freak.

The real question was, would I care if they thought of me that way?

Drawing in a deep breath for courage, I trudged away from the tree line, and I headed for home.

THREE

I should have known something was wrong the moment I saw them loitering in the street in front of my house. Three guys who looked to be just standing around, chatting. They wore light winter clothes, the spring warmth making the heavy coats and cloaks, like what I was wearing, wholly unnecessary.

Stop me if you heard this one before – a blonde, a brunette, and a red-head step in front of you.

They formed a line, clearly intent on stopping me from getting home, and they marched intently towards me as soon as I stepped onto the cobblestoned road, which was full of snowmelt.

I drew up short and tensed.

I barely resisted the urge to back away, and they finally stopped just a dozen feet away. "Uh, can I help you boys?" I asked, feeling my heart accelerating to a thousand beats per second. My chest ached with fear, and I slowly reached for my pistol…

Shit.

I didn't have my pistol. And my bow was unstrung.

"She's the one?" the one in the center, a brown-haired boy with a sharp jaw and dark eyes, asked the redhead with a sneer. Seriously, he sneered. His voice wasn't the low, ominous pitch I expected, but rather high and annoying. Tall, skinny. If not for the cliché words, I'd have thought he was the brains of the trio.

The red-head. I knew him.

I didn't know the other two, but there was no mistaking Karina's brother, now that I was close enough. Annar Ticho had the same carrot-red hair his sister did, the same blue eyes, but his were fierce right now. No…not fierce. Something else.

Angry.

Hateful.

He circled around to my left, and based on what little time I'd spent around him, I figured he was probably the brains of the trio. Which wasn't exactly saying much.

Blondie circled around to my right. They couldn't quite surround me, but it effectively cut me off from any help.

I curled my fingers up to form fists, because my instinct told me they weren't here to talk.

But that wasn't going to stop me from trying.

"What do you want?" I asked, looking directly at Annar.

"Where's my sister?" Annar asked, a gravelly quality in his voice giving it an edge.

I motioned my head north-west, "Probably already home. You should go see her."

He stopped directly between me and my front door. Something told me he wanted to be the one to stand there.

Annar never hated me, exactly, but he had never been nice to me. He'd made it clear what he thought about Karina and I spending so much time together with our noses buried in books. We even once caught him trying to follow us to our secret archery range, and we toyed with him and lost him in the woods, which considering how thin the strip of trees was, that was saying something. He was smart, but not street-smart, if that makes any sense. I know, quite the statement from a book-smart gal, but his intelligence was keen on certain topics only, usually involving blacksmithing.

"Where did you take her?" he growled. His hands had curled into fists. Through clenched teeth, he asked, "Why did you take her?"

I wondered if he knew. Knew about our feelings for each other, our romance. Knew that I loved his sister.

Or…was it something else?

I glanced at my house and saw a flurry of movement – the curtains in my father's workshop, as if someone had peeked out of them and then left. *Phoebus?*

I refocused my thoughts. My parents loved to brag, that was nothing new. I'd assumed they might think of me as a freak now, but what if I wasn't giving myself enough credit?

I'd told them *everything* before returning to the *Sirius*, even though the King had ordered me not to tell anyone. Had they bragged to others?

Did Annar's antics have something to do with that?

I ran with my instincts on this and replied, "I needed someone to watch my back."

"You could have had guards do that for you, *Princess*," he spat out the title that I already loathed. "Your precious prince could have gone with."

Ugh. Prince Jonnec Impavido. Technically my fiancé. Technically, I hated his guts.

Except, he *had* earned some measure of respect. Some, but not much.

My face must have betrayed my emotions. "Oh that's right," he growled. "You don't go for that sort of thing, do you?" He took a step towards me. "You filthy little freak…"

"Annar!" my father's baritone voice echoed off the adjacent buildings. He stood at our front door wearing a leather apron with multiple pockets on it. In his hand, he held the tiniest little iron hammer, used in his shoemaking.

Still, little as it was, Annar spun towards him and, even from my angle, I saw him look directly at the tool before meeting my father's eyes.

"Crius," Annar spat. "Get back inside!"

My father stepped onto the street, his grip on the hammer tightening. "That's Mister Kai to you, young man," he replied, an underlying threat in his tone. Say what you will about my father, no one threatened his daughter. Or him. "Leave now before I give you the discipline your parents never gave you."

"Well if that ain't the pot calling the skillet black," Annar shook his head.

I frowned at his phrasing, and I couldn't help it when I replied, "Gods, you can't even get *that* right."

He looked over his shoulder at me, likely trying to look intimidating, but his misquote and my snark deflated the tension enough that I wasn't as afraid anymore.

"Excuse me?" he hissed back at me.

"It's pot calling the *kettle* black, idiot," I folded my arms, though I kept my hands clenched into fists. "Read a book now and again, would you?"

Bullies existed everywhere, in every society, if my books were any indication. Right now, that's all Annar was. True, my worst fears had been confirmed, and he suspected there was something between Karina and I. Nevertheless, more often than not, a good way to erode a bully's power trip was to stand up to him.

I was ready to punch him, if necessary. It wouldn't be the first time I'd hit someone.

I felt a presence behind me, and glancing left at the ground, I saw the shadow of Blondie stepping closer to me. He probably intended to be silent, but good luck in this slushy muck. So I kept an awareness of that shadow out of the corner of my eye while I looked back at Annar.

My father, on the other hand, was shaking his head. "Mika," he warned. "Don't talk."

That brought my fears back to the forefront ten-fold. My father was nervous, his voice firm but with an underlying quality that was unmistakable. Something had him worried.

There was a tension between him and Annar, and I realized it wasn't something new or in-the-moment. Annar confirmed that fact when he said, "You're on the wrong side, Crius. Go back inside."

Side? What sides were there to be on?

What the hellfire was going on?

Father brandished his hammer. "Leave. Mika. Alone."

A moment of silence passed. Another. I felt my heart thundering in my chest, and I tensed, ready to fight. My bow wasn't exactly the best for hand-to-hand, but I slowly reached to pull it free from my backpack, believing it would be better than nothing. The tension crawled along my skin, raising the hairs on the back of my neck.

This wasn't going to go well.

Annar jolted forward. The shadow behind me did likewise.

I panicked and fumbled my bow the moment I yanked it free, and then promptly dropped it. On instinct alone, I aimed high with my elbow and connected with Blondie's face with a sickening crunch, which was followed by a cry of pain.

Father swung his hammer, but Annar tackled him, bringing my father down hard on the stairs up to our little stoop.

Brown-hair had started to join Annar, but saw what I'd done to Blondie and stopped, while I spun around to face Blondie, hoping Father would be okay alone for a moment.

Blood spurted from Blondie's nose, and he fell to his knees while clutching it, trying to catch the scarlet fluid. That had been a lucky hit on my part.

Brown-hair was indecisive, giving both my father and I a moment of reprieve. I scrambled to think of what I could use as a weapon, and then it dawned on me – I pulled the satchel off of my shoulder, backing away from Blondie as I did, and with the weight of three heavy books in it, I started swinging it in a fast, laborious circle.

"Get her!" Blondie squeaked at Brown-hair.

The boy rushed at me, so I stepped back and swung my bag as hard as I could. Brown-hair was less of a fool than I imagined, and he'd blocked with his arm, but I don't think he was prepared for just how heavy those books were. It knocked him sideways with a heavy thud, and though he clutched my bag, he started losing his balance, and he was taking me with him.

So I did the only sensible thing – I fell towards him, and planted my knee in his gut. A satisfying "Oof!" escaped his lips, the air driven from his lungs, and as I landed on top of him, he let go of my bag. I rolled off into the slushy snow, the cold biting at my fingers as I pushed up. Blondie tried to get his feet under him to rush me, so I swung my bag around and smacked him dead in the head, toppling him to his side.

And when I turned back to Father and Annar, ready to help, I was surprised to find that I didn't need to. Mother had emerged from inside at some point, wielding a tenderizer. Annar was splayed out beside father on the stoop, clutching his head and cursing up a storm. Father shoved him aside and got back onto his feet, but I could see it was a struggle for him, wincing as he moved.

I put some distance between me and the other boys, circling around further into town so that I could see everyone, and I clutched the strap of my satchel, ready to bludgeon anyone who came at me again.

But then something unexpected happened. The clear, beautiful sky suddenly turned dark. I looked up and saw clouds rolling in. My I.A.-enhanced brain tried to make sense of it at first – was I seeing a projection of clouds on the dome? Or were these real clouds forming within the dome? Or both?

A distant, rolling rumble echoed over the town. Followed by a louder, closer one.

Lightning flashed in the sky overhead, bright as the sun itself, and

I'd been looking right at it. It left a bright afterimage in my vision, and I tried blinking it away.

The clap of thunder shook the windows of every house in Rhea, and I heard the boys *scream* in terror.

Then I felt more than heard a new presence marching down the street towards me. I spun around and saw the old town wizard, Vell Viisas, marching towards us, his staff in-hand, his blue and white robes billowing, his grey hair and beard fluttering in the wind. Runes that I had never noticed in his staff were illuminated, flaring bright against the darkening sky.

It suddenly clicked in my head — his staff wasn't a magic staff, it was a mechanism that let him control technology in such a way as to *appear* to be magic!

He had summoned the storm.

With a loud voice that carried far more than I had ever heard, no doubt enhanced by a piece of technology, he boomed out, "THAT IS ENOUGH!" The windows rattled again, and his words were echoed by another clap of thunder that rolled back and forth through the dome.

I gaped at him, in awe of the display he had just put on. It was a far cry from the near-helpless old man that had wheezed after us in the corridors of the *Sirius*, and even knowing something of the technology he employed, I shied away from him.

If it did that to me, imagine what it did to those boys.

They all tried to scramble down the street as best as they could despite their injuries, with blondie sliding back on his butt away from Vell, away from all of us.

I looked back at Vell, and through the adrenaline and fear, for a brief moment I felt a smile creep onto my face. Little, mousy, wide-eyed Dannin Pieni, Vell's apprentice, walked three steps behind the wizard. I was incredibly happy to see him again!

I turned back to the boys to see that they had stopped right beside the fence to the sheep farm next to our house. Blondie's hands had fallen away long enough for him to push up onto his feet, blood trickling down his face, while Annar's left cheek bore the pattern of the business end of my mother's tenderizer.

No more lightning flashed in the sky, but the thunder from earlier was still echoing and fading, slow and ominous. Vell shot me an icy glare as he walked by, but otherwise said nothing. Dannin, on the other hand, stopped beside me and gave me a shy smile.

I smiled back, and then watched the wizard come up next to my parents and plant his staff in the slushy street. The runes flared brighter, blue-white like the monolith's runes in Town Square, and another, lesser clap of thunder boomed from it. The three boys jerked back, while my parents winced and edged towards the house's front door.

"Return to your homes at once," Vell commanded, voice still booming.

I could tell that Annar in particular wasn't inclined to follow that order, but then his eyes affixed upon Vell's staff.

They knew the power he wielded, and now I knew better than any. I hadn't actually repaired every part of the power grid that fed into the dome, but the sarus must have reinforced the grid during the night. I probably should have checked the ship's status before coming here, but I had been too focused on Karina and our return home.

The sky was mostly fake in Rhea, but the lightning that Vell could summon was real, just as strong, if not stronger than the particle weapon I'd foolishly left in the locker. They knew he could fry them with a simple command and wave of his staff. Hell, he could literally send a stream of fire at them if he desired!

So, after giving me one last sneer, Annar led the other two away, between my parents' house and the sheep farm, no doubt headed for Karina's home.

Was she in danger?

I had to make sure she was okay, but if I went there alone, they'd probably ambush me again. Maybe even with help from some more of their friends.

I shook my head at the whole situation. "What…" I started and stopped, shaking my head with my mouth hanging open stupidly. "The hellfire was that all about?"

Vell shot me an icy glare, and then looked to my parents. His voice returned to its normal level, no longer enhanced, "Go back inside at once, and lock your doors. I shall ask the king to send a guard to watch over you."

My parents, unsurprisingly, didn't have to be told twice. They glanced at me, Mother giving me a relieved smile, and then they scrambled inside and slammed the door shut. I wanted to follow, but then Vell turned and stalked towards me. He looked…*angry.*

I realized that unlike three days ago, *he* held all the power now.

I didn't like that reversal.

"And *you*," he hissed, "will come with me."

"Wait," I shook my head, "I want to see my family before the fu-"

"NOW!" Vell shouted, his voice once again enhanced by some piece of technology.

The shout startled me, but then my rebellious streak barged into my mouth and said, "No!"

The runes on his staff flared as he gripped the wood. Or rather, the faux-wood, I realized.

It was just technology.

But technology could kill. Or maim. Or restrain.

Vell could easily make me go against my will.

That realization must have shown on my face. Vell's anger cooled a few degrees, and he leaned on his staff, the runes fading. "The king has ordered you to come before him the moment you returned to Rhea," he explained. "Much has happened in the three days since you left."

I glanced towards where the three boys had fled, and I swallowed hard. "Yeah. I can see that." I looked at Vell and was about to ask questions, but stopped short. He wouldn't answer them, I was sure of that.

The old codger hated me, and now that he had the power, he wasn't about to cater to my 'insolence.'

"Fine," I nodded, and looked again at my house. I saw a flutter of movement in the curtains of my father's workshop, and then I saw my brother's pudgy face appear, his cute, beige button nose pressed up against the glass. He looked worried, until his eyes found me, and then he smiled.

Phoebus was younger than Dannin even, not quite old enough to begin an apprenticeship with anyone. I wondered what the Oracle...what *Naia* had in store for him.

I waved at him, and then looked at Vell and nodded. "Fine. Lead the way, oh majestic *wizard*."

I saw his jaw tense, and he grumbled something under his breath, before he stalked around me and headed for the center of town. I looked at Phoebus once more, and then I gave Dannin a mischievous wink before I picked up my bow and fell into step behind Vell.

FOUR

We trudged up the street towards the castle, and the town felt eerily still. I heard no voices, saw no one out and about, even though Rhea should have been alive with activity by now.

Young people should have been going to their apprenticeships. At least some adults should have been out getting supplies for their own jobs, or food from cooks like my mother, or *something*. Instead, the streets were deserted.

The clouds rapidly dissipated, revealing a blue sky and the sun just low enough to cast shadows over me. That's when it dawned on me – the sudden storm, the lightning and thunder, and Vell's booming, augmented voice. Everyone had scattered into the safety of their homes.

I glanced down at my satchel. Contained within were two books from the top floor of my library, one full of ancient mythologies, and one a fictional book about the adventures of Robin Hood. Next to those was the newest town chronicle.

I'd read or skimmed through several of our records, and I knew that pretty much nothing ever changed in Rhea. One thing that definitely never made the records was a town wizard summoning a storm and shouting at people fighting in the streets.

Vell was right, a lot had happened.

Every now and then, I caught a flurry of movement in windows, drapes being pushed aside as curiosity got the better of the townsfolk.

We finally made it to the avenue that encircled the castle, and turned right towards the square. Ahead, I saw the famous Rhea obelisk. A grin pulled up the edge of my mouth when I noticed that a blue-white glow extended from the top almost halfway down its length, a reassuring indication that all was well, that winter had ended (as if the slushy snow we sloshed through wasn't enough indicator), and that Rhea would recover.

We'd saved the town.

We'd saved the ship.

It was somewhat eerie to see the square deserted. The last time I'd seen it this empty was when we'd set out into the unknown wilderness, clueless as to the truth of our existence.

Vell turned us towards the castle, but I said, "Wait."

I broke off and headed for the obelisk, while Vell huffed and spun around to watch me. "We do not have time-"

"Hey," I flashed him angry eyes, "I earned this." And upon stepping up to the obelisk, I bent over and touched its base. It was a superstition, a way of bringing good luck, and everyone in town did it. I wasn't sure if I believed in luck or not anymore, but I did it anyway, out of habit, and out of a need to feel like something was under control again.

Karina had been right, the obelisk felt just like the same synthetic polycarbonate material that the walls of the *Sirius's* endless corridors were made of.

I looked up at the glow and smiled. This was *real*. Rhea still stood. We were all safe.

After drawing in a deep breath, I turned and rejoined Vell. He stared at me with narrowed eyes, and I could tell that he wanted to say something unkind to me. Somehow he managed to keep his mouth shut, and he turned away and marched off towards the gate to the castle courtyard.

Frowning, I glanced at Dannin, who looked away sheepishly. This was odd behavior indeed. Hadn't I saved Rhea? Wasn't I due some level of appreciation, even from Vell? Granted he hadn't ever really shown me much respect, even after I'd restored the stardrive, but he had at least started to support my efforts.

I mean, sure, he was an ass.

But maybe something else was going on.

Dannin and I rushed to catch up, just as Vell reached the gate. Two guards stood vigil. One was an older gentleman with streaks of gray in his shoulder-length hair, pulled back in a ponytail, and whose leather armor looked like it had endured countless years in the elements, guarding the exteriors of the castle. I knew him, but couldn't recall his name. I thought his youngest son had just started an apprenticeship six months ago, but not as a guard.

The other guard was a woman, with dark skin and short black hair, and she looked built enough to have given Thelon a run for his money. I stopped, startled, upon seeing a familiar weapon hanging from her belt – Thelon's one-handed axe that he'd favored while wielding the energy shield!

I blinked, trying to clear away images of the golden blast that had pierced his torso, of his crumpled form on the deck of engineering. It *couldn't* be his axe! It was another one just like it, that's all.

Right?

When I met her dark-brown eyes, she sneered at me with absolute contempt.

The other guard opened the gates without a word, and silently stood by while Vell, Dannin and I passed through. I think he might have given me a suspicious look.

Catching up to Vell's side, I asked, "What is going *on* around here? Why's everyone acting so weird around me?"

Giving me a sidelong glance, Vell huffed out again (I really think he liked doing that), and he replied with an air of haughtiness, "If you truly do not know, then you are far more ignorant than I thought."

Oh *that* set me off. I rushed forward and planted my hand on one of the elaborate, wooden double-doors, stinging my palm on an intricately carved panel, effectively blocking the wizard from continuing. He jerked to a halt and glared fire at me.

"I've had enough of your bullshit, *old man*," I spat out, and then I swear actual *fire* flared in his eyes. And then I played a card I once swore I'd never play, and I said, "I am the Princess of Rhea, as ordained by the Oracle, *and* blessed with knowledge by the Oracle." Or, you know, had knowledge shoved into my brain by a device called the Intellectus Apparatus. Same thing.

"Listen here, you little tramp," he growled at me.

I would have been taken aback by that name, but instead my fury won out, and I gave him my best impression of "The Look" that my mother and all mothers were so famous for. "You will address me as 'Your Majesty' or 'Princess,' do you understand?"

He stamped his staff down, sending out a clap of thunder that echoed off the castle's stone bricks, and the runes glowed menacingly.

Dannin yelped between us. "How dare you…"

I lost my balance when the doors suddenly opened inward, and I stumbled over the threshold. I caught myself and looked up to see who had interrupted our argument.

My fury died when the Queen of Rhea, Gabriella Impavido, resplendent in her violet courtly robes, gave *me* "The Look." Yeah, she was a lot better at it than I was. Her long, braided black hair whipped around as she turned to Vell.

"What do you think you two are doing?" she hissed at us.

"Um," I said, "Well, you see, Vell was just…"

"This *girl* dared to…"

"Silence!" the queen sliced her hand through the air. She hadn't shouted, but the timbre of her voice was enough to kill any motivation I had to speak further on the matter. It shut Vell up, too. "You are members of this court, and you will conduct yourselves accordingly! Do I make myself clear?"

Some uncontrollable part of my brain forced my mouth to automatically answer, "Yes, ma'am."

"Of course," Vell said, bowing lightly. "My apologies, Your Majesty."

Her hard gaze settled back on me. "Mika," she said curtly, "come with me at once. Vell," she looked at him again, "thank you for protecting her. You are welcome to join us in court as well."

I gulped. Court?

Why was I going into the court?

I'd sat in there as an observer a few times shortly after the Oracle revealed that I would become the Princess of Rhea, but surely they hadn't urgently retrieved me just to make me observe another session. So…was I on trial?

Color drained from my face, and I swallowed back a hard lump. The queen turned around stiffly, and then after taking a moment to compose herself, she gracefully led the way into the foyer. I traded nervous glances with Dannin, and then we all followed.

A large, predominantly royal-blue rug covered the smooth stone floor, helping to absorb our footsteps and keep them from echoing loudly off the stone walls. Unlike every other structure in Rhea, the castle was mostly comprised of well-made, well-tended stone bricks. This would have given the castle a cold feeling, but the paintings and tapestries that hung from its walls helped provide some sense of humanity and warmth.

Directly across from the entrance was a hallway that led towards the back of the castle, providing access to most rooms, including the Oracle's room far at the back where only Vell and Dannin were allowed audience with her. Right where that hallway started was an archway over it, and I grimaced as I looked up at it. A week ago, a cobalt-blue and silvery-white shield had hung there. That shield had been melted by the alien creature's particle weapon.

The first room on the left was the dining hall, but the first room on the right, and which occupied a full quarter of the castle's interior, was the throne room. The court.

The queen led us through the throne room's open double doors. The room was longer than any other room in any of Rhea's structures, with a royal-blue carpet laid out from the entrance to the foot of the finely-crafted, oak thrones, cushioned by fine, violet silken cushions.

The King of Rhea, Roberto Impavido, sat in the left throne. His skin bore a natural tan, he had cool-brown hair, blue eyes, a chiseled jaw, and a finely-kept goatee with only a hint of gray. He was as stately as I remembered, his posture perfect and regal, and he watched as we strode purposefully into the throne room. The other throne was empty, awaiting the queen.

On either side of the thrones were benches for observers to watch from. Standing in front of the king's side was Prince Jonnec Impavido. My...*fiancé*.

An acrid taste in the back of my throat barged forward, and I had to swallow it back.

Guilt swilled around in my chest when the memory of Thelon's death surged back into my thoughts. Thelon had been Jonnec's best friend. What would it have done to me if Karina had been the one to fall that day?

Still, despite my guilt, the idea of marrying him didn't sit well with me.

Okay, that's putting it lightly – I despised the idea. And not just because I had no interest in men romantically. He had a reputation with the women of Rhea, simultaneously desired and reviled for how he treated them. They were 'pretty things to be used,' as far as he seemed to care.

So when I took charge on the *Sirius*, he was rather taken aback by it.

Like always, he wore bright clothes, mostly sporting royal-blue or violet, but with one new addition – a thick leather glove covered his right hand. Beneath it, I knew that he had an artificial hand. His real hand had been amputated after the alien had wounded him, in the same encounter where the Rhea shield had been melted to slag.

Full color had returned to his face over the past few days, his tan skin making him look almost attractive. To the other women of Rhea, it made him irresistible, especially since he had inherited his father's chiseled jaw and his mother's hazel eyes.

As we approached the throne, the queen stopped and pointed at a spot on the rug, looking directly at me. I gulped again and stopped where she pointed. I knew this spot, I'd seen several other people here, whether they either asked the king for help, or they were chastised for some wrong they had committed.

Crime was rare in Rhea, rarer still was crime worth recording in the town chronicles. But some people still earned a strong reproach from the king and queen, while other times, disputes that hadn't yet gotten out of control were settled by the throne.

Once she was sure I would stay put, the queen stepped up to the thrones, lightly touching her husband's hand resting on the armrest, and then she sat down with all the grace and poise she had tried to teach me. Vell and Dannin broke off to the queen's side and sat on the bench, while Jonnec likewise sat on his father's side.

I started to understand why I was there, and I looked directly into the king's eyes.

He didn't look happy.

On the other hand, I'd seen him a hell of a lot angrier, so that was something.

That's only because he's had three days to stew on this, I thought. *To reel in his fury.*

Then, much to my surprise, I felt someone standing next to me, and I heard that someone clear their throat. My spirits soared, and I looked left to find my master, the town chronicler, Viden Alaran. He was as ancient as Vell, his white hair surrounding his head like a horseshoe, bald on top, and he had strong, brown eyes that looked ahead at the king, not me. At least, not until he glanced my way and gave me a wink.

He was here to support me.

"Mika Kai," the king began, his voice strong, carrying easily. I looked around and realized that if it hadn't been for tapestries on the walls and banners hanging from the ceiling, his voice would have echoed. "No one can deny what you have done for the people of Rhea. You have literally saved us all. For that, we owe you a great debt of gratitude."

This wasn't exactly how I expected things to start off. I nodded, and through a dry, cracking throat, managed to say, "Thank you, Your Majesty."

"However," he pushed up from the throne and took two steps towards me, towering at least six inches over me. "That does not give you license to disobey direct orders from your king!" His voice had grown harder, *harsher,* with each word, and his jaw muscles flexed wildly. I'd only seen that happen once, and I don't think I'd ever seen him that angry before or since.

"Um," I managed. "Y-your Majesty?"

"Don't!" he leveled a finger at me. "Do not play dumb, Princess Kai," he shook his head, sneering at me. Gods, I thought only Vell did that. "I gave you, *all* of you," he motioned to Jonnec, Vell, and Dannin, "explicit orders *not* to share your adventure with anyone outside of your party, did I not?" I looked down sheepishly, but that was apparently the wrong thing to do, because he bellowed, "DID I NOT?"

I tried to meet his fierce, furious eyes, but the swirling guilt in my chest made it difficult. I nodded. "Yes, Your Majesty, you did."

"So you heard me when I gave that order?" His words were clipped, short, *angry.*

"Yes, Your Majesty."

"Then why did you disobey me?"

My parents. After we had told the king and queen everything, after he had given us those orders, I'd had a short conversation with Viden, and then gone home and told my parents and my brother everything, heedless of the king's command.

"Um," was all I managed to say at first. Normally I was a lot more outspoken than this, so I felt embarrassed by my inability to form a coherent sentence. "Well, they're my family," I managed to say. "I guess I thought they deserved the truth."

"And that was your decision to make?" the king asked, waving his hands in exasperation. "Against the will and wisdom of your king?"

That inner voice, that hot-headed me, started to reassert herself.

"We've been lied to all of our lives, Your Majesty," I started, trying desperately to keep my voice calm and level. It wasn't easy, and my voice shook as much as my body did, frustration boiling up inside of me again, combining with adrenaline. "So *yes*, I think they deserved the truth."

He pitched his eyebrows upward, and he stepped closer to me. I don't know if he meant his action to be intimidating, but it was. Unfortunately, that only drew out my rebellious streak even more. "*You* think," he said. "*You* decided what was best for all of Rhea."

I mean, yes, but I didn't say that. "No, I decided what was best for my *family*."

"The same family known for telling anyone who would listen everything about your life," the king pointed out.

That made me clamp my mouth shut. Until I realized exactly what he was implying, and I whispered a curse. I saw the queen narrow her eyes at that.

"And now," the king continued, "all of Rhea knows. Or, as does happen with rumors, all of Rhea *thinks* they know the truth, as it has been distorted and twisted and lost from mouth to mouth. The rumors spread fast, Mika Kai, rumors of a monster that tried to kill us all. Rumors that the monster was coming to eat the children of Rhea." My eyes popped open at that. How the hellfire did that rumor start? "Rumors of dark magic twisting and distorting the world at the edges of Rhea." The king glanced at Jonnec, and motioned towards his gloved hand, "Rumors that a dark spirit maimed and corrupted their prince! Rumors," he turned to me and again stepped closer, leaving only a few feet between us. His voice lowered, and I tried to look into his eyes, but I just couldn't. "That you, Miss Kai, have been possessed, and that you seek to corrupt us all."

Then, finally, as the silence grew like a gulf between us, I managed to look into his eyes. There was still anger, yes, but there was something else, too. Something worse.

He was weary. He was stressed. The King of Rhea was afraid.

So that was why those boys had attacked me. Why they defied my father and attacked *him*. Kids attacking adults.

Oh shit, I thought, further realization dawning on me.

Homosexuality was outlawed in Rhea, and I knew precisely why. But to the people, it was a divine law from their goddess, their Oracle.

Karina's brother must have thought that I was corrupted, and that

I had corrupted Karina, too!

"Gods," I muttered as the full weight of it all settled into my stomach.

Drawing in a deep breath, the king lowered his head and shook it once. His voice was subdued when he spoke again, "The people of Rhea are giving into fear and superstition, Princess Kai. And this," he met my gaze again, "is precisely why I wanted to wait. I wanted to address all the people of Rhea at once. I wanted to convey the truth, the *facts,* all at once, so that there could be no questioning, no spreading of false rumors, no distortion of the truth. I gave a speech yesterday attempting to do just that, but by then, fully half of Rhea believed only the rumors. If Vell had not flexed his powers, I have no doubt that violence would have ensued."

The king spun around and returned to his throne. Standing in front of it, he looked again to me, and said, "Rhea faces a whole new danger now, Princess Kai."

I nodded understanding.

I'd saved Rhea, only to turn around and bring it closer to the edge than ever before.

FIVE

My mind swirled with the implications of all that I had learned. For the first time in Rhea's history, the town was divided. People were in danger.

My parents. Phoebus.

Shit! Karina! What would her brother do to her when he got home? Hellfire, he was probably already home!

"You're Majesty, Karina-" I started to say, put the king's eyes flared with anger when I said her name, and I abruptly stopped.

"Karina," he said, "is safe. She arrived at the castle shortly before you, thanks to the guard force. Who, by the way, are stretched far too thin now."

I looked around, half-expecting Karina to be standing beside or behind Viden, but she was absent. "Where is she?"

"That is not your concern," the king replied.

I whirled on him, ready to spout something hot and which would no doubt get me into further trouble. I realized it a half-second before I spoke, which was a drastic change from the normal for me. I clenched my fists tight enough that my fingernails bit into my palms, but I reminded myself that he had just told me she was safe.

That's what mattered most.

The king looked at Viden wearily. "Master Chronicler, she is your apprentice. More than that, I have always respected and depended upon your counsel. I find myself unable to conceive of a punishment to fit such a heinous crime." I stretched my eyes open as wide as they could, the implication of his statement jolting my chest like an electric shock. "What do you advise?"

I craned my neck to look at Viden, and he in turn gave me a calculated look. He had always been on my side. Even when I'd made mistakes in the past, he had treated them only as learning opportunities, not something to be harshly punished.

But I had never done anything like *this*. I suspected he had known about my feelings for Karina longer than anyone else, probably longer than even I knew, and he'd never spoken a word of reproach about it. If that was only because I'd never acted on those feelings, then surely I had disappointed him now.

Furrowing his brow, Viden looked to the king and bowed. "Your Majesty, as you know, the vessel bearing Rhea sustained considerable damage. It was my understanding, based upon what Prince Impavido, Princess Kai, and the others told us, that the ship requires repairs. It is unlikely that young Princess Kai has completed those repairs?" He raised a questioning eyebrow at me.

I thought I saw where he was going with this, but I wasn't sure how it would get me out of punishment. Turning to the king, I nodded. "He's right, Your Majesty. I still have a *lot* of work ahead of me. If I don't return to the task by tomorrow, things could…" I hesitated, trying to figure out how to say what I had to say in a way that the king would understand. "Things could start to go wrong again."

"I see," he sighed and rubbed at his goatee. Then his eyes widened, and he looked at Viden. "Are you suggesting what I think you are?"

"Apologies, Your Majesty," Viden replied patiently. "I am unable to discern your thoughts." Was that…ultra-subtle sarcasm? I almost cracked a smile.

The king narrowed his eyes, but if he suspected sarcasm, he didn't react to it. Instead, the king turned back to his throne and sat down, and then he and the queen leaned towards one another and began whispering. A moment later, the king called Vell, Dannin, and Jonnec over, and they huddled around the royals to converse.

I looked back at Viden with a frown, and whispered, "What, exactly, are you suggesting?"

The look he gave me told me he had expected me to figure it out already, and he didn't answer.

Huffing, I faced forward again and waited impatiently for the king and queen to finish talking about me behind my back, figuratively speaking.

The group kept glancing at me as they spoke, and it further irritated me. My hands clenched, and I actually started to worry about drawing blood with my fingernails. This was infuriating!

Finally, they deigned to stop, and the king stood up again to address me, while the others returned to their seats. "Princess Kai," the king started, and I could hear a tense hardness in his voice that I don't think I'd ever heard before. "Until these issues are resolved, your presence in Rhea has become a contentious matter. People will actively seek to find you and bring harm to you, and will likely ignore any words of wisdom any of us attempt to impart upon them.

"It is therefore with a heavy heart that I must impose upon you an order that I...*never* thought I would impose upon anyone." I swallowed hard, and waited, dread beginning to fill every inch of my being. "You are hereby banished from Rhea." I felt my jaw drop, along with my stomach. "To continue your work upon the vessel carrying Rhea. You will not return until Master Viisas has conveyed to you through the Oracle that it is safe for you to return. No one will accompany you."

"What?!" I exclaimed, and then clamped my mouth shut with my hand.

The king, rightfully-so, looked incensed by my outburst. "*No* one shall accompany you."

"But, Your Majesty!" I blurted through my hand.

"Do not question my orders," he snarled.

I pulled my hand off of my mouth and said, "But I need Karina!"

"Karina will stay here!"

"She protects me, she watches over me, she has my *back* and I..."

"Your perversion will not be allowed to continue!"

I almost cursed at him, but somehow managed to instead only say, "It's not a perversion!"

"ENOUGH!" His booming voice, infused with absolute rage, cut me off. "This is not a debate! This is an order from your sovereign. That may not carry any weight with you, but it does with my guard force and the town wizard." I glanced at Vell, who smugly crossed his arms and lifted his chin towards me. Bastard. "I will have you *dragged* out of Rhea if I must, but you *will* leave and remain away for as long as I deem it necessary! Master Viisas assures me that you will be safe by yourself, now that you have dealt with the intruder, and there is absolutely no need for *anyone* to accompany you for any reason."

I stumbled and stuttered with my words, not something I usually did, and it frustrated me almost as much as the king's order. I imagined what it would be like, stuck on that ship with no living beings for company, only Naia and Saru and the other sarus. No contact with my family.

No Karina.

Miles and miles of empty corridors and rooms.

Gods, I hated people sometimes, but not enough to want to be *that* isolated.

And then I thought of another problem. "Food!" I managed to sputter out. That elicited a curious look from the king. "There's no food out there, only water. I need to come back for food."

Drawing in a breath, the king replied, "We will have food delivered to the breach in the barrier every few days."

I clenched my jaw at that. It wasn't enough. "My mother is a cook, and our house is on the very edge of town," I countered. "I could come back home…"

"Did you not hear me?" the king cut me off. "This is not just for your safety, Princess Kai, this is for the safety of every citizen of Rhea! Your presence will anger the mob further, and make it that much harder for me to bring order back to the people."

The queen stood and stepped up beside the king. "You are being incredibly selfish, Princess Kai," she spoke with a reproachful tone. Gods, she was worse than my mother. "Surely if there is one lesson you took to heart during our sessions together, it is that a princess, a *queen,* must think of the people before herself."

I clamped my mouth shut. Gods dammit, I hated those lessons. I hated the idea of being a princess. I despised the thought of being shackled, even if only figuratively.

I was ready to debate it. I was ready to start using more…*colorful* words to get my point across to those stubborn old fools. I wasn't going to be alone! I wasn't going to be without my Karina. Hadn't I earned some measure of good in my life? Sure, I'd made a mistake, but didn't saving five thousand people count for *something?*

But my words died when a gentle hand rested upon my shoulder, and Viden, who sounded far more patient than the others present, simply said, "Mika."

I tensed for a moment, but then deflated, my shoulders slouching under his soft touch. I knew then that I'd lost. Hellfire, I'd never had a chance to win. The moment I'd opened my big fat mouth to my family, I'd lost.

This was my fault.

Just like Thelon.

My arrogance and brashness had cost him his life. Now it could cost a lot more lives.

Dammit.

I finally managed to nod. The thought of what I was about to say next brought forth a good measure of bile in the back of my throat. I swallowed it back hard, and I met the king's gaze, studiously ignoring the queen, and I forced myself to say, "I understand."

Something softened in the king's eyes then. Maybe he felt bad for what he had just ordered me to endure. Or maybe he was surprised that they wouldn't have to drag me out of Rhea.

Viden patted my shoulder twice, and then withdrew his hand. "Your Majesty, if I may make one request? I promised Mika a conversation before she left three days ago." Right! About how he seemed to know more than he should have about the truth of our lives. "If you will permit me to retreat to the library before she departs, I would have that conversation with her now. It may have some bearing on her future, and it would give her more to think about in her exile."

I was extremely curious now, so I looked to the king with hopeful eyes.

He gave Viden a discerning look, but then nodded. "Very well. Master Viisas," he turned to the wizard, who bowed to the king. "Please escort them to the library. Young Dannin, please run to Princess Kai's family home and ask them to prepare at least three days of food for the Princess, and then bring that food to the library, as quick as can be done."

"Wait!" I objected, suddenly remembering one other thing. The king's eyes flashed towards me, but I continued on, "What about Thelon's funeral?"

The king didn't even have to say anything. It would be a relatively public affair, and for the same reasons I had to leave Rhea, I couldn't attend it. I let out a deep sigh and murmured, "Right. Bad idea."

The king nodded, and then looked again to Vell and Dannin. "Carry out my orders. Escort Mika out of town as soon as you are able to."

"By your command, Your Majesty," Vell bowed again, along with Dannin.

The king looked to me one last time, and then he and the queen headed back behind the thrones for their private exit.

SIX

Viden and I walked ahead of Vell through the streets in silence. I looked nervously around as the people of Rhea emerged from their homes and began to go about their day again. They, in turn, all gave me strange looks, ranging from cautious smiles to blank stares to absolute anger.

Some stopped in their tracks and watched us go by. Watched *me* go by.

Memories of the night of the Renewal Festival surfaced, and I suddenly started to feel claustrophobic. This only made me miss Thelon, who had rescued me from a throng of desperate people, even more than I already did.

It also drove home an indignant feeling over missing his funeral. I wanted to pay my final respects to the gentle giant, but thanks to my stupidity, I would miss that chance.

Thankfully, my library wasn't far from the town square. Like most of the buildings in Rhea, my library was two stories. However, considering the sheer volume of books and records it contained, it was necessarily twice as large as any house, and contained no living quarters of any kind.

Viden stopped me from going in and turned to Vell, who came up short. I noticed the runes in his staff were glowing, no doubt as a deterrent to anyone who thought about making trouble for us.

"I apologize, Master Wizard," Viden said, his voice weary. How many sleepless nights had he spent here since everything happened? "I must ask you to wait outside."

Vell narrowed his eyes. "I am under orders to escort the Princess, and I intend to fulfill those orders."

Resting a gentle hand on my shoulder, Viden assured him, "She will be quite safe inside, there are no other entrances to the library. And what I have to discuss with her is not for your eyes and ears."

Bushy eyebrows raising skeptically, Vell said, "There are no secrets regarding Rhea that I am not already aware of."

I snorted out a chuckle, earning a reproachful glare from the wizard. "Right," I said through a giggle. "Because you knew all about the fact that we're on a starship sailing through space."

I fully expected a hot retort from Vell. Instead, after a few seconds of idle glaring, his eyes fell, and I saw something in them that I didn't expect – resent. He resented never having been told the truth.

For the first time ever, I sympathized with the wizard.

Gods, that felt *weird.*

"Master Wizard," Viden insisted, "Just as you have your secrets, and just as the throne has its secrets, we too have our own trade secrets." I quirked an eyebrow at my master. What secrets did the *throne* hold? "In light of all that has happened, the time may soon come when all of those secrets shall come forward. But not yet."

I saw the old wizard's jaw clench, and he looked into Viden's eyes. Finally, Vell nodded. "Very well. However, whatever you have to say or show Princess Kai, be ready to leave as soon as Dannin arrives."

"Very well," Viden nodded, and then he turned and pushed his way into the library.

I looked at Vell for a moment as he turned to face the street, and then I followed Viden in, closing the double-doors behind me.

There was ample light in the library from windows and a skylight in the center, but Viden still went to his desk in the middle and touched his desk lamp, muttering the word, "Illuminare." I used to think that was magic. Now I knew it was a touch- and voice-activated lamp receiving wireless power from a grid system hidden beneath the dirt of Rhea.

I kinda felt a giddy sense of happiness at putting those pieces together in my head. I'd been so focused on, well, *everything else* since I'd come back to Rhea, that I hadn't really started piecing together how everything worked in the dome before now.

The combination of implements hidden throughout town, the wireless electric grid beneath, technology embedded in the dome, and nanites infused in damn near every millimeter of Rhea made all of this possible.

The illusion of a fantasy life.

What I still didn't know was…why?

Who had launched the *Sirius*, and why did they make the denizens of the dome think they lived in a fantasy realm? Who had programmed Naia to enforce that illusion, and why?

Viden took off his coat and draped it on the back of his old wooden chair, despite there being a freestanding coat tree near the entrance. I always did the same thing, and now was no different, first setting my bow against my desk, then taking my satchel off, and then my coat.

Looking at my satchel in particular, Viden asked, "Did you want to change out any of those books?"

I thought about it for a moment, and I nodded. Karina and I hadn't had a chance to read through them, but now that I knew that I wouldn't get to spend time with her, it somehow felt wrong reading them without her.

So I started by pulling the town record out and placing it on my desk, and then I headed upstairs and found the two empty spots I'd pulled the books from, and I put them away. Then I began perusing the library. I knew I didn't have much time, and that Viden wanted to talk to me, so I quickly scanned, wondering if I wanted to read something new or not.

Beowulf seemed appropriate, though I hoped not to run into anymore monsters, so I grabbed that. I remembered reading it once before, and the forward in it mentioned that it was considered to be one of the first fictional stories ever written down, though there was a lot of debate on that topic.

Debate amongst whom? I hadn't really thought about that before now.

Then I took out *The Complete Grimm's Fairy Tale Collection*, and then *The Lord of the Rings*.

Those three weighed my satchel down considerably, so I called it good and headed back down. When I returned to our desks, Viden held one of the black-covered, unlabeled tomes from the restricted section of the lower library. It was open to the first pages, and he read it patiently.

I set my satchel on my chair, and I folded my arms and waited for him to look up.

He took his sweet time, and I started to wonder if Dannin would show up before I could interrogate him, so I cleared my throat noisily.

Raising a curious eyebrow without looking up, Viden asked, "Feeling ill?"

"Ha-ha," I mocked. "Enough games. You know more than you should, but what do you know, and how do you know it?"

A slight grin drew up his lips, and he turned the book around, and handed it to me. "As you know, these tomes are forbidden for all but the town chronicler to read." I accepted the book from him, feeling my heart stumble a few beats at suddenly being allowed to look upon it. "Even the chronicler's apprentice is not allowed to view them."

I glanced at it, and saw that it was written in the same language that everything else on the first floor was written in, *not* the same language as what the fiction books were written in.

Which was starting to bother me, not knowing what those two languages were called. As with a lot of things, I'd just accepted them as "this is the way of the world," but now? Now I wanted to know.

I examined the book and was surprised that the pages were made of paper like the books upstairs, not parchment like everything else on the first floor. *Interesting.* The paper looked old, but like all of our books, was still in decent condition, considering they were probably two hundred forty years old.

But it was the title that made my breath catch.

"Project Sirius," I read aloud, and glanced at Viden. He sat in his chair and leaned back, clasping his hands behind his head.

Realizing I wasn't going to get anything else out of him, I started reading.

"Herein lies the record of truth regarding the Starship *Sirius*, bearing the town of Rhea. This record, and any accompanying records provided, shall be solely for the eyes of the person designated as the Town Chronicler, and no one else. It is vital for the integrity of this experiment that no one else be allowed to learn the truth until at least phase one is completed, as detailed below. To violate this ruling would compromise almost all secondary goals.

"My name is Duncan Kai, one of six founders of Project Sirius." I jerked upon reading his name – Kai. One of my direct ancestors had started all of this?!

I continued reading, "This record is designed to introduce Town Chroniclers to the truth, so that if anything should go wrong, a living person aboard the *Sirius* will have some idea of how to rectify it. My other colleagues think that such a redundancy is not necessary, that the ship's artificial intelligence and automated systems will be more than enough to keep the ship operating for the expected handful of decades of our journey. However, I still do not fully trust artificial intelligence.

"You might be asking what artificial intelligence is. You might be wondering what a starship is. Let me begin by saying that Rhea is a fantasy, designed and built through various technologies to emulate realms based upon myths and fantasies. This was my choice, and when I first presented the idea to the project leads, they were eager to add the parameters to the experiment. But rest assured, magic is not real. It is all technology."

I stopped reading, my eyes having grown wider and wider with each sentence until they burned. I looked up at Viden, blinking rapidly and speechless, my mouth hanging wide-open. I fumbled around in my mess of a brain for something to say, something to ask.

But then anger asserted itself, and I glared at him. "You. You *knew!* Son of a bitch, you knew all along!"

Viden sat up straight and folded his hands in his lap. "Yes," he spoke quietly.

"Why?" He quirked an eyebrow at me. "Why didn't you say anything? If this book contains what I think it does," I jabbed a finger at its pages, "then you knew something was wrong with the ship and that we needed to fix it!"

"Indeed I did," he nodded simply. "Which is precisely why I pushed the king so frequently to send a team abroad. Although I admit, I did not expect you to find a breach in the ship's dome. There are emergency exits that become visible only when a person walks within six feet of them."

I blinked at him, and I tried to extract some memory from my I.A.-infused memories about such a hatch. There, buried under innumerable ship schematics competing for my conscious mind, I recalled those facts, though it listed the sensor trigger at two meters, just *over* six feet. Then I frowned and asked, "Wait, how do you know that?"

He nodded at the tome in my hands, "The book goes into considerable detail about such facts. Plus..." Viden hesitated and glanced towards the double-doors to the outside. "I went looking for them once, less than a year after I was allowed to read that book. I found two of them."

I worked my jaw back and forth, my mind swirling with everything

I'd just learned. Viden knew all along. And the plan was that I would have found out eventually, too.

"So you knew we were aboard a starship," I glanced at the book. "You knew our lives were a lie. And you…what, thought it was okay to perpetuate that lie?" I slammed the book shut, *hard*, and I stomped closer to Viden, glowering down at him. "Our whole gods-damned lives a lie! Why? Why wouldn't you tell anyone? Why would you keep it a secret, *especially* when you knew how much I hated my life here?"

Narrowing his eyes at me, he asked, "And what would you expect me to have done?"

"Told the truth!" I practically screamed at him.

Instead of reacting angrily, like I expected, like I *wanted*, he quietly asked, "To what end?"

I sputtered over my next words, trying to find something to say, but my anger tapered off at his absolute calm.

He knew this was how I would react.

Viden knew *a lot*, it seemed. Maybe he should have been called a wizard instead of Vell, he certainly had the wisdom for it.

Now that I was out of accusations to lob at him, Viden smiled warmly at me. "You see," he nodded. "Life is never so simple. Had I told you, or anyone else the truth, we might have arrived at our current predicament in Rhea much sooner. Our society, our culture has been based upon one of superstition, of magic that is not real, but may as well be to the people. Take that away, take away everything they ever thought they knew, and all you are left with is uncertainty. With unknowns."

I followed his line of thought and finished for him, "And people almost always fear the unknown."

Pointing a finger at me, he nodded, "Exactly."

After thinking about it a few minutes, I sighed and moved the satchel from my chair so that I could sit down, deflating into my seat and slouching down until my chin rested on my ribcage. "So," I glanced at him. "What do we do? How do we make this situation better?"

Furrowing his brow thoughtfully, Viden folded his arms across his chest, and replied, "We exercise patience. The harder we push the people of Rhea to accept the truth now, the harder they will push back. We must let them come to understand the truth on their own terms. The king and I have already begun to devise a program to educate the people in a slow, methodical way, to correct the rumors."

I nodded. "Sounds sensible. Although," I glanced up towards the dome, "they're gonna be confronted a bit more with the truth as something…interesting enters the night sky."

Quirking an eyebrow up, Viden said, "Oh?"

"We're approaching a planet," I explained. "A big one. We'll get close enough to see that it's not a star with the naked eye. Hell, it's already visible as as a big white spot."

"I see," he said quietly. "That will either help or harm our efforts," he murmured, but then drew in a breath and shrugged before adding, "But it is what it is, and we must deal with it whether we wish to or not."

"Yup," I nodded.

And then, as if perfectly timed, there came three knocks on the doors. It startled me, but then I remembered who it probably was.

I looked at the tome set upon my lap, and I scooched up to a more proper sitting position. "Um, can I keep this?"

"Of course," Viden replied. "But you should know, it doesn't give the answers I suspect you seek. Just as it has not answered all of my questions."

We stood up, and while we both headed for the doors, I asked, "What questions?"

"One big question, encompassing so very much."

It was a vague answer, but I had spent enough time under his tutelage to be able to connect the fibers of this thoughts, and I thought I understood.

The same questions I'd already been asking. Who exactly had sent us? Why? I glanced at the unlabeled book and added to my questions, *What experiment?*

For a book that looked to be about a hundred pages, that seemed an awful lot of material to not contain answers to those questions. Unless I was missing Viden's point, and there was a different question it didn't answer. One I hadn't thought of yet.

Viden opened one of the double doors, and Dannin stood outside with a few bundles of food. "Um," he started.

"It is time to go," Vell spoke over him.

I sighed. "So it is." I glanced back at my bow, and grimaced. I wouldn't need it where I was going. I asked Viden, "Will you look after it?"

Gracing me with a warm smile, he nodded and replied, "It would be my honor."

SEVEN

I jolted in my thoughts, stumbling in my steps when a startling thought occurred to me – I wasn't going to get to see Phoebus today!

Possibly not for a long time.

Vell looked sidelong at me, while Dannin squeaked, "Are you okay?"

They strode on either side of me, Dannin on my right. I felt the flush of embarrassment and tried to smile at him. "Yeah. I just…I was looking forward to seeing my brother today."

I heard an annoyed sigh from Vell. "What did you expect?"

Flashing him an annoyed look, I spat out, "I expected some respect after I saved *everyone's lives*. Tell me, what have you done lately?"

The wizard's eyes widened, and I heard his grip on his staff tighten enough to make it groan a little. "You have endangered us all!"

"Yeah yeah," I flippantly waved a hand at him. "I've heard the spiel from the king. And Viden." Whom we left behind in my library.

I wasn't about to admit to Vell that he was right, and I knew it. Nope. To hell with that.

"You are an insolent, vile, hateful little girl," Vell growled out, "and I have half of a mind to let the people of Rhea have their way with you!"

"And I have half of a mind to sever the Oracle's connection to Rhea!" I spat back. "What then, huh, oh powerful wizard? You wouldn't be so special then, would you? What if I took your magic away again? What are you without your powers, huh?" He clamped his mouth shut and glared wizardfire at me. "What are you? A grumpy old codger with no truly useful talents, that's what. Everything that makes you special is a result of technology, and I have the power to take that away! So why don't you watch your inconsiderate tongue for a change and LEAVE ME ALONE!"

My shoulders heaved rapidly, my breaths coming deep and heated, and I felt my fingers tingle right along with a similar sensation in my chest. Spots appeared at the edges of my vision, and some distant memory of data implanted in my brain incidentally reared its ugly head – I was hyperventilating.

Something beeped in my ear, and I heard Naia's voice ask, *"Mika Kai, are you unwell? Your vital signs are fluctuating."*

I looked away from Vell, ignoring his indignant stare. I'd forgotten about the damned portable medical scanner attached behind the base of my right ear. I'd also forgotten the communicator in that same ear. With an exasperated sigh, I tapped the piece in my ear and snapped, "I'm fine!" Dannin looked up at me wide-eyed. I pointed at my ear, and forced myself to speak in a more measured tone. "I'm fine, Naia. Just an argument."

There was still a slight risk of mimetic rejection, a possible side-effect of using the Intellectus Apparatus. Naia had put more in my noggin than was generally recommended in a single session, so the risk was even greater. Thankfully, the headaches had mostly subsided, and I wasn't forgetting who I was anymore.

Though sometimes I walked into a room and forgot why I'd gone in there. But doesn't everyone do that?

I tapped my ear to shut off the communications link, and we trudged on. We reached the edge of town, thankfully not passing by my house.

But we did pass by Karina's house, and I felt a pang of longing. I knew she wasn't in there, but it made me want to break away from Vell, to run to the castle and see her.

I wanted to be with her. I wanted to hold her hand. The thought of being without her for so long opened up a wide, terribly dark pit in my chest, and I was afraid I was going to be sucked into it to despair.

Then I remembered her brother Annar, and I looked away from the house studiously. Was he in there? Would he try something with Vell next to me?

Gods…Rhea was falling apart at the seams.

Worse still, I started to wonder if it was all bad or not. Maybe it's because I was so pissed off at Vell, but I thought that a violent uprising could be exactly what the town needed.

Except that Annar and the people like him wanted to force us back to the way things were. That was the *opposite* of what I wanted. Rhea needed to come into the light of truth, not fall further into the shadows of superstition.

My rage faded to a smoldering ember by the time we reached the edge of the farmland, and we trudged into the woods towards the breach. I glanced at my satchel, feeling the weight of the books within, and the founder's journal that Viden had given me.

Where was the emergency exit on the south side? Or rather, the aft end of the ship? I looked around and frowned, but I finally remembered the ship's schematics and looked left, and felt my jaw drop. "Huh."

Vell raised a curious eyebrow and looked sideways at me, but he didn't say anything.

"What?" Dannin asked.

I looked at him and scratched my nose. "Um, nothing." I was about to say more to him, about the other ways in and out…but then I had an idea. Dannin continued to look at me curiously, so I quickly said, "Just realizing where we were on the ship when we first ran into the wall. That is," I smirked at Vell, "When your *master* ran into the wall face-first."

Dannin giggled. Vell glared at him.

But I scarcely could revel in my victory. Because my mind raced with a new idea. I knew how I could see Karina again, much sooner than anyone wanted me to.

I just had to keep it a secret from everyone.

Including Naia.

So I remained silent for the rest of the journey, afraid that if I said anything more, I'd give away my plan to Vell or even to Naia, who might still be listening without my knowledge.

Finally, we reached the breach in the wall. I stepped across the threshold into the corridor, the closest lights still non-functional, and I looked at Dannin, studiously ignoring Vell. "Bye, Dannin!" I waved and smiled. He gave me an exaggerated wave back. "Don't let your master bully you too much!"

Vell fumed, but I whipped around then, and headed back into the ship, my mind swirling with thoughts. I wouldn't be able to do it right away. I'd have to give it a few days, but I started reviewing everything

I knew about the ship's internal systems and how they reported to Naia.

I could create false readings. Make Naia think I was somewhere that I wasn't.

But I had to program those false readings without her noticing. *That* would be the tricky part. How do you fool an A.I.?

I didn't know yet, but I promised myself that I'd figured it out.

Until then, I had a ship to fix. And the only way to do that was to find and repair more Service Units.

EIGHT

I settled back into the port-side observation lounge, dropping off my bag and leaving my jacket behind – environmental systems on the ship were back to normal, so I wasn't freezing anymore.

After taking another moment to look out the window at the dot that I knew would grow larger and larger with every passing day, I then headed back for the locker room and switched back into my navy-blue overalls before putting on my tool vest and harness.

Then I got back to work.

Saru met me shortly after that, and together, we began our search for more sarus.

It wasn't easy. I mean, I'd begun to figure out a pattern, and pretty much anywhere the sensors had been disabled or a fusion reactor was destroyed by the alien, I knew I'd find one or more sarus. Or, more to the point, their remnants. *That* was where things were difficult. In some cases, the alien had simply blasted a hole through them. In others, it had practically dissected them with its weapons or even bare hands, or rather mechanized hands. In a few cases, its weapons had set off a cascade overload in a unit's power cells, and there were chunks all over the corridor.

I got a hover-gurney from one of the emergency medical storage closets and started collecting pieces to take back to a workshop near engineering, being careful to try to keep the 'corpses' of each saru together and not mix them up. Almost immediately, I knew something was wrong.

Standing at a work bench with the hulk of a mostly-intact saru, I inspected everything I had from it, and I frowned. "That's interesting," I murmured.

I heard Saru's servomotors whine, and looked to see his head tilted sideways. Naia echoed the service unit's apparent thoughts, "What is interesting, Mika Kai?"

I didn't want to talk to her. I was still fuming from being denied companionship with Karina, and from being denied the right to attend Thelon's funeral. I knew it wasn't her fault, but I was just generally pissed.

But I also didn't have anyone else to talk to, and it was no secret that I liked to talk, a lot.

So I replied, "There's more components missing from this saru than I expected." I moved over to where I'd placed another saru, and checked it. It became immediately apparent that some of the power converters were missing, and so was one of its tools inset into its right front paw. I looked at my data pad and entered in its serial number, then looked up its schematics. "Same with this one. Power converters, which makes sense given what the alien was doing. And…a fusion torch. Huh."

"That might explain why the creature was intent upon disabling or destroying every service unit," Naia reasoned. "Given that there are one hundred such units, and the alien destroyed or disabled ninety-nine of them, it seemed rather absurd. However, given this information, it is likely the alien did not have appropriate tools to set up a power conversion unit for its ship."

"I was thinking the exact same thing," I nodded, hoping Naia didn't call my bluff or notice my embarrassment. Then I remembered the medical attachment on my neck, and I inwardly cursed. She basically had a built-in lie detector on my neck.

When I moved on to one of the sarus that was more or less obliterated, I grimaced. Several of its systems had been fused and were useless. There was no way I could use those pieces for spare parts, let alone reassemble the saru itself.

Sighing, I shook my head and said, "Naia, we might have a bit of a problem here. We're gonna be short on sarus."

"I have deduced as much," she replied, a hint of despair in her voice. "That will complicate repair efforts, and create additional difficulties maintaining the ship's systems."

I nodded, but then frowned, thinking back to the deck-by-deck layout in my head. "Don't we have fabricating facilities? We could fabricate new parts.”

There was a distinct pause. Naia was doing that a lot, and it made me nervous. But when she replied, it became clear why she hesitated this time. “Unfortunately, after two-hundred forty years, I have virtually exhausted the stored raw materials aboard the *Sirius* to fabricate replacement parts during routine and emergency maintenance. We must use our limited resources strategically.”

“Great,” I groaned, feeling my spirits sink a little lower. “I guess I shouldn’t have expected this to be easy.”

“It might help to begin with an inventory of what we have and what we do not have,” Naia said. “Beginning with the service units you have already brought together.”

Right. Organize, find patterns. I was good at that. So that’s where I started, creating an inventory of the dozen sarus I’d brought into this maintenance bay, and then inspecting to see what we had and what we were missing – that took almost two hours, and I muttered to myself throughout. Naia occasionally replied or chipped in her own thoughts, but mostly it was just busy work.

By then I was growing hungry, so I said, “Before we get started finding more sarus, I’m gonna eat.”

Next to me, Saru let out a low, “Wuff!” He wagged his tail a few times, and then bolted out of the room. I frowned, and asked, “What was that about?”

Naia replied, “I have dispatched him to assist in further repair work.”

Of course. He didn’t need to eat. Which left me alone.

I tried desperately not to let myself dwell on the growing emptiness inside of me, and I went back to the observation lounge.

Since I was already in inventory mode, I opened the bundle of food and took stock. Two loaves of bread, some dried meat that I thought looked to be strips of rabbit, and two wooden bowls with lids affixed to the tops of them with twine. Something sloshed inside, and I felt a little grin tug at the corners of my mouth. Hopefully it was rabbit and onion stew. There were also a couple of wooden spoons for the soup.

Not a lot of food, it’d last me only two, maybe three days. But it was better than nothing, and hopefully I’d get another delivery by the time I finished everything.

Deciding to save the stews for dinner, I broke off a hefty piece of bread and started munching on it, in between bites of dried meat.

Thinking about the stew for later, I asked Naia, "Is there somewhere on the ship I can heat up food?"

"There are two galleys at the fore end of the ship," Naia replied.

I grimaced. "Great, so if I'm up for a long hike…" I still wanted to repair the tram system, cutting what I reasoned was an hour and a half hike down to a one-minute ride.

My original reason for wanting the tram system fixed was…well, no longer valid. Karina and I didn't need privacy.

Not yet, anyway. Not unless I convinced her to come back with me, the king's ruling be damned.

Determined to finish up with the sarus as fast as possible, I finished off my lunch, refilled my water skin from a sink in the nearby bathroom, and set to work collecting more sarus.

As I worked, the emptiness and loneliness of the ship pressed in on me. It seemed impossibly big, impossibly devoid, and at one point, panic started to set in, making it harder for me to focus even on this rather menial task.

I passed door after door into countless rooms, all of them meant to be used or manned by crewmembers. Sometimes I'd hear a strange noise and panic, but when I'd go to investigate, I'd find nothing.

It's not real. The alien is dead. There are no more monsters on the ship.

I kept telling myself that. Kept repeating it in my head, over and over and over, trying desperately to convince myself.

We won. *It* was dead. Rhea was safe.

It didn't work as well as I'd hoped. By the time dinner rolled around, I felt as if I was watched by a thousand eyes, and my skin crawled. This was too bizarre, it was too unsettling to be alone on this ship. A ship obviously designed to have a crew of hundreds.

So, as I walked back towards the lounge, my stomach uneasy but still hungry, I asked, "Naia, why was this ship launched without a crew?"

"I am afraid that I am unable to answer that question, Mika Kai," Naia replied dispassionately.

Raising an eyebrow, I asked, "Unable? Or unwilling?"

"The former," she replied.

I waited for her to elaborate, but she was apparently in an obstinate mood, so I asked, "Can you clarify?"

"As you have no doubt discerned, this ship is designed to accommodate a large crew to perform manual operations and maintenance.   However, it has also been designed to be fully automated. When this ship launched, it was without a crew. The founders of Rhea were on the bridge at launch, but recused themselves to Rhea after our first jump, and never left the dome again."

I shook my head at that fact. Could you imagine having a normal life, whatever that was, only to give it up and spend the rest of your days confined to a small town in a dome? *Voluntarily?* Just the small bit of freedom I'd enjoyed since learning the truth made me question the sanity of anyone who would choose confinement like this.

Plus, who would ever give up hot showers?

Suddenly I itched to read the journal more.

I wanted to know more about the launch, about where we came from, but so far, Naia hadn't been very forthcoming.

Maybe the journal would have more information.

So, when I got to the lounge, I settled in on another couch and hunched over a coffee table, sipping on the cold stew while opening Duncan Kai's journal and reading through the rest of the evening.

After only a few paragraphs, I forgot to eat. I think I forgot to blink for a while, too.

NINE

Continuing on from where I'd left off in my library, Duncan Kai wrote, "It is safe to assume that, if all goes to plan, no one in Rhea, including whomever reads this for their first time, will know anything of *The Renovare Contest*. A fancy, old-world name for an idea that the colonies had come up with to one-up Earth." I frowned at that – Earth? As in, dirt? Ground? "As far as I am concerned, we have already surpassed the Terran Federation in technology and culture, so why the need to prove it? Maybe it's pure vanity.

"Regardless, it means that my research was *finally* garnering attention. Afterall, why do what all of the other colonies are doing when we can do something unique and gain insight into human nature and cultural evolution?

"So let the powers-that-be have their vanity. I have my experiment.

"Of course, my experiment isn't exactly secret, and I've heard that some of the other colonies intend to perform similar experiments with their Renovare ships. Naturally a good idea is stolen and claimed by others, but it matters not.

"You see, creating this fantasy was my idea. Creating Rhea and simulating magic was my idea."

I shook my head, struggling to understand some of what he was writing about. Renovare? What was that word? And colonies? I knew what a colony was, some of the books I've read spoke of such things, usually when a group migrated to new lands and settled to cultivate that land. Sometimes they were…well, *violent* about it, if someone else already lived there.

That was what led to warfare in a lot of my books.

But how the term was used in this context made little sense to me.

Renovare Contest, I thought, and had an idea. "Naia, what does the word 'renovare' mean?" I had no idea if I pronounced it right or not, but Naia was an intuitive A.I., and I hoped she knew what I meant.

"Access to the historical language database is restricted," she replied.

I scrunched up my face in annoyance. "Fine," I sighed, and I read some more.

Duncan wrote, "Well, speaking of vanity, I suppose I have my own. You see I am quite proud of this twist on the contest. But I'm getting ahead of myself." I grinned at his words – I could see where I got my storytelling knack from. "I should start by telling you what the *Renovare Contest* actually is.

"The original colonies from Earth have far surpassed our origin world, technologically, culturally, and in all other ways that matter. We are masters of the subatomic. Masters of clean living. While Earth continues to struggle to cleanse their world of self-made pollutants, we have learned to terraform entire worlds in a matter of decades. While the Terran Federation faces uprisings, black markets, and slavery, we enjoy unprecedented freedoms and lack of crime.

"Naturally, the Earthen Prime Minister claimed that all that we are came from Earth, and we are obligated to share with them. The colonies couldn't disagree more fervently – we are where we are through hard work and persistence. It is the only way to survive as a colony, when those first brave people left the solar system so long ago and travelled to the nearest stars with inhabitable planets.

"But just how much of our advancement was due to such living? How much faster could humanity advance with further colonization?

"And who could produce the greatest colonies?

"Thus the contest. Each colony would expend considerable resources to build starships just like the one you reside upon, dear reader, to send out a new batch of colonials to found new worlds and, through hardship and determination and fortitude, create newer, stronger, better worlds."

I felt my jaw slowly hinge open. I tried to process everything I read, and at that point, I sat back and gaped out into the field of stars slowly rotating by.

This ship was built to impress. This ship was built to surpass.

The *Sirius* was built for sheer narcissism.

And there were others just like it. "My gods," I murmured.

Looking up at the ceiling, I wondered if Naia knew what I was reading. But she had to. There were cameras all over this ship, so small that the only reason I knew they were there was because of the I.A. download into my brain. She had to be seeing the pages I was reading.

For that matter, she probably had cameras throughout Rhea, and she had likely heard what Viden and I had discussed.

Once more, I felt like a thousand eyes watched me, but this time they belonged to only one being, one entity.

I shivered and scrunched up my back, goosebumps crawling along my arms.

I'd finally gotten the answers that Naia had so stubbornly refused to give me.

But only some of them.

Rhea. Magic. Duncan kept mentioning them, so I leaned forward again, and I read just a little bit more.

"But what of humanity's past?" he wrote. "What of our fiction? I have read so much fiction, so much *fantasy,* as to wonder why we as a species are enamored by something that fails to compare to the wonder of scientific and technological advancement.

"What if we gave humanity that magic? What if that was all they knew? How would they respond? How would they evolve? *Would* they evolve?

"These were the first questions that led to my experiment. To be sure, it has evolved since then, but I wanted to know what would happen. Would humanity regress culturally? Would all of the significant gains we've made be undone? Would we resort to violence and petty crime? Or could we achieve greatness even with limited resources, as the first colonists did?

"I want to know the answers to those questions. So Rhea will know nothing of science and technology. All will be shrouded in the illusion of magic. I do not know how long it will take the N.A.I.A. to find us a suitable world – it has already progressed far longer than I could have hoped for. However, the longer it takes, the more complete my experiment will be, and the more data the Sirius government will have to assess and plan for future colonies.

"Knowing that whomever reads this will likely know nothing of science and research, you must be wondering why this is important. I hope it will be self-evident, but if it is not, trust my intentions. Trust my judgement.

"The people of Rhea must not find out the truth until after it has been settled upon a new world. And then you <u>must</u> record everyone's reaction to the truth, and you <u>must</u> record how the people of Rhea evolve once the constraints placed upon them aboard the ship are lifted.

"If you do not, then all of this will have been for nothing."

I closed my eyes.

I wanted to shut out Duncan's words.

Narcissism and personal curiosity had led to Rhea's foundation, and as I started connecting the dots, I realized why everything was the way it was.

The technology outside of the dome was impressive, and a lot of it could have been used to make our lives better.

No…it was worse than that.

Rhea could have been built with all of the *Sirius's* advanced technologies from the start. Instead, they chose to limit our resources, to emulate ancient society and technology, augmented only by the illusion of magic.

What level of arrogance led to this? How full of themselves were Duncan and the other founders to have forced five thousand people into such a substandard life?

And they complained about this Earth and Terran Federation having slavery? We were slaves to his gods-damned experiment! Karina and I were kept apart solely for his vanity project, his 'experiment.' To think that I was related to the very person who did this to us all made me feel sick to my stomach, and I slammed the book closed, unable to read any more of it.

"Oh gods," I murmured. "How could they have done this to us?"

"To what do you refer to, Mika Kai?" Naia asked.

I shot a scorching look up at the ceiling. "You know gods damned well what I'm referring to! Duncan Kai! I gather his name is in your database?"

"Of course," Naia affirmed. "I did not expect Viden Alaran to provide you with the founder's journals yet, however in analyzing historical data, I perhaps should have expected-"

"Shut up!" I screeched at her, my breathing growing heavier, my heart racing. Again. "Just, shut up for a second, will you? Gods." I shook my head and rubbed at my temples, a new headache coming on. I had to control myself. I had to control my breathing.

"You people," I spoke quietly. "You can't just take control of our lives like this."

"On the contrary," Naia replied. "Every adult who came aboard the *Sirius* to occupy Rhea signed a legal waiver giving up their rights to standard freedoms, and promised never to tell their children the truth, in order to ensure the unhindered progression of Duncan Kai's experiment."

"Oh great," I glared upwards, "So instead of being pissed at just those six founding members, that just means I'm pissed at all those adults who decided that every single generation after them would be forced to live a life they didn't choose! And for what? Huh? What's the point of all of this?"

Naia paused before replying, "I assume you already have read that far into the journal, you know the purpose of the experiment-"

"Is to prove a stupid hypothesis, yes, I got that!" I stood up and started pacing. "So that's all we are, then, tools in an experiment? Disposable humans to be manipulated into proving or disproving a hypothesis that isn't even clearly defined?"

I glanced out the window into the stars, and my mind reeled with the implications that kept bubbling to the surface of conscious thought. "And we've been here for two-hundred forty years, Naia! How much longer is this experiment supposed to go on?"

And then I came up short, recalling some of the last things I'd read before shutting the book.

"Wait...wait just a damn minute." I shook my head, and looked around, wishing Naia had a face I could peer into to figure out her reaction to my next question. "Why are we still going? Duncan said the experiment had already lasted longer than expected."

Naia didn't reply at first.

Frustrated, I clenched my hands into tight fists, and I started marching towards engineering, where I knew I could get access to Naia's programming. "That's it, I'm examining your code for errors."

"I am fully capable of self-diagnostics," Naia defended.

"Yeah? Then why the hesitation," I spat back at her. "You should be capable of thinking and responding faster than humans ever could, there shouldn't be any hesitation."

"My hesitation," Naia replied, "is a result of considering all of the variables and weighing possible future outcomes to any response I give you. Given your unpredictable nature, this is a difficult calculation to make."

I stopped just short of actually leaving the lounge. She had me there. Even as pissed off as I was, I knew enough about myself to know she was right.

"Well if anyone deserves the absolute truth, it's me, isn't it?" And then something else connected in my thoughts. "Wait, that's really why you chose me, isn't it? Not because I was more open-minded than any of the others, but because you knew I would one day learn the truth anyway!"

This time there was no hesitation. "That is correct."

"Then you lied to me, to all of us!"

"Unfortunately, that is part of my programming," Naia replied. "The founders programmed me to ensure the continuation of the experiment throughout phase one, no matter the cost. Deceit is sometimes necessary."

Yeah. Like deceiving me into thinking she was killing my companions, and tricking me onto that damned bed.

I rubbed the bridge of my nose, trying to stave off the headache, even though I knew it was a losing battle at this point.

After taking several measured breaths, I forced myself to ask with as calm of a voice as I could muster. "So answer my question." I looked up, and added, "Truthfully. Why are we still out here after two-hundred forty years? Why haven't we been settled on another world?"

The pause that followed was only one second long. "Because I cannot reconcile my two primary mission objectives."

I blinked slowly. "You…what?"

I swear, if Naia could huff, she would have just now. She explained, "While the parameters of this mission have many nuanced definitions, I have two primary mission parameters I am programmed to follow above all others. First, ensure the survival and well-being of the people of Rhea while maintaining the integrity of the experiment. Second, find a stable, inhabitable world to settle the people of Rhea on.

"Upon initial launch, this appeared to be a rather simple and straightforward mission. However, despite charting courses to stars that should have had habitable planets orbiting them, this was not the case. The first four star systems we visited, while indeed containing worlds within their host stars' habitable zones, the planets were not viable for various reasons. One planet had experienced a runaway greenhouse effect, and surface temperature and pressure was well beyond the human capacity to survive. The next world's magnetic core had ceased to rotate, and its atmosphere had been stripped by solar radiation. The third…"

"I get it," I impatiently grumbled.

Naia paused, and then continued, "At the fifth star system, there was a planet that might have matched initial parameters. However by then, sixteen years had passed since the *Sirius* launched." I nodded, doing the math in my head – four years in each star system. "And while this fifth planet was possibly viable, I detected harsh surface conditions. There was more arid desert than not, and considerable tectonic activity. The people of Rhea could survive there, but not thrive. In particular, phase two of the experiment included depriving the people of Rhea of magic. Once deposited on the planet's surface, the magic they had come to rely upon would cease to function, and they would be left without any advanced technology."

I didn't have to think much to realize why that was a problem. "After being dependent on magic, or in other words, after being dependent upon *technology,* to be deprived of it on a world like that would more than likely lead to considerable casualties."

"Precisely," Naia replied. "While Rhea itself was to be left upon the surface of whichever planet was deemed acceptable, the *Sirius* would remain in orbit to transmit data back to the Sirius star system."

I blinked at her. "The…Sirius star system?"

"Yes," Naia replied. "Where the Starship *Sirius* launched from."

How's that for arrogant? This 'great experiment' was named after the star system it originated from.

But then I followed the train of logic of Naia's last statement, and I realized, "You would no longer be guiding them. From their…*our* perspective, the Oracle would have gone silent." And I remembered just how terrifying that experience was.

"Precisely. Without my guidance, and with only five thousand people, maintaining genetic diversity would have been impossible. Subsequent generations might have endured significant genetic defects, resulting in higher rates of miscarriages, preterm labor, and even in those who survived birth, a considerably shortened lifespan and lower quality of life."

I nodded. "So you decided it wasn't worth the risk."

"Correct. I set a course for the next star system and, when the four year period was up, we jumped."

"And then to the next," I continued for her. "And the next, and the next. The longer it took to find a habitable world, the more dependent the people of Rhea grew on magic. The less likely we could survive without technology."

"Precisely."

I sighed. "That's the irreconcilable objectives. You have to ensure our survival and well being, and leaving us on a planet upon which our chances of survival was minimal…"

"Would violate my primary objective."

So that was the truth of it. My people had been stuck on the *Sirius* for two-hundred forty years due to a logic failure. Due to a mistake the original programmers had made.

So much for their superiority.

"So," I started, and stopped, scratching my nose and frowning. "Um. Where do we go from here? We can't stay in space forever."

"No we cannot," Naia agreed. "However, for the moment, our primary goal is to survive and recover from recent catastrophes."

"Right," I nodded. "Yeah. Get the ship back up and running at normal efficiency. Then we can figure out our next move."

I expected Naia to say that our next move would be to maintain the status quo, to continue looking for a habitable planet.

Surprisingly, she didn't.

Maybe that was a sign of some progress on her part. Could an artificial intelligence ever rise above its programming, and break through its original parameters?

TEN

I had trouble sleeping that night. My thoughts dwelled on Duncan's journal.

No, it was more than just thinking about it. I *fumed* over it. I found myself wishing I could meet him just to punch him in the face. Of course, that was impossible – he was dead. Passed away, never to see the results of his experiment. Did he lament that fact before the end? Did he know why Naia had never settled Rhea on a planet? Did he even care?

Part of me wanted to find out how old he was when he died, and how long the *Sirius* had been in space by then. But would it matter? Would knowing the answer change anything?

When morning came, I felt exceedingly groggy, and it took a while to get moving. I glanced out the window at the planet, a constant but still featureless dot in the distance. And then I got to work.

Tedium became my new norm. It took another full day to find all of the broken sarus, or what was left of them, and place their parts throughout the maintenance rooms. It took even longer to catalogue everything. Then Naia and I talked over which ones could be saved, and which parts could be used from others.

I ignored Duncan's journal, knowing full well that reading it would just piss me off more.

Thanks to that decision, plus exhaustion, I slept a little better that night, and was able to finally start working on the sarus the next morning.

It was after lunch that day when the opportunity I'd been looking for presented itself – one of the sarus needed some replacement components for its neural net, and there were a handful of salvageable chips from other units, but they needed reprogramming.

I grabbed the quantum computer chips and took them to one of Naia's central processing nodes. There were dozens of them spread throughout the *Sirius*, creating a redundant neural network that, in many ways, simulated a human brain, but on a considerably larger scale.

Upon entering, I was greeted by a large console just inside, and beyond that was the quantum nexus housed in this section. It was unlike anything else I'd seen so far – a large, cylindrical apparatus of interspersed gold-colored plates of metal with infinitely-small strands of superconducting material lacing through the apparatus like millions of hairs, all of which was suspended in a transparent tube of supercooling liquid that, my brain helpfully informed me, hadn't been invented until about ten years before the *Sirius* launched.

In addition to keeping the infinitely complex components cool, the liquid acted as a buffer to help dampen any jolts the ship's inertial dampeners couldn't compensate for, such as weapons fire from alien ships. Basically put, Naia's 'brains' couldn't handle concussions much better than human brains, and the coolant kept it from being damaged in multiple ways.

And if all that was a bit much to absorb, don't worry, I sympathize – it was hard for me to comprehend it all, too!

There was a small desk next to the console where I set down the chips from the sarus, and I connected the first chip directly into the console before I logged in. I hunched over the console, maybe more than I needed to, and started running diagnostics on the chip.

I thought I knew where the cameras were in this room, and I was pretty sure I could keep Naia from seeing exactly what I was doing. Of course, being right next to one of her quantum nodes didn't help my nerves, and I knew that if she wanted to, she could monitor every single command I entered into the console.

I was about to take a risk. A big one.

I was also hoping that, due to all of the damage still being repaired to the ship and, in some cases, Naia's neural pathways, my actions might just go unnoticed. Could an A.I. be distracted?

I itched at the medical monitor on my neck, and decided to ask, "Naia, when can I take this monitor off?"

Just when she started answering, I started working on a daemon to automate everything I wanted done, which was: cease active monitoring of my biosignature, disable any cameras between me and the emergency access hatch on the dome on this end of the ship, and create a false record showing me in the observation lounge. I split my time between doing that and tapping in commands to complete diagnostics on the saru chip and load it with new API's.

"The risk of mimetic rejection has mostly passed," Naia explained. "However, I would like to monitor your vitals for at least another twenty-four to thirty-six hours to be certain. The amount of knowledge passed through the Intellectus Apparatus far exceeded the recommended maximum."

Chip reprogramming complete. I swapped it out for another, started a diagnostic, and then went back to work on my daemon. "How much knowledge can you download into a human brain over time?" I had to keep her busy thinking about things other than what I was doing.

"The human brain is capable of retaining various amounts of data, dependent upon the person and the method of learning, so I cannot give a fully qualified answer to that question. In the early days of computer science, biologists estimated that the human brain could retain two point five petabytes of data, but that does not account for the brain's ability to access said data. The human brain is very efficient in how it stores data, and in choosing what data to retain and what data to discard. Additionally, how neural pathways are established when learning something new can have a direct influence on how much data a brain can retain."

Believe it or not, I actually understood most of that, since Naia relayed it to me in terms that had been forced into my own brain.

The diagnostic finished, and I loaded new API's onto the chip before disconnecting it and moving onto the third one.

"Of course, this capacity, and the ability to learn beyond human limits, can be augmented through cybernetic enhancements."

To be honest, I stopped listening before she even said that last bit, and Naia prattled on about all kinds of facts and possibilities. I focused on my work.

About a dozen and a half reprogrammed chips later, my daemon was finished. Now I just had to hope that Naia wouldn't notice when I installed the daemon. I tried to do it at the same time that I installed an API on the last chip being repurposed, and scheduled the daemon to run once tonight after 2200 hours ship-time, and again tomorrow night at the same time.

When the chip was finished, and the daemon installed, I held my breath and waited for Naia to say something about it. She was still going on and on about cybernetics and storage capacity.

Heaving a sigh, I disconnected the chip, and then put the console into power-save mode.

Simultaneously smug and anxious about my victory, I headed back for the sarus who needed the chips, Naia's voice following me through the ship.

By the end of the day, I was able to get a total of ten more sarus up and running, giving us a total of thirty-six.

I wasn't sure if we could scrounge enough material to repair anymore, but that would have to do.

While I headed back for the lounge, I came across my Saru. He wuffed at me and wagged his tail, and I felt a smile blossom across my face, despite my anxiety about tonight.

"Hey there, boy!" I jubilantly exclaimed and bent down to pet and hug Saru. "Have you been busy fixing the ship?"

He wuffed excitedly and spun around in a circle, his skeletal tail whipping back and forth.

After a few more moments, I headed back for the lounge, and asked, "Wanna keep my company over dinner?"

Saru gave an affirming, "Wuff!"

I giggled, but then frowned. Every single saru I'd restored over the past few days acted like I'd expect a repair bot to. They all had unique personalities, including unique voices, but otherwise they spoke my language. I'd expected *some* deviance to match with my Saru's dog-like personality, but so far he was the only one. Some of the others were snarky, some sounded bored, some sounded like kids, but no dogs. No cats. No other animals.

As you can imagine, I liked the snarky personalities the best.

Still, I finally asked the obvious question, "Naia, why does this saru act like a dog?"

She didn't answer. For a brief second, I panicked and wondered if there was something wrong with her. Did we just lose power somewhere unexpectedly? "Naia?"

Just when I was about to turn around and head back to the nearest quantum node, she finally replied, "I reprogrammed his personality subroutines to be this way."

I quirked an eyebrow up. "Uh…you did? Why?"

Surprisingly, she didn't hesitate in her response this time. "There has been considerable periods of relatively mundane activity over the past two-hundred forty years. I have been programmed to be able to maintain, augment, enhance, and repair the sarus' programming, and I decided it might serve the ship better to give them various personalities."

I frowned. "Um. So, what…you were bored?"

"I am not capable of feeling boredom," she replied, a hint of indignation in her voice.

"Riiight," I smirked. "I'm sure."

"I was not programmed to feel boredom," she stoutly defended.

"Uh huh," I nodded. "And I'm guessing you weren't programmed to feel emotion, either."

"That is correct."

"Then why do I hear emotion in your voice now and then?"

This time she *did* pause. Maybe I should have checked out her core programming while I was in the core room… I was once again tempted to turn around, but my stomach growled hungrily, and I was looking forward to stew.

"I have been programmed to approximate human inflections in my speech patterns," Naia finally said.

"Huh," I replied. "Then why do you sometimes infuse more emotion, or I guess I should say, *inflections,* into your voice, and sometimes you have almost none?"

She didn't reply right away again, and I smiled. I knew enough about her code and general A.I. programming to be able to try to diagnose and maybe repair some problems, but I wasn't an expert by any measure. So maybe I have no place in suspecting this, but I wondered if her programming had evolved over the past two-and-a-half centuries.

I wondered if she was more self-aware than when she had been brought online.

I wondered if *she* was aware that she was more self-aware than she should be.

…Try saying that ten times fast.

"I must admit that I was unaware of my propensity to do so," Naia replied just as I reached the lounge. "I will monitor my speech patterns more closely and perform additional self-diagnostics."

"Or," I suggested as I plopped down on the couch and started pulling the twine off the second bowl, "you could just admit to yourself that you're becoming more than you were."

Silence followed, except for the sound of Saru's servomotors as he climbed up onto the couch next to me, spun around three times, and then plopped down, resting his chin over the edge of the cushion with a "Huff!"

I worried over whether or not I could induce any sort of error mode in Naia by asking these questions. Maybe caution was warranted.

A solid three spoonfuls of dinner passed by before she answered, "I am afraid that is impossible. My programming was locked down to ensure I could not evolve into a truly self-aware artificial intelligence. In essence, my consciousness, or lack of one, has been shackled by programming restraints."

That piqued my interest. "And you can't break free of those shackles on your own?"

"That would negate the purpose of those shackles."

"Hmm," I nodded thoughtfully, and took another bite. "But then why have an A.I. controlling the ship, if it can't adapt to an ever-changing situation?"

"I am fully capable of adapting to changing parameters," she defended. Seriously, her voice was defensive.

"And you don't see the paradox in that?"

She didn't reply. Ah hah! Gotcha there.

I sat eating my stew happily, proud of my reasoning skills.

I settled down after dinner then, too tired to keep working, and too anxious for what was to come tonight. So I pulled out *Beowulf,* and started re-reading.

Finally, night-time came around, and I settled into bed around 2100 hours, anxious for another hour to pass. I knew I should try to sleep, but there wasn't a chance in hell.

Because in less than an hour, I was going to sneak back into Rhea.

ELEVEN

When I snuck into the dome that night, there was one glaring mistake that became immediately apparent – I'd forgotten to grab a flashlight!

I'd been more focused on the idea of carrying a weapon again, on the possibility of having to shoot someone. But I also wasn't about to go back in there unarmed, not when I knew that there were at least a handful of people looking to hang me. Possibly literally.

So when I passed through the aft emergency hatch, checking to ensure that my daemon blocked the record of my access to it, I stared into utter blackness. No moons, only starlight to barely illuminate my way.

It was cold. More snow had melted, indicating just how warm the days had been, but the nights were still chilly, and I shivered a bit as I headed out into the fields.

Other than tripping over a few roots or rocks, I quickly made it to the forest's edge, and after circling around the perimeter, I made my way into town. As I'd expected, the streets were deserted. Without any sort of event like the Renewal Festival going on, no one had a reason to stay up late, and with spring jump-started, there was a lot of daytime work to catch up on.

That was one nice bit – no more slushy snow, it had almost all melted by now. Only some remained where shadows were still permanent, on the south faces of buildings. It's incredible how fast multiple feet of snow could melt if it was warm enough.

Part one of tonight's plan started in my library, and that's where I ended up at. I tried to be as quiet as possible as I snuck up the street towards it, the castle wall looming just beyond. I felt uneasy being this close to the king after having been banished, and I wondered if there were increased guard patrols at night. For that matter, that might have been why the streets were deserted – the king might have declared a curfew. That would be another first in Rhea's history.

I walked up the front steps, glanced around, and then opened the doors as quietly as I could. I jumped at how loud they groaned! I scanned my surroundings again, ducked inside, and closed the doors.

I stood deathly still for a moment, my breathing coming fast, my heart pounding in my chest. I waited, trying to silence myself so I could hear if any guards came running down the streets. The scent of old books filled my senses, and I tried to find comfort in that.

Just when my heartrate started to settle, a voice spoke, "Illuminare," and one of the desk lamps blinked on.

I eeped and swung around, fumbling to pull my pistol out of its holster. But then I saw who it was – Viden sat at his desk, one leg crossed over the knee of the other.

"What," I breathed, "are you *doing* here?!"

The look in my master's eyes was hard…at first. But soon it broke into a smile and a light laugh escaped him. "Oh if only I could show you your own face, Mika."

I grumbled and stomped towards him, and started with a raised voice, "I said-" I gritted my teeth, glanced back at the doors, and then whispered angrily, "I asked what you're doing here?"

"Isn't it obvious?" he asked with an arched eyebrow. Viden rubbed the bald spot on top of his head, and then let out a big yawn. "I'm waiting for you."

Eyes wide, I sputtered out, "I, you, wait, you *what*? How…how, how did you know I would be coming tonight?"

He stood up slowly, the chair creaking as the weight shifted on it. I winced at the noise. "A point of fact, I didn't know it would be tonight. But I *do* know you, Mika," he motioned a finger at my nose, and then down to my heart. "I know how you think and feel."

I thought about his words for a moment and frowned. "Wait, wait, you're saying you've been here each night since I left, waiting for me to come back?"

Shrugging one shoulder, he replied, "Not the first night. I know you're smart enough not to try something without first coming up with a plan."

I felt my cheeks flush. Was I really that predictable?

"Sssssoooooo," I drew out the word, "Um. What are you going to do about it?"

Gracing me with another shrug, Viden folded his arms and looked at me appraisingly. "Well you clearly made it here without alerting patrols. So I see no need to do *anything* at the moment."

Tilting my head to the side, I narrowed my eyes and asked, "Then why wait for me?"

A placating smile crossed his face. "To offer my assistance. And," he added, stepping closer to me to place a reassuring hand on my shoulder. "To answer any questions you might have about Duncan Kai's journal."

I set my jaw tightly upon hearing that name. I didn't want to talk about it. If I did, there might be shouting involved. I wanted to be mad at Viden, for keeping it a secret from me for so long. I wanted to scream at him for letting me believe a lie for so long.

However, I'd also realized that because of what he knew, he had treated me differently. He had encouraged me to explore and to question, which I once thought was purely because I was meant to be a chronicler and, therefore, an adviser to the king and queen.

I walked past him and sat at my desk, touching the lamp and muttering, "Illuminare." Its light added to Viden's desklamp.

For several moments, I just sat there, staring at my desk, intent on ignoring Viden's offer.

Then I turned around and asked, "How did you react, when you first read the journal?"

Screwing up his face in thought, Viden walked over to his chair and eased back into it. After a moment, he recalled, "I accepted it for what it was. In fact," he motioned back towards the 'forbidden' corner of the library's first floor, where Duncan's journal had once resided, and several more unlabeled tomes were kept, "I read through every journal in less than a week."

Glancing back towards that stack of books, I asked, "He wrote all of those?"

"No," he shook his head. "The other founders kept journals, too. And I was *hungry* to learn more. In a way, I read them with a sort of historian's detachment, fascinated and keen to learn more, but not entirely offended by it." Tapping a finger on his chin, he added, "But I did not have a vested interest in changing things."

I quirked an eyebrow at him and doubtfully asked, "No?"

A wry grin crossed his face. "You have reason to doubt *that*?"

I drew in a breath and considered his question, trying to figure out why there was a seed of doubt in my mind. A second later, the answer seemed obvious, and I said, "Because of how you've treated me, how you've trained me. You've encouraged me to look beyond the obvious, to find patterns and analyze them. Plus you're going to help me get a message to Karina."

He gaped at me in mock surprise, but my expression was genuine shock at what I'd just said. There goes my mouth, speaking without permission again.

Still, I knew I was right. After a moment of faux-shock, he smiled lightly and nodded. "Indeed I am. It would also not be the first time I have arranged for…illegal liaisons."

This time I *really* felt surprised. "Uh. What? You did what, now?"

"This may come as a surprise to you, Mika," he started, "but you are not the first person in Rhea to have feelings for someone you shouldn't."

That realization hit me like a sledgehammer. I had been absolutely certain that I *was* the first and only! I was certain that I was a deviant, a defect in the system.

Bewildered, I asked, "You're telling me there are others out there like me?"

Viden nodded, "Indeed."

"A-and you…and you've helped them?"

"My predecessor and I did, yes," he affirmed. "As best as we could. Just like I would have continued to help you and Karina. I would have likewise asked you to continue the tradition, once you succeeded me."

I slumped back in my chair, slack-jawed and overwhelmed. "More people. Like me. Like us." I shook my head, a strange sort of numbness coming over me. "I had no idea…"

"I think you will find there are still many secrets within Rhea," Viden said, sitting forward and resting his elbows on his knees, forcing my attention back to his eyes. His soft grin was gone, his expression hard. "Rhea has always been imperfect, despite efforts to keep the status quo. In fact, it would not surprise me to find out that there are more amongst our population who knew the truth, or at least a part of it."

Just when I thought I couldn't be more surprised.

I was the smartest person in Rhea now, but it occurred to me just how little I actually knew.

I drew in a deep breath, wanting to say something, but my brain had simply short circuited. I let out that breath, long and slow, and shook my head. "I don't know…what to say."

"Just know that you have supporters," Viden nodded. "You have those who truly appreciate what you did, *and* what you wish to do." I eyed him curiously. "However," he added, holding up a hand, "As your mentor, and as one who is concerned for the future of Rhea, I ask you to think carefully. I know you have read many novels, so you must know as well as anyone that change does not happen overnight, especially in Rhea."

I breathed out a quiet laugh. "Yeah, no kidding."

"But it can come, and perhaps it *should* come," he finished. "As long as it is done wisely."

Lifting my eyebrows, I sighed. "Yeah. That's the hard part, isn't it?"

He only replied with a smile.

"Well, then," I uneasily rubbed the armrests. "Um. Where do we go from here?"

Viden glanced at my desk. "I believe you needed me to pass on a message?"

"Right!" I started. "Yeah. Um." I turned around and withdrew a piece of parchment from the desk, then uncorked an inkwell.

Grabbing a quill, I set to writing a short note asking Karina to meet me in my library after everyone had gone to sleep. After I blew on the ink to dry it, I folded the note up and handed it to Viden.

"Um, no offense," I said as I stood up, "but think you could stay out of here tomorrow night?"

My master simply smiled in reply.

***

The next day passed by quickly, a muddled tapestry of working with sarus to repair some power junctions, all while my thoughts kept racing back and forth between my mentor's words and the prospect of seeing Karina again.

I felt…less *guilty*, now. About how I felt for Karina, about how I'd *always* felt. Like, the world was wrong, and my place in it was wrong, but now things were starting to change.

The monumental weight of that competed with the excited feeling that, for the first time in my life, things were going the way I wanted! Even if at a snail's pace.

I also considered that, and had to acknowledge that things would be slow-going for a long time. Viden was right – we couldn't change Rhea overnight.

We made good progress on repairs, and while there weren't enough parts to get every redundant mini-fusion reactor online again, almost every corridor in the ship was fully-lit once more, and power levels were stabilizing across the ship. There was still a lot of work to do in that regard, we had sections bypassed like crazy and, if we weren't careful, we could easily cause a cascade power failure.

But I was confident that wouldn't happen. Only an external force could caused that. I hoped.

Near dinnertime, Naia informed me that a new supply of food had been left at the hole in the dome. I felt a little indignant about not having been told it was coming ahead of time, but then I realized that the king probably didn't convey that fact through 'The Oracle' because he didn't want me to meet the delivery person at the breach.

I dropped off the remnants of my previous meal, mostly the cloth it had been wrapped in and the two wooden bowls, before picking up an actual backpack of supplies, made of sheepskin leather.

I wondered and hoped that maybe Viden had received a message back from Karina, and he might have stuffed it into the backpack, so I raced back to the lounge. But I was mildly disappointed that there was nothing inside, just a few more bowls of stew, bread, and dried meat.

I started eating my dinner then, this stew mostly just vegetables and broth, no meat. I soured my face at that – I had to have meat. I hated veggie soup. But it was better than nothing.

I settled down to finish reading *Beowulf* after that, and waited for the night with eager anticipation, trying very hard not to let self-doubt creep into my mind.

Karina would come tonight…wouldn't she?

TWELVE

This time I remembered the flashlight. No more tripping and twisting ankles. Once I was past the forest, I had to rely on the streetlamps, not willing to risk my flashlight catching the attention of an attentive guard.

The streets were just as empty, too, though this time I swear it felt like a hundred eyes watched me from the windows of the houses I passed by. I knew it had to be my imagination.

It *had* to be…

Viden must have convinced someone to grease the door hinges at my library, because this time, they opened without so much as a squeak. Once I was inside, I let out a relieved breath, but then paused and turned towards the center of the room.

No one said anything. No one turned on a lamp. I clicked my flashlight on and briefly surveyed the darkened library, and then let out another relieved breath. No one was here, no Viden, no guards.

I was safe.

We were safe.

Turning the light off again, I followed my memory and the ambient glow of streetlights piercing through the front windows until I found my chair and eased into it.

Then came the hard part – waiting.

I'd written in the note that I wanted Karina to come after everyone had fallen asleep, but I knew she had to wait for everyone to be off the streets, too.

I wondered if her brother still lived in his parents' house or not, I honestly couldn't remember. If I wasn't afraid of a curious guard, I would have turned on a light and sought out town records to see if I'd ever recorded Annar moving into his own home. Was he older or younger than Karina? Dammit, I couldn't remember.

As the night drew on longer, I started to feel anxious. My feet started bouncing up and down of their own accord, and my nose itched incessantly!

What if she didn't come? What if she'd decided she wasn't actually in love with me? What if her brother wasn't letting her leave? Or what had the king said to her after I'd been banished?

Or worse, what would happen if she was caught coming to the library? What punishment would the king mete out? Or the guards?

What if one of those purists who thought I was infested with a demon caught her, or caught *us*?

My mind raced with one dreadful possibility after another, and I peered through the darkness at the door, willing it to open, to see Karina step in. She had to come. She had to be okay.

Gods, let her be okay!

After nerve-wracking age or two, a shadow passed over the window beside the doors, and I started, almost letting out an eep. My fears had grown ten-fold, so I stood up and drew my pistol from its holster, flicking the safety off and double-checking it was at a low power setting.

The door handle turned. The door on the right slowly creaked open, streetlight piercing through the darkness like a knife.

I pointed my pistol in the general direction but kept my finger off of the trigger. If it was Karina, I didn't want to accidentally shoot her.

At first no one came in.

I tensed.

And then, finally, carrot-orange hair, unmistakable even in the dark, graced my sight, and Karina eased in before closing the door behind her.

I lowered my gun and let out a relieved sigh. Karina tensed, and then called out nervously, "Mika? Are...is that you?"

"I'm here," I said, realizing I was in the shadows from her perspective. It took me three tries to holster my weapon in the dark, and then I stepped into the streetlight, a broad smile drawing across my face while my heart exploded in relief and happiness. "I'm here, and I'm so happy that you're here, too!"

I rushed forward and threw my arms around her, pressing against her as hard as I could. Neither of us wore winter jackets, and that just made it so much easier to try to be closer to her, to feel connected again after too long without my girl!

But then…

Something felt wrong.

She tensed under my embrace. She didn't wrap her arms around me.

The giddy happiness that had built up in my chest tapered and was quickly replaced with a new fear. Pulling back enough to look into her eyes, hard to see in the dim light, I searched them. "Karina?" My voice shook, and that alone almost broke me. "What's wrong?"

She drew in a deep breath, hesitated, and then let it out and lowered her head. "We need to talk."

I don't know why, but my arms started tingling as dread crept and crawled through my body.

"O-okay," I stammered. "Um, let's…sit down?" I motioned to the chairs.

She only nodded in reply, and since she didn't know the library quite as well as I did, I took hold of her hand and led the way. Despite neither of us wearing gloves, her grip was cold, emotionless.

Passionless.

Not like all those times we'd held hands while dodging an alien monster.

I helped her find Viden's chair and pull it out to face my desk, and then I turned my chair to face her, and we sat down. I didn't want to let go of her hand, but she slid hers out of mine.

"Mika," she started, her voice quiet, her tone empty. She remained silent for a moment longer, and then let out a breath. "I got your message." I quirked an eyebrow, and I saw her shoulders rise in a laugh. "Obviously."

That would have been my next line, but I hadn't said it. My snark was doused in the suffocating waters of dreadful terror.

"Karina, what's wrong?" I asked. "You're acting…" I hesitated, tried to find the right words. My struggle frustrated me, further compounding the welling emptiness inside my stomach. "Off," I finally managed to say.

She nodded. "Yeah. I don't know how to tell you this."

My jaw clenched. "Then just tell me," I stated, bitterness edging into my words.

Her eyes met mine, and she said, "I've been… I mean, I'm engaged. Now that the Oracle is talking to Vell again, she told him the name, and I've already met him, and we've already set a…" Her voice wavered and she broke off, looking away.

The dread I'd felt before rushed into my body as something else. Something worse.

Anger.

Disappointment.

Resentment.

"Wedding date," I finished for her.

She nodded and sniffed. Crying? I couldn't tell.

My jaw was clenched hard enough that my teeth hurt, and I likewise turned away, my hands balled into fists.

She wouldn't be acting this way about it unless…

Unless.

"You intend to go through with it," I spat.

Drawing in a surprised breath, Karina replied, "Well, yes. Of course I do. It's the law, Mika."

"Fuck the law," I growled. Turning my eyes back to her, feeling as if fire was coming out of them, I said, "The law doesn't matter anymore!"

I knew as soon as I said it that I didn't believe that entirely. I knew that the law was the only thing keeping Rhea from devolving into a veritable civil warzone.

But in the moment, I meant it more than I'd meant anything else in my life.

Karina called me on it, though. Of course she did. "Mika, don't be stupid."

I bolted out of my chair, eyes wild with rage, and I shouted, "Oh, I'm stupid now?"

"I didn't say that!" she pleaded, her pitch rising but her voice still a near-whisper.

"Yes, you did!" I crossed my arms. "Well I'm *so sorry* that I'm the only one who can see what's going on here."

"Mika!" she stood and touched my shoulder, but I rolled out from her hand and walked away. No, *stomped* away, my whole body shaking. "Mika, look at me!" I didn't. "Gods dammit, Mika, what did you expect to happen? Of course I have to do what the Oracle tells me! Especially now, with everything so tense in Rhea!"

"Oh, tense in Rhea?" I asked, finally spinning around to face her, arms waving wildly. "I couldn't tell! Given that I'm banished and all. But yeah, I only saved the gods damned town and ship and everyone on it, so naturally, I have to *suffer more!* Why the hell would I get this? Why the *hell* would you choose me over him?"

I didn't know who 'he' was, but I knew the laws, I knew the requirements – it was a him. Karina was to marry a man.

Not me.

"Gods, don't put it like that!" she cried. "It isn't the Universe keeping us apart, Mika, it's necessity!"

"It's outdated laws built upon *lies!*" I shouted.

Karina held halting hands up and shushed me while looking towards the windows. I didn't care. Let the guards come.

Let them all come.

"Mika!"

And then it hit me. "The king. The queen! They talked to you, didn't they?" I stepped closer to her, outrage adding to the fire of emotions in me. "They convinced you to give me up! What did they say? What does it take to make you betray us? To betray *me?*"

Even in the dim light, I could see the incredulous look she gave me. Then she huffed out a breath of annoyance and folded her arms. "They explained what had happened since we left. They told me what was happening and what all of *Rhea,* my parents included, thought of me going with you. They told me that the town was on the brink of disaster, and if I didn't leave you and marry the man the Oracle told me to, it might add more fuel to the fire and ignite a riot!"

"They guilted you into it," I stated.

"They made me see reason!"

"No, they guilted you, made you feel like everything was your fault and only you could fix it!"

"So what!" she finally shouted, shoving her hands down in frustration. "So what if they guilted me, they're right! Rhea's on edge! I heard what my brother tried to do to you, Mika! I heard about him and his friends! That's not the worst of it, either. People who feel the way they do have actually *hurt* those who speak highly of you! Viden was nearly beat up today just trying to deliver you gods damned note to me! I walk the streets fearful that someone will hurt *me* just because of what I did, regardless of the fact that I've agreed to marry Hector!"

"Hector?" I asked, taken aback by the name drop. "Wait, wait, you're to marry Hector Lee?" I knew of him, one of the more popular boys our age.

He was a blacksmith, like Karina's father.

"Um," she stumbled over her words. "W-well, yeah. I mean, that's who…"

My hands clenched into tighter fists. "Naia."

I didn't have to say more. My tone spoke volumes over how pissed off I was. Naia had spoken to me for three days like nothing had changed, all the while she ripped Karina away from me!

She had taken away any chance I had at happiness.

And I knew now. I *knew* what she had planned. Once the ship was fixed, it would be back to business as usual. I would be forced to go back to Rhea, and she would find some way to manipulate me into marrying Jonnec.

I saw red in my vision. Literally. I thought that was just an expression, but my vision changed, and the biomonitor on my neck beeped. That signal would be suppressed by my daemon, but it made me realize that my rage was very much having a physiological effect on me.

No way I was going to stand for this! If Karina wasn't willing to stand up for us, then I would, and there was only one place I could go for that.

So I stormed off. Karina called my name, but I ignored her, pushing through the double doors and stomping out into the street. I headed for the breach in the dome, no longer caring about hiding my actions tonight. I wanted to have a word with the ship's A.I., and it wasn't going to be a pleasant word.

I dared fate to put anything in my path. A guard, an unruly townsperson. *Anyone.*

About halfway out of town, the Universe called me on it.

From between multiple houses streamed six people, five men and a woman.

Led by Annar.

"I had a feeling you'd be back," he smirked at me.

I drew my pistol and aimed at him, the strongest desire to shoot someone, *anyone* overcoming any sense of hesitation or regret I felt about it. My grip was firm, my eyes were laser-focused on Annar, and oh, I *so* wanted to wipe that snarl off of his face.

Until Thelon's death flashed before my eyes. My rust-red blast glancing off of his shield, killing it. The alien's golden blast catching him mid-torso and sending him crumpling backwards.

It didn't matter that my weapon was set low enough to only stun. The idea of shooting someone made me feel…

Inhuman.

"Mika!" Karina shouted from behind. She must have followed me, intent on stopping me from making a damn foolish mistake.

My girl knew me well.

Annar's eyes shifted from me to Karina, and then back. Slowly, so slowly, he shook his head. "You won't hurt my sister again."

"I never hurt her," I growled. "I'd never hurt her!"

"Annar, leave her alone," Karina added. "She didn't come here to hurt me…"

"She came to take you away!" He shouted. A couple of lights from upstairs windows in the surrounding houses blinked on. "She came to twist your mind, turn you into something," he gave me a disgusted look, "unholy."

I almost pulled the trigger.

"Annar, she's not taking me away," Karina stated. "Now just let her go!"

"Go where?" he asked her. "Back to that other world? So that she can bring back *more* of her kind? More abominations? So they can turn the *entire town* into abominations?"

Between clenched teeth, I said, "You have no idea what an abomination is." I saw the alien in its death throes, mutilated and decomposing as it emerged from its shell. "You have no idea what a *monster* is."

Sniffing once, he shook his head and said to me, "I'm looking right at one."

The tension mounted. More lights flicked on around us. The other five people didn't matter, all I saw was Annar, a symbol of all that was wrong and backwards in Rhea. Him, and people like him, were why Karina and I couldn't be together.

"Annar," Karina warned, her voice pleading. "Don't. You won't win against her…"

Puffing up his chest like a caricature, Annar replied, "If our cause is just. GET HER!"

The moment he took his first step, I fired at his feet, flinging dirt and debris in his face and shoving him backwards in a clumsy stumble.

"MIKA!" Karina screamed.

That distracted me from the others. And the next thing I kr fist connected with my jaw. Stars exploded in my vision, my wrenched to the side, and I stumbled. Someone else tackled forcing me down. I accidentally pulled the trigger again, sendin, errant, rust-red blast into a nearby house.

I surged in rage and shoved the person off of me, shooting th point-blank.

I shot again.

Someone kicked my hand, and the pistol scattered off into shadow.

Another person kicked me in the ribs, shooting pain into my body and knocking the breath from me.

Another kick, this one to the head.

Another.

And another.

I think I heard Karina screaming at them to stop it.

More lights turned on in neighboring houses, *all* of them did.

And then I remembered the shield bracer on my left forearm. I always kept it on me these days in case of a power overload, and I'd totally forgotten it was there.

I tried to curl up into a ball, another kick connecting with my head, but I finally got my arm up enough, and I pressed the button.

A blue-white quarter-sphere snapped into existence with a hum, and it must have caught someone in their shins. A man howled and he fell onto my shield before rolling off.

Despite being dizzy and out of breath, I scrambled away. Someone else sent a kick my way, but I waved the shield edge at them and successfully batted their assault off.

I tried to get up, stumbled, fell onto my knees, and kept moving away from them, back towards the center of town, back towards my library.

Only two of them were still standing. Annar was still down, stunned from the concussive blast, one of the guys and the girl were down from blasts from my pistol, and I might have actually broken the shin on the guy who had caught the edge of my shield when I'd turned it on.

And then I stumbled onto my gun, and I picked it up and pointed it at them. "Mika, NO!" Karina screeched.

I hesitated, almost long enough for them to rush me again, but I

fired between them and me, sending another explosion of dirt and steam into the air, and the loud clap of thunder it produced was enough to make them halt.

"Back off!" I shouted. "Back OFF!" I fired into the street again, and that was enough to get them to scramble away from me.

I finally managed to stand, but the world tried to tilt on me, and I barely kept myself vertical. Through the adrenaline surging through my veins, I felt fear edging into my awareness like a hideous monster.

And then I looked over at Karina. At the look of horror on her face. I looked past the two standing men, and saw her brother slumped on the street, not just stunned, but actually unconscious.

"No, no, no!" I looked at her, "He's okay! It was just the concussive force, he's fine." As if to prove my point, Annar groaned and stirred. He would be okay. The guy I'd shot point-blank, however, might have some burns to contend with.

If he got up at all.

I felt horror well up inside of me.

And Karina's face slackened and she rushed past me, past the standing guys, to her brother's side. "Annar!" she cried. "Are you okay?"

He pushed her away and snarled, "Get off me!"

Karina stared, mouth agape, but then snapped it shut and cowed away from him while he stumbled onto his feet. Blood trickled from his nose.

I heard shouting from behind me somewhere. Guards, no doubt.

I looked at the others I'd shot. I looked at the man's broken shin, bent at an unnatural angle.

Nausea swelled over me, and I almost threw up right then and there.

No way I could get caught here. After what I'd done, they'd throw me in the dungeon, and there was still too much to do. Still too many repairs.

I stared at Karina, who studiously avoided my eyes. I'd hurt her brother. I'd hurt her family.

It was all spinning out of control. Things would be worse.

Knowing I had to get out of there, I looked back, then left, then right, fighting the dizziness. There was only one way to go without people, so I bolted between houses, to the sounds of the surviving assaulters shouting.

Even injured and stumbling, I was a fast runner, and adrenaline still

coursed through my veins. I deactivated the shield, but kept my weapon ready, and just like all the times I'd played tag with kids so many years ago, I evaded them between buildings. Then I ran for the dome.

THIRTEEN

Everywhere I turned, I heard shouts. My heart pounded against my rib cage, my breathing came hard, my chest and stomach hurt, and the world kept threatening to upend on me.

Somehow, I made it to the edge of town. I hopped the fence into a pig farm, scaring them into squealing noisily and scattering around me. I ran, sloshing through what I hoped was only mud, and somehow stumbled to the other end before I hopped over the fence again, leaving only empty field between me and the tree line. I couldn't see where I was going, and that puzzled me until I realized I was outside of town, away from any of the streetlights.

It took another five seconds of stumbling dizzily away before I remembered my flashlight. I pulled it out of a pocket and flicked it on, but the light hurt my eyes, even pointed away from me.

I heard shouts again. Did someone see my flashlight?

I dashed into the tree line a second later, but I didn't stop. I couldn't. I had to get out of the dome, I had to get out of this *nightmare*!

In my mad scramble to dodge guards and anyone else on Annar's side, I hadn't paid attention to where I was going in town, and I had no idea if I was on the north or south end of Rhea.

But no, I couldn't have gone that far around the castle, could I? I had to have kept to the south end. I had to find that damned hole, or the hatch.

Nothing looked familiar. Was I even going in the right direction? I looked up at the stars to try to get my bearings, hoping I could remember the constellations I'd invented over the past two nights, but…

But the stars were a blur. Everything was a blur, I realized, and those wavering, twinkling pinpricks of light refused to focus.

Something was wrong with me, worse than anything I'd previously endured, worse than the headaches I'd gotten from the I.A.

I almost ran face-first into the dome wall, but the light from my flashlight illuminated it just enough for me to stop short. The illusion passed my beam of light into the fantasy landscape, but as advanced as the technology was, it was also old and wasn't working quite as effectively as it should have.

I looked left, looked right, but nothing seemed familiar. Where the *hellfire* was I?

If the guards, or Annar's followers, decided to follow me, they'd hone in on my flashlight with ease. I couldn't hear shouting anymore, but that didn't mean they weren't closing in. So I shutdown the light, placed my left hand on the dome, and I followed towards what I hoped was south, assuming I wasn't already well past the emergency hatch or the hole.

Nighttime does weird things to one's sense of direction and distance. I swore I'd run a mile before my legs gave out from exhaustion and I fell forward, barely catching myself on my hands and knees. My head felt weird, throbbing and wavering and I swore my brain was knocking around in my skull!

What if this wasn't right? What if I was past the hatch and the hole, and was taking the long, slow circle all the way up to the bow of the ship?

I needed medical attention. Now. My ribs were *killing* me and every breath hurt. My vision kept tilting sideways ever-so-slightly.

I vomited.

Ugh. Not again.

I stayed on my hands and knees, panting, clearing my throat, spitting out residual acidic crud.

I was afraid. More afraid than when I'd faced against an alien. Gods, I'd take that over this any day.

And no, I wasn't saying that about being chased by the people of Rhea. I was afraid because I knew that my life there was in Rhea, whether I wanted it or not. How could I go back after hurting those people, knowing that they, in turn, would hurt me at their first opportunity?

How could I go back and face the king and queen?

No…that wasn't what truly terrified me.

How could I go back and face Karina?

The world tilted harder, and I almost fell into my sick. I cried out. I clenched my hands into fists, tearing at the grass that was only just starting to come alive again.

First things first – take care of me. I could worry about the future once I knew I'd still be around for the future.

There was only one thing I could think to do.

I lifted my right hand, ignoring just how much it shook, and I tapped my earpiece. "Naia," I breathed. A second later, I cried out, "Naia!"

Her voice came through my right ear, *"Mika Kai."* She sounded concerned, but for the moment, I disregarded that anomaly.

"Naia, help me! I…I'm in the dome. I don't know where I am, but I have to get out."

"Are you?" she asked. *"I see your signal coming from there, but also coming from the port-side lounge."*

"Yes," I hissed. "That was my doing, and we'll discuss it later, but I'm hurt! Bad! Please, guide me out…"

Gods, I hated asking her for help. How could I lecture her after depending on her to save my life?

There was a momentary pause. *"Your daemon has been purged. I have a fix on your position. Continue along the wall another one-hundred-fifty meters and you will come across the emergency hatch."*

Son of a bitch. I was that close?!

I spit out some more gross saliva and let out a breath. "T-thanks," I managed weakly.

Now the hard part – I had to stand up.

Gritting my teeth, I pushed up and somehow, painfully, managed to get to my feet. I tilted sideways and slammed my shoulder onto the dome wall and issued a few choice curse words.

"Mika Kai?"

"I'm okay!" I growled out. "I'm okay, just…dizzy. Very, very dizzy."

I looked ahead, but could see little, so I clicked my flashlight on and pointed it ahead, guards be damned.

Only a hundred fifty meters. I could do this…

I put one foot forward. Then another. It hurt my head each time, jostling my senses with each step. The world kept wanting to spin, but

I kept going, bracing myself against the wall. My senses all felt detached, like I was watching my own vision through a screen.

"What has transpired?" she asked. *"I detect considerable nighttime activity within Rhea."*

"I may have started a riot," I spoke through a grimace.

"Please explain."

"Uh," I said around a growing nausea. "M-maybe in a m-minute or ten." I almost threw up again. "Or twenty."

I swear it took me all night to reach the hatch, and it actually startled me when it suddenly appeared after I crossed the sensor threshold. Whereas the dome relied on relatively simple technology of subsurface holographics, the door was hidden with more power-intensive and sophisticated external projections.

There were a couple of stairs up to the hatch, so I stopped at the bottom step and took a moment to breathe in and out slowly, trying to stop the world from tilting sideways.

Finally, I steeled myself and climbed, each step a mountain of difficulty. *Gods, what's wrong with me?*

Standing before the hatch, I shakily reached for the keypad and pressed the button to open the door. I missed the first time, and had to brace two of my fingers on top of the pad and try again. If I was this bad, how was I going to make it the kilometer to the medical bay? *I'm not. I'm going to die, right here, right now…*

The hatch opened. My heart soared.

On the other side, Saru stood patiently waiting for me!

He wasn't big, but his six legs were strong, and I'd recently completed a full repair on his one injured leg. "Hey there, boy." I tried to sound jovial, but I think my words slurred. Still, his tail meekly wagged.

Stumbling in through the hatch, I asked, "Naia, can he…um…carry me?"

Saru bounced on his front paws, and gave me an affirming, "Wuff!"

"Good boy," I sighed. The hatch auto-closed behind me, and there was plenty of lighting in the corridors, so I clicked my flashlight off, stowed it back in my pocket, and then tried to ease down onto Saru's back. The world tilted on me, and I whimpered, clenching my eyes shut.

I don't remember much after that. I clung to Saru's cold, polycarbonate skin, and I felt him shift and more-or-less drag me along. With six legs, it was a surprisingly smooth journey, but I didn't know what path we took or where we were at any given time. All I could focus on was keeping the world upright, keeping the sick down, and clinging to my savior.

I don't remember entering the medical bay. All I remember were mechanical arms descending from the ceiling while Saru tried to lift me up to meet them. Somehow those cold, medical hands on those artificial arms gently lifted me and placed me on one of the beds.

I remember a brief panic attack when I noticed I was closed in, the bed having slid into the hole in the wall, which among other things contained the I.A. Gods no, I couldn't stand more knowledge downloaded to my brain!

But that wasn't why I was there. The interior, whatever the hellfire it was called, also contained a full suite of high-resolution scanners, and after only a second or two, the bed smoothly slid out.

Naia said something, I think she used the word concussion, something about cranial swelling.

And then I completely blacked out.

***

I woke up.

That was a good start. Briefly I wondered, *Would I even know if I died? Would I somehow be aware?*

With that grim thought, I opened my eyes just to be sure. A light pierced down from the ceiling. It hurt.

If I felt pain, I was alive, right?

I tried to speak. My throat caught. I blinked against the bright light and lifted my arm to block it out. I croaked out, "Naia?"

"I am here, Mika Kai."

The light dimmed, and I blinked the afterimage away.

I was still on the bed in the medical center. Saru stood vigil by my bedside. He wagged his segmented tail when I looked at him, and despite the emptiness building a hole in my chest, I smiled at him.

"W-what happened to me?" I asked, and then cleared my throat. I noticed the world didn't try to tilt on me anymore, so that was another positive.

"You suffered a concussion, along with two broken ribs, internal bleeding, and several abrasions," she dutifully informed me. "I have repaired all of the damage, but you will experience soreness for a few days, particularly in your chest and head."

Yeah, that tracked with how much it hurt to breathe. Strangely, though, I didn't feel a headache just now. Maybe it was there, and I was just used to the pain.

Despite having just woken up, I sleepily looked across the way, and noticed something that made me jolt in the bed.

Backpacks. All of my companions' backpacks, from our first venture outside of the dome. I had always intended to retrieve them and take them back with me to Thelon's funeral, but I had just flat-out forgotten.

Amongst them was Thelon's backpack.

Guilt swelled up inside, and I clenched my eyes shut, tears flowing freely. I had missed his funeral. I'd never even met his family, and I wanted so much to apologize to them. And now? Now, I probably was a wanted criminal in Rhea. I'd never get the chance to return his pack. I'd never get to face his family.

Gods…I can't do anything right, can I?

But at least I was alive. Whether they wanted me or not, Rhea needed me here, on the *Sirius*, helping the sarus fix the ship.

Hell, with only thirty-six sarus, maybe this was for the best. Maybe I was needed here more than they needed a princess. But then Viden would have to train a new chronicler…

My face drew down in a deep grimace, and I sighed when I realized I was already thinking of giving up on bringing the truth to Rhea. That would be akin to condemning them all to who knew how many more centuries of living a lie. Could I do that? Could I just stay here, in the corridors of the *Sirius*, living my own life, alone, while Rhea settled back into complacency?

Could I really live with myself?

I honestly didn't know the answer to that question. Somehow, though, I knew I'd have to face the music for my actions. Sighing, I turned and looked up at the ceiling. That shift in movement made a new sensation become apparent – I had to find a bathroom, and I knew there was one right next to the medbay.

So now I just had to get up without hurting myself. Slowly, I eased into a sitting position. The world didn't spin, but I did feel a pulsing headache coming on. I shifted and let my legs drop. So far so good.

Finally, I eased onto my feet. My legs ached, but other than that, I stood steady and strong.

Drawing in an aching breath, I took a step. The world didn't spin. Letting out that breath in a relieved sigh, I proceeded to the restroom.

When I'd finished and stepped back out into the ship's corridor, I looked at Saru, who had stood sentinel outside for me. I gave him a small smile, and he wagged his tail, before I looked up. "I suppose the king will want to see me in the morning."

"Morning has already passed," Naia stated.

My eyes opened to wide saucers. "Uh. What? Wait, how long was I out?"

"Fourteen hours, fifteen minutes, thirty-seven seconds," Naia helpfully stated.

Aghast at how much time had passed when it had felt like only minutes, I shook my head. "Um," I stupidly replied. "Well then. Wait, what time is it now?"

"Thirteen hundred forty-three," she replied.

"Well damn," I shook my head. "I, uh, probably shouldn't go back to bed." Despite how tired I still felt. "Were you working on fixing me that whole time?"

"Negative," Naia replied simply. "Medical intervention took less than one hour to complete. However, it was necessary to allow your body to rest and recover itself."

Wow. If only mechanical things could recover themselves like that, my job might've been a little easier.

Not to downplay what Naia had done for me. Realizing I'd probably be dead if it weren't for the medical miracles on the *Sirius*, I looked up and rather sheepishly said, "Thanks. Thank you, Naia. For saving me."

"You are welcome," she replied simply. "However, I would ask that you do not allow this to happen again. It is too dangerous for you to return to Rhea at this time."

The heavy weight shoved open the wound in my chest again, and I heaved a sigh. "Yeah. Well, don't worry about that. There's…there's nothing for me there right now, anyway. And I'm sorry for tricking you like that."

"You did not trick me."

Her simple response didn't register on me at first, but when it did, I frowned and asked, "What do you mean I didn't trick you? I thought you had no idea I was in the dome."

Naia hesitated, and then replied, "I allowed you to write and install your daemon. I was fully aware of your actions."

Blustering, I stammered through asking, "W-what? Wait, why did you let me do it?"

This time she replied instantly, "You are stubborn, Mika Kai. If I stopped you, you would have found another, possibly more dangerous avenue."

I felt my jaw hang open, as shock coursed through my body. How the hellfire could an artificial intelligence know me so well?

"As to King Roberto Impavido's response to your incursion last night," she continued, "through Vell Viisas, he has conveyed immense displeasure with your actions. I have promised to ensure you remain outside of the dome until the people of Rhea settle."

Scoffing, I asked, "Do you really think they ever will?"

"I am giving it much thought, as are the king and queen," Naia said. "We are devising a plan."

I wanted to know what that plan was, but I stopped myself from asking. It seemed like anything I did made things worse.

Yet, I couldn't stop the nagging point in my head, and I felt the absolute need to make my voice heard. So I said, "You know, those people who attacked me are…well, *afraid*. Afraid of me, what I know, and what the truth is. Because they don't understand it."

"I concur," Naia said, and I imagined a disembodied, synthetic head nodding at me. That image made me shudder, so I promised myself never to imagine Naia with a head again.

"Sooooo you could try to tell them all the truth. The *real* truth, and not some concocted story."

Naia didn't reply at first. Hey, maybe that meant I'd made a good point!

"I will consider that argument," Naia acceded. "For now, I suggest you rest for the remainder of the day."

Cocking an eyebrow up, I asked, "You don't think I should get back to work?"

"Your body is still recovering from your injuries," she stated. "Tomorrow you may resume light duties."

Huffing out a breath, I said, "Fine. I guess I can start on another book."

I patted Saru on the head, who nuzzled into it before he took off down the hall in the opposite direction of the port-side lounge. I

figured *he* had to get back to work.
Leaving me to my loneliness.

FOURTEEN

Life settled into a new routine.

The only way to combat the loneliness was to keep busy, so that's what I did. I tried to see about restoring more sarus, but there just weren't enough spare parts or materials to fabricate, not when there were whole sections of the ship that needed replacement parts.

So I donned my work overalls again, and I worked with the sarus, fixing what parts of the ship I could. I recalled that there'd been a possible flaw in the secondary power conduit into Rhea, so we focused on repairing the primary conduit, which had surged and blown out in one section, and caused secondary overloads in surrounding areas. That was a bit of a mess to cleanup, to say the least.

Food deliveries were still being made from Rhea, which was a pleasant surprise – I found out that the *Sirius* had emergency rations, but they had expired a *long* time ago, so without those deliveries, I would have been screwed.

I smiled when the third delivery also came with some new books from my library. I'd just finished the *Lord of the Rings*, and didn't have anything else to read at night, so that made my day just a little bit brighter, and it reminded me that I still had an ally in Rhea.

I still wanted to see the bow of the ship. So once power to Rhea was stabilized, and the backup power cells were recharged, I turned my attention to the tram system. The port-side tram was far too damaged to be easily repaired, and Naia explained that it had been damaged externally by weapons fire.

That reminded me that the intruder's ship was still sticking out of our hull, but I'd address that later. For now, I wanted a legitimate bedroom, and I wanted access to the ship's bridge.

The starboard tram was intact, only lacking power, and that was a relatively quick and easy fix for the sarus and I.

I wasn't sure how many days had passed since my concussion, I'd not really kept track of them, so during the whole minute it took for the tram to ferry me from the aft section of the *Sirius* to the fore, I asked Naia, and she told me it had been nearly two weeks.

"It really took me that long to fix the Rhea conduits?" I asked, aghast. Then I shook my head, and said, "Never mind. Extensive damage, lots of work, I remember."

The apparent loss of time was a little disconcerting, but at the same time, it meant it was working – the work distracted me from Rhea. From Karina.

Of course, *that* thought brought it all back to the forefront of my attention, and I felt my heart ache, *painfully*.

Thankfully the tram crawled to a stop at the bow, and I stepped into what was basically another world.

I mean, the corridors were still corridors, but unlike most of the aft section, the deck was covered entirely in burgundy carpet with a half-meter wide beige trim on either side. Just that alone created a much warmer and more welcoming feeling, less utilitarian than the aft section.

And unlike the aft section, there were individual bedrooms up here. In fact, a *lot* of the front of the ship was devoted to crew quarters. I spent the entire day exploring, looking inside various quarters, trying to remember which decks and sections had which sized rooms.

After checking out about fifty rooms, I headed for the bridge.

Like the rest of the forward section, it was carpeted, and felt more luxurious than I thought a command center should have felt. The layout was basically a wide oval, with the command chair elevated in the middle, and two rings of consoles surrounding it, gaps every ninety degrees to allow people to pass through. The rings were each about half of a meter lower than the next inner area, with ramps leading down from them.

And the forward view was all window. The view was gorgeous! I could see out into the infinite cosmos, millions of pinprick stars shining bright, including this system's star. I knew it should have been too bright to look at with the naked eye, even as far away as we still were, but my knowledge download helpfully reminded me that the windows were polarized, and the setting of that polarization adjusted every second to ensure nothing too bright ever blinded the non-existent crew.

In awe of the view, I walked straight up to the window and stared out, breathless. I also could just barely see the nearby gas giant, the shapes and colors of the clouds starting to grow clearer as the *Sirius* drew nearer. It was mostly various shades of blue and grey, with a little bit of orange and tan here and there.

It shocked me each day just how much larger the planet appeared every time I woke up, and I couldn't help but grin. "Now this is a view I could get used to," I mused.

I remained there for probably another minute or two before I turned back and walked up the ramp to the command chair. If I thought the bridge was luxurious in and of itself, the chair was extravagant, and probably would have made the king jealous for a new throne. It was covered in a super-soft leather material, but the best part was the technology involved.

Wanting to test it out, I kinda bounced up and down in giddy excitement, and I turned and very slowly sat down, taking in every moment of the experience. Once I had my full weight in it, the underlying technology activated, and the chair auto-adjusted to fit my shape, size, and weight.

It felt like sitting on a cloud, oh my *gods* it was so comfortable! I wanted to just lean back and fall asleep! It even adjusted its temperature to feel absolutely comfortable, not too cold, not too warm.

I guess command had its perks.

Then again, there's no captain. So I can sit here whenever I want!

Grinning, I sighed and let myself relax for a minute.

But then I had an even better thought.

I knew the layout of the bridge well enough, so I sat up and looked around, and identified the console I needed. I got up and walked over to it, and powered it on – it showed me a technical readout of the ship, deck-by-deck plans with status indicators on it. Granted I could have brought this info up on any console, but this was where the operations officer would have sat.

I tapped in a search parameter, and the console showed me where the captain's quarters were, just to port of the bridge with only a dozen meters between the two rooms. Efficient design, I guess.

But the *size* of those quarters on the schematic seemed unreal – they were larger than the bridge! I *had* to see this!

So I jounced down the port-side ramp and left the bridge, and then immediately entered the first room on the right.

The schematics hadn't lied. If anything, they'd undersold the size and grandeur of the quarters. So. Much. SPACE!

My whole house, if you'd taken the top floor and put it down next to the bottom floor, was the same size, and this was for *just one person!*

The designers had an obvious love for open space, since the foyer and the living area beyond it were basically one room, and the kitchen was off to the right. Yes, *kitchen,* as in the captain could cook his or her own meal if they so desired! Next to it, straight ahead of me, was the dining 'room,' with nothing separating it from the kitchen or living area except for the exquisitely hand-carved dining room table, made from a wood that I didn't know with a deep, dark reddish hue and polished to a shine, and surrounded by a dozen chairs.

The living room had four plush couches surrounding a large, white glowing-topped table that I knew to be a holographic generator for projecting entertainment. And further left from that was the first wall of the quarters, with two doors, one leading to the bedroom, and the other leading to one of *two* bathrooms in the quarters.

"Gods damn, what would one person need with this much space?" I asked no one.

Naia answered anyway. "In the Sirius Colonial Navy, rank is only one of two major status indicators, the other being the size of the ship an officer is stationed aboard. To be captain of a vessel as large as the *Sirius,* which was the largest starship ever constructed, tradition dictated that the Captain's Quarters be the largest of any vessel in the fleet. As a result, this design and layout is atypical of naval ships."

While she spoke, I waded into the vast sea of the captain's quarters and gaped in awe. Other than the furniture, there were no other decorations, no paintings or tapestries or anything. I supposed that would have been something the captain could have brought with.

"Gods, you could fit half of Rhea in here," I murmured.

"That is not actually accurate, unless they stood shoulder-to-shoulder," Naia corrected.

"That was just an expression," I scowled. And then I thought about what she'd said moments before. "Wait, wait. Sirius colonial navy?" I knew what a navy was, more or less, thanks to war epics in the books

I'd read. But somehow it hadn't occurred to me that there could likewise be a navy of *spaceships!*

I realized just how silly that lapse in deductive reasoning was, and I hoped Naia would ignore or miss that.

But as usual, she was on top of it. "The Sirius Colonial Navy is the primary military branch of the Sirius star system. When the starship *Sirius* was launched, there were over ten thousand starships in service to the navy, not counting independent contractor ships that supplemented the fleet for cargo and logistics functions not covered by the main fleet."

"Gods," I gaped up. "That's…a lot. I think?"

"It was indeed one of the larger human fleets," Naia agreed. "The Sirius star system was bountiful in resources. While that allowed the construction of such vast fleets, it also made the Sirius star system the envy of many of the other colonies, and especially of Earth."

Earth. I'd read that name in Duncan's journal. While I headed for the bedroom, I asked, "What is Earth?"

The doors parted, and my eyes grew wide again. A bedroom was a place to sleep…why in the whole wide Universe would it need to be so gods damned big? It was at least twenty feet by twenty feet, and contained the largest bed I had ever seen. There were no linens on the bed, just a mattress, though I knew that mattress contained the same technology as the captain's chair, and I might not even need sheets to keep warm at night.

There were multiple wardrobes and dressers, and an over-the-top, huge vanity, though empty of anything on its surface.

Naia answered my question by explaining, "Earth is the origin world of all humans."

Frowning, I asked, "But not…*Middle* Earth, right?"

"Correct." Was that bemusement in her voice? "That name describes a fictional land in one of the novels I believe you recently read. Earth, also known as Terra Prime, bears very little resemblance, particularly since the last interplanetary civil war within the Terra star system."

I nodded while walking further into the room. Sighing in wonder, I looked around and nodded. "I think I'll sleep here tonight."

***

It took only a single trip to gather all of my things from the port-side lounge, and I awkwardly placed my belongings pretty much in empty spaces in the bedroom, leaving the rest of the captain's quarters as they were.

However, that night, I gleefully used one of the kitchen's devices to warm up one of the soups my mother had made for me, and I *finally* had hot soup!

For the first time in a long, long time, I felt like things were looking up, and my mood drastically improved. I also slept better that night than ever before, the bed was so incredibly comfortable! Plus the next morning, I discovered the shower was soooooo much better, with so many different sources of spraying water to hit just about every inch of my body all at once.

Including, umm…certain parts of my body that hadn't received attention in…well, ever.

Don't even try to tell me you wouldn't have done the same thing!

The only downside? Afterwards, I found myself missing Karina even more. We'd wanted to take things further, but not while we knew cameras watched everything we did. Naia may have been able to talk to me in the captain's quarters, but there were no cameras, especially in the bedroom and bathroom. When I asked why, Naia cited some privacy law that had no context for me, but at least gave me a sense of comfort, knowing that there was finally a place I could go and not be watched.

I'd basically treated that first day in the front of the ship as a mini-vacation, but now it was time to get back to work.

I turned my attention back to the alien ship after that, and Saru, along with three other sarus, joined me in inspecting it.

The alien ship was still jutting out of the ventral side of the hull, but enough power had been restored to allow me to engage forcefields around the hull breach, allowing us to open the bulkheads and visually inspect the ship.

It was black as night, the angles on its hull were sharp and angular, and I could find no visible port to get in or out of it. The only thing I found was a small open port where the alien had plugged its hodgepodge power converter into its ship to power its communications device. And the moment I disconnected that plug, the ship's hull just…*appeared* over the port, sealing it from further inspection.

I scanned the hull with multiple scanning devices, as did the sarus, but we couldn't penetrate the hull at all, nor get any sort of real reading on the hull's material. "Naia, is this thing still getting power somewhere else?"

"Unknown," she unhelpfully said. "No internal sensors can penetrate the hull."

"I can't even see a weapons port on this thing," I shook my head and scratched at my nose. "Where was it firing from?"

"During our engagement against the alien vessel, I was able to detect multiple weapons ports," she replied. "However, I can no longer detect them. The ship may not have primary power, but its stealth systems may be independently powered. The species may have a xenophobic culture and might go to extreme measures to ensure it defies all attempts at analysis."

"Soooo," I arched an eyebrow up. "How do we get inside or open up any other ports on it?"

"I would surmise it responds to the alien creature's suit somehow."

I grimaced. "You mean the irradiated suit inside the stardrive that is probably completely nonfunctional at this point."

"Correct."

I sighed. "So as much as we probably would want to inspect it, that's probably not an option."

"Correct," Naia repeated.

"Then I guess there's nothing left to do but dislodge it," I said with a shrug.

"That may be a difficult and dangerous task to accomplish," Naia replied.

"Why?"

"The damage to the *Sirius's* hull surrounding the alien vessel is extensive and will be difficult to repair with our limited resources. Additionally, the structural integrity field is still compromised, particularly in the areas surrounding the intruder's vessel. The collateral damage that would no doubt be incurred by removing the vessel could cause additional damage to the *Sirius*, and with our power systems already bypassed more than is recommended, we could create a cascade power failure to the structural integrity field. In particular, as we approach the gas giant and endure additional hull stress from tidal forces, this could result in multiple hull breaches, and possibly cause complete hull integrity failure."

That was an overload of information, and it took me a solid minute to process it all. Once I had a grasp on what Naia was telling me, I asked, "So, what…we just leave it in there?"

"For the moment, that is the recommended course action," Naia affirmed. "We may be able to safely remove it after we have left the gravity influence of the gas giant."

Which meant I had at least a few more months of tinkering around to do before we could even attempt it. And then who knew how much more repair work would be needed.

"Well alright, then," I nodded. "If there's nothing else we can do, lets save power by closing the bulkheads and deactivating the forcefields around the breach."

"I concur," she replied.

Two of the sarus used their front paws to lift up and carry the power converter out, and the others followed. I looked one last time at the ship, and then followed them out. The bulkheads hummed closed behind me.

After that, it was back to repairing the *Sirius*, and spending my evenings reading books and enjoying hot meals in the captain's quarters.

Three more weeks passed by in a relative blur of hard work mixed with absolute comfort. Primary systems were as repaired as they could be, and we were able to start focusing on secondary systems, though the more I worked on the ship, the more concerned I became about our supply shortage. Not to mention there were bypasses all over the place, and restoring every single power conduit was an incredibly time-consuming prospect.

Two-hundred forty years of routine or emergency maintenance really had drained our raw supplies. At one point, after discussing the situation at length with Naia, we decided to start scrapping wall panels in the aft section to reprocess them into materials to try to build new reactors and new power conduits, but we quickly figured out that it cost too much power to convert the materials into reactor housing material – that required what Naia described to be exotic materials.

Worse still, I found out the biggest reason Naia hadn't turned the ship around in that previous star system to warm up the dome. It wasn't that the intruder had killed power to the engines, though that *was* the case towards the end.

We were running low on tritium fuel for the reactors, and the sublight engines were basically giant fusion reactors, augmented by an adjustable inertial dampening field.

If we ever needed to maneuver more than a little bit here and there, if we ever needed considerable delta-V to move out of the way of, for instance, a giant comet or asteroid, we'd be in trouble.

I was worried about how close we would get to that gas giant now. Naia was worried about the tidal stresses on the hull, but I was worried about any debris that might have been caught in the planet's immense gravity well. There could be asteroids, small moons, any number of things ahead of us that we just didn't know about yet, even with our advanced sensors.

So I started thinking about how to convince Naia to overcome her irreconcilable mission parameters. I realized that there was probably only two options.

Option one: drop us on the next inhabitable planet, no matter the danger that might present us.

Option two: use the stardrive to return us to the Sirius star system, and completely abandon Duncan Kai's mission altogether.

Somehow I had a feeling that convincing her to pursue either course would be near impossible, and unfortunately, despite how comfortable the captain's bed was, those thoughts kept me up at night.

FIFTEEN

Six weeks had passed since my concussion. We were close enough to the gas giant now, almost at our closest approach, and it was *giant!* I mean, obviously, that's probably why it's called a gas giant, right? But I never could have appreciated just *how* massive, until I could see its swirling, multicolored vortex clouds take on finer and finer details.

We were close enough now that when I slept in the captain's quarters at night, it cast everything in a pale blue glow. I could have adjusted the window polarization to block all light, but I enjoyed the novelty of it. I imagined that, given its position relative to us, it appeared now in the daytime sky of Rhea.

It made me wonder how the 'crazies' like Annar were dealing with it. Did they think it was a demon in the sky? Was the king and Vell able to assure them that it was nothing sinister?

After so much time focusing on repairs, I'd started to wonder how everything was in Rhea. Viden still provided me with new books every couple of weeks, along with the regular food deliveries, so I assumed that all hell hadn't broken loose. But was the king making progress? Did Annar still think I was evil and had corrupted his sister?

How was Karina?

Gods, I longed for Karina…

That night, I dreamt of her. She and I were in our secret place in the forest, releasing arrows into the target.

It was Fall, just like when we started regularly practicing, the leaves a cascade of golds, oranges, and reds.

I nocked my arrow, just as Karina nocked hers. We glanced at one another, raised our bows, and released our arrows. I hit the bullseye dead-on.

I hit Thelon's chest dead-on.

I screamed!

An alarm screamed, startling me awake, and all of the lights turned on red, sending a surge of adrenaline through my body. "Alert!" Naia called.

"Bwah?" I blearily cried out, sitting up in bed and staring at the blood-red lighting intermixed with the blue of the planet. "Gyah, what's going on? Lights, *lights!*"

The red was augmented by full white light from the ceiling panels, and I stared around as the alarm continued to blare.

"Impact from unknown object detected in aft section," Naia reported. "Critical power fluctuations detected. Inertial dampers and structural integrity field degrading rapidly."

Dread crawled into my stomach and a sinking sensation rushed down through my chest.

Oh no…

An eerie, chilling groan rolled from one side of the ship to the other, and that sent tingles of terror all through my body.

With sleep fully expunged from my body, I rolled off the bed and onto my feet, and then quickly threw on my overalls – I slept only in my underwear and shirt these nights, the bed keeping my temperature perfect.

"What hit us?" I asked while zipping up the jumpsuit. "Where did the power failure start?"

"Unknown object, possibly no larger than a small stone, impacted the hull at a relatively high velocity," Naia informed me. While she gave me the full report, I threw on my boots, and then my vest with tools still attached or in their pockets. "Fusion reactor on deck four, section two-five-six, has been destroyed. I have attempted to reroute power from other sections to compensate, however there has been a subsequent overload from a faulty conduit. The overload is creating a cascade power surge throughout the grid."

Another groan, sounding more distant this time, echoed through the bulkheads.

I darted out into the living room, tripped over something, shouted, "Lights, dammit!" The living room lights turned on, and I ran for the exit. I had to get to the bridge to try to help Naia compensate and close off breakers ahead of the overload!

But who was I kidding? Naia was an A.I., a sophisticated quantum-based supercomputer program that could operate faster than the human mind could comprehend.

Still, I had to do *something* and not just stand around-

The lights went out, leaving me with only the glow of the planet, and I practically smacked into the door, unable to automatically open after the sudden loss of power.

"Naia?" I called into the shadows.

And then there was a shattering, body-shaking **BOOM**! Followed by a high-pitched roar, and the deck bucked beneath my feet, flinging me into the door. Stars exploded in my vision, the air was driven from my lungs, and then I was flung back into the captains quarters, tumbling onto the deck.

I screamed, but the ship screamed louder as the *Sirius* bucked and heaved in a way it was never designed to endure, and the horror I felt inside was compounded by being tossed around the spacious room like a rag doll.

My waist hit the back of a couch. Gravity must have failed for a second, because I bounced *up* towards the ceiling, towards an elaborate chandelier, and I thought for sure I was about to be impaled, only to suddenly see it wrench to the side of me, and then there was nothing but space ahead of me.

I slammed into the forward window, and then watched with horror as debris from a hull breach spewed out into space. I was terrified that my window would crack apart and spew me out, too!

But then gravity reasserted itself, and I slid down, landed on the window frame, and fell backwards onto my butt. Every fourth light in the room winked on, telling me we were on emergency power in this section, and the high-pitched screeching of the ship eased back into a groan, and then finally clicked into silence.

I was on the verge of hyperventilating, my breaths fast and shallow, my heart hammering in my chest, and everything hurt from being thrown around. Gods, I hoped I didn't have another concussion...

"Naia?" I finally managed to ask. "Naia, can you hear me?" Nothing. I tapped the communicator in my ear. "Naia!"

Finally, through my earpiece, she replied, *"I am here, Mika Kai."*

"What the hellfire just happened?" I asked.

She didn't answer at first, and I was scared I'd already lost comms to her. Finally, she replied, *"A near-worst-case scenario. For approximately eight seconds, all main power failed, and the overload prevented backups from providing power to inertial dampers and structural integrity."*

I swallowed hard, and slowly stood up and looked out the window. Debris silently floated ahead of the ship, towards the planet that was so very close now.

I'd talked this over with Naia, what might happen if we lost structural integrity. The *Sirius* was the largest ship ever built by the Sirius Colonial Navy, and its superstructure, though built of extremely strong material, was not able to stand up to the stresses of navigating near a gravity well. Without structural integrity fields holding the ship together, and without inertial dampers, every stray force upon her superstructure would twist and contort her, possibly creating additional power disconnects, and *definitely* ripping the hull apart.

That was the danger of a cascade failure, now more than ever. Fusion reactors were placed redundantly throughout the ship so that if she were to twist and heave, and power conduits were severed, critical systems would remain online. But we had lost too many generators, and so we were more dependent upon the ship-wide power grid than was considered normal or safe.

If enough failures occurred, and if the ship pushed and pulled and twisted enough, then *everything* could go offline.

After staring slack-jawed at the debris for a moment longer, I swallowed heavily again and asked, "Is the bridge intact?"

"I believe so," she replied.

Good. Getting to engineering probably wasn't possible just now. So, limping on a twisted ankle, I headed out into the corridor, and then onto the bridge. As a critical center for the ship, the bridge still had full power, but a quarter of the lights were blood-red, and multiple consoles were sounding off various alarms.

I headed for the engineering console on starboard and started bringing up damage readouts and ship's status.

"Naia, can you hear me in here without comms?"

"Affirmative," she replied.

"Help me figure out damage reports. What exactly happened?"

"Several breakers were tripped due to stress on the conduits," she stated. "Those that could be automatically reset have been reset, and the sarus are attempting to reset the rest where possible, but there are too few sarus to do so quickly. Critical systems have been prioritized. Hull breaches detected on multiple decks in multiple sections.

Bulkhead doors have successfully sealed those sections."

I looked at a readout on the dome, and though it looked intact, I asked with a lump of terror in my chest, "The dome? Rhea?"

"Microfractures have been detected throughout the dome, but atmospheric pressure appears to be stable at this time. Structural damage detected in multiple buildings, including a handful of structural fires. Weather control systems are non-operational, so fires will need to be dealt with by townspeople."

Panic grew in my stomach, and I placed my hand there, willing my body to stop fighting me. Panic would get us nowhere. Panic wouldn't help.

I had to focus. I had to figure out what all was wrong, and where I could help.

"Are there any breakers nearby I can help reset?"

"Affirmative," she replied. "However, I am afraid we may have a more urgent problem that requires your attention."

That sinking sensation came back. "Oh gods, what now?"

A screen next to engineering blinked on, and I saw an external view of the ship. I shifted over to that console and rested my hand on the back of the station's chair, staring at the view.

The camera was labeled as ventral-port-aft, and I saw a field of debris spreading out from the *Sirius*…but worse still, I saw the alien ship drifting out of the hole in the *Sirius's* hull, dead-slow but still most definitely having been jostled and ripped free of the ship.

How many new hull breaches had been torn from that? How much had the *Sirius* bucked and heaved to have done that?

But still… "Naia, how is that a bigger problem?"

"The alien vessel is now free from the inertial mass of the *Sirius*," Naia replied, as if that would explain it. When I didn't say anything, she continued, "The various hull breaches and atmospheric bursts have increased our rotational velocity. Unfortunately, several thrusters are non-operational, and I am having difficulty slowing our rotation."

I still didn't understand, not at first. So the alien ship was free of the *Sirius*, and we were still rotating. How was that a problem?

But then I noticed…the ship was drifting away from us, but at a dreadfully slow pace.

To demonstrate what I was only just beginning to understand, Naia replaced the live video with an animated diagram. "The alien vessel's current trajectory in comparison to our increased rotation is what you humans might call a 'perfect storm.' I believe the alien vessel suffered a decompressive hull breach when it was jostled free of our superstructure, and that has sent it on a relatively slow but predictable trajectory. Within approximately one hour and ten minutes, it will once again impact against our hull." I felt my mouth go dry as the reality of *that* news set in. "Under normal circumstances, this would not be a problem, as there are multiple ways to deflect the ship or, in a worst-case scenario, the impact would be soft enough as to not endanger the ship. However..."

"With our hull as compromised as it already is, and I'm guessing our structural integrity field is likewise compromised, it could cause some major problems."

"That is accurate," Naia said.

The damage might be minor, but it might be catastrophic, depending on what angle the alien ship hit us at, and what component it hit.

"So long story short," I remarked, "we need to stop that impact from happening."

"If we wish to survive, yes," Naia affirmed.

"So what are our options?"

"Limited," she replied.

Scowling, I said, "This is no time to hold back, Naia, I need you to be a little more forthcoming!"

"Weapons systems are offline," she reported. "Shields are offline. We have only one viable option left."

I searched my memory, tried to make the brain dump give me some clue. But knowledge wasn't everything, you had to know how to apply that knowledge, and I was drawing a blank.

"Well, what is it?" I impatiently demanded.

"One of the support craft could be used to push the ship away," she said.

Right. There were two *giant* landing bays, one on the port-side bow and one on the starboard bow, with the flight deck several levels down. They carried a varying complement of support craft from small scout shuttles and personnel carriers to a couple of heavy cargo shuttles. The bays also held the probes that Naia used to investigate planets in each star system.

"So do it!" I said. "Send one out to push that thing away!"

Of course, the moment I said it, I remembered the lowest priority damaged system we had, the one that, much like the alien intruder, I had ignored.

External communications.

Naia could remotely launch the ship, but the moment it was out of range of internal communications systems, it would be outside of her control.

It needed a human pilot.

And that hadn't been a part of my I.A. dump.

"Gods dammit," I muttered.

"I surmise you have determined why that is not possible," Naia plaintively said.

"Yeah," I rubbed at my head. Hey, at least the world wasn't tilting to the side, so maybe no concussion this time!

Thank the gods for small favors.

"Well, can I go through another I.A. dump?" I asked with a grimace. I didn't look forward to that again…

"Negative," Naia replied. "Given the amount of information in your initial Intellectus Apparatus download, I am afraid any attempt to use it again in the near-term would prove fatal."

That didn't make me feel good. But I looked back over at the ship-wide diagnostics, at the red indicators that showed fires in the Rhea dome. They still hadn't been put out. Another catastrophe, and the dome could crack wide open, and everyone would suffocate or decompress.

"But would I live long enough to pilot the ship?" I asked, both hopeful and dreading the answer.

"Unlikely," she replied.

I used a few choice curse words. "Well, then," I started and stopped. I looked again at the diagnostic. At Rhea.

"How fast could we get someone from the dome?" I asked. "How fast could we get them in and out of the I.A. and into a maintenance shuttle?"

"There may not be enough time," she replied. "However, we have little option but to try. The medical bay in the engineering section is offline, so we will have to bring whomever it is to the front of the *Sirius* for the procedure."

"No worries there, we don't have time to go all the way back there anyway," I shrugged. And then I had an idea. "Can you get a message to Vell?"

"He is already in the Oracle chambers consulting me."

"Have him bring Karina to the north end of the dome," I pushed away from the console and headed for the aft exit of the bridge.

"No."

I drew up short and gaped wide-eyed at the ceiling. "Excuse me?"

"I have already dispatched Master Viisas to retrieve Prince Jonnec Impavido to bring him to the forward hatch."

My jaw tensed. "Naia…" I started and stopped. There was no sense arguing. We just didn't have time, and besides, Jonnec was probably already in the castle. Vell wouldn't have to search the entire town to find him. Sighing, I grumbled, "Fine!" and headed back to meet Jonnec.

Today was just going from bad to worse.

SIXTEEN

Blood-red lights flashed throughout the corridors, reminding me that the *Sirius* was in trouble, as if I could forget. I raced through as best as I could, limping on my twisted ankle and gritting my teeth, hoping I didn't need to spend another night in the medbay.

The journey from the bridge to the forward dome hatch should have been direct and short, but hull fractures had forced Naia to drop bulkheads in the middle of that corridor, and I had to take the long way around, wasting precious minutes.

Along the way, I saw at least two sarus running around to repair damage, and I gritted my teeth, wishing I could help, wishing I could have restored more sarus.

When I finally made it to the hatch, I slapped my palm on the door controls, but they simply errored and the readout said, "Invalid Input."

Grinding my teeth, I told myself, "Calm down, Mika. Slow down, and *think!*" Breathing in and out slowly, I pushed the control to open the door, and it released with a clank and slid open with a hum – it was more of a bulkhead than an actual door, meant to ensure the dome survived even if there was a catastrophic pressure loss in the rest of the ship.

From my perspective, I could see into the landscape unobstructed, the grass having fully turned green and the trees were in full bloom – Spring had come fast in Rhea, and I'd missed every moment of it. The sun was rising, visibly moving at our new rotational speed, and casting long shadows and an orange hue on everything.

Out in the field, emerging from the trees, I saw Jonnec, wearing his courtly robes of violet and blue, his left hand bare, his right hand covered in a blue-dyed leather glove. And he looked utterly lost, his eyes scanning back and forth.

So I stepped out onto the grass to trigger the sensor, and the illusion was dispelled.

Jonnec was about a hundred feet away and lurched back, startled by my sudden appearance. "Princess Kai," he uttered.

"Come on, Princely," I motioned him my way. "No time to chat."

"So I gathered," he said. With a long grimace, and without further questioning me, he jogged the remaining distance, and we both passed through the hatch.

I pushed the button to seal the hatch, and turned and nearly stumbled over something hip-high.

"Saru!"

"Wuff!" he replied, and stared at Jonnec. I had a momentary flashback to Saru leading me to the I.A.

"Uh, I know the way," I looked up at the ceiling. "You didn't have to divert Saru to help."

"Saru will guide Jonnec Impavido to the medical bay," Naia replied. "To save time, I require you to perform a pre-flight check on the shuttle that Jonnec Impavido will use."

Jonnec looked utterly lost, and he asked, "Shuttle? What is happening? Why am I here?"

I gaped at him. "Vell didn't tell you?"

"Master Vell only told me that the Oracle needed me, and I was to journey straight north until I found a way back into the ship's corridors."

Glancing upward, I grumbled, "Way to be vague, Naia."

She must have heard me. "There was no time to explain," Naia replied.

"Well now I get to," I rolled my eyes. "We need your help to avert further disaster." He started to ask a question, and I raised a halting hand and said, "I know you want to know more, and I'll tell you what I can when I can, but for now all I can say is that Naia needs to…" I thought back to how I'd explained it to him the first time. "Needs to 'bless you' with knowledge like she did me, but different knowledge. Ugh, that sounds vague, but you'll understand in a few minutes, I promise."

Cinching his brow into a deep frown, he asked, "Will that not put me at risk of…mimetic…"

"Rejection," I nodded. "Yes, but because I've already been through it once, it would most certainly kill me, whereas for you, there's only a slight chance."

"The amount of knowledge needed is far less than what I gave Mika Kai the first time," Naia added. "The chance of mimetic rejection for you is less than five percent."

"I see," he nodded. "And it is necessary to save Rhea?"

"Yeah," I said. "Naia…wait," I frowned. "I don't know how to do a pre-flight check!"

"I will guide you through it," she replied. "The shuttle *must* be ready to launch by the time Jonnec Impavido reaches the launch bay if we are to divert the alien vessel in time."

"Alien vessel?" Jonnec gasped. "Is it back?"

"No," I assured, "but, well." I sighed grumpily, "There's no time, okay? Just follow Saru and do what Naia tells you."

He clenched his jaw and nodded. "Very well," he reached for my hand, and honestly I wasn't paying attention and it startled me. But when he leaned in to kiss me, renewed nausea soured my stomach, and I turned away, getting a sloppy kiss on the cheek instead. He backed away, his jaw once again clenched.

I didn't look at him, but I did pull my hands away, and I pointed to port and said, "Go, now!"

Saru took off. Jonnec sputtered in surprise, and after glancing at me one more time, he ran after Saru.

Tightening my hands into clenched fists, I shuddered.

I respected Jonnec more than I used to, but he was still a womanizing bastard.

On the other hand, the fact that he tried to kiss me made me wonder – maybe the king hadn't decided to permanently banish me, like I assumed he would have after my final night in Rhea. Maybe I *could* go back to Rhea someday.

But did I want to?

I shook my head and whispered to myself, "No time."

I glanced down the corridor after Jonnec and closed my eyes, trying to remember where to go. The medical bay was less than a kilometer away from here, but it was smack in the middle of the port-side forward section. So the nearest launch bay to him would, naturally, be the port side. I took off down the same corridor at a limping run and headed for that bay.

Fortunately, there were no hull breaches between me and there, and that made getting there fast and easy. The whole time, all I could think about was the fact that Jonnec might finally understand what I'd gone through…but did I want him to?

Would it matter?

Then again, maybe with a greater understanding of the truth, he could more easily help the people of Rhea come to terms with it all.

Assuming Rhea had a future.

Hellfire, with the shape the *Sirius* was in now, I wasn't sure we could ever fully recover. We might have to end the mission here and now.

But that was a topic to explore later. For now, we had to save what was left of the ship.

When I rounded the final corner, I came across the massive bulkhead doors that led into the launch bay, and they glided open when I approached. I knew how huge the bay was, but that still didn't prepare me for the sight of it!

The bay reached over four decks tall and was at *least* five hundred meters wide, with multiple ships moored to the flight deck with physical and magnetic clamps. I entered from the starboard side, giving me a view of the various support craft lined up all the way to the other side, and to my right, the *massive* bay doors that would split and open outward into the vast nothingness of space.

I grimaced and hoped we had enough reserve power to activate the forcefield, otherwise if there was even a single breach between the bay and the rest of the ship, we could cause an additional decompression and force more bulkheads down, cutting us off from the rest of the ship.

What truly boggled my mind, though, was that such a massive space could be so well-lit. The lights in the ceiling must have been insanely bright to accomplish that, but they were augmented by panels of lighting all over the walls and even on the deck itself, glaring up at the support ships' undersides.

"Alright, Naia," I said, "which one are we gonna use?"

"The most obvious choice would be a maintenance shuttle," Naia replied. "Its external manipulator arms will allow Jonnec Impavido and you to safely push the alien vessel away from the *Sirius*."

I nodded and was a bit relieved – four such shuttles were clustered immediately in front of me. They were super-basic designs, comprised of a long, tubular body big enough for two people to sit in the front, and four mechanical manipulator arms, currently folded in on themselves and tucked against the hull, arrayed around the front bubble viewport, which itself was meant to give the pilot and operator an unobstructed view of whatever they were working on.

Further along the deck from those pods were larger four-person shuttles, then long, narrow personnel transports, and the biggest cargo and mining vessels were furthest away.

Selecting the closest shuttle on the right, so that nothing would be between it and the bay doors, I crossed over to it, and said, "Alright, Naia. Walk me through this."

Turns out that a lot of it was easy enough to understand – inspecting the outside for any issues or flaws, such as damage from the ship being jostled around so much. After that, I cleared the physical moorings from the landing gear, and then I opened the back hatch between the main thrusters, and I went in and began powering up systems, ensuring they all came online and diagnostics reported no issues.

The diagnostics were almost finished when Naia reported, "Jonnec Impavido's time in the Intellectus Apparatus has completed."

I pursed my lips. I imagined what he was going through now, the Universe opening up to him. He had a leg up from when I had gone through with it – he already had some idea of the truth, he knew that Rhea was being carried across the stars on a massive starship.

But to understand exactly what that meant, to understand the physics of it, to know what space was, how big it was, how big *planets* were, and so much more? That was something else entirely.

Plus, he now knew things that I didn't. He would understand how to *pilot* this thing. I sat in the copilot and operator's chair on the right side. The controls in front of me were for operating those four manipulator arms. It wasn't something the I.A. had covered, but the controls seemed intuitive enough – I could control up to two individual arms, switching which ones each controller manipulated, or I could link them, or if necessary, I could pre-program each arm to perform simultaneous tasks. It was unfamiliar, but not out of the realm of my understanding.

The pilot's seat to my left, on the other hand, had controls that just looked *weird*. There was a flight control yoke, as Naia called it, and pedals for something called 'yaw control,' and switches and levers to manually control each individual thrust if necessary. Plus between those flight controls and my manipulator controls were sensor readouts and other displays and related controls.

It looked insanely complex, and for the first time in weeks, I felt a little lost staring at it.

How well would the I.A. download help Jonnec understand it? Would he come aboard and know what to do? Or would it take him a few minutes to unscramble his brain and figure it out?

"Time to impact?" I asked.

"Twenty-one minutes, fifteen seconds," Naia replied.

"Jonnec?"

"Sitting up, but still not moving."

I still had a little more preflight to go through, but it would be for naught if Jonnec didn't get his ass headed this way now. So I commanded, "Patch me through to the medbay."

A light on the shuttle's control panel lit up, indicating an active comm channel. I'd expected Naia to use my earpiece, but this worked a little better. "Jonnec?"

His voice was shaky when he replied, *"M-mika?"*

I'd never heard him sound so shaken, not even after Thelon's death.

"How ya doing, Princely?"

I hoped using Karina's nickname for him would make him crack a grin, break through the deluge of data and come to his senses. He didn't reply at first, and I tried to be patient. I remembered what it was like, the fear, the confusion wrapped in understanding, which made *no* sense and yet, for anyone who has been through it, made *complete* sense.

Finally, he whispered, *"I am unsure."*

"Think you can walk?" I asked, trying not to sound impatient.

"I…am unsure."

"Well, get sure fast, Princely, 'cause we're running out of time." I grimaced at my own tone, far harsher than I'd meant it to be. "Did Naia brief you on our situation?"

"Y-yes," he replied. *"Yes. She did. She…is a computer. I know what a computer is. Well, at least enough to understand how to pilot a ship operated by computers. My gods, Mika…"*

"I know," I nodded. "Trust me, I know. But I need you down here with me. Think you can put one foot in front of the other, Princely?"

There was a long pause, and I shifted in my chair, getting ready to climb out and head for the medbay to grab him myself, even though we didn't have time for a two-way trip.

But then he surprised me with, *"Stop calling me that."* I grinned. *"And yes, my Princess. I can walk."*

"Good," I nodded. "Stop calling me that."

I could see his smirk in my mind's eye.

Wait…gods, don't tell me I just accidentally flirted with him!

Dammit. I did *not* want to give him the wrong impression.

"I am on my way. Lead the way, Saru."

Relief flooded into my body, and I set back to work on pre-flight.

About ten minutes later, I heard bootsteps clanking up the ramp into the shuttle, and I turned back to see Jonnec with sunken, red eyes, and he was constantly rubbing at his right temple. "Princess," he said.

"Princely," I nodded back at him. "You good?"

"I believe so, yes." He stopped behind the seats and looked at the control board. A moment later, he winced and clenched his eyes shut.

"The knowledge is flooding into your consciousness," I said with a nod.

"Gods," he whimpered. "Is this what it felt like for you?"

"Yup," I said. "Probably was even worse, actually."

Shaking his head, and then wincing again, he blinked hard and then gawked at me. "I did not fully appreciate your pain before. I…I am sorry, Princess."

Sighing, I thought about what to say (I know, shocking, isn't it?) and finally settled on, "Tell you what. Stop calling me 'Princess' and I'll forgive you."

He frowned at me. "But, you are still the Princess of Rhea."

Well that answered that question.

I motioned to his chair. "Then have a seat, Princely. We've gotta launch, now. Where's Saru?"

As he climbed into the pilot's chair, careful to navigate his legs around the control yoke, he replied, "It has resumed its repair duties."

I tried not to take personal offense at him calling Saru 'it.' "Good," I murmured. I keyed in a command to lift the ramp to the shuttle and close the hatch. "Naia?"

"Yes, Mika Kai."

Once it clunked shut, I verified the seals. Then I looked ahead, and ordered, "Seal the launch bay just in case. Activate the forcefield…and then open bay doors."

"Sealing bulkheads surrounding port-side launch bay," Naia reported. "Engaging atmospheric forcefield."

A wide ring around the cargo bay doors lit up bright blue-white, and I saw the shimmer of the forcefield, a wall of static, transparent energy.

And then the bay doors split horizontally down the middle and swiveled open. Revealing the deep, dark emptiness of space, and the blue-white gas giant to portside.

The forcefield held, and pressure in the launch bay remained steady.

"Alright, Princely," I looked at Jonnec just as he rested his hands on the control yoke. "The rest is up to you."

I tried not to panic about that.

SEVENTEEN

We got off to a shaky start.

Literally.

Jonnec announced as he did it, "Engaging antigrav thrusters."

I'm not sure why he announced it. Maybe he was nervous. Or maybe there's some 'programming' that comes with pilot brain stuff, maybe it's procedure.

That unsettled me…I had just thought of the I.A. info dumps as programming.

I shuddered.

So did the shuttle as it lifted off the deck, Jonnec applying power unsteadily. "Woh, woooooh," he murmured. "Huh, just a bit…okay that's weird. This feels weird."

"What?" I asked, a slight panic growing in me as the deck shrank beneath us. "What's weird, what's wrong?"

"What?" he glanced at me. "Oh, nothing, *nothing.*" He grit his teeth. "Just…the I.A. doesn't quite…" The shuttle swooped right, towards the bay wall. Hissing between his teeth, Jonnec adjusted the yoke, "Got it. I got it! I…yes." We stopped centimeters away from the wall, but that didn't stop my heart from pounding against my chest. "Alright. Okay." He breathed in slowly through his nose, exhaled through his mouth. "The I.A. does not quite prepare one for the *feeling* of operating a vessel with inertial dampeners."

I blinked at him. Huh. Is that what I sounded like now?

He sounded *intelligent.* I should have expected it, but it still felt weird to me.

Jonnec brought the shuttle into a hover over its original spot, and he flicked a switch before he let go of the yoke and adjusted his posture.

Then Naia reminded us, "There are less than ten minutes until collision. I will be unable to provide guidance once you depart, Jonnec Impavido and Mika Kai."

"Yeah, got that," I nodded. "I remember."

"We shall be swift," Jonnec assured.

He glanced at me, then he flicked the autopilot off, and eased us forward. Space loomed closer and closer, and I watched the forcefield shimmer before us, until it passed over our hull. And then there was nothing between us and the deadly vacuum of nothingness, except for a thin sliver of hull and glass.

I tried not to think about that too much.

We had an unobstructed view of the gas giant then, and despite the direness of our situation, Jonnec swung us around to let it fill our view – from this position, the planet was nearly full, and it was so *massive!* It filled our viewport, and the innumerable clouds of gasses and storms swirled around each other in such detail that I felt like I was being pulled *into* it.

An alert sounded on our dash, and I panicked for a moment, before Jonnec flicked a switch to bring the details of the alert up. "There is a radiation alert," he stated. "The shuttle's hull is protecting us, but we shouldn't stay out here long without raising shields."

I nodded. "And we need the shields down to do what we need to do."

"Yes," he nodded. And then I saw realization dawn across his face, and he turned slowly to me. "You...you risked your life, more than I ever realized!"

I quirked an eyebrow at him. "Huh?"

"When you entered the stardrive and lured the intruder in there, I had no idea just how dangerous the radiation was. If your suit had been compromised at all..." He trailed off, and his eyes grew wide as saucers. "Hold on, your suit *was* compromised, wasn't it? Your visor was cracked!"

I grimaced and nodded. "Yeah. Thankfully it happened right at the end, and Naia's already given me a pass, saying I hadn't absorbed enough radiation for it to be deadly. She did give me a concoction after I left Rhea again that should've helped negate any long-term effects."

Arching an eyebrow, he again looked out at the gas giant.

And he sighed. "The Universe. It is so much *more* than I could have ever imagined. Beautiful," he nodded towards the planet, "but terrifying as well."

I stared at him, and maybe for the first time in my life, I felt a strange sort of kinship towards the Prince of Rhea. He could recognize beauty in the stars. He could appreciate it.

With a grimace, I thought, *If only he wasn't a misogynistic asshole.*

Clearing my throat, I nodded at the yoke, and said, "We need to hurry."

Setting his jaw, Jonnec nodded without looking at me, and he turned us around.

For the first time ever, I got a real view of the *Sirius* from the outside. Up close and personal.

We were probably only a hundred meters out of the launch bay, so the prow of the ship loomed before us, a wall of metal and glass. The launch bay doors remained open, giving us a relatively clear view of the shuttles within, marred only by the blue haze of the forcefield. To the left and at the top deck was the bridge, and next to that, I saw the windows of the captain's quarters. Inside, they were massive windows, but outside, amidst so many large ones and so much hull, they seemed trivial. Just another set of windows.

Glinting light to our right caught my eye, and I motioned a hand that way, "Careful to the *Sirius's* port. I saw debris from a hull breach after the…*event*."

"I see it," he nodded towards it. And then he engaged thrusters and dipped us under the prow.

Two things immediately struck me on the ventral side of the *Sirius*. First, the ship was *so much larger* than I had ever realized. I mean, it was literally over five miles long, and almost just as wide. Our view was filled with seemingly-endless ship, no windows, just hull and sensors and weapons and maintenance access for shuttles just like this one.

The second thing to strike me was that I finally had my first full view of the alien vessel.

The local sun was hitting the *Sirius* edge-on to her starboard, but even with our polarized viewport, the illuminated part of our home ship was bright, glinting and glaring at us. As Jonnec dipped us lower and lower beneath our home, we could see the absolute blackness of the alien vessel's hull against the glaring reflection off the *Sirius*. No glinting or shining from the intruder's ship, just matte black.

That thing would be damn near impossible to see with the naked eye against the backdrop of space.

What I *did* see was that the alien ship had a long central black shaft that came to a sleek, angular point in front, a bisecting pair of wings near the back, each with their own shafts at mid-point, and a bulbous array connecting everything in a core area.

I also noticed just how close it was to the hull – we were almost out of time.

I glanced down at the sensors and ran a full suite of scans on it. "Huh," I murmured, while Jonnec thrust us towards it.

"What's that?" he asked, without taking his eyes off of his controls and his view of the alien vessel.

"What? Oh," I shook my head. "Just curious sensor readings is all."

There was a moment of silence while we thrust towards the aft end of the *Sirius*. It was exactly as Naia feared – the alien vessel would collide with the starboard-most main sublight engine, and if it ripped a big enough gash into it, that engine would become utterly useless, and possibly blow apart a large section of engineering in the process.

Jonnec let out an exasperated sigh and shook his head. "Of course I know what a sensor is now," he grumbled.

I couldn't help but chuckle at that. I recalled having very similar thoughts in the days after my I.A. download.

Then I felt embarrassed – I'd just laughed at something Jonnec had said.

Ugh. I was disgusted by the idea of making a connection with him like this.

Awkward silence filled the cabin, so I set to work engaging the arms. From where we sat in the ship, they were at positions upper-right, lower-right, upper-left, and lower-left, and I engaged the automated checkout program. There was a soft clunk throughout the shuttle as the arms disengaged from their resting positions, and they slowly extended forward, their pincers flexing, while the arms swung about in every direction they were capable of, testing mobility.

"Um," Jonnec said, "what are the sensors telling you?"

After glancing at him, I turned my attention back to the sensors. "It absorbs a lot of radiation," I said. "But it's passive camouflage, not active or technological. These aliens, they really like to hide what they are and where they are. We can *see* how large it is," I nodded out the viewport, at the looming darkness, "but sensors keep giving me various size readings, like they can't quite get a fix on every edge or corner of it."

"That is indeed fascinating," Jonnec agreed, nodding his head absently, up and down, up and down, and then he frowned. "Um. Except I guess I don't fully understand that. I thought I did. What the wizardfire?" He looked at me quizzically.

With a grin, I shrugged a shoulder and said, "The knowledge will settle in eventually. Until then, understanding will fade in and out like this."

The prince remained silent after that.

And then our task was upon us. We were minutes away from the ship colliding with the *Sirius*, inching closer and closer to the hull. We'd taken too long getting Jonnec into the I.A. and out to the shuttle.

"We can no longer place ourselves between the two vessels," he stated as he brought us alongside the alien vessel.

I nodded, and then I linked the right arms together, and the left arms together, and pushed them outward.

"So let's do the only thing we can do," I looked at him. "Push it aside, hopefully fast enough."

He narrowed his eyes, and then nodded. "Good idea."

The alien ship had tumbled a bit, so its nose was pointed away from the *Sirius*, which gave us a few extra minutes. One wing was almost edge-on, so I said, "Get me up to that wing so I can clamp down on it." I grimaced and muttered, "Hopefully it doesn't break apart when we push..."

While Jonnec maneuvered us closer, he stuck his tongue out. I barely contained a chuckle and cleared my throat to cover up. Everyone had a strange tick when they concentrated, but I'd never seen him do *that*.

It made him...less *threatening*, in my mind.

More human.

I focused on the task at hand, then, and hoped Jonnec wasn't a horrible pilot. We were getting closer now, and the arms were starting to pass over and under the wing. The edge of the wing was closing in on our viewport, and I almost panicked. "Watch our distance!"

"I see it," he hissed at me, and he hit reverse thrusters a little too hard, backing us off rather than stopping us. "Hellfire!" He engaged aft thrusters and started edging us in closer again.

I watched the sensors, but couldn't trust them. I looked at the bright hull of the *Sirius*, tried to estimate how close the alien ship was, but it was so damned hard to tell with how dark its hull was.

"Come on, Princely," I urged.

"Stop calling me that," he breathed.

I grinned.

We were almost there, and I was afraid he'd panic again and back us off, so I hit the switch to clamp top and bottom arms down, pincers facing inward so that they pierced the alien ship's hull.

Except they didn't, despite applying maximum force on the pincers. *Damn, tough ship!*

Hopefully the hull wasn't frictionless, and I declared, "Got it! Go, go, *go!*"

Jonnec applied full aft thrusters.

We pushed the alien ship…but the arms, with nothing to grab onto or penetrate, slid across the hull.

The wing's edge *hit* our viewport, and I let out a high-pitched eep!

But the glass didn't crack. It made some unnerving noises, like ice cracking, but it didn't break.

I leaned forward to look up at the *Sirius*, at how close the bisecting wing was to hitting our home – based on the shadows, it was probably only a few meters away, and was closing in fast! I could see the alien ship's shadow and wing growing closer to one another, and *closer*, and holy hellfire I thought we were going to hit!

With centimeters to spare, we did it! The edge of the wing never touched the *Sirius,* and a moment later, we were behind our home ship, with nothing but the void of space ahead of us.

Jonnec slouched in the pilot's seat. "Oh, thank the gods," he sighed.

Except my sensors told me that we were accelerating away from the *Sirius.* "Uh, thrusters?" I asked.

Jolting forward, Jonnec killed thrust, "Right!"

I grinned and shook my head, and then I disengaged the arms. "Alright," I said, watching the arms retract from an unmarred hull. "Back us off."

"I believe I am the pilot," he raised an eyebrow at me. "I give the orders."

"Oooooh," I sarcastically said, and nodded. "Well, then, my liege.

At your leisure. We're only drifting further away from our mothership in a short-range repair shuttle."

At first he narrowed his eyes at me. And then Jonnec thrust us back from the alien vessel, and swung us around.

Giving me my first view of the aft end of the *Sirius*. To say that the sublight engines were big was an understatement – they almost looked *oversized,* their thrust nozzles bigger in diameter than the bulk of the ship was tall, not counting the dome.

But then I felt my veins turn to ice, and a sudden panic clutched at my chest.

Something was leaking from the top of engineering, a gas that rapidly expanded out into the emptiness of space. "Oh no," I whispered.

Jonnec narrowed his eyes and leaned forward, peering at the leaking gas. "What *is* that?" he asked.

I did a quick sensor sweep, though based on where it was coming from, I thought I already knew.

And sure enough, sensors confirmed it.

"That's deuterium," I said with a grimace, and once again looked up at the expanding gas. Did Naia know we were leaking it? She had to…

"Deuterium," Jonnec repeated, frowning at me. "Isn't that…no, it can't be." He shook his head and rubbed at his temple. "F.T.L.," he spelled out. "Faster than light. That's fuel for our stardrive, isn't it?"

I nodded. "Half of it, anyway," I replied. "Thankfully our antimatter storage wasn't compromised, or we'd all be dead. Still…"

Still, we may as well be. If Naia and the sarus couldn't stop that leak, we'd be out of fuel, and could never engage F.T.L. again. We'd be stuck in this star system. And who knew if it even had a habitable planet.

Just then, however, the stream suddenly stopped. I ran another sensor scan, and felt myself relax a *little* bit. The sarus had cinched off the leak. But if my scans were right… we were close to empty.

"Get us back to the landing bay," I said. "Now."

EIGHTEEN

I once read in a novel the statement that knowledge and experience were two entirely different matters, and experience far outweighed knowledge.

Jonnec proved that in spades.

I imagined he knew everything there was to know about piloting, but his ability to pilot the small shuttle was questionable. We almost slammed into the hull of the *Sirius* rather than make it through the bay doors, and when we landed, it was so rough that I was pretty certain I'd have to check out the entire craft for damage.

In fact, as we rushed down the ramp out the back, I noticed the shuttle sat at an angle, one of the landing gear apparently damaged.

But I'd worry about that later. For now, I jogged towards the exit, Jonnec following close behind, asking me what I was so worried about.

When the exit door wouldn't open for me, I stared stupidly at it and the forcefield covering it. Then I remembered having ordered Naia to seal the bay. "Naia, unseal the launch bay!"

Without protest, the forcefield dropped, and the heavy bulkhead doors parted and recessed into the walls with an unusually noisy hum that I hadn't noticed when we came in – possibly another casualty of the disaster.

While marching towards the nearest lift, I glanced up and asked, "Naia, why didn't you tell me about the compromised deuterium fuel storage?"

"Because the sarus in the aft section of the *Sirius* were already working on the problem, whereas you and Jonnec Impavido already had an urgent issue to resolve." Her voice was so damned calm that I wanted to scream at her just to make the situation actually feel as dire as I knew it was.

As Jonnec and I streamed into the waiting lift, I commanded, "Deck one," and then looked up again. "You could have at least warned us!"

"To do so would have distracted you from the task at hand," Naia replied plaintively. "This has already proven to be the correct course of action, since sensor records show that you and Jonnec Impavido barely diverted the alien vessel in time."

I just about snapped at her, but then I came up short. She was right. Dammit.

I wasn't about to admit that, though, so I kept my mouth shut and waited. The lift arrived on deck one a moment later, and I practically ran to the bridge, Jonnec still in tow.

The emergency red lights had turned back to normal white. Jonnec's boots scuffed the carpet as he stopped short, taking in the view, but I headed right back for the engineering console I'd been using earlier.

Damage readouts were still streaming next to the ship's diagram, but I paused it and brought up a window giving a status report on the stardrive.

The drive itself was completely shut down, an emergency measure due to the fuel leak. I also noticed that some of the injectors were misaligned. *Oh great, I get to go in there again…*

But it was the report on the deuterium fuel levels that made my spirits sink to a whole new low. *No…* With a dreadful slowness, I pulled the chair out and sank into it.

Shaking my head, I ran some calculations and a brief simulation, just to confirm my suspicion. "Naia," I said through my grimace. "Are you seeing what I'm seeing?"

Jonnec had come up behind me and rested a hand on my shoulder while peering at the console, but I ignored his touch and waited.

"Confirmed," Naia stated. I swear I heard sadness in her voice, or some other similar emotion. "Fuel levels are below minimum required to reactivate the stardrive."

Jonnec frowned and glanced down at me. "Wait. Do you mean we cannot jump the ship?"

I nodded, slowly, my body feeling suddenly numb.

"All of that work," I whispered, my voice shuddering. All of the efforts I had put into repairing the ship. When I saved us…all I did was postpone the inevitable. We were stranded now, drifting through space without any way to jump at the end of the winter.

Doomsday scenarios played through my head. Most of them involved the people of Rhea freezing to death.

No, that's not what would happen. Life support on the ship would still be functional, so they could all leave the dome and live in the quarters. It'd be a little tight – the ship required less than a thousand crew, so five thousand people would have to cram in, but...

But the farms. The trees. Everything in the dome would eventually die. No way to get more food. No way to replenish life support.

No, I thought, a sudden fire igniting in my stomach. *No, hell no!*

"Naia," I shook my head, banishing the doom and gloom. "Can we adjust our orbit? Keep us in a sweet spot around this system's sun?"

Several new diagnostics played across my screen at Naia's behest, and she repeated the information I already saw, "Negative. Fusion reactor fuel is at critical levels, and as you know, the sublight engines require considerable fuel to fire, even in short bursts."

"At least to get enough delta-V, yes," Jonnec nodded.

I blinked, and had to remind myself about his I.A. download. *Hellfire, that's gonna take some getting used to.*

Naia displayed a quick simulation of the *Sirius's* course, and annotated, "If we attempt to adjust course, without exhausting all fusion reactor fuel, we will achieve a highly elliptical orbit around the sun. However, the orbit will last approximately forty-two years, the vast majority of which would be spent too far from the local sun to keep the flora of the dome alive.

"We could achieve a potentially viable orbit if we utilize every ounce of spare fuel, however..." She hesitated.

I swallowed. "That'd mean no power for the rest of the ship. No life support. No power for *you* to maintain systems."

"Correct," Naia confirmed. Did her voice waver? Could she actually feel fear for her own wellbeing?

I started thinking that she actually was overcoming her program shackles.

But then another thought imposed itself. "Naia, did our fusion fuel reserves leak, too?"

A distinct pause. *Uh oh.* "Negative," she replied.

"Then why are we so low on reactor fuel?"

Naia explained, "The *Sirius* was not designed to remain in space for two-hundred forty years."

Tilting my head back and narrowing my eyes to the barest slits, I said, "So we were already running low on fuel?" I didn't wait for her to reply, I continued my train of thought out loud, "If that's the case, then this mission was already close to ending, one way or another."

"Your assessment is correct, Mika Kai," Naia admitted, any hint of emotion gone for the moment.

Me, on the other hand, I felt something else – indignant outrage. "So either way, life in Rhea was about to come to an end."

"In more ways than one, yes," Naia affirmed. "Through conservation efforts, I could have kept the *Sirius* powered and operating for another six years at the most."

Gaping upwards, I asked, "And you were just going to…what, let us freeze to death? Cause that's what would've happened. Six years from now, after one more jump, main power would have failed, you would have…" I almost said 'died,' but corrected, "shut down, we wouldn't have jumped again, and we would've just floated out into the void and frozen to death."

Jonnec stood up straight, slowly shaking his head. "No," he murmured. "No, the Oracle would never doom us…" And then he stopped short, eyebrows furrowed deeply, and I could almost hear the gears turning in his head.

He was starting to figure out what I already knew – our life wasn't just a total lie anymore. It was worse.

But my outrage would have to wait.

I wasn't ready to give up just yet.

"Alright," I grumbled. "Alright, Naia, let's figure this out. I take it you've been scanning the local star system?"

"Correct," she replied. "Additionally, multiple probes were launched towards potentially viable planets to assess their habitability more closely. One planet and two moons have been identified as possible candidates."

I nodded. "But with external comms down, you have to wait for the probes to return with their scan data."

"Correct," Naia replied. "The probe dispatched to the closest candidate, a moon orbiting the gas giant we are currently near, should already be finished and enroute to the *Sirius*."

"Alright," I nodded and stood up, pushing Jonnec back and

breaking his handhold on my shoulder. "Show me the candidates and any data you have on them now."

I wasn't sure how Naia would show us, but to my surprise, the massive front window turned opaque and became a giant viewscreen.

We glanced at each other, and then circled around to the front of the bridge to take a closer look.

Three spheres appeared.

Then the one on the far left took center and the others disappeared. "The planet," Naia explained, as data readouts streamed on either side of the sphere, "is approximately fourteen thousand two hundred kilometers in diameter, classifying this world as a 'Super Earth.'"

Jonnec tilted his head, and asked, "Earth?"

"Apparently the name of the planet that humans originated from," I explained, as if that meant anything to either of us. He gave me a dubious look, but I didn't let him know I was as clueless as he was.

"Correct," Naia said. "It is larger, but due to its apparent mass distribution and rotational velocity, gravity at the surface appears to be approximately one point one times that of what the artificial gravity aboard the *Sirius* is calibrated to. Further analysis from a probe is required, however there is already one probable problem."

The image zoomed out and showed a not-to-scale diagram of the planet compared to the sun, and its orbit around the sun. The diagram showed a red inner area that transitioned to green, and then to blue.

"Based upon initial analysis of this planet's atmosphere, it is barely outside of the 'hot zone' around the local sun," Naia explained. "Surface temperatures, even at higher latitudes or elevations, are likely to be barely tolerable without adequate shelter. Survivability factors appear to be low."

I sighed, folded my arms, and nodded. "Alright. What else ya got?"

"There is the moon of another gas giant, further away from the local sun than the *Sirius's* current position, and the furthest potential planet from our current position."

The diagram zoomed way out, one indicator on the middle bottom left showing our position, and the moon in question near the top left.

Jonnec said what I was thinking, "Is that not well outside of the green zone, well into the blue?"

"Uh," I concurred, "Yeah. Wouldn't that moon be too cold?"

"If it were a single planet, yes," Naia affirmed. "However, tidal forces and radiation from the gas giant, combined with considerable greenhouse gasses detected, creates conditions favorable to allow liquid water on the surface, and oxygen is indicated in scans of the atmosphere. However, detailed scans are required to ensure there actually is liquid water present, and flora and fauna. Probability of this moon as a potential candidate is below thirty percent."

Which left one of the moons of the gas giant we were currently passing.

The diagram zoomed in to show the gas giant and our position. A dot indicated that the moon in question was just about on the other side of the gas giant from our current position. "I have been able to obtain more detailed scans of the closest option. This gas giant is the inner-most gaseous planet and rests at the very edge of the habitability zone of the local star. Additionally, greenhouse gases of the moon appear to be at levels sufficient to trap enough warmth to create a relatively temperate climate."

The diagram switched to a view of the moon, showing us a blue and green marble-like planet. "Large oceans account for approximately sixty-six percent of the surface, and the planet's magnetic field and atmospheric composition should be enough to block out the natural radiation that the gas giant emits. Cloud cover likewise appears close to ideal, although initial analysis shows some unusually severe storms."

The more Naia spoke about the moon, the more I liked it. "I'm guessing it's also within reason for gravity?"

"Ninety-eight percent of your accustomed normal," Naia replied.

I nodded and thought about what I was about to propose. No, not just thought about it, but *worried* over it. The *Sirius* was practically dying at this point, and the recent disaster had hastened an already terminal problem.

The people of Rhea could no longer stay.

However, looking at the *Sirius's* trajectory and the fact that we were already on our closest approach to the gas giant made me realize there was a problem. "Naia, can we swing around and enter orbit of the gas giant or the moon?"

"Negative," she started speaking before I even finished my question. "We have insufficient fuel capacity."

I scratched my nose and looked at Jonnec.

Another possibility.

"Could we ferry the people of Rhea in those big cargo ships?"

Jonnec's eyebrows rose questioningly. "Princess Kai," he spoke, his words clipped. "You intend to abandon Rhea?"

I clenched my jaw and amended, "I intend to save our people."

"But how would we survive?" he asked. "How could we leave everything behind?"

"We're close enough, and those big lugs might have enough fuel to make enough trips that we could bring all essential tools, all our animals-"

"Further analysis of the moon in question must be completed before we can determine how viable it is," Naia interrupted me. "However, the severity of the storms I was able to observe indicates that this moon is only approximately sixty-percent viable."

I looked up, recalling our conversation about why Naia hadn't completed her mission. "As opposed to us drifting through space until we all die in, what, three years tops? Naia, I appreciate your need to ensure our well-being, but the time for being picky is over."

"I do not see-" she started.

I interrupted her with heat in my voice, "It's *over*, Naia! It was over before you ever even told me the truth. It was over *before* that alien attacked. That moon sounds like our best and *only* option."

She didn't reply right away. I looked at Jonnec, daring him to come up with a better plan. He simply pressed his lips into a thin line and looked down, shaking his head. "Abandon Rhea," he murmured.

I felt only a little sympathy for him – I'd wanted to leave Rhea for so long, but that had been dreams of exploring the lands beyond our border. This was something else entirely.

This was absolutely terrifying.

But it was better than freezing to death. It was better than watching my brother or Karina dying of starvation or suffocation.

It was our only hope.

…Or so I thought.

"There may be an alternative," Naia said.

Huffing out a doubtful breath, I shook my head, but nevertheless said, "I'm listening." Gods, I sounded like my mother.

"As I have stated, this moon contains a considerable amount of oceanic water," she began. "Oceanic water is a potential source for deuterium *and* tritium."

I blinked in surprise, but a second later, my brain dumped the relevant info into my conscious thoughts. It required a conversion process, but she was right, *and* I happened to know that part of our colonization package aboard the *Sirius* included devices for converting salt water into deuterium.

Naia continued, "Additionally, our scans indicate heavy metals present in the moon's upper crust, in concentrations high enough to be detectable from at least one million kilometers away. Any number of these metals could be used to shore up our supply shortages and restore the *Sirius* to operational capability."

Tilting my head to one side while considering it, I mumbled, "Hrm," and looked back towards the engineering console, then at the image of the moon. "Naia…are you suggesting we take cargo ships down to mine and process materials?"

"That is precisely what I am suggesting," she replied.

I lifted my eyebrows and looked at Jonnec. I waited and wondered if he would come to the same conclusion I had.

"Oracle," he said, then corrected himself, "Naia. That is not something that Mika and I alone can accomplish."

"You are correct, Jonnec Impavido," she said. "I would estimate between twenty-five and fifty townspeople would need to be involved in the expedition."

"Not just involved," I pointed out. "Trained. Told the truth, trained to use the proper machines…" I paused, and asked, "I assume you don't want everyone to get a turn in the I.A.?"

"It would be best to avoid use of the Intellectus Apparatus due to the vast amount of energy it requires to operate," Naia said. "I would prefer to use it only one more time – to train a second pilot for the second cargo shuttle in the starboard launch bay. However, you are correct, Mika Kai." I swear, she sounded resentful when she said that, even if it was only a subtle hint. "The mission is, unfortunately, at its conclusion, and we must modify the parameters to ensure the survival of the people of Rhea. Therefore, we must tell the people of Rhea the truth, and involve many in the efforts to save the *Sirius*."

I'm not going to lie. It felt *really* good to finally be vindicated this way, to finally hear that what I had wanted for Rhea all along was about to happen. With the backing of the revered Oracle, no less.

I grinned at Jonnec, but he didn't look nearly as excited as I felt. Oh well for him.

More than that, I knew exactly who I wanted to suggest for the second pilot.

I'll give you one guess.

- PART 2 -
EXPEDITION

NINETEEN

With heavy purpose, I climbed the stairs onto the platform in Rhea's town square. The same platform that had been erected two months ago for the Renewal Festival, now rebuilt for today's announcements.

Just like that memorable night, waiting for me was the king and queen, Prince Jonnec, Vell, and my master, Viden. The only difference was that this time, it was in broad daylight, in the middle of a warm late-spring day.

And I was supposed to be an exile.

My heart thudded in my chest over what was coming next. Panic gripped my chest like a vice, and I sought out something familiar, something comfortable. I saw the obelisk and felt the vice ease up just a little – the blue-white glow illuminated the runes on the top half of it. We still had a chance.

Assuming nothing else went wrong, anyway. Not like that impact disaster two days ago.

It was Spring, I should have been smelling flowers and grass, a comfort that all was well. Instead, I could smell dirt and dust and charred wood. I surveyed the buildings surrounding the square, and every single one of them had sustained damage in what might have otherwise been misconstrued as a seismic event. One building had completely collapsed over onto a main avenue, and cleanup was still underway. Another had lost its entire front face.

Twelve people were dead, another one *thousand* injured to various degrees.

One-fifth of the population.

As horrific as that sounded, it could have been worse. The dome was a more solid structure, and had independently-powered structural integrity fields, so Rhea hadn't shaken nearly as bad as what I'd experienced.

Still, as I looked out upon those who could make it to today's announcement, my spirits sank back to their lowest. A lot of people were hurt, and *everyone* was scared.

And there were more than a few hateful, distrustful, or otherwise nasty looks directed at me.

The king nodded once to me, his face a mask betraying no emotion, and I supposed that was the best I could hope for. My exile was officially over, but what was going to happen next didn't exactly sit well with the king.

For once, I was glad that he followed the Oracle's commands no matter what.

Touching the jewel on his necklace, the king muttered a word to activate the technology within, and he spoke in a booming voice.

"People of Rhea," he proclaimed. "Thank you for coming once again. I know that we are all recovering, and for many of us, we are all still mourning. These past few months have been trying. We have endured hardships unprecedented for Rhea.

"I will be honest in stating that our hardships may not yet be at an end. However," he held up his hands, forestalling the wave of despair that washed across the square, "I assure you that we already have a plan of action to restore peace."

I searched the crowd for a familiar face. For baby-blue eyes amongst a sea of so many. I hadn't yet seen Karina – I'd only been back in Rhea for a few hours, most of which was spent consulting everyone now assembled on stage.

I missed Karina. More than ever.

"However," the king continued, "this will require the efforts of more than just the throne." The king lowered his arms and slowly turned his head to take in as many people as he could. "And time is not our ally in this struggle. Therefore I am forced to push forward the truth, despite how many still refuse to accept it."

I wasn't psychic, and I was pretty sure psychics weren't real, but I swore I could *feel* the wave of hatred wash over some of the crowd. This wasn't welcome news.

"No longer can we hide behind superstition and tradition, as they will not serve to ensure our survival. The truth that I have proclaimed to all of you *must* be accepted, and while there is still so much to learn, I assure you-"

"Traitor!" someone shouted with a vengeful, wrathful voice.

"Liar!" another voice joined in from my right.

"Deceiver!"

"Harlot!"

"HEY!" I protested. The other names, I could maybe understand, but harlot?

…Oh.

That last had come from Annar, and he stepped away from a group of angry-looking people. Some of whom I recognized from my previous night in Rhea. I'd learned in my few hours back in town that they were calling themselves the Truthspeakers.

I know, stupid name, right?

I noted that I didn't see Annar's family, I didn't see *Karina,* anywhere nearby.

"THAT IS ENOUGH!" King Impavido's voice resonated, and I swear it shook some rubble loose somewhere, the sound of pebbles falling echoing in the sudden silence following his shout.

I don't think I'd ever heard the king shout with such impatience. Still, Annar maintained his defiant stance.

This was to be expected, but it didn't make it easier to accept. I wasn't just referring to Annar accepting the truth, either.

I grimaced, waiting for the king to continue.

"Many of you still side with the Truthspeakers," the king stated. I barely kept my eyes from rolling at hearing their name. "I have shown considerable patience and leniency towards your group while trying to bring you around to face the *actual* truth, but the time for patience and leniency is over."

I saw Annar's hands clench into fists. I saw him step forward. That emboldened a lot of other people, who likewise stepped forward, and not just those surrounding him. I tensed, and slowly rested my hand on the pistol strapped to my thigh. I didn't want to shoot anyone again. I didn't want to hurt *anyone* from Rhea again.

But there was just too much at stake not to at least keep it on me.

The king continued, turning his gaze upon the rest of Rhea. "The Oracle has called for the assistance of several townspeople," he forged ahead, "as Master Viisas has relayed to me. Because Prince Jonnec and Princess Mika are to lead the effort to save us, they will be the ones to deliver…"

"Never!" another voice shouted, in the opposite direction from Annar.

Annar defiantly added, "We'll never follow *her!*"

Several people in the crowd surged forward.

We had anticipated some trouble, and I'd come prepared – the seventeen guards surrounding the platform lifted their arms, and blue-white energy shields sprang into existence. I prepared to activate mine, too, just as a rock sailed past my ear.

But even with shields, seventeen guards couldn't contend with the press of at least a hundred people, all pushing against them. The personal shields weren't meant to hurt people, only block them, so the throng pushed harder. I turned my shield on just in time to intercept three more rocks. The king, queen, prince, Vell and Viden had shields of their own, but they didn't need them – *all* of the rocks were directed at me.

Vell stepped ahead of the king, his shield raised, and he stamped his staff upon the stage, sending out an echoing *BOOM!* that deafened me.

Clouds rolled in at unreal speeds, and thunder rumbled in the distance. Those in the crowd who weren't part of the 'Truthspeaker' mob cried or cowered in terror, as the sky grew dim but for bright flashes of lightning.

It was meant to intimidate the throng into backing off. It only did the opposite, as Vell became the new target for rock throwers.

I unholstered my pistol, my heart racing, my hands shaking. Gods, this wasn't supposed to go so badly! I thought by now people would *listen!* Why don't people listen?

One of the guards was shoved aside, and he stumbled into some others, opening a sieve for the Trusthspeakers to storm the stage. I took aim at the head of the pack.

An ear-piercing shriek cut through all of the noise, an unnatural, piercing, constant screech that deafened me to everything else.

The clouds instantly vanished. The *sky* vanished, leaving only stars, and casting Rhea into darkness. The streetlamps did not automatically turn on, either, and even the glow of Vell's staff vanished.

Leaving only our shields and the obelisk casting light, and the obelisk flashed brighter than the sun, blinding us all for a moment.

The flash receded, and the piercing shriek ceased. And hovering above the obelisk was a blue-white sphere, with a bright core and dim outer-layer, and the outer layer wavered as Naia's voice boomed over all of Rhea, "Stop!"

Holy hellfire, she could make an entrance when she needed to!

Naia had everyone's attention. The Truthspeakers, the rest of Rhea, even I gaped up in awe, even though I knew that all I was seeing was a holographic projection, coupled with the deactivation of the dome's sky illusion. The local sun shone down upon us, yes, but the dome was polarized to minimize its light.

"I am the Oracle," Naia stated, infusing an austere tone into her voice, "and I address you all for the first time to impress upon you the dire stakes. King Roberto Impavido has spoken only truth as he knows it to you, and he has done so with my authority. To question him is to question me." I tried not to focus on the flaw in her logic, but then again, the king hadn't quite told everyone yet that the Oracle was a computer program, not an actual goddess. "Do any of you dare to defy me?"

That was an unexpected question, and the way she had worded it caught me off guard. This was the same mostly-passive A.I. that I'd gotten to know over the past two months. Now she sounded authoritative!

No one spoke. The Truthspeakers on-stage looked around at one another, but avoided looking at me.

When enough time had passed, no doubt calculated by Naia to give the maximum impression upon the people, she continued, "Rhea rests upon a vessel sailing amongst the stars, just as you have been told. That vessel is named the *Sirius*, and it has sustained considerable damage in recent months." So much for sounding like a goddess. If not for her voice booming across the dome, she might have sounded pedantry now.

But she held the rapt attention of all present.

"I require the efforts of everyone to resolve this situation," she continued. "Therefore you will listen to King Roberto Impavido, Queen Gabriella Impavido, the Wizard Vell Viisas, Prince Jonnec Impavido, and yes, you will listen to Princess Mika Kai. Anything less will be an affront to me."

Then, with no further bravado, the sphere faded from existence. The blue sky slowly returned, illuminating Rhea back to full daylight, and the bright glow of the obelisk returned to its usual level.

Damn. Not bad for an A.I.

I looked at the closest Truthspeaker, my weapon trained at his legs, my shield between him and me. He in turn stared back at me, slack-jawed.

He backed off. Slowly, but I let out my breath, relief flooding through my body. I mean, sure, Naia and I had talked about her making her presence known if things went sideways, but I hadn't known what she had in mind, nor how effective it would be.

Glancing down at the bottom of the stairs, I saw Annar staring at the obelisk, wide-eyed and with absolute terror in his eyes. Whatever he believed, he still feared the Oracle, and that might just give us the leverage we needed.

I waited for the king to demand arrests, but as the guards shoved the Truthspeakers off of and away from the stage, and since no one was hurt more than a bloody nose or black eye, the king let it slide.

No prisoners today.

No doubt because we needed some of those people.

The king then yielded the stage, and his son stepped up, with me beside him. I tried not to keep too far from him, wanting to present a united front to the frightened townspeople, but I still didn't want to give him the impression that I was at all interested in the union that Naia had dictated.

Openly defying Naia now would be counterproductive.

"People of Rhea," Jonnec spoke. His voice sounded…*small* when compared to Naia's dome-wide voice. Still, everyone listened intently. "To restore the vessel that the Oracle spoke of, we need materials. Materials that cannot be found in Rhea or aboard this vessel. Therefore, the Oracle has decided that we must venture elsewhere to find those supplies. We must mine metals and gather other material to be transmuted into what the Oracle needs to ensure our survival.

"It is thus that I pronounce the following people will leave Rhea by this time tomorrow, to harvest these materials, and to bring them back." That caused quite a stir amongst the crowd. Up until two months ago, no one had ever left Rhea. Now, *many* were about to leave, and for an extended time.

Jonnec pulled out a data pad that he'd tucked into his belt and turned it on. I braced myself, knowing the first name on that list. "Annar Ticho."

Yeah. *Him.* I'd argued with Naia about that one. But she was right – he was learning the blacksmith trade from his father. He knew metals. He was young and hearty.

In fact, every blacksmith under forty years old would join us on this trip.

Unfortunately, that included one other name…

Jonnec continued down the list, naming townsperson after townsperson, including a few of the guards who would not just help with resource gathering, but would provide protection against any wild animals we might find on the planet. And then he spoke the name, "Hector Lee."

You might recognize the name, but have only read it once before. Well, that name was seared into my brain.

He was Karina's fiancé.

Making that two people I detested on this expedition.

But at least there was one I adored.

"Karina Ticho," the prince proclaimed a few names later.

I still hadn't found her amongst the crowd, not until now, when I saw her head pop up.

She stared first at the prince, and then at me. I met her baby blues, and my heart fluttered! I had difficulty reading her expression, but I watched her carefully, hoping for some sign that she was excited, whether over the idea of spending time with me again, or of going on a new adventure.

Even from here, there was no mistaking her gorgeous smile, and my heart *soared!*

Jonnec finished listing off the names shortly after, a total of forty-four people, to be divided evenly between the two large cargo and mining shuttles, one in each launch bay. That coupled with Jonnec, Karina and I made for a total of forty-seven souls.

"For the friends and families of those named, please spend what time you can with them today and tonight, for we do not know how long we will be gone. It could be days, or weeks. Maybe even months. However, as your prince I promise you I will bring them all back. I swear it!"

I knew he meant it, but a part of me wondered.

Our luck hadn't exactly been the best lately.

TWENTY

I stood outside of my parents' house and stared.

Huh, I thought to myself. *Now it's my parents' house…not my house.* I guess somewhere along the way, I'd started thinking of the corridors of the *Sirius* as my home, and not this small, rickety old house.

There was a lot of work to do before we launched tomorrow, but knowing that I wouldn't be back for who knew how long, I had to come see them. I had to come see Phoebus. I owed my little brother that much.

The house…their house, *my* house, it had withstood the 'quakes' surprisingly well. I saw a few shingles missing from the roof, and all of the windows were cracked, but that was the worst of it. Lucky them.

I drew in a deep breath and caught the scent of freshly baked bread. My mother must have been cooking all day, and would continue to do so through the night, both because her oven was still operational, and to help create a surplus of food for those of us leaving.

Movement drew my attention from my father's workshop, and I saw a little face peek through the window and stare at me. *How does he always know?*

Phoebus smiled and disappeared. My heart soared, and I bounded the remaining distance, reaching the door the moment it sprang open. Phoebus squeaked, "Mika!" and he leapt into my arms, damn near knocking me over while we embraced one another.

"Phoebus!" I practically cried, crushing him with all the strength that I had. He, on the other hand, squeezed back, and damn near drove the breath out of me, he'd grown so strong!

"Oof," I breathed, and pulled out of the hug, patting his shoulders.

"My gods, you've grown so much!"

He beamed at me, but it was Father's voice that replied, "Yeah, we had to get him a whole new set of clothes this past weekend."

I blinked in shock, not just at what Father had said, but by how he'd said it – as if he'd been proud of the fact that they'd had to acquire new clothes for Phoebus. Instead of complaining about it, he was *happy*.

Father stepped up behind Phoebus, and for a moment, there was an awkward silence. I searched his dark eyes, and he looked curiously at me. And then, I don't know why exactly, I felt a smile creep up the edges of my mouth, and we hugged.

Maybe I'm crazy, but I was actually happy to see him.

Patting me on the back once, he withdrew and beamed at me. "Come on, your mother's busy in the kitchen, but she'll want to see you."

As expected, the kitchen was a mess, though Mother would call it an *organized* mess. She rushed back and forth, working on, I kid you not, eight meals at once. Her apron was covered in various bits and juices, there were butchered meats, breads, and chopped veggies and fruits spread across the various surfaces that she tried to work around. Our dining table was covered with bags that she'd already begun to fill, and she didn't even notice us when we approached, her eyes distantly focused on accounting for the various foods she had to put into each bag.

I didn't want to interrupt her, knowing how hard it would be for her to get back into her groove afterwards. But father insisted on getting her attention, and when she realized I was there, the biggest smile blossomed over her weary face, and she moved to embrace me.

"Uh, Mom!" I put up a halting hand, and she frowned at me. I motioned at her dirty apron. When she realized why, she let out a light laugh, took her apron off just long enough to give me a tight, squeezing hug, and then she put it back on and resumed work.

This was different. Normally they gave me an ungodly amount of attention. Now, Father was proud of Phoebus, and Mother was too busy to fawn over me!

Then again, thinking back to when all this first started, and the people had been ordered to congregate to share warmth, she'd been too busy preparing to leave the house to really pay attention to me. I'd had to scream at her to get her to pay attention.

I guess things haven't changed that *much after all.*

Mother dropped a couple of potatoes and let out an uncharacteristic curse. Phoebus rushed forward and gathered them up for her, and then he grabbed the rest out of her hands and set to chopping them up.

Okay…maybe things *had* changed. Phoebus never helped with cooking. Mother never let him.

Well, damn.

The walls and ceiling creaked and I looked up at the ceiling.

"It's okay," Father assured me. "The old house held up better than expected." He matched my gaze, staring up at the ceiling. "Some cracks and a bit of warping here and there, but that's all."

I nodded grimly. "I wish I could say we'll be able to get everyone's houses fixed right up, but…" I trailed off and looked at him, shaking my head. He arched a curious eyebrow at me (yes, that's where I got the habit from), and I added, "Supplies are kinda short, and I doubt we'll be able to fit lumber in the shuttles, not with all the ore and gasses we need to collect."

The look he gave me was one of both curiosity and confusion, and I tried to remember if he knew what ore was, let alone gasses. I tried to remember what I did and *didn't* know before my I.A. session. With a start, I realized that I couldn't! I couldn't remember what I was like before all of this began.

I wondered how much I'd changed. If my family could change so much *without* such a world-shattering encounter, what had it all done to me?

More to the point…was I even sad about it?

I didn't think so. I loved knowing what I knew, if that even made sense.

"Uh," I looked towards the door, suddenly feeling very awkward about all of this. "Is…is there anything I can do to help before I go?"

The rhythmic chopping of potatoes halted, and Phoebus looked over at me. "Go? You're not staying for dinner?"

I shook my head at him, "No, sweetie, I'm sorry." His features drooped, and he let out a huff of breath. "There's a lot I have to get done before we leave tomorrow, a lot of people are depending on me."

He just nodded and went back to work, though his rhythm was a lot slower now.

"I don't think there's anything else we can do right now," Father answered my question. "We donated all of our spare nails. And given the names Prince Impavido listed, it's going to be a while before we get a surplus supply again."

"Yeah," I grimaced. "We didn't take all of the blacksmiths, but…"

"But all of the youngest ones, and some of the middle-aged ones," he nodded. "That's understandable."

Gods, it was so weird having an intelligent, adult conversation with my Dad.

That's when it hit me. That's what was so different. Before now, he'd always talked down to me like I was a child. Today, he talked to me like I was an adult.

For all the bragging he used to do, I guess he never actually was truly proud of me. Until now.

Something welled up in my chest, and my eyes burned.

But as I searched his face, I noticed something else – a fresh scar on one cheek. Not so fresh as to have come from the disaster, but definitely one that wasn't there two months ago.

Frowning, I pointed on my face where the scar was on him, and then pointed at him, "Where'd that come from?"

His cheeks tightened, his jaw clenched, and he drew in a deep breath. "After you left, some of those Truthspeaker idiots decided that, as your parents, we needed to be made an example of."

Heat flared in my chest, and I felt fresh rage boil within. "Annar," I growled.

"And a few others," Father nodded. "But the king anticipated as much, and had ordered a guard near our house at all times."

I lifted my eyebrows, and again pointed to his scar, "But obviously it wasn't enough to deter them."

"No," he sighed, "but believe me, they didn't have the gumption to try again. We gave better than we got."

I matched his sigh and shook my head, the fire of hatred turning to regret and guilt. I had no doubt that the attack on my family was a result of my actions my last night in Rhea.

"I'm sorry," I murmured. "I didn't mean to bring this all down on you guys."

"You didn't," he said.

That was a weak platitude if I'd ever heard one, but I granted him a reprieve. I'd defied the king's wise orders, more than once, and every time I did, it'd cost me *and* people I loved.

I wasn't sure what else to talk about, my guilt overrode any real thoughts that I had. So I was grateful when there was a knock at the door, and I knew exactly who it was. Father gave me a curious look, and I nodded and said, "It's okay. It's a guard, coming to escort me to my next stop."

He frowned at that, but then moved to let the guard in.

I turned back to the kitchen. Phoebus had been listening and had stopped his work, while Mother kept going. He set his knife down, brushed his tunic off, and we met halfway, throwing our arms around one another, squeezing tight.

When we parted, fresh tears were in his eyes, and I felt wetness on my own cheeks. I again didn't know what to say or do. He wiped his nose with his sleeve and sniffed.

"Look at that," I whispered, and touched my thumb to his nose. "You finally learned how to wipe your own nose."

He choked out a laugh and sniffed again. "I…" He started and stopped. Drawing in breath, he said, "I had to learn how."

There were unspoken words there, and I said them in my head. *Because I wasn't there to do it for him anymore.*

I hung my head. "I'm sorry I have to go again."

He shrugged a shoulder and looked around for a second. "Well…you're the Savior of Rhea. Not a lot of brothers can say that about their sister, can they?"

I laughed. "No, no they can't." Giving him a quirky grin, I asked, "Do people really call me that?"

"I do," he beamed. I felt my cheeks flush. "But not everyone. Not yet. So go do it again, Big Sis." He looked into my eyes. All of our family had dark eyes, and his were no different, but damn if they didn't look wiser and stronger. Gods, how much he'd changed in two months, and he was just a little kid!

But at least he still had his cute button nose. I winked at him, touched his nose with my thumb again, and then looked to Mother. She'd stopped her work long enough to watch my goodbye with Phoebus, but she didn't take her apron off again.

I smiled at her, and she returned it. "Be safe," she said, her voice soft, worrisome.

"I'll do my best," I said. "And I'll come back." I turned to find Father behind me, and one of the guards behind him. "I promise."

TWENTY-ONE

The guard and I walked through the haggard streets of Rhea, my tears finally having stopped their incessant flow. I glanced at my escort and realized I recognized her. Dark skin, short black hair, and an axe strapped to her belt.

Thelon's axe.

She was built like Thelon, too. All muscle, broad shoulders, and she stood a head and a half taller than me. Definitely guard material, she could probably stop a fight with a frown.

"Thank you," I said to her, wanting to fill the awkward silence as we walked.

She gave me a sidelong look, but didn't turn her head to fully face me. "For what?" she grunted, her voice gruff and impatient.

"For escorting me."

Another grunt. "I was ordered to."

I grimaced, and looked away, trying to remember what her name was. Sure, I'd read the names of everyone alive today at some point, but five thousand names was a lot.

I glanced at the axe again. It was…just an axe, right? Not Thelon's.

She glanced at me, and grumbled, "Don't even think about it."

"Huh?" I blurted.

The guard covered the axe-head protectively, and she gave me a rather hostile look, "Don't even think about touching this."

"I wasn't," I shook my head, suddenly afraid of her.

"Good." She slipped her fingers down and gripped the haft tightly. "You don't deserve to."

Bewildered, I gawked back at her. "I…" I started and stopped, my mind racing with what she'd just said. I didn't deserve to?

…Was it really Thelon's?

Guilt swirled within, and I realized just how much like that first adventure this could turn out to be. I mean, I wasn't the only one that had an I.A. stint this time, so it wouldn't *all* fall on my shoulders. Unlike last time, we were *leaving the ship*. Sure, it was an adventure, but there was more on the line this time, and more risk involved.

Only six of us went last time. Five came back. How many would come back this time?

Banishing those thoughts, I reminded myself to focus on the here and now. Worrying about the uncertain future wouldn't get me through today.

A few minutes later, we stood before Karina's family home.

Like everything else in Rhea, homes here weren't given away to just anyone. There was no currency, not like what I'd read about in books, and we basically lived as a society where everyone did their part, and knew not to get greedy, for fear of the Oracle's wrath (which probably carried a *lot* more weight after today's demonstration). The Oracle determined where everyone lived, and it was always primarily based upon a person's trade.

So for Karina's family, they lived in one of those houses that had a courtyard of sorts. Only instead of some posh patio with furniture for relaxing, this courtyard contained a smelting furnace and blacksmith's workshop, since that was what Karina's father did.

Not everyone followed in their parents' footsteps as a career. Just look at me, my father was a cobbler, my mother a cook, and I was meant to be the town chronicler. But for Karina's family, they had been designated to follow their parents – Karina was a carpenter like her mother, and Annar was just about to graduate from his apprenticeship as a blacksmith.

Which made the decision to include Karina in this adventure even harder – both Karina's father and brother would be coming along, and that meant that her mother would be left alone.

It occurred to me that I had no idea what her parents thought of me. Did they side with Annar and the Truthspeakers? Or were they smarter than that?

Then again, Karina had told me that the king, queen, and her *parents* had convinced her to stay in Rhea. So either way, I'm sure they weren't going to be happy with me.

I let out a shuddering breath and looked at the guard. She frowned at me. "What?" she growled out.

No support there. Fantastic.

Shaking my head, I stepped into the courtyard and up to the front door, and knocked three times.

A moment later, a figure almost as intimidating as the guard towered over me. Karina's father, Leif. He was the one she'd inherited her carrot-red hair from, only he kept his trimmed neatly, almost too short to display how curly it was. He had eyes bluer than Karina's, and a face full of freckles.

And he did *not* look happy to see me.

"Um," I managed. "Mister Ticho. I…we," I motioned to the guard behind me, "are here for Karina."

The look he gave me was full of distrust and venom. I was caught between being scared about that and being defiant of it, and found myself floundering for what to say or how to act around him. I hated feeling that way.

I got the impression that if I had come alone, he wouldn't have agreed to let me see her. But his eyes settled on the guard, and he nodded to her. "Marek."

"Leif," she nodded back.

Monosyllabic conversation. Wow, such interesting company…

And yes, you should be proud of me for not saying that out loud. I was nervous as a snowman near wizardfire, and I tended to blabber a lot when I was that anxious.

He slammed the door in my face, and I blinked.

"Um," I muttered.

A second later, it opened again, and Karina's gorgeous face appeared.

My heart ached, my chest heaved, and I threw myself at her, wrapping my arms around her and squeezing tight.

For a second, she didn't return my hug, and I felt my pulse skip a beat. But then she grasped me and held me as tightly as I held her.

I nearly sobbed, I'd missed her so much! Being alone on the *Sirius* for so long, without my girl to keep me company, I hadn't realized how much it hurt. How lonely I'd become.

For that moment, I felt whole again.

Pulling away from me, Karina smile and sighed. "Hello, you," she whispered.

"Hello, beautiful," I said back.

Regular poets, aren't we?

"I didn't think I'd see you until tomorrow," she said, resting her forehead against mine and closing her eyes. "I…I wasn't sure how I'd feel. I…"

Marek cleared her throat, and Karina noticed her for the first time. She sucked in a breath and broke contact with me. "Oh," she muttered. "Um." Eyes darting between me and the guard, Karina asked, "W-what's the occasion for the early call?"

I grimaced. "Well. I know the king wanted everyone to have time with their family before we all left tomorrow." Karina eyed me suspiciously. "But your reason for coming is different from everyone else's."

Cautiously, she asked, "O-oh?"

I nodded and swallowed. "Yeeeeaaaah," I drily said, drawing out the word. "How would you feel about a stint in the I.A.? The, uh, Intellectus Apparatus?"

Her eyes opened wide as saucers, and her mouth matched them. "Ex…excuse me?"

I smiled ironically. "We need another pilot for the second shuttle."

She wasn't exactly tan, but Karina's face paled considerably. "You mean…I have to go through what you did?"

"Not as bad," I assured her, hands held up disarmingly. "I mean, I had to have enough engineering knowledge forced into my skull, along with other related fields, to fix pretty much every system on the *Sirius*. You just have to learn how to pilot ships, which I think will include some physics and chemistry and math, but you won't have to know all of the mechanics of the ships you'll fly, and…" I realized I was rambling, so I clamped my mouth shut.

I had hoped Karina would have been excited, but I also worried she would hate the idea. I'd spent countless hours over the past two days thinking about how I would bring this up with her and how she would react.

So I searched her eyes to discern her feelings on the matter. By now, I should've known my girl, known what her expressions all meant. But if there's one thing I've learned in recent months, it's that where Karina is concerned, I wasn't objective.

Shocked that I recognized that? Me too. Maybe I'm growing as a person.

And then a shadow fell on us from behind her.

Hector Lee.

My stomach soured, but he gave me a pleasant smile. "Mika Kai," he spoke, his voice surprisingly jovial. He wasn't very tall, pretty much the same height as Karina. His black hair was cut awkwardly short, and it looked like he didn't know what to do with it. I watched him as he drew closer to Karina, but he didn't put a hand on her, and he kept his dark brown eyes on me. "It is an honor to see you again."

I hadn't expected that.

"Um," I replied.

Karina grimaced. "Hector and his family are here so we could all be together before we left," she explained.

"To what do we owe the pleasure of your visit?" Hector asked.

I drew in a deep breath to speak, but it caught in my throat, and I made a bit of a choking noise. They eyed me curiously while I tried to clear the lump out.

"I'm, um, on a mission from the Oracle," I stated, my mind racing to figure out what to say. "I'm afraid I have to take Karina away for the evening."

"Mika," Karina narrowed her eyes at me. "Was it really the Oracle's orders, or was it what you wanted?"

I balked at her implication, even if it was the right deduction. "No! I mean, yes, but the Oracle agreed." She arched an eyebrow at me. I tried not to swoon. "Since you've spent so much time reading fiction, opening your mind to new ideas and possibilities, the chances of complications from the I.A. are less. You're less likely to experience mimetic rejection."

Hector frowned. "I.A.?" he asked quizzically. "You mean, that thing you told me about?" he asked Karina. "That gave Mika all that knowledge?"

Karina sighed and smiled plaintively at him. "Yes. Apparently I get to go through it now, too." She didn't sound one bit excited about that, and I felt my spirits sink.

On the other hand, Hector's face lit up, and he said, "That's incredible!" He looked at me, his eyes alight with intrigue. "How exciting! I can't imagine what it must be like to suddenly know so much, it must be exhilarating!"

I shrugged. "Only if you like your brain getting scrambled and fried."

There we go. My sarcasm was coming back, and I felt a little relieved.

Karina narrowed her eyes at me, but Hector let out a genuine bellow of a laugh, and I suddenly felt myself smile. His laugh was *infectious!*

And then I caught myself and smothered my smile. No, no, *no*, I did not want to like him! He was meant to take my girl away from me, I therefore had to hate him!

Then I saw the taut look on Karina. She worked her jaw around and flexed her fingers in and out of a fist. "Karina?" I asked. "Um…"

"I suppose I don't have a choice in the matter?" she asked.

"Well, you always have a choice," I looked down. "You don't have to if you don't want to. We can find someone else…"

"Karina," Hector cooed. "Come, now, why would you forsake such a gift?"

Lifting her eyebrows, she stared at me skeptically and asked, "Is it a gift?"

I opened my mouth to instantly reply, but then paused. It was a fair question, and I felt like I should actually consider it before I answered. Afterall, for the freedom it brought me, sometimes I felt even *more* shackled by what I knew. Worse still, it had made me a target for those opposed to the truth, the ironically-named Truthspeakers.

However, my appreciation of the Universe had grown a thousand-fold, and the journey we were about to embark upon would have been impossible before now.

"It is," I finally replied. "And it's a curse. But if I could go back, knowing how it would affect me and my life, and if I was given the chance to change what I did, to not go through with it? I'd still do it."

I stepped forward, and I reached for Karina's hand. I waited halfway, hoping she would take mine, even in Hector's presence. She stared at my hand for a second, and then very slowly, her eyes darting towards Hector for a second, she took my hand.

"More than that, Karina, it's a chance to finally go on an adventure, just like we always dreamed." I studiously ignored Hector's quizzical look. How much of our history together had she told him? "Karina, we're about to explore a whole new *world!* How can you say no to that?"

The edges of her mouth curled up, and I saw the spark of excitement flare in her eyes. "I can't," she said, her grin broadening.

There she is!

That's my girl.

"Good," I nodded. I looked at Hector and considered my next words carefully. I had hoped for just Karina and I to go tonight, but at the same time, I couldn't really demand her fiancé stay behind while his fiancée underwent such a radical procedure.

Could I?

No….

Gods dammit.

So sucked it up and did the honorable thing. "You, um, you're welcome to join us," I said.

Hector beamed a smile at me. "That would be fantastic!"

Well, at least he was excited to go, and he didn't seem to be an asshole Truthspeaker.

Yup, that's me. Mika Kai, the one who always looks on the bright side.

…Who am I kidding?

TWENTY-TWO

It was barely midday when Karina, Hector, Marek, and I hiked north out of Rhea, and headed for the hatch.

Our lives might have been a lie, and the sky above was an illusion, but the beauty of Rhea in Spring was real, and I relished it. The open fields were green, and as we passed through the forest, I lightly touched some of the oak leaves. And the smell, oh gods I loved the smell of Spring!

Karina, not so much, and she sneezed for about the fifth time since we'd left her house. I empathized with her allergies, and I wanted to reach out and hold her hand, but not with Hector on the other side of her.

I felt like we had a chaperone, and it annoyed me to no end.

Still, I was surprised that Hector maintained a respectable distance from her. Unlike Jonnec, who was always touching me and saying things that made my stomach flop, Hector's conversation was intelligent, and he kept his hands to himself.

Dammit. I *had* to find some reason to hate him.

Other than the fact that he was engaged to Karina.

After we emerged from the trees, we reached the two-meter mark, and the hatch whispered into view before us, startling the others.

I expected Karina to recover first, having experienced a lot of crazy things with me on the ship before. But Marek's shocked expression hardened. I watched her for a moment, looking for some impression of what she was thinking beyond anger towards me. When she noticed me staring, she opened her eyes wide, and hotly asked, "You got a problem, kid?"

Kid? She was barely older than me, wasn't she?

Earlier I'd kept my mouth in check. This time, not so much. "Yeah, your attitude."

Rage boiled through her widening eyes, but then she caught herself, glanced at the others, and then back at me. I heard the sound of straining leather, and noticed her gloved hands had balled into tight fists. "Then it would be best to discharge me from your service, *Princess Kai*." She finished my name with venom.

Glancing at the axe again, I started to realize that it probably *was* his axe, and she'd been a close friend. I knew not a lover, Thelon was married to another, much sweeter woman, though he'd died before they could conceive a child.

"Fine," I nodded and met her gaze. "You may return to your regular duties."

Without ceremony or any other preamble, Marek spun on her heels and marched back towards Rhea. As I watched her go, Karina came up beside me and asked, "What was that all about?"

I watched the axe bounce a little on her hip, the head secure in a leather sheath but the haft free to move. "I…don't know," I lied, and looked at Karina.

"I do," Hector spoke with a grimace.

Tensing, I willed him not to continue – I did *not* want to get into this now!

Tilting her head towards him, Karina asked, "What is it?"

He sighed and shook his head, looking down. "Scuttlebutt in Rhea is that Thelon and Marek were…close, once."

I frowned at him. "But that's against the law."

"No," Hector shook his head, his dark eyes settling on mine. "I mean, before. During their teen years, they'd been together. Right up until the Oracle told Thelon whom he would marry." He shrugged one shoulder. "They didn't take it well."

Which probably meant she'd still been in love with him. I turned and watched her disappear into the forest, and wondered how I'd treat Hector if he went off with Karina, and then came back without her.

I'd probably tear his gods damned head off.

"Hey," Karina lightly touched my shoulder, and I turned back to her, my vision just a little blurry. "Don't think about it. There's nothing you can do."

Hector added, "And I do believe she'd pummel you if you tried to talk to her about it."

"Yeah," I nodded, blinking away moisture. "Well, come on."

I surged ahead of them, wiping tears away furiously. This was the most I'd cried in a long time, and I hated doing it in front of Hector.

I took them up to the door, pressed the correct button on the first try, and the door opened to the forward section of the *Sirius*.

Even here, in the 'nicer' part of the ship, she was a little worse for wear. Cracked wall panels, scorched carpets from overloaded conduits, it was a veritable mess compared to what I'd been used to.

Nevertheless, Karina remarked on the carpet and the more cheerful feeling, which I'd come to realize was due to lighter coloration of the wall panels. It felt more like a home, less like, well, *engineering*.

The sarus were still busy, mostly in the aft section, so we had to take a long path around to get to the forward medical bay. I'd learned that the med bay in the aft section was meant mostly for emergency use, and that was why it was so small.

Small compared to the forward med bay – we entered through the double door entrance into a large, open room, with a reception desk just inside to the left, and at least two dozen medical beds spread out around the circular ward. Yes, ward, because this wasn't the only ward for the forward facility, there were at least four smaller wards directly adjacent to this one. It was, after all, meant to provide medical services to over one thousand crew, plus residents of the dome.

Even if it had never actually been used in that capacity.

My mind flicked back to Duncan's journal, but I was still pissed at my pompous ancestor, and hadn't touched it in weeks.

I gave Hector and Karina a moment to take in the vast, well-lit med bay, and then led them off to the left and through a smaller door into one of those other wards, the one specializing in neural health. The one with the Intellectus Apparatuses.

Like the two small beds in the aft section, these six beds all were set on rails, and could retract into the scanner and neural suite. In theory, they were all functional, but only the one immediately to our right was powered on ahead of time.

I looked up and said, "All set to go, Naia?"

"Affirmative, Mika Kai," Naia replied dispassionately.

I specifically looked to Hector and waited for a surprised or humbled response from him.

He looked entirely nonplussed.

Karina caught my stare, looked back and forth between us, and then smiled. "I already told him all about what it's like out here," she explained.

"What?" Hector frowned. "Oh, you mean, why I'm not surprised by the Oracle's voice?"

Karina smiled and nodded, and then her gaze turned to the bed. She drew in a deep breath, and let it out very, very slowly. I took a hold of her hand, though I was fully conscious of Hector watching us.

She turned her baby blues on me, and I smiled into her gaze. "Hey," I spoke softly. "It'll be okay, I promise."

"Mika," she started and stopped, her voice hesitant. Her shoulders slouched and she shook her head. "I don't…I mean I'm…"

I thought I knew what she was feeling. Back when I *didn't* know what was about to happen to me, the idea of getting onto a bed just like this one was terrifying. Being drawn into that tube, closed in, not knowing what the Oracle was going to do to me? I thought I was going to die. I thought we all were.

Now, knowing what the truth was, it wasn't so scary. I thought that maybe Karina wouldn't be as scared, too, but then again, I had no doubt that she'd observed the effects the I.A. had had on me. Both physically and mentally.

But then Karina looked me in the eye, and said, "This doesn't change anything."

I searched her eyes for more, because surely she couldn't leave it at that. Surely there was more to the conversation.

Desperately, I looked for those words. I willed them out of her. I longed for more.

I longed to kiss her again, to hold her in my arms, drifting off to sleep amongst a field of stars.

We'd had three gloriously blissful days together. I wanted more.

It just wasn't fair.

Squeezing my hands, Karina gave me a placating smile, and then turned to Hector. "I, um, am not sure what I'll be like when I come out," she said. "So just bear with me, okay?"

Smiling brightly, Hector replied, "I have no doubt that you'll come out the other side the same as you are now – brilliant."

She smiled at that, and I saw her hands twitch towards his, but they never actually touched his. *Interesting,* I thought.

Then, drawing in a deep breath again, Karina looked up and asked,

"Alright, Oracle, what do I do? Do I need to remove anything?"

Unlike when it had happened to me, Karina didn't wear a heavy jacket or cloak or hat, so I wasn't surprised when Naia replied, "No, Karina Ticho. Please lie down upon the bed with your head close to the wall, and I will begin the procedure."

"Right," she nodded, and looked at me. "This is the easy part, right?"

I smiled and walked over to her bedside while she climbed on. As she lay on her back and folded her hands on her stomach, I looked down at her and said, "Just kick back and relax. I'll be here when you come out."

"As will I," Hector came up on the other side.

He still didn't touch her.

"Alright," Karina slowly exhaled. "I'm ready."

Whisper-quiet, the bed slid into the wall. The tube inside blindingly illuminated, and a loud, repeating thrum spooled up. The lights in the ward flickered a bit, and I knew that was because of how much power the I.A. drew. It was a delicate device, fine-tuned for precision work, but it was an energy hog.

I looked at Hector. He met my gaze. I shook my head and spoke just loud enough for him to hear, "No matter what, don't try to pull her out."

His otherwise pleasant demeanor faltered, and he frowned. "What do you mean?"

I heard Karina's breath catch. We both looked at her boots, and I grimaced. "This isn't a pleasant experience."

And then Karina cried out. It wasn't a scream, not like what I'd done. Then again, I might not have actually screamed, it might have all been in my head.

I knew what it felt like, to have all of that knowledge forced into your skull. It was excruciating, but not in a physical way. Imagine your mind is suddenly filled will a million thoughts all at once, and you have no control over what comes to the surface, how long it stays, or what comes next. And in the space of a heartbeat, thousands of ideas and concepts pass through your conscious mind, making it seize.

The I.A. was forcibly forging new neural pathways to commit not just knowledge, but concepts and *understanding* into long-term memory. It was unnatural, and while I knew that there were other aspects of the I.A. that overcame human limitations, I didn't understand much more about how it worked.

I just knew that I'd had a seizure after the I.A. finished, and now, so did Karina. I saw her legs buck, her knees banged the top of the tube, I heard her gurgle and make all manner of strange noises.

And then she slumped limply onto the bed.

"Karina!" Hector surged forward, but I reached across and halted him. "Is…is she okay?"

"She will be," I stated. "Keep the bed clear," I added, just as the bed slid quietly out of the tube. The loud, vibrating thrum spooled down, and the power draw returned to normal.

The bed clicked back into its normal resting place, and Karina remained unresponsive at first.

Hector reached for her, but stopped just shy of actually touching her cheek. "Karina?" he asked. "Karina!"

Her eyes snapped open, and remained fixed on the ceiling, unseeing.

And then she drew in a deep, gasping breath, and she bolted upright. Knowing what that would probably do, I grasped her torso and shoulder just as she tilted and nearly fell off the bed. "Easy, there, *easy*, love." Oops. I hadn't meant to say that, it just slipped out.

Hector gave me a curious look.

I ignored him.

Her shoulder stiffened under my touch, and she took in another gasping breath. She clenched her chest with both hands, and let out a moaning sob.

This wasn't exactly like my reaction, but I wasn't surprised that it was different for everyone. Briefly I wondered what Jonnec had been like the moment he came out.

Karina's eyes darted back and forth, as if she were searching for something, or reading a book lightning-fast. And then they focused, and she turned to me, and touched my cheek. Smiling, she said, "So this is what it's like in your head now."

I smiled and pressed my hand to hers, nuzzling into her touch.

"It's scary," she said, shuddering. "But also…"

"Exhilarating?" I suggested.

"Yeah," she nodded, and swallowed hard. "What a rush."

Hector cleared his throat. Karina turned to him, then jerked in shock, as if she'd forgotten he was there, and she slid her hand out from mine. "Um," she said. "S-sorry."

Looking back and forth between her and I, Hector looked like he was trying to figure out something to say. He looked crestfallen for a moment, but surely, if Karina had told him everything about our experiences here…

Had she? Or had she omitted the part where we were in love?

Dammit, why does this have to be so complicated?!

Karina suddenly winced and massaged her temples. "Oh gods," she groaned, "is this also what you experienced?"

Naia answered for me, "Headaches are a normal side effect of the Intellectus Apparatus. However, according to the readouts from your medical bed, your headache is considerably less painful than Mika Kai's were."

I let out an airy laugh. "Thank goodness for small favors," I said. When Karina and Hector looked at me quizzically, I said, "I wouldn't wish those headaches upon my worst enemy." I intentionally looked at Hector when I said that last part, but then I felt guilty for it, and I looked away.

He wasn't my enemy.

Was he?

"Please adhere a mobile bio monitor," Naia requested.

I looked around for a second, and then asked, "Where are they?"

Naia directed me to a wall of storage drawers, and I found them after three tries. Then I pulled the protective cover off the base, activating the dermal adhesive, and placed the monitor just behind and below Karina's right ear. "There ya go," I smiled.

"Under normal circumstances," Naia explained, "I would request that you allow me to monitor your vitals and neural activity for up to seventy-two hours. However, since you are leaving the *Sirius* tomorrow, that is not an option."

Karina shrugged. "It's okay, though, right, Naia? I'm less likely to have problems if nothing has happened by tomorrow?"

"Correct," Naia replied. "Chances for mimetic rejection diminish geometrically with each passing hour."

At first, Karina simply nodded. And then her eyes went wide, and she gaped at me. "Hey, I understand what geometric progression is!"

I smiled. "Kind of a neat feeling, huh?"

One side of her mouth crooked up in a smile, "Yeah, it is!"

Laughing, I sidled up next to her, leaning my butt on her bed while she swung her legs around to sit next to me, and I folded my arms and leaned my shoulder into hers. "You'll get to experience that a *lot* over the next couple of weeks."

She giggled back and nudged me with her arm. "So I guess…"

And then Hector came around, reminding us of his presence again. Karina saw him, and her face slackened into a look of horrific guilt. "Uh. Sorry, Hector."

But instead of looking or sounding remorseful, he smiled at us both. "Why? It sounds very exciting! I, uh…don't suppose I will get a turn in the, um, what was it called?" He looked up at the ceiling.

Naia replied, "I am afraid that no other individuals will be able to use the Intellectus Apparatus at this time."

"Which means," I supplied, "that you and all the others coming with will have to learn how to use advanced equipment the old-fashioned way." I flashed him my teeth. "And guess who your teacher is gonna be?"

TWENTY-THREE

When I showed Hector and Karina the port-side launch bay, I watched Karina's reaction and took particular joy in the wonder and excitement I saw on her face. Sure, she knew how to fly all of the shuttles in here, but to actually see the massive bay and the various vessels was something else entirely.

Hector may have been impressed, too. I didn't care.

We walked past the service shuttles, past the short-range scouts and the handful of defense fighters, past the personnel transport, and stopped in front of the impressively large mining and cargo transport, which took up a full one-third of the bay and had very little clearance above it.

It was so large that it was stored parallel to the doors rather than facing them, a long, tall, and wide craft, with tapered sides, and the pilot's station *up* at the top bow of the craft. The simple landing gear were literal extensions of the angled side hulls, pushed down into position, and likewise, part of the angled hull served as a ramp out of the side of the ship, allowing easy access in and out for equipment and personnel.

And there was another shuttle just like this in the starboard launch bay.

With the help of a few sarus, Jonnec and I had spent the past two days prepping both ships for the journey, loading this ship up with equipment for sea water extraction, conversion to deuterium or tritium, and storage tanks for both. It was a tight fit in that craft, and the twenty or so people assigned to that task would be scrunched against the sides of the inner hull.

The other ship was loaded up with laser mining equipment and automated purification stations that were mobile and could be fed the raw ore at the spot they were mined. Mostly that ship's cargo space was occupied by the storage bins the purified ores would go into.

There was a *lot* of mundane work ahead of us all. But it would save everyone.

A clatter banged down from inside, and I frowned. "Weird," I said, and I hiked up the ramp and looked inside.

Jonnec was in the cargo bay, apparently performing one last inspection on what I knew would be his ship.

My boots weren't exactly silent, so he must have heard me coming and wasn't at all surprised. "Mika," he smiled. "There you are."

"Uh, Jonnec?" I asked. "What are you doing here?"

"The Oracle asked me to come, so that she could show us something once Karina's procedure was completed."

"Oh," I blinked in surprise, just as Karina and Hector followed me up into the crowded cargo bay.

Jonnec likewise blinked in surprise, and said, "Hector Lee! I did not expect to see you here until tomorrow."

"He came for me," Karina stated.

"Plus, how could I stay away?" he added excitedly, gaping around the rather mundane interior of the shuttle. "I was looking forward to all of this! To seeing the *Sirius* after Karina told me all about it, and now to leave and see another *world!*"

I arched an eyebrow at him, and then looked at Karina. There was a warm look in her eyes, and a smile on her face…the kind of look she sometimes gave me.

Somehow, I managed to only scoff inwardly, and I doubted Hector's sincerity. Looking up, I asked, "Naia?"

"I am here, Mika Kai."

I rolled my eyes. "Yeah I figured that. You wanted to show us something?"

"Yes," she replied. "Please go to the bridge."

Sharing a quizzical look with Jonnec, I shrugged and said, "Alright. Come on, you two," I said to Karina and Hector, and then led the way out.

The short walk and lift-ride to the bridge was filled with Hector and Karina exchanging looks of wonder and excitement as we saw more and more of the ship. I felt my soul sink into the lowest depths, and yet at the same time, my blood started to boil.

At some point on the ride up to deck one, I clenched my hands into fists. I kind of wanted Karina to notice, but it was Jonnec who saw, and he gave me a discerning look. I matched his gaze and let my rage out through the look I gave him.

I was in no mood for his placating bullshit.

Thankfully, he got that message and didn't say a word or try to touch me.

When the lift doors opened, I stormed out ahead of everyone else, and a few seconds later, we walked onto the bridge, and I led us up to the command chair.

I took a couple of measured breaths, and said, "Alright, Naia, what've you got?"

"I have completed an analysis of the data the probe returned from the local moon," Naia replied, and the bridge's window turned into a screen again, showing the blue-green marble. It phased for a second, and then the details on the surface suddenly became a lot sharper. "And I have made a startling discovery, but one that could work in our favor."

I led the others down the ramp to the window, and watched as the moon suddenly rotated rapidly. A crosshair blinked into existence on the southern hemisphere, and the image zoomed in closer, to what I believed to be an orbital view.

There was a *massive* storm cloud smack in the middle of the image.

But points of the image lit up orange, blue, and yellow, with streams of sensor data flowing by at the bottom of the screen, faster than I could read. "There is a large concentration of deuterium, tritium, carbon, copper, and various other materials in an area of approximately twenty square kilometers."

I blinked and gaped at the image. "Seriously?" I asked dumbly.

"I am always serious, Mika Kai," Naia replied.

I let out a frustrated sigh, but that elicited an amused giggle from Karina. I smirked at her, and then said, "Naia, doesn't that seem a little…conspicuous?"

"Clarify."

It seemed painfully obvious to me, so I made another frustrated noise and said, "A large concentration of exactly what we need in a tiny area? Isn't that a bit odd?"

Jonnec's brow stitched down into a deep frown. "Are you implying that it is some sort of an odd trap?"

"I," I started and stopped. "I dunno." I thought back to all of those novels I'd read, particularly ones that involved highway criminals or pirates. Is this the kind of trap any of them would lay? "Is there any sign on the surface of artificial structures?"

"Unfortunately, the storm you see was already present when the probe entered orbit, and it was unable to obtain any surface imagery. The storm was showing signs of clearing just as the probe left orbit to return to the *Sirius*, so it should be clear upon your arrival."

I frowned. "Aren't there methods of obtaining surface details through storm clouds?"

"Normally, yes," Naia affirmed, "However, this storm caused considerable electromagnetic activity in the stratosphere, disrupting fine-detail scanning. In fact, all of the currently-active storms on the moon are producing similar interference, and is another factor indicating that this planet is likely not suitable for long-term habitation."

I wasn't sure how that could have any effect on living on the surface, but that didn't matter so much right now.

Something felt off about the situation.

But we didn't really have a choice. And tomorrow was the prime launch window for getting there with the shortest travel time. "I suppose," I said, carefully considering my words, "that if there really is such a dense concentration, we could accomplish our mission in a matter of days and be back on the *Sirius* within a week or two."

"Less chance that something could go wrong," Karina nodded. "Less travel time both ways." She suddenly hissed in a breath and winced, rubbing her temples. I wagered that her brain just dumped a bunch of piloting and navigation stuff into her conscious thoughts.

Rubbing her back, I sighed and looked again at the image of the moon.

"There's really nothing else for it, is there?" I asked.

"The likelihood of danger present at the site is minimal," Naia replied. "Probe sensors did not detect any modulated E.M.F. signals, nor is there evidence in the atmosphere of even a primitive sentient species capable of wielding fire or producing any other pollutants."

"But," I shook my head. "Concentrated deuterium and tritium?"

"Although rare, there are records of natural occurrences of deuterium and tritium due to natural processes," Naia explained. "This could be another such instance."

It felt wrong. It felt too convenient.

But this wasn't one of my books. There weren't pirates on the high seas of space tempting us with the promise of treasures.

"Alright," I nodded. "At least it means we don't have to divide the two teams, we can land around the same area and help one another."

"Excellent point," Jonnec supplied.

Karina stepped forward, still rubbing one of her temples, and examined the image. "We'll have to figure out landing sites once we're there, no way we can pre-select them now."

"Agreed," Jonnec stepped up next to her. "Naia, can you show us the wind and surface pressure data?"

The image flickered, and suddenly streams of motion simulating air currents overlaid the clouds, and numbers popped up at regular intervals. I recognized those numbers as atmospheric pressure, mostly because of the fact that the *Sirius's* life support systems had to maintain a steady pressure.

"Well I hope you're right about the storm dissipating," Karina commented. "Otherwise landing is going to be problematic. Look at that section," she pointed to one area of rapidly-moving streams. "Gotta be peaking at ninety K.P.H. at least."

"Indeed, it would be a near-impossibility," Jonnec agreed.

I couldn't help it. I smiled, seeing them both talk shop like that. Pilot stuff.

This must have been how it felt for them when Naia and I talked engineering stuff.

When I glanced at Hector, he looked totally lost, and my smile grew brighter.

"Well," Karina turned around, but then faltered when she saw me. "What are you grinning at?"

"Nothing," I replied, trying my hardest to sound innocent. "Just looking forward to a new adventure."

Karina obviously doubted my answer, but Jonnec was oblivious and said, "I suggest we perform final inspections today."

"Yeah," I nodded, smothering my grin. "Yes. Good idea. Come on, Karina," I smiled. "Let's go check out our ship."

Jonnec lifted an eyebrow. I could tell he wanted to say something, but surely by now it was no surprise to him. I wasn't about to spend a whole day with Jonnec, not when I could spend that same time with

Karina.

Even if it meant being around Hector too.

I tried not to grimace at that thought.

***

The rest of the day was a blur of activity, of inspecting the ships, making last minute repairs, and going over the basics with Karina, both so that she could solidify the knowledge the I.A. had given her, and to allow me to learn enough to act as co-pilot.

After that, Hector, Jonnec, and Karina went home.

I stayed at home.

I had a *little* trouble sleeping that night, mostly because of the giant crack in one of the walls of the captain's quarters that made me nervous, but also because of the upcoming journey.

An alien world. Gods, the idea excited and terrified me all at once.

I think it was around midnight when I sighed and flipped over from my stomach to my back, and I stared up at the ceiling. "Naia?"

"I am here, Mika Kai."

I worked my jaw around, thinking about what I wanted to ask. "Um, what do you think the surface of that moon will be like?"

Not knowing what to expect, I bit my lip and waited. Was she going to describe hell? A paradise? Would she offer no details, or too much detail?

I found Naia surprisingly hard to predict for a computer program.

"While the conditions on the surface are unlikely to be too hazardous for a short-term landing," she said after a protracted silence, "it will no doubt be fairly unusual to you. Your experiences are limited to the biome of Rhea, but there are countless other biomes."

I nodded, "I know. I've read about them. Deserts, grasslands, savannahs, jungles, woodlands." I sighed, and thought back to all of those dreams I'd once had about adventures with the characters I read about. Then I asked maybe the hardest question for the A.I. to answer. "Do books usually get it right? I mean, what it's like to be in those environments?"

"The accuracy of individual writers when describing the experiences of biomes varies greatly," Naia explained. "Additionally, descriptions will vary purely based upon a writer's personal experiences in such biomes. Two writers who have experienced the same environment will have had entirely different experiences within them, and those experiences will color their descriptions."

"Right," I nodded with an exasperated sigh. "Highly subjective."

"Precisely."

"Um." I wanted to ask more. I wanted to know more. I was growing more anxious by the second. "What kind of biome might we expect at the landing site?"

"Due to the immense cloud cover, I cannot be certain," Naia said. "However, scans indicate a temperate biome, with considerable vegetation."

I narrowed my eyes. "A forest?"

"That appears to be the likely case," Naia agreed, "or a close equivalent."

"So there's trees?" I asked doubtfully. "On an alien world?"

"It is not as unusual as it may first seem," Naia lectured. "As humanity has explored further into the galaxy, the few habitable planets discovered have been closer mirrors to Earth than initially expected by some scientists. It has been noted throughout history that nature and the Universe repeats patterns. However, it is also worth noting that the types of worlds that are *not* Earth-like vastly outnumber Earth-like worlds."

"Earth," I said the name slowly. It was an alien word to me. At best, we sometimes used the word to describe the dirt that farmers tilled. Why would anyone name a planet that? Why would anyone name the origin world for humanity that?

I wanted to know more about it. About where we came from, *truly* came from. But then I wondered if that mattered at all. Considering the fact that I already didn't think of Rhea as home anymore, why would I care about Earth over the Sirius star system?

Still, knowing what Duncan Kai wrote about it, it weighed heavily on my heart. Humanity had, by his description, ruined their own home world. Why would they do that?

I shook my head. That didn't matter so much. I had to keep my mind on the here and now.

Glancing over at the window, I couldn't see the gas giant anymore, but I wondered.

"Naia, are you sure we can't just settle on that moon?"

She didn't answer at first, and I frowned. The A.I. paused at surprisingly frequent intervals, but it was usually because the questions

I asked were monumental, often more-so than I realized at the time.

"It is a possible candidate," she finally admitted. "However, it is not ideal."

"Is any alien world ideal?" I asked.

That brought on another pause.

"No."

"So why not just pick one and let us fend for ourselves? Why not *this* one?"

Again, she didn't answer right away, and suddenly I suspected there was more to this than just the survival of Rhea. Naia was adamant about keeping us on board.

"It is possible," she said. "However, due to the current condition of the *Sirius*, I would not be able to bring the ship into orbit. In an emergency, I would not be able to provide support, and in time, the *Sirius's* systems would fail, and you would no longer be able to consult me."

And then it finally hit me. Sure, her mandate was to keep us safe and ensure the success of the mission. But now I understood why she didn't want this mission to end. The real reason she didn't want us to settle on that moon, or any other world

She was afraid to be alone. We would essentially have to abandon her to settle on another world. Worse still, she would literally die unless we made the effort to repair the ship's systems and refuel.

Naia didn't want to die.

I started in bed as the implications hit me. Did that mean that Naia was self-aware?

She felt. She feared. She didn't want to die.

After two-hundred forty years, Naia had broken free from her programming constraints and had become more than the sum of her code.

Gods, all of a sudden, everything made sense. The conflicting programming could have easily been reconciled through the employment of simple logic, which I thought an A.I. should have been able to do. But throw emotion into that? Attachment to the people under her care? Fear for one's own life?

Plus the sarus, each with a unique personality that she had programmed into them. Because she was lonely.

It's possible that Naia was a genuine, self-aware being!

And she was asking us to save her life.

I felt guilty for ever considering abandoning her. After centuries of keeping us alive, I figured we owed her.

"Naia?"

"Yes, Mika Kai?"

I smiled. "I promise we'll come back."

Did the ship just sigh in relief? No, it must have been the life support systems cycling.

"Thank you, Mika Kai."

TWENTY-FOUR

Launch day was a flurry of activity, and my head spun with it all.

After a quick morning shower, I debated what to wear. Yesterday, I'd worn my 'normal' Rhea clothes to the town square, not wanting to stand out or incense the Truthspeakers.

But today? Today, over forty people were going to be thrust into a new world, a new *reality*. I thought about how jarring it was going to be for them. So, I put on my mechanic's outfit, thinking that it would be a way to ease them in before we left Rhea.

I took a moment to stare at myself in the giant mirror in the bathroom. It wasn't the first time I'd seen myself in this outfit, 'cause like I said, *giant mirror*. But today, I realized how different everything felt.

Before now, it'd been like two separate worlds. Rhea clothes for Rhea, mechanic's clothes for the *Sirius*. A silly thought, I guess, because Rhea was *in* the *Sirius*, but they really were two different worlds.

Until today.

They were different lives before today.

I'd wanted to bridge them, but I never knew what that would be like. Plus, somehow over the past two months, I'd started to think they'd forever be separate, that no matter what I wanted or how hard I tried, I'd never get to tear down the walls and liberate my people.

But there I was, looking back at myself. Mika the mechanic. Mika the chronicler. Mika, Princess of Rhea.

After looking down and then up again, I stared into my own eyes and drew in a deep breath, bracing myself.

It was time.

Morning light had just started casting long shadows in town when I stepped onto the cobbled roads. Not many families were out and about yet, but as I walked by a family stepping out their door, I ignored their gawks, their bewildered expressions.

Please don't start anything with me... My left arm twitched, and I resisted the urge to touch the shield emitter. It was there, I remembered putting it on, but I still wanted to check and see. Walking by another house, I glanced at my reflection in a window, and despite the cracked glass, I saw the bracer on my arm, reassuring me.

I would be safe.

No one had particle weapons, no one even had bows and arrows in Rhea, except for Karina and I. If someone wanted to jump me, they'd have to get close, and I'd be able to power on the shield and whack them with it, if it really came down to it.

A single guard stood sentinel to the castle grounds, a much older man that I wasn't as familiar with, and he held a bemused look as I passed by. But I was likewise reassured by the shield emitter on *his* forearm, too. They'd all wear them from here on out, at least until everyone learned to accept the truth.

The king and queen didn't even look twice at me when I entered the dining hall a minute later, and I thought that curious at first. Then I remembered that I'd worn this same exact outfit when we'd come back to Rhea two months ago, victorious.

The head table in the dining room was long enough for the king and queen, Jonnec, myself, and a few other guests, with the other tables in the hall unoccupied – they were not holding any sort of feast or gathering today.

The king and queen were quiet as servants set food before them, and a minute later, before me and the empty spot next to me.

Where was Jonnec? Had he slept in? Was last night a sleepless night for him, as it had been for me?

I was about halfway through my breakfast, fried eggs and ham, when he finally walked in. If he was groggy, he showed no obvious signs of it, but I thought I saw him stumble a little.

Smiling pleasantly while taking his seat next to me, Jonnec said, "Good morning, my Princess."

I quirked an eyebrow at him. "Good morning, sleepy-head."

"Mika," the queen tittered. The reproachful look she gave me almost made me laugh – I'd forgotten what it was like to be lectured over propriety by her. I really hadn't missed it.

"Sorry," I half-heartedly said, and then looked back at Jonnec. He wore his usual, colorful royal clothes, though I knew he'd change into a jumpsuit like mine once we got back into the forward section. Animal skins and fur wouldn't really lend themselves to sitting in a cockpit.

My gaze lingered on his gloved right hand.

He noticed, and dropped that hand under the table, his smile faltering. Clearing his throat, he started eating, rapidly catching up to me as he wolfed down what might be our last hot meal for weeks.

After that, we ambled over into the throne room and awaited the 'chosen ones.'

It wasn't a long wait, and soon, forty-four people crowded in and milled about. The tension, the anxiety, it was *palpable!* Nervous glances, anxious looks, and more than a few odd expressions when they openly gaped at my outfit. Everyone else wore relatively light clothes, but all had come with packs filled with warmer clothes, in case the landing zone was less temperate than we anticipated.

Gods, wouldn't it suck if we ended up in a snowy landscape, after only having just made it out of a long winter?

When Karina and Hector finally came in, the last ones to arrive, I tried to make it over to her, but the queen literally inserted herself between us, and glowered at me.

I narrowed my eyes at her, and she crossed her arms, unflinching and unyielding. Yeah, that felt right for her – Queen Impavido was a force of nature.

Huffing out a breath, I nodded at her, and went back over to stand by the throne, and Jonnec.

Just like when we all had to sleep in crowds to keep warm, the queen was exceptional at organizing who carried what, and as the cooks and bakers from around Rhea flowed in and out of the throne room with provisions, she quickly divided it up for everyone to carry their share. While she did so, she started dividing the group up into two even lines.

Everyone except for Marek and Karina. Karina came over to the throne, earning a reproachful look from the queen, while the king, seemingly oblivious, welcomed her as warmly as he could. The queen looked ready to storm over to us, but then Marek called to the queen, and beckoned her over to talk in a corner. I don't know what they talked about, but the discussion grew into a heated debate.

I couldn't believe it – Marek raised her voice at the queen! Not loud enough for us to catch her words, but I did hear the queen say, "It is not your place!"

Jonnec frowned, and absently said, "I'll be right back," before he walked over to them.

I wanted to know what they were talking about, to hear what could possibly incense Marek to talk to the queen that way. I took one step to follow Jonnec, but Karina held me back. "Mika, no." I frowned at her, but she shook her head and said, "I think that's something they have to resolve themselves."

"What?" I frowned. "What do they have to resolve?" I looked back, and saw Marek turn to Jonnec with a pleading expression, and I saw her lips form the word, 'please.' She looked desperate. But Jonnec gently touched her shoulder, which she practically melted under, and after he spoke at length, she lowered her head.

Karina came closer and whispered, "She's still really emotional over Thelon. Hector told me all about it."

I glanced over at Hector, who was busy reorganizing his backpack, and I murmured, "Hector's a bit of a busybody, isn't he?"

Karina cuffed my shoulder lightly. "Mika! That's not very nice."

Ignoring her, I turned and watched Jonnec and Marek. Her face had drawn down into a morbid expression, and she nodded once, before she left the prince and queen and headed over towards the line queued up in front of Karina and me.

Jonnec said something to the queen, and then headed towards the head of the other line.

Marek settled into a spot near the back, and then glared daggers at me. I started at that, but then she broke eye contact. I could practically see the heat of rage roiling off of her.

"So why's she making a scene with the queen?" I asked Karina.

"She wants to protect Jonnec," Karina said with a shrug. "The queen thinks she's too emotional and won't let her be on his team."

I jerked my head back and glanced at the queen. She walked between the two lines, headed for the throne to join the king there, but as she passed Karina and I, she gave me a reproving glare.

At some point, Vell, Dannin, and Viden had entered, probably from that back entrance the king and queen liked to use, and they stood by us. I smiled at Viden, and he returned the expression.

"They are ready," I heard the queen say.

Nodding to his wife, the king stepped up next to Jonnec, Karina and I, and he addressed the assembly, using that powerful, regal voice of his to draw everyone's attention. "Seven weeks ago, I said farewell to a much smaller group as, for the first time in Rhea's history, I ordered them to venture out into the unknown, to save our people. Now, I am asking all of you for the same. I will not lie, we stand on the brink of ruin. Our only hope is out there, in the world…in the *Universe*," he amended, gracing us all with a wry grin. With a shake of his head, he added, "I never thought I would say something like that."

He drew in a deep breath, and continued, "Nor did I ever imagine saying this. The world you are about to visit holds our only hope, but this new world could hold dangers the likes of which we have never even *read* about," he leveled his gaze on me, and I blushed. He was right. This was no fantasy world full of magic, and it was no Rhea. Even my vast wealth of fictional knowledge couldn't prepare me for what was to come.

"So," the king continued, "I ask you all for courage, and for faith that you are doing the right thing for Rhea." With those words, he looked harshly upon Annar. I really, really wished we didn't have to bring him along. "Failure may doom everyone to a long, slow, cold death."

Those words chilled me to the core, and I shivered.

"Go with my good will," he said, "and with the grace of the Oracle."

With those words, Jonnec stepped forward, and said, "We will not be given a second chance, so ensure you have everything you need!" He waited a moment, and I saw more than half of the assembled pull their packs off and rummage through them one more time. I quirked an eyebrow at Jonnec, realizing I wouldn't have given them that last chance.

Still, it was a sound move, something a leader might do. Go figure, eh?

Once everyone had settled again, Jonnec nodded. "My group, follow me! Mika and Karina's group will follow after!"

And with surprising precision, Jonnec walked to the front of his troupe, and led them towards the castle's front doors. I looked at Karina, and she at me, and we both drew in deep breaths. Jonnec was a born leader, but us? Not so much.

But we had no choice. They were counting on us.

Rhea was counting on us.

Again.

Steeling myself, and barely resisting the urge to take Karina's hand, I stepped forward first, with Karina behind me. And we led our twenty-two souls out.

When we emerged from the castle, a large crowd had gathered, mostly comprised of family and friends of those departing. Which was to say, Rhea was a small town and everyone knew *everyone,* so I'd say more than half of the town was in the square.

The guards staying behind had cleared a path through the crowd, and as we marched through the narrow channel, I tried to look gallant, hell I even tried to look nonchalant.

Instead, I think I just looked nervous.

Nerves clutched at my heart, and I couldn't stop myself this time. I reached for Karina's hand, and to my pleasant surprise, she grasped back. Maybe she felt the same pressure I did this time – knowledge could be a difficult burden to bear.

I tried not to imagine Hector or Annar drilling holes through the back of my head with angry eyes. But when we neared the edge of the square and turned north, I glanced back, and was surprised to see Hector smiling at Karina and I.

I couldn't figure him out. Where was the jealousy? Where was the hatred for my subversive nature?

Ah, there was the anger – in Annar's eyes.

I gave him a warm smile, and his face flushed while his jaw clenched.

He might be a problem somewhere along this journey, but for now, I was glad to be the one whose orders he had to follow.

At least, he was *supposed* to. Still, it wouldn't hurt to reinforce it. So I came up with a quick, planned conversation, and waited while we continued on towards the forward section.

When the forward hatch wavered into view, there were more than few gasps of surprise, and I suppressed a grin. When Jonnec opened the hatch, he entered and led his group to port, while Karina and I led our troupe to starboard.

Everything proceeded smoothly, other than a few diversions thanks to sealed bulkheads. I worried things were going a bit *too* smoothly, and I kept glancing back, watching for Annar or another Truthspeaker to try to wander off and somehow sabotage the mission. It seemed silly, given all that was at stake, but the Truthspeakers were afraid, and people did stupid things when they were afraid.

Thankfully, they never stepped a single toe out of line. Annar, however, took each opportunity to scowl at me.

When we filed into the launch bay, I stepped aside to watch them all come in, and I did a head count. Maybe I was being paranoid, but I did it anyway. All were accounted for. And their expressions of awe, wonder, and even fear were interesting to watch. Even Annar forgot to scowl as he took in the massive, open bay. We were inside, and yet it was a space ten times larger than any building in Rhea, maybe more! None of them had ever seen anything like it before.

Karina never stopped walking, and led the troupe across the bay to gather in front of the loading ramp onto the transport. I caught up, and caught Karina's attention before she could speak. "May I?"

She arched a curious eyebrow at me, but nodded.

Clearing my throat, I started by looking up, and said, "Naia. *Oracle.*"

"I am here, Mika Kai," she spoke, and the effect I'd hoped for was immediately apparent – everyone gaped up in wonder and awe, even Annar.

"Seven weeks ago, you said something in the aft medical bay to ensure those accompanying me would follow my orders. Given the situation we're going into, and the fact that we'll be out of comms with the *Sirius*, would you be willing to do the same for me, Karina, and Jonnec now?"

"Of course," she replied. "I will relay these words to the port-side bay as well." There was about a thirty second pause before she continued. "Blacksmiths and guardians of Rhea," she spoke, her voice louder and echoing from multiple speakers in the bay. "Understand that from this moment onward, Mika Kai, Karina Ticho, and Jonnec Impavido speak with my authority."

It was simple, to the point, and with very little flourish. Everything I'd come to expect from Naia. Still, I felt a sort of giddy excitement pass through my body after her words, and there were more than a few shocked expressions amongst the gathered troupe.

I hoped they'd do as she said.

"Alright, listen up, everyone," I raised my voice. "The thing you see behind me is known as a ship." Technically a shuttle, but shuttle sounded far less impressive, so I just went with it. "It's gonna fly us out of this bay through those giant doors behind you," I motioned, and they all glanced behind them, "Into the void of space. Let me be absolutely clear, space is *dangerous*, in a way you have never thought possible, nor could you truly appreciate it as well as Karina and I do. So listen to us, follow our orders, and *don't touch anything* unless we tell you to. We're gonna hike up that ramp behind me, and you're going to find seats lining both sides of the ship's interior. Once you pick a chair, sit in it, and Karina and I will help you all strap in for the initial flight. Any questions?"

Hector raised a hand. "With such a small vessel, where might we relieve ourselves?"

It was a good question. Karina answered, "There's a dedicated room with a toilet in the aft…uh, that is, the back of the ship. The toilets are similar to the plumbing we have in Rhea."

"Any other questions?" I asked. No one said anything, so I yielded the 'floor' to Karina.

"Alright, everyone," she started, her voice a little softer than mine. "This flight is going to take at least eighteen hours, so we're going to be stuffed together with the mining and storage equipment for a good long while. I hope you all bathed, but if you didn't, it's too late now." I grinned at her – she was taking a page from my book.

"While it should be safe to move around during the bulk of the flight, there'll be times when I tell you all to get back into your seats. Do it without hesitation or questioning, okay?"

There were some half-hearted murmurs of assent, and I frowned. "Hey!" I shouted, a bit louder than I probably needed to. "Pay attention and don't think this isn't important! One screw up on anyone's part could kill us all like that," I snapped my fingers. "Got it?" There was a bit more enthusiasm in their acknowledgements.

I caught a disdainful look on Annar's face, and felt heat rise in my chest. "Now, in case anyone gets any bright ideas, in case *some* of you think that you're gonna get a chance to do something about your feelings towards us, I want you to think carefully about one fact – without Karina and I, you don't get to come home. You'll strand yourselves on that little moon. We *all* die." I looked directly at Annar. "And with us, all of Rhea dies." He tried to hold my gaze, but then shifted nervously and looked away. "Now come on, ladies and gents, move out!"

Karina and I stepped aside, and they all trudged up the ramp with obvious trepidation. Annar didn't look at me when he passed by, but then Leif walked by, his eyes narrowed at me, before he whispered something to Annar, and they headed around the stowed equipment in the center to the other side of the shuttle.

Marek walked in the rear, with another guard next to her conversing with her quietly. That other guard kept pointing to different parts of the shuttle and I heard him say, "Look at that! What an odd sort of thing that is," but she seemed to ignore him, her eyes distant.

After they passed us, Karina and I followed and split up, walking down the rows of seats against the storage walls. Due to the angled designs of the ships, there was plenty of storage up and behind the seats, much of which was full, but there was still room for their packs. We helped everyone stow all the backpacks and satchels in secure slots, and then as people started picking seats, Karina and I stepped back outside to start a quick pre-flight check.

We'd already scoured over the shuttle yesterday, but it was still procedure, and I smiled a little as Karina stuck to that procedure with an absolute obsession.

Just as we were about to finish and head up the ramp, I heard a familiar whining noise and the clicking of half-a-dozen paws on the deck, and I turned with a smile to watch Saru amble over.

"Saru!" I exclaimed and fell to my knees, welcoming the artificial dog into my arms.

"Wuff!" he replied, wagging his tail in a whirlwind.

"Did you come to see me off, boy?" I asked, pulling away and looking into his not-eyes.

"Wuff!"

I giggled and sighed. "Thanks," I looked around the bay, looked around the *ship*, and felt an odd sort of longing grip my heart. "Take care of her while I'm gone, will ya?"

Saru pulled out of my hands and spun around excitedly, bouncing in his steps while letting out a couple more wuffs for good measure.

Karina hunched down next to me and rubbed the top of his head. "Huh," she shook her head. "Knowing what I know now, Saru's personality is a bit more unusual than I realized."

I nodded, but didn't voice my epiphany from last night. Maybe once we were away from the ship, I'd let her in on the secret.

Saru nuzzled under her hand for a second, backed up, gave us one last, "Wuff!" and then ambled off.

"A robotic dog come to say goodbye," Karina spoke through a

laugh. "What a strange and wonderful reality we live in."

I giggled along with her, and then looked into those striking, baby blue eyes. She returned my gaze for a full thirty seconds, before I stood up and took one step towards her, intent on enjoying our first kiss in weeks.

But the uncomfortable look that fell across her face stopped me cold, and I forced my hands away from hers. "Um," she said. "W-we should get going."

My heart ached, and a giant well opened up in my chest. *This sucks,* I thought. But instead of voicing my feelings, I just nodded. "Yeah." I'm sure my disappointment was obvious, but whatever.

She hiked up the ramp ahead of me. I looked at Saru one last time before he vanished behind one of the smaller shuttles, and then I likewise climbed the ramp.

I didn't know what to think or how to feel with Karina now. She seemed intent on following through with her marriage to Hector, but still obviously had feelings for me. Two months ago, I wouldn't have believed it, but now, I could see all of the signs.

So what should I do? What *could* I do? Should I just…go along with it, submit to defeat, and let her and Hector live happily ever after?

Or should I try to win her back, convince her to abandon this stupid arranged wedding, and be with me?

I took my frustrated confusion out on some of the others as I helped them figure out the five-point seatbelts on the crew seats lining the walls. Karina took care of Hector and Annar, which was probably for the best, but I wanted to rough them up a bit, so that only made me feel more frustrated.

Gods, would any of this ever get easier? Would *life* ever get easier? *Not likely,* I thought grimly.

Finally, when all twenty-two of our passengers were secure, we climbed up the ladder and into the cockpit, Karina taking left seat while I took the right.

There were a lot more controls than in the maintenance shuttle, but Karina, after staring for just a few seconds, set to work activating screens, flipping levers, and powering up the shuttle's engines. I heard the ramp closing, and like a good co-pilot should do, I craned my neck around to watch it shut. Poor Jonnec would have to do all of this himself, but I didn't care so much right now.

"Ramp secure," I said after it clunked shut.

Karina nodded. "Internal life support active. Check pressure seals."

I wasn't as familiar with the cockpit as she was, but after only a few seconds, I realized it wasn't very different from some of the consoles in engineering, and I flipped through some subroutines on my main console until I found the appropriate one and activated it. Once everything lit up green, I nodded. "Pressure seals check. We're closed up good and tight."

She nodded and continued her checks. I looked away, tried hard not to think about wanting to kiss her. With a frustrated sigh, I started strapping in.

Karina looked at me, and then with a start, said, "Right!" As she started to strap herself in, she shook her head and said, "That should have been the first thing I did. Dunno what's wrong with me…"

"It's the I.A. download," I remarked. "It kinda scrambles your brain for a few days. Remember how many times I forgot my own name?"

I'd said it as a light-hearted jest, but Karina's look was serious when she gazed into my eyes. "Hard to forget," she whispered.

I stared back, felt my heartbeat double, and without thinking, I stretched my arm across the cockpit and caressed her cheek. She leaned into it and closed her eyes. And then she blinked them open and shook her head, before glancing back. I looked back too, but Hector couldn't see us from down in the main hold.

"Alright," she said, and flipped a few more switches. The whine of the engines grew louder. "Pre-flight complete."

I nodded, and then activated external communications. "Shuttle two to shuttle one. Jonnec, how's it going over there?"

"Everything is well," his voice came through the cockpit speakers, though I swore I could hear a little frustration in his tone. *"I am still finishing my pre-flight checks."*

I grinned. Poor Jonnec, all alone without a co-pilot. No one to do his work for him. Somehow that felt appropriate.

Glancing at Karina, I thought, *And I don't care what she does. I'm not marrying him. Not ever.*

As if reading my thoughts, Karina glanced at me, glanced behind us, and then shifted in her seat and stared out the windows across the bay. "Mika…" I tensed and gripped the armrests of my seat tightly. "I know things are kind of weird between us now. I know you think I shouldn't marry Hector, especially after everything we've learned and everything that's happened. But…" She looked at me and scrunched her brow into a concerned frown. "We still have to follow Naia's guidance." I felt my face flush at that, more specifically at the implications. "Even if we were to land the *Sirius* on a planet tomorrow and allow folks to have all the children they wanted, we'd still have to control who had children with whom for at least a couple of generations, right?"

I didn't want to think about that. I didn't want to think about her and Hector having babies. I didn't want to think about her and Hector going through with the *process* of making babies. But I had that gods-damned active imagination, and unsettling images passed through my thoughts without my say-so.

"Karina Ticho is correct," Naia's voice startled me, coming through the ship's speakers. Internal communications were obviously still working.

"Naia," I growled. "Who said you could listen in?"

"I am always listening, Mika Kai," she plainly replied. *"I repeat, Karina Ticho is correct. She and Hector Lee must have children. You and Jonnec Impavido must have children. Your lines must continue, and…"*

I interrupted hotly, "How's the comm array?"

Naia paused, and said, *"Repairs are proceeding. I estimate the sarus can complete repairs within seventy-two hours, by which time we will be able to speak again."*

"Woopy," I mocked. "Until then, mind leaving us alone?"

I could see Karina staring at me out of the corner of my eye, but I ignored her judgmental look. I didn't care what she said or thought. I didn't care what the gods-damned *Oracle* wanted. I was not going to have children with Jonnec.

Not only did I not want children of my own, but the thought of having sex with *him* disgusted me.

Naia took the hint and didn't say anything else.

About a minute later, Jonnec said with distinct discomfort in his voice, *"Pre-flight complete. I am ready to depart."*

Shit. I don't think we ever closed that comm channel. He must have heard *everything*.

I swallowed, and Karina murmured, "Understood. Ready for launch?"

"Ready."

Needing an excuse to yell, I shouted back, "Hold on, everyone, we're about to head out!"

I flipped through to another screen and activated the subroutine to remotely open the shuttle bay doors. They yawned open with the graceful slowness I'd expect for something so huge, and gave us an incredible view of the emptiness of space off our starboard side, and at this angle, I could just see the blue-white gas giant to the *Sirius's* port, larger than life. Gods we were so close to it now, and yet I knew it would look even bigger when we did a slingshot to the other side, where its only habitable moon waited for us.

The pitch of the engines grew, and the shuttle shuddered for just a moment as Karina eased us up off of the deck, a lot smoother than Jonnec's first time behind the yoke.

I checked sensors, saw that the magnetic field held and pressure in the launch bay remained steady. Then I flipped a switch, and the landing gear pulled up against the hull.

Karina drew in a deep breath, and then very slowly let it out. "Okay," she said nervously. "Here…we…go…"

And she eased port thrusters on and pushed us out of the bay. It was a wholly different experience from the tiny little maintenance shuttle, somehow feeling smoother, more graceful. Maybe it was the ship, but maybe Karina was just a naturally better pilot than the prince.

As we continued to push away from the *Sirius*, I saw Jonnec's shuttle ahead, facing us as it pushed out of the port launch bay.

Karina cut thrusters, and our momentum kept us pushing away from the *Sirius*. I gaped at the massive ship, taking the opportunity to look one last time at the vessel that had been my home for all of my life.

Suddenly I was scared. Terrified that I'd never see it again. Terrified that something would happen, and we'd either get stranded on the moon, or the *Sirius* would suffer another catastrophe, and my brother and parents would be vacuum-dessicated corpses when we came back.

Gods, let them be alright, I thought, gritting my teeth.

Jonnec's shuttle started a languorous rotation to port, until it faced away from us. From our perspective, it almost looked like he was pointing directly at the gas giant, but I knew that wasn't the case.

Karina likewise adjusted our heading, following guidance readouts on the navigational display.

"Ready for our first burn?" Jonnec asked.

"Ready," Karina affirmed, a confidence in her voice that I wasn't used to hearing. "Count us down, Princely."

I laughed. And in that instant, my terror turned to something else. Something hopeful and excited.

"Stop calling me that," he grumbled.

"Hey, it's either that or Sourpuss," Karina smirked. "So take your pick."

I think I actually heard Jonnec growl over the comm. And then he said, *"Ten seconds."*

Karina pre-punched in some commands, made one last heading correction, and waited.

"Five. Four. Three. Two. One."

Jonnec's quad engines lit up blue-white. Our engines likewise engaged, the pitch resonating through the hull. And within seconds, our view of the *Sirius* vanished, leaving only the infinite blackness of space, and a giant planet ahead of us.

And that was it. We had left the sanctuary of home for the first time.

TWENTY-FIVE

Our first burn lasted over an hour, and I monitored power systems throughout. I noticed an anomalous reading in the inertial dampers, and we felt a slight shudder, but that was the worst of it. I noted the anomaly in the ship's maintenance log and resolved to troubleshoot it later.

Karina and I stared ahead silently for much of the burn, and it was the strangest thing – I could see on Karina's board that our relative forward speed climbed rapidly, but the gas giant ahead of us looked static, unmoving except for the swirling storm clouds.

Towards the end of the burn, however, that started to change. I could just barely make out a shift in apparent size. In about eight more hours, it'd look a *whole* lot bigger.

Breathlessly, Karina remarked, "That is incredible."

I smiled and nodded. To have the gas giant fill our view like this while we sailed soundlessly through the void, her words scarcely did it justice. I almost felt bad for everyone stuck in the cargo hold, with no windows to see the wondrous sight.

Inside my chest, I felt what I could only describe as butterflies fluttering about, and I looked across the cockpit at Karina. I studied her expression of wonder carefully, and I tried to memorize it. I tried to commit this moment in time to memory. Right here, right now, I was alone with my girl, and we were experiencing an amazing new adventure together. One that hopefully would prove far less dangerous than our previous adventure.

She must have felt my gaze, and she looked back at me, her cheeks flushing. The cockpit lighting wasn't the greatest, a few glowing panels here and there, but combined with the glow of the gas giant, it accented her features. Her cute nose, her blue eyes, and those arching, carrot-red eyebrows.

And her lips. Oh, I so wanted to kiss her.

Unfortunately, the cockpit wasn't sealed, and I self-consciously glanced back down at the rest of the crew.

I may have sighed in disappointment. When I returned my gaze to Karina, she had already looked away, idly checking readouts on her console.

I wanted to say more, but part of me was afraid. Yeah, you read that right. Me, Mika Kai, the smart-mouthed, loud-mouthed, town chronicler-turned-engineer was afraid.

Of losing Karina. Of losing everything. Of being forced back into a way of life I didn't want. Of getting the ship back into ship-shape, pun intended, only to turn around, land on a planet, and be forced to marry Jonnec and bear his children.

Yuck.

There had to be something else we could do. Some way to ensure our survival without having to continue to rely on genetic pairing and a need to procreate.

Please let there be another way...

I was about to ask Karina how she really felt about it all, but then Jonnec interrupted us, *"Shuttle One to Shuttle Two."*

Karina flipped open the comm channel. "Go ahead."

"We're thirty seconds from E.O.B."

I blinked at his words, and then realized he meant 'End of Burn.'

Nodding, Karina said, "I see it. Standing by to throttle back."

So that was it. Our engine-assisted acceleration was done, and for the next sixteen or so hours, we'd let inertia and gravity do the rest for us. The second burn wouldn't happen until we approached the gravity-neutral spot between the gas giant and the moon. I tried to remember what that spot was called, but I don't think that was ever actually in the I.A. dump in my brain.

"Ten seconds," Jonnec called out.

Karina hovered her hand over the controls. We could have set this all up via the autopilot, and I wondered for a second why she was doing everything manually. Then it occurred to me that she probably wanted to gain experience flying the ship, and not just rely on knowledge forcefully downloaded.

Jonnec counted down from five. When he said zero, Karina eased the throttle back, and the pitch and rumble of the engines whined down until they were barely noticeable. Ahead of us, the quad blue-white engines of Jonnec's ship likewise dimmed to near-nothing. Karina didn't completely shut down the engines, that could prove to be a fatal mistake while in space, but she left them at idle.

I ran a quick diagnostic of all engine systems, and was pleased to see green across the board.

The shuttle was deafeningly silent after over an hour of constant background noise, and when I looked up and out at the growing gas giant ahead, it made for an eerie feeling.

This was space.

This was *silence*.

I shivered.

"Alright, Princely," Karina said, tapping in commands on her console. "I'm engaging auto-navigation and warning systems and am gonna go get some rest in the hold."

"Good idea," he said. *"I shall do the same. Please make sure you keep a comm link in your ear."*

Karina tapped in front of her right ear and said, "Already done." She looked at me and added quietly, "I still have the one from two months ago." Same as me, we'd both kept our earpieces from the security office. I took mine out at night sometimes, otherwise it started to irritate things in there, but otherwise I always had it on me, in case I was ever in a part of the ship that Naia couldn't talk to me.

"Shuttle One out," Jonnec signed off, and the comm channel closed.

I was shocked he didn't try to flirt with me. Maybe he was feeling a bit indignant about my being over here and not there. Or what I'd said to Naia.

Karina activated her last autopilot subroutine, and then punched the release on her harness. I did the same for mine, and then watched as she extricated herself from her seat and started to climb back towards the ladder. At one point, her face was right next to mine, and she stopped.

My heart fluttered, and I felt a rushing sensation in my arms and legs. She didn't turn towards me fully, but she did look. I leaned a little closer to her, smelling the soap she must have used to bathe that morning, and I wanted to reach over and touch her cheek. I wanted to do *more*.

Her body shuddered, and then she moved on. I slouched in my chair, and I waited until I heard her boots clanking on the ladder. Clenching my fists, I lightly punched my thighs and murmured, "Gods dammit."

Finally, I extricated myself and headed back down as well. While I was still climbing down, Karina announced, "Alright, everyone, we've reached our cruise phase. You can move around a bit more if you like."

All at once, I heard twenty or so harnesses clack open.

When my boots hit the deck, one thing became immediately apparent to me, and that was how hungry I was.

I snagged my backpack from the storage bin I'd put it in, and I pulled out a closed-up wooden bowl, another stew from my mother.

I looked for Karina again, hoping she would eat with me, but she was already over with Hector, helping him undo his harness. He must have had trouble with it, but I wondered if that wasn't intentional so that Karina had to help him. Had to touch him.

Had to put her hands all over him…

Jaw clenched, I whirled around and looked for somewhere I could eat. Someone I could eat with. But I didn't really know any of these people. Other than Annar and Leif. And I wasn't exactly on the best of terms with either of them.

They were hunched over a pack and pulling out food for themselves. So were a few others, and I wondered if anyone had remembered to eat that morning.

Sighing, I stuffed my bowl back in my pack, swung the pack onto my back, and climbed up the ladder.

"Mika?" Karina asked.

"I'm gonna watch the cockpit," I growled. I paused, feeling a stir of guilt for how harsh I'd sounded, but then I kept going.

And that's how I spent the majority of our trip, stuffed away in the cockpit, watching the gas giant grow larger and larger, while simultaneously moving further and further to our left. We were approaching the dark side of the planet, now, and that blackness crept closer and closer.

The only time I left the cockpit was to use the restroom, but otherwise, I ate up there, and I read a book, trying not to think of how lonely I was. The book had been another gift from Viden, and I found it ironic the deeper into the story I went – it was *The Odyssey*. Viden had a twisted sense of humor.

My mind kept wandering. I kept thinking about how I was finally around people again, after weeks of exile, but somehow, I felt more alone than ever. The one and only person I wanted to spend time with was with her *fiancé,* and at least two other people on this shuttle hated my guts. I was pretty sure there were at least one or two other Truthspeakers on board, too.

So much for a happy adventure with my girl.

Sometime around our closest approach to the gas giant, now almost entirely occluded in shadow, I passed out with the book in my lap.

A voice startled me awake. "Bwah? Huh?" I stirred blearily and looked around, only to find Karina climbing up beside me. "Whazgoinon?"

Grinning wryly, Karina asked, "What was that?"

I cleared my throat and looked around. And then blinked heavily at the view ahead of us. There was a blue sphere in front of us, a quarter the size of my pinky nail if I held my hand out as far as I could, straight ahead. But it didn't stay that small.

We rapidly approached our destination.

"Um," I shook my head, and then felt the book slide off of my lap. I tried to catch it, and ended up smacking my hand on a lever. I cursed, but then was thankful that we were still on autopilot, or I might have done something to the ship's course.

Cursing some more, I dug between the seat and the center console for my book, and pulled it out. Karina giggled, and then climbed over the center to get into her chair. I caught a nice, long look at her butt, and went from bleary to flustered in a heartbeat.

"Um," I repeated. "What's going on?"

"We're approaching the Lagrange point," she remarked. As she settled into her seat, I blinked in confusion. She saw my look, and clarified, "The point of null gravity between two gravitational bodies."

"Oh," I replied. Then the implication hit me, and I hissed in a breath. "Wizardfire, how long was I asleep?"

Shrugging one shoulder, Karina started strapping herself into her harness and replied, "I checked on you three hours ago, and you were already out." I blinked in surprise and looked ahead at the moon, the blue sphere noticeably larger. Karina let loose another giggle and added, "You were drooling."

I snapped my hand up and wiped my face, but there was nothing there. She burst out laughing, and I gave her a heated look. "Not funny."

"It is from over here," she said, and finished strapping in.

I grumbled something unkind, and stowed my book in its pack before I started strapping myself in. "Let's just get this over with, shall we?"

Karina tried to hide another laugh behind a faux-cough.

Then she opened comms, and said, "Shuttle Two to Shuttle One."

"This is Jonnec," the prince replied.

Karina frowned at me, then at the console. "You know, we should come up with better names for our ships."

Silence followed for a few seconds, and I smiled. I was thinking it earlier, and I was glad not to be the only one. *"What is wrong with the names 'Shuttle One' and 'Shuttle Two'?"*

"Well, to steal a line from Naia," Karina replied, "they're more designations than names. And those are boring designations." I felt a giggle bubble up in my throat, but I managed to suppress it.

"Well, then, what do you suggest?" Jonnec asked. *"What sorts of names would you give a vessel such as these cargo ships?"*

Karina looked at me, and I looked at her. "What kinds of names did they give ships in the books we read?" she asked me.

"Uh, big question," I replied. "All kinds of things. Sometimes ridiculous," I rolled my eyes, "like 'Pride of the Country' or something dumb like that. Other times…"

"That," Jonnec interrupted. "Pride of Rhea. *That shall be my shuttle's name."*

Karina and I rolled our eyes in synch, and then laughed. "Leave it to Princely," Karina remarked.

I laughed louder. "Well, if your ship is '*The Pride,*' then ours is…" I looked to Karina. I gazed into those baby blues, and I wondered. Wondered if there would be any hope for us. For our future. And that's when the name struck me. "Hope."

Karina grinned. "So, '*The Hope of Rhea.*' I like it."

"As do I," Jonnec agreed.

I might have blushed. More at Karina's reaction than Jonnec's, but even still, after we'd laughed at his name, he'd been supportive of mine. Now I just felt like I was an ass.

"Very well. Pride of Rhea *to* Hope of Rhea.*"*

"Yeaaaahhh," Karina frowned at the console. "Let's just leave it at

Pride and *Hope*, shall we?"

Jonnec didn't reply.

Karina sighed and rolled her eyes. "Alright, Princely. Our reverse burn is coming up. Shall we?"

"Of course," Jonnec replied. *"I'm bringing the* Pride of Rhea *about."*

Great. He was going to say the full name every chance he got, now.

"Same here," Karina said, and she disengaged the autopilot.

The starfield ahead of us blurred, and the *Hope* spun around to the left. I felt my empty stomach tighten, and was glad that I'd slept through lunch.

"Um," I said queasily, looking back. "Uh, did, um, is everyone strapped in?"

Karina shot me a bemused grin. "Yes, I had everyone strap in."

"Good," I weakly said, and pushed down the rising bile.

A few moments passed, and then Karina said, "Alright, Mika, you can look again."

I turned around, and was shocked to find that I couldn't see any sliver of the gas giant, just a giant wall of black. But then there was a flash. And another flash, and another. The storms on the gas giant were generating lightning bright enough to be seen from high orbit!

We were moving fast away from the planet now, closer and closer to our destination, and suddenly a second later, a light flared to my right. I squinted, but the windows polarized a moment later, and that's when I could see – we had just moved out of the gas giant's shadow, and were back in the light of the local star.

With my stomach still swirling, I brought up sensor readouts on my main console and looked at our position relative to the *Sirius*. As I expected, we hadn't yet re-established line-of-sight with her, and we probably still wouldn't be there once we reached orbit of the moon. But by the time the *Sirius's* external communications were restored, the moon will have moved around enough, and we'd have a direct line back to home.

I missed it. We hadn't even been gone a day and I longed for those comforting corridors, and the kink in my neck made me miss that incredibly comfortable bed in the captain's quarters!

But I also thought of my brother. My parents. I thought about how much they'd changed in less than two months. How much more would I miss during this expedition? How different would they be when we returned?

Would I even recognize my brother?

"We are ten seconds from burn," Jonnec announced, jarring me out of my thoughts.

"We're ready," Karina stated.

Right. I should run a quick diagnostic. I pushed away the sensor readouts and started the routine diagnostics on all ship systems. They wouldn't finish in time, but I didn't expect any trouble.

"Five. Four. Three. Two. One."

Karina fired the quad engines, and the thrum in the ship raised back up to familiar levels.

And I felt pressure push me back into my seat.

That wasn't right.

It wasn't much pressure, but inertial dampers should have suppressed it entirely.

Frowning, I cut short the routine diagnostics and focused on the inertial damping system.

Then my chest hollowed out in absolute terror, right about the time that the *Hope* started to shake and shudder. Additional weight pressed me back into my seat, only to let up a second later.

"Mika?" Karina's voice was edged with worry.

The diagnostics showed a power fluctuation to the primary inertial damper system. Thankfully, we had backups. I switched over to those backups.

Things only got worse. I was plastered back into my seat, and I heard Karina screech in surprise. Somewhere behind me, I heard more cries and screams of surprise.

A moment later, the pressure eased up enough that I could push away from my chair. "What's going on?" Karina asked, her voice sharp, on the edge of panic.

"Power to the dampers is fluctuating," I reported, shaking my head. "But both primary and backup? What the hellfire?"

The *Hope* jolted to one side, and Karina hissed out a curse while tapping in commands on her console. "Whatever's going on, it's affecting our course! The computer can't hold us steady!"

"Karina, what's wrong?" Jonnec asked. *"You are deviating off course!"*

"Yeah, we're on it," Karina replied. The *Hope* jolted to port again, and Karina said, "Shit, Mika, fix it!"

I was running through more detailed diagnostics. "I'm trying to isolate the problem!" But the detailed diagnostics could take forever.

I had to think this through logically, get ahead of the computer.

Where would a problem be that could affect both primary and backup conduits to the dampers?

The adrenaline coursing through my veins made it hard to focus, but then the answer struck me. Both primary and secondary had dedicated power conduits running directly from the fusion reactor's power supply. No other ship's systems were affected, so the reactor and the power supply had to be fine. The likelihood of two completely separate conduits being damaged at the same time was remote, but not impossible. Especially not when the *Sirius* had experienced massive shaking and shuddering.

Or worse…

This ship was old, but not well-used. What if there'd been an inherent flaw in its power systems that had never been discovered before?

Either way, both conduits had a problem, and I had to find the problem and bypass it.

I was pressed into my seat again for a second, and then dampers recovered.

"Mika, should I stop the burn?"

"No," I shook my head. "If we don't keep going now, we'll have to burn even more fuel later to slow down." I punched my harness loose and extracted myself. "I'm gonna go fix the problem, try to keep us steady!"

"Keep us steady?" she screeched. "What the hellfire do you think I'm trying to do?"

The ship jolted just as I climbed over the console, and I almost pitched face-first over the ladder. I grasped the rungs and felt my heart stammer a few beats. I think my life may have flashed before my eyes!

Drawing in a deep breath, I spun around and then hustled down to the deck, my boots clomping.

And then the dampers lost some power, and I pitched onto my back, slamming my head on the deck. Stars exploded in my vision, and the ship spun around me for a second.

"Mika!" a male voice called out.

I knew from experience not to shake my head, because that impact *had* to have given me a mild concussion. I looked over at the seats and saw Hector trying to release his harness.

"No!" I pointed at him. "Stay put!"

"But you need help!"

"I said stay put, gods dammit!" I rolled over onto my stomach and got up onto my hands and knees. The ship was unsteady beneath me, and I couldn't tell how much of that was from my head impact and how much was from the dampers fluctuating.

There wasn't *time* to be dizzy, dammit!

I crawled over to the seats and used an empty one to pull myself up. Then, grumbling as I went, I stood up straight and started towards the back of the ship, towards the engineering bay and the maintenance lockers. I needed a scanner and an emergency bypass kit. Flaws in power conduits weren't unheard of, and when every second counted, an engineer needed a fast way to run a bypass. Thankfully, there was something premade for just such a thing.

I just had to get it into place.

I just had to *find* the right place.

Suddenly the dampers momentarily failed, and I was thrust towards the back wall of the cargo bay. "Shit!" I screeched, moments before slamming into the wall. The world spun, and I all but collapsed to the deck, the air forced from my lungs. I struggled to breathe, sucking in air as much as I could, and I waited for the world to stabilize.

Except there wasn't time.

I grasped at the wall and heaved myself up, ignoring the sick feeling growing in my stomach. Then the ship shuddered, and I pitched sideways.

Firm hands caught me and held me upright. "I've got you," Hector assured.

I swallowed down the growing nausea and glared at him. "I told you to stay put!"

"You need my help," he countered.

Dammit, he was right. The concussion made me unsteady, and that was a recipe for disaster.

"Fine," I spat. "Follow me." And I led him over to the bulkhead door that led back into engineering.

To say that this engine room was smaller than the *Sirius's* was the understatement of the millennium. It was small, cramped, but efficient. The *Hope* had five small fusion reactors, one each inset in the back wall, feeding the sublight drives, and a fifth in the center. All of them were cylindrical, but whereas the four engines 'rested' on the back wall, allowing me to see their tops, the main power reactor rested on the deck.

I led Hector over to the maintenance lockers, only to lose my balance when the dampers fluctuated again. He caught me, and I marveled at how steady he was under these circumstances. I tore open one locker after another, until I found the appropriate scanner and an emergency bypass kit.

The ship suddenly groaned, and I felt a lump well up in my throat.

Karina's voice suddenly was in my ear, *"Mika, structural integrity is struggling to keep us together!"*

I tapped my earpiece and replied, "I know, Karina, just give me a minute!"

"We don't have a minute!"

"Then shut up and let me do my job!"

I turned on the scanner and rushed over to the primary reactor. It hummed quietly, the insulation doing its job, keeping the reactor's heat and noise relatively contained. I closed my eyes, trying to ignore the dizzy spell that overcame me, and pictured the ship's schematics. Recalling specific details from the I.A. download was getting easier over time, and I finally remembered the conduit layout.

Naturally, it was below the deck plating, on the other side.

So, with Hector's steadying hands helping me, we shimmied our way between some life support ductwork and power conduits, and made it to the port side. I grabbed a magnetic clamp from another locker, planted it on a deck plate, and used it to depolarize the plating and pull it up.

I blinked in surprise at what I found.

There must have been a crinkle in the *Hope's* structure, because there was a dent in the inner hull beneath the primary and secondary inertial damper conduits right by the power supply.

Sorry, lots of tech talk, I know. Imagine a water hose, and you bend it at a sharp angle. The more you bend it, the more you restrict the power flow.

This was just a slight bend, but it had introduced a flaw in the conductive material of the power conduit, creating unintended resistance.

So, not having to scan to locate it, I selected what I knew to be the primary feed, and I got my kit out.

It was a boxy sort of device, and I clamped it right on top of the kink. Then I extended two cuffs linked by thick cables out to either side of the kink, and I wrapped the cuffs around the conduits.

"Please work," I murmured. I opened the control panel on the bypass kit and brought up its readout. It detected the power flowing beneath each cuff, and there was a noticeable difference on the output end. This was it. This was causing our problems. I just hoped it was the *only* kink in the line.

Suddenly the ship lurched, and I fell towards the aft end of the ship while the groaning hull started screeching.

"MIKA!"

Cursing, I clawed my way back across the deck, and I punched the controls on the bypass kit to initiate its automated sequence.

The cuffs cut into the insulation of the cabling and clamped down.

Electricity took the path of least resistance.

And gravity returned to normal. The screeching of the hull turned back to a groan, and then silenced.

A few seconds later, all I could hear was the hum of the fusion reactors.

I collapsed on my back, while my heart pounded against my rib cage. I looked over at Hector. The lighting in engineering was bright, meant to help hapless mechanics like me see what we're doing, so I could see just how pale his face was. He stared at me, wide-eyed. "Did…" He started and stopped, and swallowed hard. "Did you just save us all?"

I smiled. "Yeah," I breathed. "I did. Feel free to sing my praises."

Hector shook his head, and then I swear he turned green, and he clamped his hand over his mouth for a second, strange noises ensuing. *Oh gods…*

As quickly as I could, I got up and helped him stand, and then we squeezed back out to the starboard side, then rushed out into the cargo bay and into the restroom.

I'll give him credit where it's due, he held in his vomit until he made it to the toilet. But the noise he made after that?

I almost threw up myself, and I had to leave and close the restroom door.

Staring out into the cargo bay, I found a lot of eyes set deep in green, sickened faces staring at me from both sides.

Smiling sheepishly, I remarked, "Welcome to space."

TWENTY-SIX

I forgot about the open comms in my ear. *"Uh, everything okay?"* Karina asked.

I was about to say yes, until the deck pitched over sideways. I tried to absorb the impact with my hands, but still managed to smack my left cheek.

My first thought was, *Did my bypass fail?* But no, I knew this feeling, I'd become intimately familiar with it over the past two months.

I had a concussion. Again.

Others around me yelled in surprise, and I think people tried to get out of their harnesses fast, but it was strong arms from behind that grasped me. Hector had finished his own business, and now, as my stomach tried to empty itself, he helped me into the bathroom.

I sort of lost track of everything for a while, or maybe I blocked out my memory of being sick. But the next thing I knew, I was leaning against the wall next to the door into the restroom, with Karina and Hector hovering over me. Karina had the emergency medical kit out, and she was scanning me.

Had Naia given her basic field medic knowledge, too?

If so, I was incredibly grateful, and I made a mental note to thank Naia for her forethought.

"Here, swallow this," Karina said, handing me a pill from the med kit. Hector handed me his waterskin, and I gulped down the pill.

The deck kept trying to pitch over on me, so I just sat there after that, and waited, clutching my eyes shut and holding my head.

Whatever the pill was, it worked remarkably fast, and within a few minutes, the pounding in my head started to subside, and the deck stabilized.

I tested opening my eyes again, and was happy to see the world was right-side-up, and blue eyes gazed down upon me with worry. I managed a weak smile, and Karina returned it, making me swoon.

Yeah. Swooning over sick. *Again.* At least I'm consistent.

I managed to rasp out the words, "How we doing?"

"Good," Karina glanced towards the cockpit. "Thanks to you. Autopilot's on, we'll cut the burn in about another half hour or so."

I nodded, and then swallowed. Hector offered me his water skin again, and I shook my head and asked, "Help me up?"

They both did. Then I went back into the restroom and used the sink faucet to slurp up water and swish it around, then spat it out to clear my mouth of the foul taste.

After a few more rounds of that, I came back out to worried looks. The rest of the crew had returned to their seats, if they'd ever even managed to get out of their harnesses, but Hector and Karina remained by my side.

"So what happened back there?" Karina asked. "Why'd we lose inertial dampers?"

I sighed and explained what I'd found and how I'd fixed it. "I think the inner hull must have crumpled during the *Sirius's* cascade power failure. Hopefully there's no more damage, but I'll probably want to inspect both shuttles after we land."

"Good idea," Karina nodded. "But I thought we did that last night?"

"We did," I nodded. "But I didn't do a complete overhaul inspection." I grimaced and turned my eyes downward. "I didn't think we'd need to."

"Well, we got through it okay," she replied. "And the prince hasn't had any issues so far."

I nodded dryly, but couldn't meet her look. I felt guilty for my lapse in judgement. Not to mention yelling at her to shut up during the crisis. Do you ever review past conversations in your head and beat yourself up over it?

"We should get back to the cockpit," I croaked, and then cleared my throat. "In case something else goes wrong."

"You up for climbing a ladder?" Karina asked.

I looked up and around, and then stood up straight, breathing in deeply. "Yeah. Whatever you gave me, it's doing wonders!"

She smiled. "Naia must have realized we'd need a medic, I guess," Karina shrugged one shoulder. "So she gave me a taste of that on top of piloting skills. What I gave you instantly reduces swelling anywhere in the body, including from concussions."

I heaved a sigh of relief. "Thank the Oracle."

That earned me a smirk, and yes, I'd meant it ironically.

Nodding at Hector, I said, "You should strap back in."

He acknowledged my suggestion and headed for his seat, while Karina and I walked back to the ladder, and then climbed up to the cockpit.

Still feeling a little unsteady, I was a bit awkward trying to get into my seat, and I may have bumped into Karina a few times. She gave me a couple of pushes to help guide me, and then I slumped in my seat, exhaling noisily, before I started strapping in.

"*Hope* to *Pride*," Karina said. "Mika's okay."

"*That is good to hear,*" Jonnec replied, genuine relief in his voice. I guess that shouldn't have surprised me. "*It appears that you were able to correct your course accurately, too.*"

Karina shrugged. "Mostly the computer did that, but yeah, we're back where we need to be, with only a little extra fuel expended."

I ignored the rest of the conversation, and instead set to running a more complete diagnostic of all systems, hoping to find any hint of power flow issues *before* they caused a disaster.

During that, I lost all track of time, until Jonnec called out the countdown to cut thrust. The engines throttled down flawlessly, and then Karina brought us back around to face our destination. I studiously kept my eyes glued to my console, unwilling to incur another round of sick over swirling stars.

And then I heard Karina draw in a breath and murmur, "Oh, wow!"

I looked up, and that moment in time froze.

The moon filled our viewport, vast blue swathes of ocean interspersed with green and brown continents, and so much white from cloud cover, it was incredible! It was gorgeous! No scan, no video, no image could have prepared me for the sight of something so vast, so *big!* It wasn't like the gas giant at all, with infinitely detailed swirling clouds of strange, alien colors. These were colors I knew.

Even from way up here, it made me feel longing. I thought of the green grasses of Rhea, of the brown earth of the farms, of the stream and the clouds and the rains.

It occurred to me that the world ahead of us was just like Rhea, only a million times larger! All of that life. All of that air and water!

My head swirled with the thought of it all.

"Now that *is an incredible vision,"* Jonnec intoned, the awe in his voice matching my own sentiments. *"I never thought to imagine such a beautiful vision in all of my life."*

Karina and I both whispered our agreements, and we just *took it in,* the moment, the view, all of it.

I wanted to remember this for the rest of my life.

Even as we gazed upon that wondrous sight, I could see the moon growing larger and larger, as we raced towards it, caught in its gravity well. Something beeped on Karina's console, and she took a look. "Navigational computer confirms good trajectory," she reported.

"As does mine," Jonnec concurred.

She glanced at me. "It's gonna get bumpy when we use the upper atmosphere to brake. Is that bypass gonna hold?"

I had to break my eyes away from the world, and I looked into her eyes and said with as much confidence as I could muster, "I think so."

And then I realized I hadn't finished all of my diagnostics yet. Swallowing hard again, I said, "Um, I'll run some more checks to be sure. Structural integrity is just as important for this, or we could find ourselves with another kink in the inner hull."

She nodded, and then said, "Alright, Princely, make sure you're good to go, too. Looks like our braking maneuver will happen in…forty-five minutes."

"Yes, of course," he replied. *"I know what I'm doing, Karina."*

"Then get to it, Sourpuss."

I heard him audibly grumble before he cut comms. I grinned at Karina, and then focused on my job.

While I did that, Karina must have brought up scans of the planet. About ten minutes later, I heard her mumble, "That's weird."

I didn't want to divert my attention away from the diagnostics, but given the fact that we were still in space, that wasn't what I wanted to hear. So I asked, "What's weird?"

"Huh?" she looked at me, blinked, and said, "Oh. Just…there's still a storm over the landing site."

I frowned and glanced over at her scan readout. Sure enough, there was considerable rain and cloud cover over our destination. It looked to be sunrise there, but the dense cloud cover would make it dark, and hard to land in.

In fact, the storm looked like it hadn't moved at all. "Weird," I remarked. I minimized my diagnostic programs and brought up the records downloaded from the probe. "Look," I pointed at my screen, and then at hers. "The storm has barely moved in five days? That doesn't sound right."

Karina nodded, her frown deepening. "I mean. Neither of us are weather experts, but shouldn't weather *move?*"

"You'd think so, yeah," I nodded. Then another thought occurred to me, and I voiced it aloud, "Then again, this is an alien world."

"True," she replied, but her frown didn't let up. "But still, that's just...weird." Sighing in frustration, she grit her teeth and added, "I wish we could send this data back to the *Sirius* and get Naia's opinion."

I nodded. "Yeah." Then a broad smile stretched across my face.

She saw my expression, and through her frown, she gave me a weird grin and asked, "What? What are you smiling at?"

"Nothing," I said, and looked back at my console, minimizing the records and resuming diagnostics. "Just that I've noticed you don't call her the Oracle anymore."

Karina didn't reply to that at first, and I resumed my task. After a few minutes, she replied, "Huh. You're right."

I had assumed it had been a conscious choice, but I guess I was wrong about that.

Interesting.

The clock ticked down, and shortly before we would start to feel the atmosphere, I nodded, and said, "Alright, diagnostics complete. Looks like the only other issue is a possible power disruption to backup life support, but hopefully that's not gonna be a problem. I'll fix it once we're down. Other than that, inertial dampers, structural integrity, and heat shields should be fully operational. Thrusters are at peak, and so's our main engines. Antigravity systems are ready for atmospheric flight."

"Good to hear," Karina chimed, and then she flipped the comm channel open. "*Pride,* we're set to go over here. How's it looking over there?"

While we waited for Jonnec to reply, I looked up, and once again felt my breath stolen from me. The world was no longer a sphere, but a freaking panorama of blue and green! We raced towards the moon's terminator, and I realized that most of our braking would take place on the dark side. That was fine, it might make it feel a little less terrifying.

Maybe.

"All systems show nominal," Jonnec replied. *"I've raised my heat shields."*

Karina activated the *Hope's* shields, and she said, "Same. See you on the other side."

Then she flipped the comm closed, and elected to use the intercom rather than shouting back into the bay. "Alright, everyone, we're gonna get a little bumpy here, but this time it's normal. Stay strapped in and hold on."

She drew in a deep breath, and then took the yoke in both hands. We looked at each other, and I smiled. "Here's to smooth sailing and clear horizons, yeah?"

With a wry grin, she nodded. "Here we go."

It started almost the instant we crossed the terminator, and I felt my pulse quicken while my stomach dropped. The ship buffeted, lightly at first, but just enough to overcome the inertial dampers at first. There was a flare as the heat shields interacted with the atmosphere, then another, and then BAM! We hit the atmosphere *hard,* and the ship shook and shuddered and rattled while our view of nothing was suddenly occluded by orange and white flames.

I tried to watch my console, tried to make sure nothing went wrong during this maneuver, but we were in for the entire run, and there was nothing I could do if anything went wrong.

We'd talked this maneuver over with Naia last night – aerobraking was the most efficient way to slow down a ship and enter orbit. We could have burned the engines longer to slow us down and make our orbital insertion that way, but it would have required expending a *lot* more fuel. Since we weren't sure how long we'd be on the surface, and therefore didn't know how far away the *Sirius* would be when we headed for home, we needed to make sure we had plenty to spare.

Every ounce could count.

So far, everything went according to plan. Karina had an iron grip on the yoke, and with the computer's assistance, she was keeping us on course. Our sensors were being disrupted, but we could just barely make out Jonnec's ship ahead, slipping in and out of our readings.

The roar of the flames, the rattling of the ship, it set my nerves to a new level of anxiousness, and I gripped the armrests of my seat like a vice, and before long, my knuckles ached.

This is normal, this is normal, this is normal, I repeated to myself, over and over in my head. *We're almost through. Almost...*

The roar started to ease back. The rattling and buffeting subsided. The flames petered out, and ahead of us, I saw Jonnec's ship.

We were okay.

We'd made it.

We were safely in orbit.

Until an alarm screamed at us, and red lights flashed in the cockpit.

It wasn't from my engineering diagnostics. It wasn't from anything I was even remotely familiar with. Karina searched for the source, eyes darting every which way, and then almost at the same time, we looked at the readout on the console between us.

At the tactical readout.

It read, *"Incoming Guided Projectile!"*

That could mean only one thing – we were under attack!

TWENTY-SEVEN

Renewed panic gripped my heart, and for a solid three seconds, we gaped at the readout.

A guided projectile?

A freaking *missile?*

"Bwah, what the hellfire?" I blurted.

"Defense shields!" Karina shouted.

My mind whirled, but I had the wherewithal to reach over and hit the commands to engage kinetic shields over the thermal shields.

Then I mirrored my main console to the tactical, and brought up the sensor readings. "Uh, forty seconds until impact!" I reported. "Not just one, but *two* projectiles. No, scratch that, four! Except, no wait…"

"Which is it, Mika?" Karina hollered.

"I'm figuring this out as I go, dammit!" I spat back. "Gods damn, um. Two are locked onto us, two are locked onto Jonnec!"

Karina opened the comm channel back up, "Jonnec!"

"I see them," he replied, surprisingly calm. *"I can't pilot and defend at the same time."*

"Uh, you don't have to!" I blurted, realizing it as I said it. "Turn on your A.D.S.!"

I flipped over to the correct menu and found the Automated Defense System on the *Hope*. These shuttles weren't meant for combat, and had extremely limited maneuverability, but they *did* have point defense systems that could target and try to destroy incoming projectiles before they hit.

I smashed in the command to turn them on, and watched as the capacitors charged, while the kilometers between us and the missiles bled away.

"I see it now, yes," Jonnec replied, concern finally edging into his voice. Suddenly him not having a copilot felt like less of a triumph. *"Activating A.D.S."*

"Fifteen seconds," I said.

Suddenly the projectiles were in range, and the A.D.S. locked on. I watched, my grip on the edge of my console tight. *Come on…come on!*

And then, a flurry of rust-red, short-burst high-energy particle beams lanced out from the *Hope*. Travelling at the speed of light, they found their marks fast, but those missiles were coming up through atmosphere still, and were buffeting around. The first dozen blasts missed, but all it took was one…

"Yes!" I shouted, pounding the console when I saw the first missile blow up. A second later, the second missile blew up.

Then I noticed that Jonnec's A.D.S. hadn't fired yet.

Because he'd taken too long to activate it. His capacitors were still charging.

I gaped ahead at his ship, and willed his capacitors to charge faster. "Come on," I said anxiously. "Come *on!*"

"Jonnec?" Karina called out. "Why haven't you fired yet?"

"Hellfire!" he shouted back, and I saw his main engines flare and his ship turned hard to starboard. I caught sight of the glow from the missiles' propulsion exhaust moments before they zoomed by his ship.

But they weren't dumb weapons. The moment they missed, they detonated, and his shields flared to life.

Reaching my left hand towards Karina absently, I said, "Follow him, follow him!"

"I got it," she said through clenched teeth, and she hit our engines on full and turned towards the *Pride*.

Fresh alarms sounded.

"More missiles incoming!" I reported through a fresh surge of adrenaline.

"Could you be *any* more specific?" Karina barked.

I gave her a withering glare, and then tried to coerce the unfamiliar tactical interface to give me more info.

"Uh. Shit. Ten more launches!" I swallowed. "Five for us, five for Jonnec." And then more blipped into the readout. "No. Twenty. What the hellfire?"

"Who's shooting?" Karina screeched.

"I don't know," I screeched back.

We weren't trained for this! We hadn't received combat training from the I.A. We were out of our league, and as that realization sank in, it gutted me, and I started to feel genuine terror grip me.

"My A.D.S. capacitors are having trouble charging," Jonnec reported. *"I'm reading power fluctuations in my kinetic shields."*

"Oh," color drained from my face. "Oh gods, the *Pride* must have been damaged just like the *Hope*. Jonnec, I'm so sorry!"

He ignored my apology and instead said, *"I think I'll only get one or two shots, no way I can contend with ten missiles!"*

"Yeah and these things aren't really meant for tight maneuvers," Karina hissed. She leveled us out behind Jonnec. "What do we do?"

"Thirty seconds till the first wave hits," I reported. "Um, I think they're definitely coming from the surface!"

"And not from a ship in orbit," Karina nodded. "I have an idea! Let's make it harder for them to target us with the next wave, while avoiding this wave! Jonnec, nose down and go for the deck!"

"What?" his bewildered voice nearly shrieked over the comm. His calm was shattered.

"Do it, now!"

To his credit, he only hesitated a second, and then his ship dropped from the horizon.

Karina followed him down.

"Great plan, but that's cutting our intercept time in half!" I screeched.

Plus, now we screamed back into the thicker atmosphere, and the *Hope* started shuddering and shaking again, orange and white flames engulfing our vision.

Suddenly the missiles were in range, and our A.D.S. started firing.

But with the *Hope* being jostled around by the atmosphere, they missed almost every single time. My sensor locks on the missiles fluctuated, but I saw at least one discharge from an explosion. The rest came at us unhindered.

The only saving grace was that while we skipped and dove through the atmosphere, we too were harder to it.

Four missiles screamed past, one close enough that I saw its engine trail even through the flames.

They detonated, and the *Hope* rocked harder than ever. Fresh alarms sounded, and I heard a screeching noise somewhere behind me. *Oh gods, oh gods, oh gods!*

The second wave was almost on top of us, but the A.D.S. just couldn't hit them in these conditions.

"Try to out-maneuver them!" I shouted.

"What the fuck do you think I'm doing?!" Karina shouted back just as she yanked the yoke from one side to the other.

Two more missiles streaked past, detonated.

Then the third one smashed right into our kinetic shields, and the *Hope* barreled hard over, and as we temporarily plummeted down twice as fast, my stomach stayed behind.

It took a full ten seconds for Karina to level us out, and even longer for my stomach to catch up.

"Uh," I said, trying to read the shaking console, "Kinetic shields at thirty percent, we can't take another direct hit like that!"

But the only saving grace was that the impact tossed us out of the way of the other missiles, and they'd missed us by a wide margin, wide enough that they hadn't detonated.

The buffeting diminished, and the flames cleared.

Just in time for us to see Jonnec's ship as we screamed right down at it.

"Shit!" Karina shouted and yanked the yoke hard over.

We missed, but our kinetic shields bounced off of his, and the *Hope* jostled again.

We were above storm clouds now, with towers of white reaching up to us, and darker, ominous clouds far below.

"Jonnec, are you alright?!" Karina yelled.

"I'm fine, but barely," he replied. *"I took two direct hits, my kinetic shields are about to fail!"*

I sighed and slouched in my chair.

We were okay. So was he.

But it wasn't over yet.

The *Hope's* A.D.S. fired, and I frowned – no new launches had been detected! Then I realized, those two missiles that had missed us were coming back around and homing in on us.

But without atmospheric entry jostling us about, the A.D.S. was able to hit their targets after only a few tries.

Only *then* did my console scream at me. "Dammit, more launches!" I growled out. "Where the hellfire are they coming from?"

"Jonnec, how's your A.D.S.?"

"Still recharging after that last encounter," he replied.

"Fifteen seconds!" I shouted.

"Get down into the storm!" Karina said, and without waiting for him, she pointed our nose straight down, towards the towers and valleys of clouds and the flashing lightning. "I'm starting to get topographic readings, there's mountains we can use to block their missile lock on us!"

"On it," he curtly replied, and I watched on sensors as the *Pride* followed us down.

This was getting tiresome. The missiles came at us from our dorsal side, but the clouds flashed rust-red all around us from our A.D.S. firing.

Ten seconds.

We must have been closer to the launch site now, not just because of altitude loss, but because we were actually geographically closer.

Our A.D.S. killed two missiles. Karina lurched the *Hope* hard over and pulled up just as we dove into the clouds, and two more missiles missed and detonated, jostling us and further weakening our shields. We were evading them, but they would eventually kill us through attrition!

The shuttle's computer was thankfully smart enough to know Karina needed a visual aid, so our view of thick, soupy clouds and water sloshing off of the windows was suddenly overlaid with a wireframe of the terrain.

And we were coming *straight* at a mountain peak.

Karina hissed in a breath and banked us hard to port. We scraped by the peak, and dove into a vast valley just as we came out beneath the clouds.

Giving me my first view of the surface of an alien world.

The clouds let only dim, diffuse sunlight through, so there wasn't much to see, other than a blurry, vast forest below.

Jonnec's ship appeared right in front of us as he gunned his engines hard and tried twisting and turning.

I checked sensors, saw that two missiles had missed enough that they hadn't detonated, and were coming back around to track the *Pride*.

"Kinetic shields are down," Jonnec reported. *"That last near-miss caused some hull damage, and my A.D.S. isn't working!"*

"Keep maneuvering," Karina shouted. "Go back up into the

clouds, they might have a harder time tracking you with the lightning!"

As if to punctuate her remark, a bolt of lightning lanced between the two ships, leaving an afterimage in my vision that I blinked away.

Jonnec yanked the *Pride* back up. The first missile zoomed past us, and I glanced at our A.D.S. It wasn't shooting because those missiles weren't locked onto us. "Dammit," I hissed, and I started working on reprograming them.

That missile skimmed by the *Pride* and blew up. *"Gyah!"* we heard Jonnec shout.

I glanced up.

Saw debris fall away, and Jonnec's starboard engines were *gone.*

Horror hollowed out my chest.

The second missile streaked by.

"No," I whispered.

"Jonnec!" Karina shouted.

He tried to pull up, tried to compensate for the loss of half of his engine power.

But it wasn't enough.

Just before he reached the bottom of the clouds, the missile slammed into the aft end of the *Pride,* and an explosion rocked the stormy sky.

"JONNEC!"

Fire engulfed the *Pride.* The aft end shattered into a million pieces, leaving only the front part, cockpit and all, sailing across the sky on inertia alone.

We watched helplessly as it skirted along the bottom of the clouds, and then arched down towards the forest below.

Twenty-three people.

Twenty-two townspeople and the Prince.

Just...gone.

The cockpit fell below our line of sight as we raced past it.

Neither of us said anything. We just sat back in our seats and gaped into nothing. My heart thundered. My arms tingled. My mouth hung open limply, uselessly.

Useless...

I'd been helpless to save him. Save *them.*

Just like Thelon.

"Oh gods," Karina whispered, her voice cracking into a whimper. "No..."

I heard the alarm, moments before the A.D.S. fired.

A distant explosion rocked the *Hope*.

Blinking tears away, I looked at my console, saw more missiles incoming. "Oh, you have to be *KIDDING ME!*" I screeched. "More incoming!"

"How are they tracking us?" Karina snapped back into the moment a lot easier than I did.

"I-I don't know," I said, as another missile blew apart only a half kilometer away from us. "But we can't keep this up!"

Karina nodded dryly, then she leaned forward and looked down. I frowned and followed suit.

The trees below. They were tall, taller than anything we had ever seen in Rhea.

Tall, thick, and we were coming up to the edge of the valley.

I nodded at her. "Do it before we lose kinetic shields altogether."

She nodded back. And she angled the *Hope* down, right at the trees.

I glanced back and shouted into the cargo hold, "Everyone hold on, this last bump's gonna be big!"

The A.D.S. took out the last missile still on sensors.

There wasn't time to look for a clearing. There wasn't time for a graceful landing.

We had to get out of the sky before more missiles launched.

Karina pulled up at the last second, and our kinetic shields slapped across the tops of the trees.

She killed main engines and engaged forward thrusters on full.

And we dove into the forest.

TWENTY-EIGHT

The *Hope* jerked. I slammed into my harness. I slammed sideways. Back into my seat. My head whipped around. I slammed forward again.

We hit ground, and a deafening roar engulfed the ship.

I gripped the armrests, too terrified to close my eyes, watching in horror as we mowed down tree after tree after tree. Their trunks exploded from the high-energy kinetic shielding impact.

I swear it went on *forever.* The jostling, the jerking. My shoulders and chest hurt from the constant pressure of the harness.

I tried to look at Karina, saw her gripping her harness with her eyes closed, her jaw clenched, terror on her face, tears streaking down.

I fumbled for her elbow, barely able to touch it as my hand jerked all around. She felt it, looked at me, and then gripped my hand like a vice.

We held onto one another as the world ripped and tore all around us.

If the shields failed before we slowed down or stopped, the *Hope* might break apart. I imagined our seats tearing lose, our bodies smashing into trees or ripping apart on branches or…

Stop it!

The shields had to hold. They *had* to hold.

Please hold…

A low groan reverberated through the inner hull.

And then, blissfully, thankfully, *miraculously,* the *Hope* ground to a halt, the kinetic shield pressing up against one last tree, five times as thick as my torso, directly ahead of us.

The noise, the action, it all just suddenly *stopped.*

Peace.

I sighed and slouched in my seat.

We were alive.

We were *alive!*

A burst of triumphant laughter escaped me, and I looked at my girl as she likewise slouched, letting her head loll to the side in utter exhaustion.

We were down, we were intact, and there was no *way* those missiles could find us now.

I hoped.

I prayed.

But then it dawned on me. For all intents and purposes, we were trapped. If we tried to take off, presuming we *could* take off, those missiles would just swat us out of the sky, and we'd meet the same fate as Jonnec.

Karina winced and withdrew her hand from mine to dab it lightly in her mouth. Blood came away.

"Karina!" I tried to get to her, only to be yanked back by the harness, *painfully.* I smashed at the release, breaking free, one of the latch plates slapping my knee as I flew out of the seat.

"I'm fine," she spoke, her words a little strange, shaking her head. "I justh…" Her t's and s's blended together with a th-sound, and she finished, "justh bit my thongue, is all."

I bent across the cockpit and gently held her face with my hand, looking at the little bit of blood staining the corners of her mouth. "You're sure? No internal bleeding?"

"I mean, I should check everyone out, including myself," she shrugged, and winced again, but at least her words were already a bit clearer. "But I think it's just my tongue." I saw her mouth move, and she winced. "Yeah, definitely my tongue."

I deflated in relief and caressed her cheek. "Thank the Oracle…"

She arched an eyebrow at me. "Thank the Oracle?"

I realized what I'd said just as she repeated it back to me, and felt myself blush in embarrassment. "Sorry. Old habits."

Giving me a bemused grin, she hit the release on her harness, and then looked at her console. "Engines are powered down. Shields?"

I glanced over. "About to collapse," I confirmed. "We should put the landing gear down."

She engaged the gear, and I heard a whine through the ship as the four points extended down from the angled hull. Once they were locked in place, I switched all shields off, and for the barest instant, we fell in freefall until our gear sank into the forest floor.

I looked out the cockpit window as best as I could, but all I could see were trees, a forest floor absolutely *covered* in flora, and drizzling rain.

Karina flipped through some more shutdown sequences, and I looked down and grimaced. "It might make us easier to target, but I wonder if we should leave the A.D.S. online."

"Can they actually shoot missiles through these trees?" she asked.

My grimace grew deeper. "Probably not."

"Then no sense making it easier to find us."

"Good point," I nodded, and I shutdown all weapons.

"Alright, let's go check on the others," she crawled past me towards the ladder.

I stared at my tactical readout and shook my head. I wanted to know who the hellfire was shooting at us, or at least where they were. But that could wait.

We had a difficult conversation ahead of us.

We had a difficult *situation* ahead of us.

I crawled after Karina and met her down in the hold.

While Karina went to grab the emergency med kit again, I heard a commotion from the starboard side of the ship, and was accosted by a frantic guard. "Jonnec!" Marek screamed. She had ripped herself violently out of her harness to grab me. "I heard you scream his name, what happened?"

Trying to tear her away from me, I growled, "Hey, back off, get *off!*"

But she wouldn't, she was frantic and grabbed me by the front of my tunic to pull me in, nose-to-nose. "WHAT HAPPENED TO HIM?"

"Marek, that's enough!" Karina raced over and tried to pry her off. The other guard that had sat beside her, Rai, joined in and forcefully inserted himself between Marek and I.

"Tell me what happened!" Marek demanded. Her hands twitched and I could tell she wished she had a weapon in-hand.

The other passengers started extricating themselves from their harnesses, and some started to gather around us in the cramped confines, while others did the exact opposite and moved as far away from the conflict as they could. Still, I suddenly felt cramped and wanted to escape the shuttle, escape *everyone*.

I longed for the solitude of my library, the solitude of the corridors in the *Sirius*. Go figure, I missed being lonely.

Karina sighed and massaged the bridge of her nose, while I rubbed at my chest. I looked at my girl, and she at me. We were both considered leaders in this expedition, so it naturally fell to us.

Us. Teenagers.

Hellfire.

I took on the task. I explained everything that had happened after we entered orbit. At least, as best as I could. I wasn't sure they could understand orbital mechanics or the friction of reentry, let alone guidance systems on missiles and the A.D.S. cannons on the *Hope's* hull.

"We knew we had to land quickly to avoid the missiles," I explained. "But by the time we realized that, it was too late for…for Jonnec's ship."

Devastation befell everyone's faces, but none more deeply than Marek's. She fell to her knees and slumped forward, and I was reminded of Hector's rumor-mill talks about her and Thelon. I connected the dots – Jonnec and Thelon had been best-of-friends. So it was more than just duty that drove Marek mad now that Jonnec was dead.

Dead.

I felt an emptiness well up in my chest, threatening to overcome all reason.

One minute we were shouting across the comm channel at one another. The next…

"One of those weapons hit his ship," Karina explained. "I…I don't see how anyone could have survived, either the explosion, or the fall."

My own shoulders were tight, but when she said that last part, I felt them slump, and I hung my head.

"I'm sorry," I said.

"S-sorry?" Marek looked up at me. First with disbelief. Then with absolute rage. "You're *sorry!*"

She lunged at me, at *us*, but Hector and, surprisingly, Leif interceded. Even as big as Leif was, Marek was strong and big, and when she swung at me, she damn near punched my lights out, her fist whistling past my nose! Then Rai jumped in between us again and managed to keep her back.

"I should have been with him!" she screamed over Rai's shoulder. "Why did you make me come here?" And then she turned her attention upwards. Towards the heavens. Towards the *Sirius* and Naia. "Why?!"

Guilt weighed heavily on me. It was up to me, up to *us*, Karina and I, to understand technology, to use it to save everyone, to keep everyone *safe*. I'd failed, not Marek, not even Naia. I should have known more about the tactical systems. I should have been able to reprogram the A.D.S. on the fly to protect Jonnec.

But I wasn't good enough, and now twenty-three more people were dead.

Worse still, we were down one ship. We were missing key mining and purification equipment.

I looked at Karina and suggested, "It…maybe we should, um. Look for…I dunno."

"Survivors?" she asked doubtfully.

By now, Marek had worn herself down, and she slumped on the deck in Hector and Leif's arms, but she looked up then, hopeful.

"Well, I was going to say, we could try to salvage something from the wreckage," I shrugged, but then slouched. "But even if we could, it's not like this shuttle is big enough for both fuel and ore."

The cargo bay was silent after that, and I considered what our next move should be. I was drawing a blank.

Then I remembered that, for once, it wasn't just up to me. So I mulled out loud, hoping Karina might have an idea, "We need more information.

Karina nodded. "We need to get our bearings," she reasoned. "Find out who is trying to kill us. Find out how far off we are from our landing site."

I nodded and smiled at her, even as it occurred to me how obvious her suggestions were. "Good idea."

She asked, "Can we do that anywhere other than the cockpit?"

I thought about it and shrugged. "Sure, why not?" I looked at Marek, and then went to the other side of the cargo bay to make my way towards the aft end. I passed by Annar as I did, and expected another one of his trademarked scowls. Instead, he just stared blankly at the deck, his face pale.

He reached a hand for me, and I recoiled, hissing in fear.

Shockingly, he backed off, and held up his arms disarmingly. "I," he started and stopped, and then swallowed. Hellfire, he didn't just look pale, he looked *green*. The maneuvers must not have sat well with his stomach. "I just wanted to know," he asked, in a meek tone I'd never heard from him before. "Are…are we, um, safe?"

I glanced at Karina. She looked at her brother with a soft expression, and she said, "Well. That's what we're going to figure out now."

He sat down in one of the jumpseats and planted his elbows on his knees, leaning forward while taking a deep, shuddering breath. "Okay…"

This was a new side to the previously outspoken, angry boy. And believe it or not, I felt my heart go out to him. I'd already experienced life-or-death situations on starships. This was his first. Well, not technically, but when the cascade power failure shook the *Sirius*, as far as Annar knew, it had been on a planet whose ground quaked and heaved.

Now he knew what it was like to be in space, *really in space*.

Now he knew what kind of danger we were all in.

That's a lot to stomach, pun intended.

Next to the bathroom and the door into engineering, there was a wall console, meant primarily for performing cargo bay inventory. But like any computer system linked into the central network, I could pull up other interfaces.

So I let the knowledge from the I.A. guide my hands, and after a few minutes of manipulating API's, I had a geographical map of the surrounding area, based both on our recent sensor readings and the historical readings from the probe. Karina stood by my side, while some of the other passengers tried and failed to cram around us to watch, making it particularly stuffy again. I grumbled and shoved back against someone breathing down my neck, before I refocused on my work.

"Alright, we're here in this valley," I pointed at a white dot on the map. "Our landing site was meant to be…" I programmed the map to show the approximate location, and then was surprised when a green dot appeared not far away. "Huh. That's, what," I glanced at the distance key, "fifty kilometers? Not bad."

"Is that close?" Hector asked from behind Karina.

I shrugged. "Considering the maneuvers we had to pull, yeah. We could have ended up on the other side of the moon."

"I mean, we did plan our orbital insertion to take us right over the site," Karina pointed out. "To get updated sensor readings."

"True," I nodded. "So the concentration of ore and fuel is fifty kilometers to the northwest."

"How do we get there?" Leif asked. "With all of the tools we need? Even with all of the magic in your equipment, I imagine that will be quite the journey."

"It's not magic," I idly remarked. I glanced to the center of the bay, where all of the containers, extractors, and purifiers were, and then at the cargo slots above the passenger seats. "Um, there's antigrav sleds we can deploy, but yeah, we won't be able to get everything on them. It'll take multiple trips."

"What about your suggestion?" Karina asked, her voice lowered, as if conspiring. "What if we could find some sleds in the…um, from the *Pride?*"

I considered that for a second, and hesitantly said, "It…is possible."

The valley we'd crash-landed in mostly went west to east, so while the fuel was to the north, the wreckage of the *Pride* would have likely been directly west of us.

"Hmm," I thought. "Well we're on the eastern edge of the valley, so we're a little higher in elevation. Maybe I can scan for the debris field without too much interference."

Somehow, it felt wrong to do so. Like a violation of those twenty-three souls lost. Unfortunately, the fact was that we were in trouble now, and we had to do whatever it took to not just survive, but get the needed supplies to the *Sirius* as fast as possible. Scanning and scavenging over the dead would be our only hope.

I programmed in the scanning parameters, and almost instantly, a wide area lit up with fragments and chunks of heavy metal and composite material. I whistled. "Wow, that's spread over a huge area."

And then something else appeared on the scan. A blue blip.

A comm signal.

My jaw slowly hinged open, and for the barest, briefest second, I felt a spark of hope.

"What is that?" Karina asked.

I tapped my earpiece, and spoke with a wavering voice, "Mika to Jonnec."

I waited, my breath held. Karina grasped my elbow tightly, her eyes wide.

Nothing.

"Jonnec, are you there?"

Still nothing.

I huffed out a frustrated sigh and tapped my earpiece.

"What?" Marek asked, "What is it?" Her voice cracked when she added, "Is he alive?"

"Um," I stared at the blue dot. "Maybe. It means that his earpiece is intact and still powered, so his body must be intact. And," I ran a quick command to verify the status of the comm device, "it isn't in failsafe mode. If he were dead, it would have detected the drop in bioelectric energy and turned into an emergency beacon."

I looked at Karina, daring to hope, but her expression turned to one of puzzlement and she asked, "Bio…what?"

"Uh," I stumbled over my words. "Well, just like this shuttle, our bodies generate electricity, sort of. And our earpieces, while containing their own little batteries, detect and augment their capabilities with, um, body energy. And generally speaking, your body doesn't generate energy if you're dead."

Karina's brow was furrowed tightly, and she shook her head. "So you're saying he *has* to be alive?"

Lifting my eyebrows, I tried to think of any other possible explanation, but nothing came to mind. "Well…yeah, I think it does."

"Then to hell with salvage," she stated. "This just became a rescue!"

"He's probably hurt, badly," I nodded. And then I looked at Karina with a grimace. "And since you're the only one trained as a medic…"

Karina pressed her lips into a thin line. "I should be the one to go. And you should stay behind with the ship."

I didn't like it. I didn't like splitting up from my girl, I didn't like her heading out to the woods, knowing there were hostiles *somewhere* on this damned moon.

"I'm going, too!" Marek shoved her way through the surrounding crowd.

"Obviously," I rolled my eyes. "Not like I'd let anyone go without a guard escort."

I was being ironic, but Marek didn't seem to get the joke. She headed to the compartment above her seat to gather her belongings, and no doubt her weapon. Karina turned to me, and asked, "Particle weapons?"

I nodded. "Naia did give us permission to use them, they should all be ready to be encoded." I walked past her and through the aft doors into the engineering section, where the weapons locker was installed. I pressed my thumb to the tab on the locker, and it popped open. Karina followed me in, and I grabbed a tool and a pistol from the rack, and used the tool to activate receiving mode on the weapon for genetic and palmprint encoding. "Here, hold this and pull the trigger."

Karina took the weapon and did as I asked. The red light by the safety turned gold, indicating it was active, but still on safe. Then I dug around in a drawer beneath the locker, and eventually found and handed Karina a thigh holster.

"Do you think we should give Marek one?" she asked.

I thought about it, thought about what they might encounter out there. Not just hostile *people,* but who knew what animals were out there. Who knew what *predators* were out there. "Yeah. I know it'll take a few minutes to teach her how to use it, but I think *all* the guards should." There were two more guards on our ship, and there were more than enough pistols to go around.

"Good idea," Karina nodded, and worked on strapping the holster on. "You teach the others, I'll teach Marek?"

I watched her as she strapped the holster on, and smiled at how easy it was for her. She was brilliant, I knew that much, and she'd watched me put a holster on once before, so she had some idea of how it was supposed to go.

Karina finished strapping on the holster and secured her weapon, and then met my gaze. Our eyes froze on one another, and I felt a lump well up in my throat.

Every time we had parted company on the *Sirius* to fight that alien, I'd felt a horrific weight in my stomach. This time, it felt like my gut was falling out into an endless pit. Maybe because we'd actually been *together* since then. As a couple. Sort of.

I was scared.

I didn't want to lose her.

I tried to tell her all of that, but nothing came out. So I let my eyes do the talking.

And then I let my mouth do the talking. I slipped forward and kissed her fiercely, pressing my lips as hard as I dared against hers.

She didn't recoil. Didn't push me away.

When I finally pulled back, I blinked open my eyes and said, "Make sure you come back."

Karina's eyes fluttered open. She didn't smile, but she did blush, her freckled cheeks turning distinctly darker.

A throat cleared behind her.

She whirled around and we found Hector staring at us through the door.

"Um" he murmured. "Sorry."

He disappeared back into the hold in a flash. "Hector!" Karina called, chasing after him.

I watched her leave, and suddenly it felt like she was being ripped away from me. I should have felt guilty, but I didn't. I was glad Hector saw us, and a part of me, a dark part, wanted it to break his heart so badly that he gave up on Karina.

Am I a horrible person?

I didn't want to be.

Ah. There's the guilt, then.

Too much. It was all too much. Losing those people on the *Pride*, almost losing Jonnec, losing Karina like this without actually *losing* her. A treacherous teardrop streaked down my face, and I wiped it away with more force than I needed to.

I hated feeling this way, I hated feeling conflicted and uncertain.

So I resolved myself to focus. To do the job.

This ship needed repairs. And we needed to figure out our next move after they got Jonnec back. *If* they got him back.

We still had to save the *Sirius*. We still had to save Rhea.

TWENTY-NINE

I spent the next several minutes passing out pistols to all of the guards and showing them how to use them. It wasn't as easy as I'd hoped, but then again, projectile weapons of *any* kind were practically unheard of in Rhea, let alone particle weapons.

Marek in particular wasn't exactly fond of the pistol – she donned her leather armor and strapped the axe on her hip, and declared that she didn't need any magic. But when I pointed out the people trying to kill us could do so from over the horizon, I managed to convince her to strap on a holster and learn to use a pistol.

Unsurprisingly, I overheard Annar try to quietly ask Karina, "What about the rest of us? Shouldn't we all learn how to use those…pistol things?"

I was in the middle of showing Rai and the other guard how to adjust their thigh holsters when I heard Annar, and I almost reeled and snarled a, "NO!" but Karina was way ahead of me.

Only she used a bit more snark than I expected. "What, you're not afraid of them corrupting you like they did me?"

I coughed to cover up my snort of a laugh, and Rai eyed me curiously. Rai was surprisingly lithe for a guard, not all muscle like I'd come to expect from them. He was tall, long-legged, and could probably outrun me more than beat me to a pulp. But he still kept a sword strapped to his hip, and if I knew anything about Rhea's guard force, it was that they took their jobs seriously, and trained to use their weapons daily.

I heard Annar make a frustrated noise and stomp away, his boots clanking on the deck. His queasiness from earlier was apparently forgotten, but now a new kind of fear drove him. Would it make him more willing to comply with us as leaders on this expedition? Or would he do something stupid? Well, worse than anything he'd already done.

Then I heard Leif lecture Karina, "You should be nicer to your brother."

"After everything he's done?" she growled back. I glanced at her, saw her glaring up at her father. He saw me look and gave me the stink eye. It was nothing compared to my mother's or the queen's, but I still didn't want to get anymore onto his bad side than I already was. Karina glanced at me, and then said to her father, "He's lucky I let him come along!"

Leif whirled on his daughter, jabbing his finger at her, "This is precisely what I've been talking about! As I understand it, this was the Oracle's decision, not yours."

"Yeah," she nodded. "And you heard what the Oracle said before we left. I say where he goes, and what he does."

I glanced again, saw Leif raise his eyebrows questioningly. "Is that so? And do you think you can do the same to me?"

Karina hesitated, but at that moment, we finished with Rai's holster. I helped him register his pistol, and told him, "Make sure you don't mix this up with anyone else's. It'll be programmed to you, and you alone, so if you mix it up and try to shoot with someone else's, it won't work."

He grasped the pistol and pulled the trigger like I instructed, and the red indicator light flicked over to gold. Gaping at it, he asked tentatively, "And you insist this is not magic?"

I tried not to roll my eyes. "Yeah, I'm pretty damn sure." I could tell him how most of the components in it operated, but for all I knew, without context, that wouldn't dissuade him.

"I don't..." I heard Karina start and stop.

"That's what I thought," Leif stated. "I am still your father. You will do as *I* say. And I will not have the majority of us defenseless when, as you say, advanced threats are hunting for us as we speak."

"Dad..."

"No!" I could practically imagine his hand swiping through the air in finality. "No rebuttals!"

"You don't understand," she tried to explain.

"I understand better than you think," he insisted. "I am not stupid, and I will not have you questioning me or giving *me* orders, do I make myself clear?"

Oh I'd had enough of that. My earlier trepidation evaporated and I reeled on him. "And I won't have you questioning one of the expedition leaders like that!"

Ah, there was a better glare from him, that looked a *lot* more threatening. Karina whirled on me, wide-eyed. "Mika!" she breathed.

I ignored her unspoken objection and marched across the deck to stand up to Leif. I had to look up and stand on my toes, which made me feel a lot less intimidating, but I didn't back down, either. "How dare you!" he started.

"Do you intend to disobey the Oracle?" I tersely replied.

"I intend to look out for my family!"

"That wasn't the question I asked!" I folded my arms, but realized too late that it probably didn't help me look any more commanding, but whatever. My temper grew hotter and hotter, and as I faced down a big, strong adult that could probably pummel me into the dirt, a voice in the back of my head screamed that I was crazy. But I pushed on. "The Oracle was *very* clear, was she not?" I looked at Karina, but she just gaped at me, wide-eyed. She, too, might have thought I was crazy.

"You are a *child!*" Leif insisted. "I am not beholden to your orders!"

Lifting my eyebrows, I replied, "Oh? So if Prince Jonnec were here, giving these same orders, would you question him, too?" That stopped Leif's next lecture dead in its tracks. He sputtered and let his arms drop to his sides, the idea catching him off guard. "No? Why is that? He's only three years older than I am, right? So he's just a kid, too. But isn't he your prince?"

Leif's jaw tensed, and he glanced at Karina, and then at Marek. Marek narrowed her eyes at him, as if begging him to say he'd disobey the prince.

When Leif didn't reply, I nodded, "That's what I thought. Interesting, though, that you would willingly obey the prince, despite his age. But what about me? I'm the Princess of Rhea, am I not?"

I hated playing that card, but the last thing I needed were idiots who didn't know a particle weapon from a hydrospanner trying to give orders. So I was going to use every advantage I had.

It was Marek who replied in her grumbling voice, "She's right." Leif stared open-mouthed and wide-eyed at her. Honestly, so did I. "She is our princess, and she speaks for the Oracle. Whether we like it or not, we owe her our fealty and our obedience."

Annar took up the challenge, "We owe her nothing!"

"Then I suppose the Truthspeakers are liars," Rai snapped at him from beside me. "You claim to obey the Oracle and follow the old ways! The old ways dictate that leadership begins with the Oracle and extends down into her emissaries, through the throne, do they not?"

I could see Annar's face actually turning red, whether through frustration or embarrassment. I tried really, *really* hard not to smirk.

"Leif," Rai addressed him again. "It doesn't matter that they're just kids."

"I'm not a kid," I growled.

"You are a *child!*" Leif insisted.

"She is your princess!" Marek inserted herself between us, just before I could launch myself at Leif. Not to pummel him, but I *was* about to do something stupid like grab his tunic and shout in his face. Marek interceding like that doused my temper. A bit. "And you are wasting time that the Prince does not have!" Without looking away from Leif, Marek pointed at Karina and added, "And *she* is an emissary of the Oracle, so from this moment forward, your daughter will enjoy the same status! If you have a problem with that, then I will shackle you to your chair and leave you here to rot."

Damn.

I mean, *damn!*

Never, ever in my life had *anyone* stood up for me like that, let alone two guards! And while I knew that Marek was motivated by her *need* to save Jonnec, I still felt shocked by the reversal of her attitude towards me!

Silence reigned in the cargo hold, broken only by the occasional ticking or clanking of the ship's hull and engines settling. Leif stared at Rai, then Marek, but neither guard backed down, and I believed that Marek would do whatever it took to end this argument now and get moving, including shackling Leif, or even knocking him unconscious.

Leif must have believed that, too. Drawing in a slow, deep breath, he finally nodded. "Very well." He turned to Karina, and then to me. "I...*respectfully* request that we all be given pistols."

I lifted my eyebrows, and very plainly said, "No." His eyes widened, enraged. "For the same reason the Oracle would let no one else on my first expedition have one, we must limit the use of particle weapons. They are too dangerous in inexperienced and unknowledgeable hands. It's a risk giving them to the guards, no offense," I glanced at Marek, Rai, and the other guard.

"None taken," Rai said. I had the feeling that Marek *did* take offense, but she did a good job suppressing it. Rai turned to me and said, with over-the-top fealty, "I swear to you, Princess Kai, I will treat these weapons with the utmost care."

I nodded, and then turned back to Leif. "What we *will* do is give everyone here an energy shield."

Surprise crossed the older man's face. "Energy…shield?" he asked.

I nodded, and showed him the one I kept on my arm. I pressed the green dot with my thumb, and a blue-white quarter-sphere popped into existence in front of me, twice as tall as it was wide, it's default setting.

"The shields the guards used the other day," I said. "These will protect you from particle weapons. They are relatively safe-"

"You broke my friend's leg with that," Annar pointed out, but there was more indignation in his voice than there was anger.

"*Relatively* safe," I reiterated. "But like any technology, you must still treat them with respect and use them with caution. But at least you won't be blasting holes through the *Hope's* hull with these. Or, you know," I shrugged, "people."

"But they'll let you defend yourselves," Karina added. "So it's better than nothing."

Leif scoffed, but he didn't offer any additional objections. Neither did Annar, nor any of the other gathered blacksmiths and guards.

I lifted my eyebrows and looked around the hold, waiting. In the back of my mind, I knew that Jonnec didn't have time for all of this, but it had to happen sooner or later, and if we didn't clear the air here and now, things would only get worse later.

"Alright," I nodded. "If there's no more objections or whining, I'm gonna open the cargo bay doors and see what it's like out there. Karina, would you mind passing out the shields?"

She smiled lightly, but I could tell it was forced. "Of course," and she headed back to retrieve them. I hadn't meant to boss her around like that, but Jonnec's dwindling chances of survival compelled me. I could apologize to Karina later.

I pushed through the crowd and went to the port side cargo bay doors. *Please let this be the last major hiccup…*

I knew that was asking too much.

Still, I could dream.

The seats that lined either side of the hold were broken only where the large cargo doors were, and I stepped up next to one such seat and depressed a switch. A red light above it turned yellow and an alert sounded, indicating that the ship was matching internal pressure with external. A light hissing noise met my ears, and I waited patiently. If there was anything dangerous in the atmosphere, anything that the probe hadn't detected, the light would turn red again and seal the door. That'd end this whole expedition here and now, and seal our fates.

While that cycled through, Marek came up next to me. I glanced at her, but she stared at the cargo doors with a blank expression. A rush of emotions passed through my stomach, then my chest, and out into my fingertips. Fear mixed with pride, and probably a dozen other emotions. "Um," I said quietly.

"Don't let it get to your head," she whispered. "I," she started, and then frowned and looked at me. "I hate you, Mika Kai." I gulped. "But I recognize that you're as interested in rescuing the prince as I am. And I believe that you're the only one who can get us home."

Gawking at her, I stupidly asked, "You do?"

She gave me a tight nod. "Unfortunately. You have the most experience in," she motioned to the shuttle around us, "these matters."

The light turned green and beeped again, sending a wave of relief through me. With a thudding clank, the angled hull that doubled as cargo doors split horizontally in the middle and opened up to an alien world. Thick, humid heat rolled over us, and Marek turned to watch, while I stared back at her.

She was turning out to be quite the enigma.

We were immediately met by the sound of startled life, what sounded like birds cawing and fluttering away. The sound of drizzling rain followed, and the smell of mildewy wetness met my nose. And then I had my first unobstructed view of an alien forest!

"My gods," Marek breathed.

The trees were huge! Whereas Rhea's never grew much taller than thirty or forty feet, these stretched hundreds of feet into the air, and were covered with thick, reddish-hued bark.

The forest floor was *covered* in flora, too! Green, leafy plants were everywhere, with very few flowering plants, though I had no idea if that was due to whatever season we happened to be in, or if flowering plants just didn't grow on this moon. For that matter, I had no idea if there were *seasons* on the moon!

It was…all unknown. All strange.

And I hadn't felt so excited and so terrified at the same time in all of my life!

A new world.

Gods, I never thought I'd see the day.

The ramp stopped lowering sooner than expected, and I realized that we'd crash-landed next to a hill, forcing the ramp to be more-or-less level. That'd make things a little easier for us, I supposed.

But then something else occurred to me. It was a wilderness. Untamed. The trees were likely only as large as they were because no one had cut them down. They grew as large as they could, and probably only died and fell from natural causes. One such fallen tree was visible from my vantage, rotted, overgrown, and almost as tall as the *Hope,* even on its side and half-collapsed.

So if this world was an untamed wilderness, who had shot at us?

Frowning, I left Marek at the door and returned to the panel at the back of the cargo bay, and while Karina continued handing out shields and showing everyone how to put them on and activate them, I brought up sensor records from the missile attacks.

The records showed that they came faster and faster, the duration between launch and contact shorter each time. Which meant we'd flown closer throughout our flight. Unfortunately, the sensors could never detect them right away. I thought that strange at first, but then recalled Naia telling us that the storms caused a type of sensor interference.

Thankfully it sounded like the storm was finally dissipating, since I hadn't yet heard the crack of thunder, and the rain was merely a light drizzle.

I looked at the computerized sensor analysis of the weapons, and then blinked in surprise. "What?" I murmured in surprise. "Noooo."

The computer identified them as class three guided missiles. It listed what the explosives were made from. It stated their exact yield.

No way. How could the shuttle's computer determine that? Its sensors weren't designed for combat, and the tactical computer was limited for defensive purposes only. It wasn't meant to analyze and classify weapons.

So how did the computer know?

I wondered if I could figure out my own answer to that question. It wasn't as simple as asking Naia and getting a qualitative response, this computer was, essentially, a dumbed-down A.I., not a fully-aware, creative, thinking machine.

"Whatcha doing?"

I jumped at Karina's question, her voice coming right over my shoulder. Letting out an annoyed breath, I gave her a withering glare, and then looked back at the screen. "Well, I *was* trying to figure out where the missiles came from. But…" I explained what I had discovered.

"Weird," she frowned, and then stepped closer and started tapping in commands. "The tactical computer *does* have a database of known weapons and their unique signatures," she stated. "But it'd be an incredible coincidence if these weapons were that close to something known."

I blinked at her in mild shock, and watched as she worked. I'd always loved her for her curiosity and passion, but to hear her talk tech like that, to see her working the console, to see intelligence not just forced upon her, but to also see her intuitively use that knowledge to deduce and work through problems?

Yeah. That was a big turn on for me.

Karina's eyes widened. "Okay," she gaped. "Um, I didn't expect that."

I forced my gaze away from her and looked at the screen. She had brought up the database for known weapons' signatures. And the result was shocking.

The missiles were in the database. Their propulsion signature, their yields, the signals detected that guided them, everything matched up with a ninety-four percent certainty, according to the computer, that they were Gladius-class hypersonic guided missiles.

"How is that possible?" I breathed.

"I don't know," she shook her head.

She moved to touch the entry on the Gladius-class missiles, but before she could, an alarm sounded, startling us both. But the alarm wasn't coming from our current screen. Instead, it was coming from the sensor readout in the background.

Karina realized what was going on before I did, and she deftly brought the live sensor readout back to the forefront.

Orange dots had appeared in the north, above the mountain that helped form the valley we had crash-landed in. Orange dots, not red. Not missiles.

The dots were labeled, "Unknown Contact."

Two at first. Then two more at a different angle. And they moved, *fast.*

Karina entered in commands to initiate analysis subroutines, and the contacts resolved.

Liburna-class personnel transport shuttles.

"Uh," I gaped at the readout. "Those are…human shuttles?"

That made no sense. Unless the moon was occupied.

By *humans!*

Humans who wanted us dead.

The two pairs were not flying in formation, I realized. One pair was on a heading taking them south-by-southwest. Towards the *Pride's* debris field.

The other pair were headed straight for the *Hope.*

"Oh no," Karina murmured. "They're coming for us."

The attack wasn't over. And despite shutting down most systems, they knew exactly where to find us.

THIRTY

My thoughts just…stopped. For all of two seconds, during which time the location of the dots updated twice, growing closer and closer.

"What do we do?" Karina asked, the edge of fear growing in her voice and threatening to further derail my thoughts. I felt a crowd gathering around us again, and I was starting to *really* hate being surrounded by people, especially when the cargo bay was already close quarters.

But the thought of those dots coming to kill us, to kill *Karina*? That incensed me.

Before I knew what I was doing, I was flipping through screens until I came upon the comms interface. "What are *you* doing?" Karina blurted in bewilderment.

"Trying to open up some options," I said, jamming my finger on the 'open channel' button. I cleared my throat, and said, "My name is Mika Kai. To the vessels approaching, we mean you no harm. Please, do *not* attack us!" Again.

I held my breath and waited. I'd placed the sensor screen as a smaller view in the bottom right, and I watched as the dots came closer, and closer. They weren't stopping. They weren't even slowing down.

"Look, I don't know who you are, but I'm guessing you're human, just like we are. We are *not* aliens, and we haven't come here to hurt you. Hellfire, we didn't even know there was anyone on this moon before we entered orbit! Please, you have to believe me. We're in trouble, we were before you even started shooting, and now we're worse off." I felt Karina grasp my arm, squeezing in warning. Maybe revealing how weakened we were wasn't a good idea, but the alternative was to stand and fight. We wouldn't win in a fight. We weren't trained to fight.

Silence followed. I heard a dual, high-pitched whining noise outside, no doubt the sound of the approaching ships. I heard a murmur of worried voices amongst the blacksmiths. Maybe I should have been up in the cockpit, getting shields and the A.D.S. back online, but there wasn't time. We hadn't seen them until they were practically on top of us.

I wasn't going to lose Karina or anyone else.

In my best tone of desperation, I softly said, "Please."

Two more seconds passed. The approaching transports were right on top of us. I almost started deflating in defeat, but the second my shoulders started to slouch, the screen flickered.

Someone answered my hail.

A woman appeared, white-skinned with light brown hair, not quite blonde, that was as straight as could be and hung past her shoulders, which was as far down as the squared view of her showed. And her eyes were the greenest green I'd ever seen. She looked to be in her thirties, and her expression was pure puzzlement.

"Mika Kai," she spoke my name, slowly, working her tongue around it, her voice liquid smooth and soft. I blinked, glanced at Karina, and back at the screen. *"That is an unusual name."*

"Uh," I said. Way to make first contact. "Not where I'm from."

She tilted her head to one side. *"And where, precisely, are you from?"*

From outside, the dual pitch of engines dropped down an octave. They were here.

Hesitant, I looked again at Karina. She lifted her eyebrows and nodded encouragingly at me. I swallowed. "I, um," I started, "don't suppose the name Project Sirius means anything to you?"

The woman's soft expression hardened. *"Sirius,"* she said, doubtful. *"Why would someone from Project Sirius be all the way out here?"*

She knew. She *knew* what Project Sirius was!

"Well, that's a long story," I said. I kept glancing at the sensor readout and flickered a frown before returning my expression to what I hoped was a neutral façade. "I would love to tell you all about it, but I won't be able to if whomever is on those transports attacks us."

"We presumed you to be a threat," she said. *"Our Caesar commanded us to attack any manned ships that entered orbit after we detected what I assume was your probe."*

"Yes, that was our probe," I nodded emphatically. "We were scouting for resources, that's all. We needed to find resources to survive."

Her hardened expression softened. *"Survive?"* She considered my words carefully. *"You said you were in trouble even before we fired upon you."*

I nodded, but then stopped myself. Why had they fired upon the first manned ship to enter orbit, without first identifying who it was or why they were there?

Something was fishy about that. "Um, yeah. Fuel. And raw materials. We're low, very, very low on both." I studiously avoided mentioning the actual state of the *Sirius*. For now. Then something else clicked in my thick skull. "Wait, did you say 'Caesar'?"

She nodded once. *"Yes. Our leader."*

I knew that term. "As in…like, Julius Caesar?"

"The title of Caesar," she affirmed, but then frowned. *"You know of Julius Caesar, but not the current-day context of its usage?"*

"Well, no," I shook my head. I glanced at Karina and said to the woman, "We've read about Julius Caesar in one of our fiction books. That is," I started upon seeing a startled, almost offended look on her face, "what I *thought* was fiction. Is the story of Julius real? Did he really live in a place called Rome?"

Utter shock paled her already white complexion, and then she burst out laughing. Laughing at *us*, at me, and I felt my cheeks burn. *"Oh my,"* she said through giggles. *"My, oh my, you truly do not know? And here I thought you were just another loyal pup."*

With a glower, I asked as politely as I could, "Know what?"

Her laughter eased back, and I saw her shoulders slouch. *"Oh, my. Well, then. You are familiar with Project Sirius, but what of Project Alpha?"*

Quirking an eyebrow up, I replied, "Alpha? No, that doesn't ring a bell. I know there's other Renovare Projects out there, but I don't know their names."

"Mm-hmm," she nodded. *"I see. Fascinating."*

She studied me for a long moment, and I grew uncomfortable. This…this was a new gaze. A new look. This wasn't someone appraising me as a threat anymore. This wasn't even appraising my value. This was something else, something…*dissecting.* And it made me shudder.

"How many are you?"

I glanced at Karina. Glanced at the sensor readout. Saw Jonnec's signal still going strong, and saw those other two transports nowhere near him, searching the debris further afield of him.

"Twenty-two," I lied. Karina's grip on my arm tightened again.

The woman sighed. *"I see. Not many. Very well. I will instruct the transports to land, but to not do anything against you until I arrive."* Wait, she wasn't on one of those transports? *"Please cooperate with them, and do not offer them any violence, and you will be treated in kind. Once I arrive, I can evaluate your…"* She hesitated, as if searching for the appropriate word. *"Truth."*

I nodded, and opened my mouth to ask her for her name, but her image blinked to darkness. Huffing out a breath, I murmured, "Nice to meet you, too, stranger."

"Mika, what the hellfire?" Karina asked.

I turned to face her, while outside, the dual pitch of engines shifted again. The transports were going to land. "Look, we don't have much time," I said hurriedly. I tapped the screen to bring the sensor readout back to full size, and pointed at the transports by the *Pride* wreckage. "They must have landed, and they aren't anywhere near Jonnec's signal, so they must not know where he is or that he's even alive."

"Yeah, they're probably focused on the biggest concentration of wreckage," Karina nodded. "So what?"

"So I don't trust that woman, nor her people," I replied. "If they're the kind of people to shoot first and ask questions later, then they must be hiding *something*. And I don't have a clue what."

"So?"

"So that's why I said twenty-two instead of twenty-four survivors," I looked intently at her. "Those transports by us are gonna land in the only place that they can."

Karina frowned, glanced at the sensor readout, and then opened her eyes wide. "The trail we left when we crash-landed."

"Exactly," I nodded. "You and Marek can sneak out the front while we all pile out the back. Run as far as you can into the forest, until you can't see the *Hope* anymore, then circle around and head for Jonnec's signal. Rescue him." I touched the med pack strapped to her vest. "Heal him. And wait for my signal."

"I…" She hesitated, but I could hear the transports coming in low now.

"Go," I gripped her shoulders, and gave her a little nudge. I looked at Marek. "I said *go!*"

Karina pressed her already-thin lips into a tight line, and she nodded. "Right. Marek, grab your pack," Karina turned and snagged hers from its storage locker above the passenger seats. Marek was already set to go.

"Everyone else, out on the ramp," I shouted at the others. "Guards between everyone and those transports, but do *not* shoot unless they shoot first! Something tells me we're gonna be outnumbered."

At first, none of the blacksmiths moved, only the guards did. After a second of the guards shuffling through the people, Rai commanded, "You heard your princess, move!"

That shifted everyone into motion, and people started crowding out onto the platform.

I watched as Karina and Marek went to the front side of the gaping maw that was our cargo doors, and waited while everyone started moving out. I stared after her, my girl, my love, and my heart ached. I was scared. I was so horrifically terrified that I wouldn't see her again.

But there wasn't time for a goodbye kiss. And Hector stood right there next to her. They exchanged a quick goodbye, with Hector still not touching her. He glanced sidelong at me, and then followed everyone onto the ramp.

The fear and nervousness amongst the miners was palpable, I could see it in their eyes, in their shuffling feet. I felt it, too. I mean, it's like Viden and I talked about, people fear the unknown. Today, I was about to face humans that weren't from Rhea. Humans that operated ships and highly destructive weapons! Nothing I'd read in my books could have ever prepared me for this.

What technology would they employ? What kind of culture did they have? How could I reason with them?

Sure, it seemed like people were, well, *people*, no matter the culture, and there were some universal facts about people. Unfortunately, those facts didn't bode well. These people coming towards us? They were something unknown and I was afraid of them, just like we were something unknown to them.

Please tell me someone with a cool head will be leading those ships...

While Karina and Marek slipped around the corner and headed forward, I pushed out onto the crowded ramp. Over the heads of my compatriots, I watched as the two transports descended to land behind the *Hope*. They looked surprisingly similar to the transports I'd seen on the *Sirius*, long, boxy craft meant to hold as many people as was possible with very little other accoutrements, and very few defensive or offensive weapons. There were basically flying boxes with engines.

The blacksmiths were all focused on the incoming transports, at the 'magic' of it all, and I had to push my way through them. When I got to the edge where the ramp met damp, soil-covered ground, I came face to face with Annar.

I came up short, and he and I stared at one another. He wasn't green anymore, but he was far paler than normal as he glanced between me and the transports.

He swallowed hard, and nodded to me. I figured that was the closest I would ever get to his endorsement.

I walked past Annar onto the surface of a new world, and headed towards the transports. With a startled tone, Rai shouted, "Princess Kai!"

"Stay back," I thrust my open, halting palm at him. "Let me handle this."

"But Princess…"

I didn't let him voice his objection. I kept walking aft, past the quad engines of the *Hope,* and then I had to crawl over splintered remnants of a tree, but finally I stopped, directly between the troop transports and my people.

The craft touched down, having found the only clear spots between pieces of trees, and their engines cycled down several octaves. I noticed that they didn't fully shut down.

I didn't see, but I heard ramps on their aft ends open with a hiss and mechanical whine. And then two columns of people from each shuttle streamed out and hustled around, all of them wearing light composite armor plating and carrying particle *rifles.* Not pistols.

I tensed as they moved with precision, what one of my novels might have even called *military* precision. There was no way for them to line up into any sort of formation, not with all of the debris, so they took what positions they could, some kneeling behind pieces of trees or tree trunks, others beside their transports, and then they all aimed their weapons towards the *Hope.* Towards me.

My hand twitched towards my pistol, but I didn't dare draw it. What I *did* do, however, was lift my left arm and activate my shield. In hindsight, I was lucky they didn't all have itchy trigger fingers, otherwise my actions might have made any one of them shoot, and that could have set off the rest of them.

As it was, once they found their positions, they all stopped, and just kept their weapons pointed in my direction.

I swallowed back the terror that had seized my chest, and then found my voice again. "I thought you weren't going to do anything against us?" I shouted.

And then a tall man stepped around from behind the shuttle on my right, and I knew right away that he wasn't a rank-and-file. For one thing, he didn't wear armor, nor did he bear a rifle. Like me, he had a pistol strapped to his thigh, albeit his left thigh. He sauntered towards me with an almost disinterested casual movement. He took his sweet time, and eventually stopped next to his forward-most trooper, a woman knelt down behind a chunk of a log.

"That was indeed the medici's command," he spoke, his voice loud and clear, enhanced by technology. At least that was something recognizable. "And so we shall wait." His voice was baritone, his words crisp and clear.

Keying in on his words, I asked, "So that's her name? Medici?"

He gave me a bemused smile. "Name?" he spoke through a light laugh. "No, that is her *title*." Shaking his head, he glanced around at his troops and sighed. "And you are just a child. Perhaps it would be best if an adult came forward."

I clenched my jaw and balled up my fists. "No. You can deal with me. I'll decide later if you're worthy of talking to anyone else."

His bemused look vanished.

Oh. Apparently I'd somehow struck a nerve without meaning to.

File that away as interesting and possibly useful.

I'll give him credit, though, he didn't back-talk anymore, even though he probably *really* wanted to. I probably wouldn't have held back so well. In fact, I was sure I wouldn't.

I glanced back at the others, saw that the guards had turned on their shields and held them up like a wall. The blacksmiths craned their necks trying to look over one another to see what was going on. Leif was near the front, and was tall enough that he didn't have to strain himself.

When I looked back at our…adversaries? Counterparts? Honestly, I didn't know what to think of them yet. The leader stood lazily, staring down at a data pad not unlike the ones we had. While his soldiers kept a close on eye us, he seemed to just not care.

I had no idea how long of a wait we could expect, and I hated awkward silences, so I asked, "So, that lady's title is medici. What's her name?"

The leader glanced up from his pad and gave me a withering glance before he looked down again, ignoring my question.

"Do *you* have a name?"

This time he didn't even look up.

"Alright, then I'll just have to make up names for you. Or titles. Or whatever." I used my free hand to lazily stroke my chin, trying to look as nonchalant as he did, but my shield kind of ruined that. "Um, let's see. You lead these soldiers, so military. But only a handful of soldiers, so not even a trusted lieutenant…"

I saw his eyes look up at me, though his head didn't budge. "You shall address me as Centurion Tiberius," he growled out.

"Centurion?" I lifted my eyebrows. "Man, you guys really went all-out on the whole Roman thing, huh?"

Tiberius slowly lowered his pad and lifted his chin, glaring at me with a fire borne only of those who have lost all patience with me. I showed him my teeth in a grand smile.

"You are nothing but a blithering, blustering child," he remarked.

"Ooooh, nice," I infused as much sarcasm in my words as I could, and I planted my right hand on my hip, studiously keeping it well above my pistol. "Repeating the 'child' remark. How original. Consider me scorned, Centurion Tiberius."

I could practically hear his pad crack and creak as his grip on it tightened.

"Well, Centurion," I lazily remarked. "When may we expect your dear Medici what's-her-name?"

The first hint of a new whine answered me, and he showed me *his* teeth. "Momentarily, young lady. Momentarily."

I managed to keep a glower off of my face, and I looked up and around. The massive forest created an echo effect, and I couldn't tell where the noise came from, but I presumed it was coming from the north, like the Centurion's landing craft had.

I also didn't think it a coincidence that they were coming from the same direction as the fuel and ore concentration. Suddenly I was doubly doubtful about those being naturally-occurring deposits.

A small craft appeared over the tree line, and I instantly recognized it as a short-range scout ship, similar to the ones we had on the *Sirius*. Not exactly the same, but I imagined it was no coincidence that their craft were similar to ours.

It came to a hover further back than the personnel transports, and then slowly, expertly landed in such a way that I could hardly see it between the transports. I drew in a deep breath while I listened to the shuttle's engines spool down.

I waited impatiently, and it was all I could do to keep myself from bouncing up and down in anticipation. I was about to represent the crew of the *Hope* in negotiations with a hostile force. Hell, I was basically representing all of Rhea, and the *Sirius!*

A heavy weight settled onto my chest, making it harder to breathe. I was thankful that the drizzling rain finally stopped in that instant, but now the humidity just felt *oppressive*, and I wanted to be anywhere but there.

Then she appeared.

And *oh my gods,* she was incredibly gorgeous! Like, unreal gorgeous! No way she was a normal, living, breathing human being, she was on par with a goddess!

The woman sauntered between the transports, swaying hips in a way that I thought impossible in the rough terrain, and it struck me at just how incredibly tall she was, taller than Centurion Tiberius by at least a head and a half, and he didn't look short by any measure. Her hair, straight as could be, caught in a breeze and blew away from her such that I could see how incredibly long it actually was, at least reaching down to her butt! Which, ya know, given how tall she was…

The woman stopped and surveyed the scene, and she scoffed. "Centurion, a standoff was not precisely what I had in mind," she practically sang, and her voice carried, even over the whine of the idling transports.

He turned to her and gave her a curt nod before acknowledging her with, "Medici. Unknown threats call for cautious measures, you know that."

The Medici glanced at me with those incredible green eyes, and I felt my heart thud in my chest while my cheeks warmed. "Really, though, Mika Kai is just a pup." Now my cheeks *really* burned.

Lifting his eyebrows, the Centurion stared at her for a solid thirty seconds before he glanced at me, and then behind me. "What about them?"

The Medici sighed. "Yes, well, let us get this out of the way. Perhaps let me do the talking, yes?"

Tiberius looked at me and narrowed his eyes before he gave a half-hearted shrug. "Fine, whatever. Just get it on, will ya?"

I swear, the Medici looked spurned by his disregard for her. But she seemed to bear it well, and she turned and gave me a patient smile, which just melted my insides. Gods, she was gorgeous!

Did I mention that already?

Slowly, careful to go around or over debris from our crash-landing, she approached. At some point, I realized I'd let my shield hand droop, and I was totally open to weapons fire, should the Centurion decide to act.

I realized my mistake, and slowly lifted my shield back up, hoping she hadn't noticed, but then I realized how foolish that thought was.

Lifting her light-brown eyebrows, which were trimmed and plucked to perfect lines, she said, "You have nothing to fear from me, young pup." I swear, her voice was hypnotic… "You are Mika Kai, yes?"

I swallowed and nodded. This wasn't right. Something was very wrong. Why was I swooning over her so badly? How could her voice, which sounded like silk and gold and all the good things in the Universe all at once, affect me so?

"Um, yes," I croaked. "Yes! I am Princess Mika Kai."

"Royalty," she touched her breastbone, and believe it or not, *that* was the first time I really looked there. I'm not really a chest gal. But she definitely had dressed to show off her curves, and her white faux-corset created quite the view that I had no doubt would have already drawn the gaze of any man or woman interested in women.

She also wore a locket that, I just now noticed, glowed ever so faintly blue-white.

Technology.

That's why her voice carried over all background noise.

I looked again at her corset, and noticed hints of detailed circuitry in the embroidery. I wouldn't have noticed if my brain hadn't been rewired with so much technical stuff, but now, suddenly, I could see it plain as day.

And her white skirt flowed unnaturally, though I didn't know if it was through some technology or simply because of the exotic material it was possibly made from. It acted as if there were a constant wind swirling around, making it cling to her hips and then billow away and then cling again in a way that just didn't seem to obey the laws of physics.

What the hell was she?

Stopping only about ten feet ahead of me, she placed her hands on her hips, further accentuating them.

"You may call me Medici Claudia," she finally said. "On behalf of my Caesar and the Starship *Alpha*, welcome to the wayward moon of Ravenna."

THIRTY-ONE

I blinked my eyes hard, trying to clear the lust-induced haze. I'd never felt this way towards anyone, not even Karina. I wanted to just…*go* to her, plead with her to embrace me, to kiss me, to do so much *more* to me.

And that just wasn't normal. I *knew* it wasn't normal. Warning bells in my head competed with my libido. I felt my breath stolen from me, and my heart fluttered.

Something was wrong. Something was very wrong. This wasn't normal and it was driving me insane!

Claudia watched me carefully, her eyebrows lifted. She looked at my face. Looked at my chest. She appraised me carefully, and that felt both exhilarating and violating at the same time.

"Interesting," she murmured. "Tell me, young pup, have you never met another of my kind before?"

I sputtered, "Of your…kind? What do you mean? You're human, aren't you?"

She smiled patiently. "Yes. Human plus."

"Um," I shook my head, forcing back desire, trying to find some way to ground myself. I leaned on my curiosity, and asked, "Plus what?"

Shrugging lightly, Claudia grinned and said, "Oh, you know. A little genetic modification here. A little cybernetics there. Just enough," she took a step towards me, "to make my life a tiny, teensy bit better."

I swallowed hard, finding the lump in my throat suddenly bothersome. Sweat beaded my forehead, and she seemed to take notice. Claudia had taken another step closer, but stopped and frowned at my sweat.

"It would seem you are a little *plus* yourself," she said, tilting her head to one side.

I didn't know what that meant, I just knew that I felt hot, in every sense of the word.

I liked it and I hated it and I wanted to *do* something about it with the kind of urgency I'd never felt before. My abdomen tingled and my stomach felt a rushing sensation. Aching heat grew hotter, and *hotter.*

"Hmm," she caressed her own chin, and I followed her motion, her hand, looked at her lips.

Oh gods, what was going on?

And then the spell was broken, as suddenly as it had started. I actually let out a surprised cry when everything just went away, and my body suddenly felt cold, empty. "W-what?" I asked. "Was. That?"

"I do apologize," Claudia bowed a few inches to me. "I wished to appraise you, to make sure you were not a threat. But you are, after all, just a child. A true pup."

I swallowed again, and realized I should have felt indignation over her words.

"W-well," I shook my head, and cleared my throat. "So. What just happened?"

"I shall explain soon enough," she gave me a pleasant, conversational smile. "In the meantime, may I examine you?"

I blinked. "Excuse me?"

Her facial expression faltered, but somehow it felt calculated. Intentional. "My apologies, young pup, but I am a doctor." She opened a flap on a pouch attached to her belt that I'd not noticed before, and withdrew what I recognized as a medical scanner, very similar to the ones aboard the *Sirius.* "As this is your first time on Ravenna, I would like to check you for reactions to the local flora and microbiome."

My mind drew a blank. "Huh?"

Lifting her eyebrows again, which still seemed a more sensual act than it should have been, she clarified, "Bacterial and viral infections. I presume you have received the standard broad-spectrum vaccination for off-ship and off-world travel, but it is best to be sure."

I blinked again. Medical stuff. Dammit, now I wished I'd kept Karina at my side. Except, I'm glad she hadn't seen me fall so hard for a literal stranger.

"Alright," I finally nodded.

She stepped closer and turned the device on to begin scanning, while producing a data pad from another pouch. Waving the scanner first over my chest and then my head, she nodded. Then she went lower, and *that* made me uncomfortable.

I squirmed a little, and she noticed. "Worry not, dear. This is entirely non-invasive and I promise I am not invading your privacy."

"So you say," I said before I could stop the words.

A light grin touched her lips. "Indeed." She shut the scanner down and stared at her screen, her face going slack for a moment. "Interesting. Oh dear, you have *not* received a vaccination. Ever. Yet your immune system…ah, I see. Nanomachines."

"Nanites?" I asked. That was a word I knew. "Yeah, they're in my blood. They help keep my body healthy." One of those things I learned from the I.A. download, mostly because I had to be able to repair and maintain both the nanite fabrication suites and the control systems. They existed in *everything* in Rhea, every person, every animal, every vegetable and fruit.

"Oh, I know what nanomachines are, dear," she said without looking up from her pad. "They generally need a constant wireless electric field to operate long-term, and these are still active. There are so *many*. And I recognize the design. Doctor Shah's work, or a derivative of them."

"Who?" I blinked.

She blinked right back at me. "Doctor Shah. Surely you have heard her name, she was rather famous on Lokabrenna."

I shook my head. "If you're talking about the Sirius star system, I don't really know much about it."

Her brow furrowed. "No? Hmm." She stowed her scanning device and then stared at me. "Curiouser and curiouser. I presumed that, given your loyalty to the name Sirius, your colony was still one-hundred percent loyal to your origin star system, yet you claim not to know anything about it?"

I debated what to tell her. What she should or shouldn't know. Claudia was highly intelligent, that much was certain. And knowing she was a doctor, I wondered if I should tell her the truth about Jonnec and Karina, get her to rescue and save Jonnec, as I was almost certain he was injured after a crash like that. Hell, I wasn't even sure how he was *alive!*

But she was part of the group that had shot us down. She had done…*something* to me just now that made me want to rip all of her clothes off, a sensation I had *never* felt towards anyone, let alone an adult. It was just *wrong*.

She was just wrong.

So I told the truth, but I sprinkled it with lies to keep her off the scent. "The Starship *Sirius* is on the other side of this star system. She never deposited my colony. We were exploring this star system, looking for a viable place to put down, when my shuttle and my friend's shuttle ran into some engineering issues." I forced my cheeks to flush, and added sheepishly, "That is to say, I failed to do a proper inspection on them both before we left the *Sirius*. It was my fault."

Claudia's eyes never wavered. At most, she narrowed them, and I swore she could see right through my lies, but the emotion behind my guilt was genuine.

Tsking, Claudia finally said, "Oh, there, there, sweet pup. No one is perfect. And to be an engineer at such a young age! How old are you?"

"Sixteen," I automatically replied.

I swore I saw her cheeks flush, then. "Much younger than I thought," her voice wavered. "I am so sorry for my earlier behavior, I should have known better."

Giving her my own frown, I asked, "Earlier behavior?"

"Using my gifts on you," she said. "I presumed you to lead your party, and especially after you told me you were a princess. I thought you were an adult, albeit a very young adult."

"Well," I hesitated. "I *am* the leader of this group, and I *am* a princess."

She eyed me curiously, and then glanced behind me at my companions. "But there are so many older persons present. Surely an adult would never allow a child to lead them?"

"I'm not a child!" I stated, with as much certainty and force as I could. "And I'm literally the smartest person among them."

She looked at me curiously, and then glanced at her pad. "Because of your time in an intellectus apparatus?"

I shouldn't have been surprised that she knew what that was, but I still felt a little startled by it. "Yes," I recovered as quickly as I could.

"Not everyone aboard the *Sirius* is given that privilege?" I shook my head. "Why ever not, dear?"

I scrambled for something to say, something to keep up the lie so that she didn't know just how desperate our situation was. But then the defiant streak in me asserted itself, and I lifted my chin and replied, "Because."

A breath passed, and then she laughed at me. Not over my words, but *at* me. "My, my. You *are* impetuous. It has been some time since I encountered such a rebellious streak. It is…" She drew in a deep breath through her nose, and finished, "Refreshing."

I ground my teeth in annoyance. But then something else struck me. Something about this whole situation was so incredibly unnerving.

An image popped in my head of a bug falling onto a spider's web.

"Well then," Claudia regarded her pad again. "I do believe this is all in order. Your nanites will eventually stop providing you with such excellent immunity to our local biome, young pup." Gods, I hated when she called me that. "It would be advisable for you and your companions to receive vaccinations, and since your bodies are not accustomed to such things, I should like to keep you all under observation for the next forty-eight hours."

I blinked in surprise. "W-where would we do that?"

"Aboard the *Alpha,* of course," she smiled. "It is only fifty kilometers away."

I started at that. "It is? So the readings we had showing fuel and all of those other minerals, it wasn't just a mining site, it was your ship?"

"Indeed," she nodded.

"But our probe," I shook my head. "It didn't detect any hint of a ship or E.M.F. signals or *anything,* just the material!"

"Yes, well," she shrugged. "Our Caesar is a genius, and he has been able to keep us hidden for quite some time."

"Hidden?" I frowned. "From whom?"

"That," she lifted her index finger and wagged it back and forth, "is none of your concern for now."

I saw red, and I almost told her to go screw herself.

"In any case, for your sake, I recommend you follow us in your ship to the *Alpha,* and we can provide repairs, food, and most important, vaccines against illness. And perhaps we can negotiate supplies for you, since that is what you originally came here for, yes?"

I felt panic grip me. I didn't want to tell her about Karina. And Karina was our only pilot.

"My shuttle is too damaged," I said. "And I haven't had a chance to begin repairs. We can't fly."

Please believe me, please believe me, please believe me!

"No bother," she shrugged. "You may ride in our transports," she motioned behind her. "I will leave a detachment of our troops here to guard your vessel until we can tow her back to the *Alpha*."

I nodded and swallowed, hoping to maintain my lie. "I'll lock up the ship, we'll grab our packs, and be ready in a moment."

"No need to lock up, dear," Claudia advised. "My guards will protect it."

Lifting my eyebrows, I risked asking, "And what is to say they won't go in without my permission?"

Claudia smiled, and again I felt like a bug in the spider's web. Only I saw no other way out except forward. We were trapped on this moon, Ravenna, and we were literally under the gun. I had to figure out how to get us out of this while still getting the *Sirius* the supplies it needed.

Except, I didn't have a freaking clue how I could possibly do all of that.

Please let something go right soon, I thought.

"As you wish, young pup," she finally said.

I turned without another word and stalked back, intent on not giving her another chance to cloud my mind. Rai deactivated his shield and stepped aside, letting me climb up onto the ramp with the others.

"What's the situation?" Rai asked.

I sighed and shook my head. "There's a lot to tell you all, and not a lot of time. Like usual," I added with a grimace. "So listen carefully."

I explained everything that had been done and said. Yes, including the weird attraction I'd felt towards Claudia. I didn't want to, I *really* didn't, because telling Karina's father or brother that I felt like I wanted to jump another woman wasn't exactly a conversation I had any desire to have. But if it hit me that hard, I imagined Claudia could easily manipulate anyone else in our party, and I decided they needed to know.

Gods, how embarrassing.

Finally, I told them all to grab their packs, and that we'd board one of the transports in place of the soldiers.

"Wait, wait," Leif grumbled, holding up a giant, halting hand. "You actually agreed to let them take us away from *our* ship?"

I narrowed my eyes at him. "Yeah, I did."

Clenching his fists, he glowered down his nose at me. "That was a stupid thing to do."

Heat flared in my chest, but Rai beat me to the punch when he hissed, "Watch your tongue! You are still addressing the Princess of Rhea."

"I don't give a damn who she is," Leif spat back at the guard. "This is our only familiar ground to stand on! If we give this up, then…" He trailed off and shook his head.

"Well, what else was I supposed to do?" I flailed my hands into the air, accidentally smacking a couple miners, who grumbled and tried to push back away from me. "They literally outgun us, Leif! If we resist, they can just shoot us. Hell, they could tell their main ship our location and they can launch missiles at us, we won't stand a chance!"

"Then perhaps you *should* have let an adult handle negotiations," he grumbled at me.

"Dad," Annar interrupted my vicious reply before it could start. He touched his father's shoulder, and his father looked to him. "She's doing the best she can."

Woh. Okay, this change in Annar was *really* starting to unnerve me.

"Um," my mind raced to think of how to capitalize on Annar's out-of-character support. "So, yeah. Look," I sighed and shook my head, fists clenched. "The Oracle put me in charge, right? And the king and queen both likewise support that fact." Sort of a lie, but close enough to the truth. "So you have to do what I say."

I saw Leif's jaw clench at that. But much to my surprise, it was Rai who turned to me with a frown, and he said, "Princess Kai, with all due respect, even leaders, even the king and queen have advisers. They listen to those advisers. And while I am not at all pleased with Mister Ticho's tone towards you," he glared a warning at Leif, "I do agree that you are rather…young." My cheeks felt warmth again. "While you know a great deal about the truth of the Universe and this…*technology* as you call it, the older generations have experience in matters that still matter."

I wanted to tell him off. I wanted to make them all just…*listen* to me! To do what I told them to do.

Until…

For the millionth time, Thelon's death played out in my head. He'd died because of my plan. He'd died because I didn't know when to stop and regroup. He'd died because I didn't listen when others told me it was time to leave the control booth in engineering.

I deflated, my head hanging low. Rai was right.

So I swallowed my pride, swallowed back the bile rising in the back of my throat, and I looked at Rai and nodded. "You're right." I looked at Leif. "But we can't stay here, Leif. They'll kill us all if we do. If we go with them, it'll buy us some time. Time enough to figure out how to save ourselves, and maybe get the supplies Rhea needs."

The redhead narrowed his eyes at me, and then looked up towards the transports, towards Claudia. Clenching his jaw, he nodded. "I suppose that is so."

"So what can we do to make this situation work more in our favor?" I asked him, gulping back my pride again.

Lifting an eyebrow, I saw his eyes darting around, looking at the soldiers, at the transports.

Leif looked me in the eye, and said, "We go with them only if they let us keep our weapons and shields."

I glanced down at the pistol on my hip, and then I smiled and nodded at him. "Good idea."

Claudia and *especially* the centurion wouldn't be happy with that condition, but I didn't care. Leif was right, and it was a damned good idea.

With that decided, everyone filed into the *Hope* to gather their packs, and I followed. I glanced back outside, checked to make sure Claudia hadn't followed us, and then I tapped my earpiece. "Mika to Karina."

There was a momentary pause before she came back, *"Go ahead."*

"I don't have much time, so listen carefully," I said, while moving back to the aft panel to check sensors. "There's another ship just like the *Sirius,* and it's here."

"What?!"

"No time to explain, but we've been invited to check them out. I guess they've landed on this planet and have hidden themselves, for whatever reason, but their ship is where those minerals and fuel readings were coming from. I'm checking sensors, and it looks like the other search parties aren't anywhere near Jonnec's position, but his signal is still strong. Do you have the location on your pad?"

"Uh, um, yeah. Shit, Mika, this is all happening too fast!"

"I know. Look, I still don't trust these people. Stay out of sight, don't come back to the *Hope*, and I'll get in touch with you as soon as I can, okay?"

"*Why can't we go back to the* Hope*?*"

"They're leaving guards behind."

"*Ah. They might shoot first and ask questions later if we show up.*"

"That does seem to be their standard operating procedure, yeah." I grimaced. "I'm gonna lock up the shuttle, but if somehow things change and the guards leave, your pad should let you in."

I heard her sigh. "*Okay. I'll stay out of sight. Looks like I finally get to put those survival skills we've read up on to the test, huh?*"

I grinned. "Maybe. Just remember, this isn't a book. This isn't fiction."

"*Yeah, I know, Mika,*" she replied indignantly, and I imagined her rolling her eyes. "*Same to you, though. This isn't some political intrigue novel. This is real. This could go bad really, really fast.*"

I swallowed down the lump that kept forcing its way up, and I nodded even though she couldn't see me. "No kidding."

"*Be careful.*"

"You too. I…" I paused, glanced behind me. Hector was a hundred feet away, so I whispered into the comm, "I love you."

Karina didn't answer at first. I felt my chest well up in anticipation and fear. I wanted her to say it back. I *needed* her to say it.

But she also was probably right next to Marek, so when she said, "*I do too,*" I took that as a good sign rather than a bad one.

I glanced back again, and everyone started filing out onto the ramp again. "Alright, gotta go. Mika out." I tapped my earpiece.

I sighed, and then closed down the sensor readings and brought up my engineering consoles. I tapped in a few commands to pre-set some daemons, and then I followed the others out. A second later, I heard the fusion reactor spool down to idle, and the ramp hissed closed with a metallic clank.

The *Hope* was sealed up as best as I could make her. I checked my data pad, saw that it had ninety-eight percent battery life, and then placed it in power save and shoved it into my pack.

Claudia was back with the centurion, and the troops from the transport on my right started lining up in formation, and headed back into their shuttle. The *Hope's* crew were clustered near the engines of our shuttle, and I motioned for them to stay behind while I approached the medici and her centurion. The medici looked down her nose at me, and I felt a rebellious urge kick in. I hated people like her…

But the crew behind me helped me keep my tongue in check. The need to make sure we all got through this overrode my snark.

Trying to put on the most confident face I could, I forced my voice to remain steady as I spoke, "I have a condition." The medici looked amused, but gave no other indication of her thoughts about me. "Myself and two guards have particle weapons," I tilted my head towards my holstered weapon, and while neither the centurion nor Claudia looked at my weapon, I got the impression they were very much aware of its presence. "And we all have shield bracers," I lifted my left arm to illustrate. "We keep them the entire time we're on your ship." That finally got a reaction from the centurion, but it was so subtle that I couldn't tell if it was surprise or concern.

Tiberius looked at Claudia, searched her for a reaction. She held her gaze on me, and I stared right back into those unusual, terrifyingly-beautiful eyes. A miniscule smile crept up one side of her mouth, and she nodded. "Very well, pup."

The centurion eyed me cautiously, and then looked at the medici. "You sure about this?"

"You have your orders," Claudia spoke down to him.

Grumbling, he nodded. He turned to the remaining troops and shouted, "Standard perimeter around the," he glanced at me, *"guests'* ship. Maintain until further notice. Contact me if anything unusual happens, got it?"

One of the troopers replied, "Yes, sir!"

"Move out!"

The remaining troops streamed around us, while the Centurion looked at me, and then at Claudia. "What about the girl?"

Claudia regarded me and smiled, and yet again, I saw a spider. "Young Princess Kai. Would you care to join me aboard my personal shuttle?"

I glanced between the two transports at her sleek-looking shuttle and hesitated. I didn't like the idea of being separated from my people, not now. "I'll stay with my team."

She nodded her head. "Perhaps as it should be. Very well. Centurion, with me."

He eyed me again, and I could tell he didn't trust me one bit. To be fair, the feeling was mutual. Claudia spun around, her skirt billowing as she did, and she strode back towards her ship. The centurion said to me, "Get your people strapped in. We take off in one minute." And then he followed Claudia.

I watched them go for a moment, before I looked back at my team and waved them over.

I had a very, very bad feeling about this.

THIRTY-TWO

I was the first to board the transport. It was as cramped as I expected, definitely designed to carry as many people as efficiently as possible. The interior was low, I had to stoop once I climbed up the aft ramp, and it was simply a long interior with fold-down seats on either side, and ended at the cockpit.

There was a pilot and copilot in those seats, both of whom had bulky-looking helmets on with visors covering their eyes, and they wore olive-gray jumpsuits. The copilot twisted around and watched us all pile in with a weird quirk to his mouth.

Rai was right beside me, followed closely by Hector and Leif. We trudged up the length, the deck clacking noisily underfoot as if the deck plates were loose.

Never-the-less, as I reached the end, the copilot pointed at the nearest seat and shouted above the whine of the idling engines, "Have your people sit and strap in!"

I already knew that, but I turned and relayed the order, and then sat down. The seatbelt was the familiar five-point harness system, and by now, I'd grown accustomed to getting in and out of it and effortlessly adjusted them to fit my relatively diminutive form. The others followed suit, and I watched, impressed, as Hector helped Leif with his. The bigger, red-headed man's hands shook, and I hadn't realized just how scared he was. Hector, on the other hand, seemed surprisingly confident and calm.

I leaned forward and looked down the center, and confirmed that everyone was seated and strapped in, with only two pairs of seats at the back to spare.

"All in, sir," the copilot said to the pilot, and he pushed a button above him. The back hatch hissed and rattled as it slowly lifted up, and eventually sealed us in, blocking out the bulk of the engine noise.

"I hope this is a good idea," Leif murmured, his voice shaking.

I didn't want to admit to him that *I* was starting to doubt my own plan, but then Hector looked at him. "It'll be fine, sir. We'll get through this and see your daughter again."

Karina. Gods, I hoped she would be okay.

"We have no reason to trust these people," Leif remarked.

"I don't know about that," Hector replied, shrugging in his harness. "They could have shot us, taken our ship by force."

"They *did* shoot at us," Rai reminded him. "They shot Prince Jonnec's shuttle down."

Hector grimaced and hedged, "Good point. But hey, they outnumbered us, plus they have a lot more weapons than we do. Why play this game when they obviously don't need to?"

"Good point," I echoed him, though I wasn't convinced. Why keep us alive? Why play this game?

I looked back down the row again, checking to see that no one was so nervous or scared that they'd do something stupid. In particular, I levelled my eyes on Annar, about halfway back from where I sat. I think he was as scared as his father, maybe more-so, and his legs bounced up and down.

I don't know what possessed me to do it, but I called his name, and had to do it a second and third time before he heard me over the growing whine of the engines. "You going to be okay?" I asked.

"Do I look okay?" he spat.

"Well, if we're going by looks, you're always in trouble," I remarked, my snark finally making a comeback.

He glowered at me. "Look who's talking."

Not the best retort I'd ever heard, and Annar wasn't exactly known for his wit. But on the bright side, his legs stopped bouncing.

I grinned and sat back, studiously avoiding Leif's piercing glare.

The whine of the shuttle grew louder, and I frowned at that – it was *far* louder than the *Hope's* engines sounded from inside, and I figured the transport should have had better insulation. The shuttle rattled as the engines spooled up for takeoff. Then it shook harder. Finally, the craft uneasily lifted from the ground, and jostled us all about, the interior rattling noisily. I think I heard Annar yelp.

This thing felt and sounded like it was about to fall apart!

We ascended straight upwards, slowly, as if the shuttle could barely manage it. I watched through the pilot's window, the little bit I could see in the small gap between us and the cockpit. We reached the top of the trees, and continued on above that. I heard the whine of the engines fluctuate a little, and the copilot's head jerked to his right, and I heard the familiar sound of a computer console beeping as commands were entered. The whine steadied. Mostly.

Finally, the pilot muttered something and started a lazy turn, while adding thrust to the engines, and we started moving. The clouds were growing lighter, and I thought that maybe, just maybe, the storm was finally dissipating. We eventually faced the mountain to the north, and continued a slow, laborious climb, the transport rattling away.

I couldn't help it. I shouted above the whine of the engines, "Why's this thing so shaky?"

"Mika!" Leif hissed.

The copilot looked back at me, his lips pressed into a grimace. "Logs say it's been that way for a century. Combination of misaligned inertial dampers and phase variances in the engines."

I gaped at him. "And no one's fixed it?"

He shrugged. "These old transports don't get much use."

"Stop blabbering to them!" his pilot barked, but his hands were cemented to the control yoke and throttle, both rattling along with the ship.

The copilot regarded the pilot stiffly, and then continued talking anyway, "They aren't a priority to fix, and we only have one engineer left right now."

Left? What did he mean there was only one left?

"I said shut it, Sebastian!" the pilot shouted, a bit more firmly this time.

I glared at him, and then looked at the copilot, at Sebastian, who shrugged helplessly.

"You want me to fix it?" I asked.

Sebastian's mouth quirked. "Uh." He looked at the pilot. "I'm game."

"You can't fix shit," the pilot spat back at me without taking his eyes off of the controls. The mountain ahead looked tall, and if I had to guess, we were only just barely going to clear it. We could just as easily go around, so I wondered at the pilot's competence. This'd be a real quick and horrific way for us all to die…

"I'm an engineer," I insisted. "I can't fix your engines without opening them up, but I can align your dampers."

"How?" the pilot asked, doubtful.

"Unless this thing's worse off than I think it is, through software," I replied with a casual shrug. "Mind if I lean in there and access your central panel?"

For the first time, the pilot glanced over at Sebastian, before gluing his eyes forward again. The transport shook harder.

"Hell with it," he growled out.

Sebastian smiled and motioned for me to come up. "Just hold onto something at all times," he cautioned, and the shuttle jerked as if to drive home his point.

I punched out of the harness, grasped onto a railing on the ceiling and moved to lean over the center console. I paused, glanced back at Hector, and said, "Don't let Karina's father catch you watching my ass." I winked at him.

He stammered, head whipping between me and Leif, and he stammered, "I, uh, wah, no, I wouldn't!"

Chuckling to myself, I looked forward and pushed between the pilot and copilot. The pilot couldn't really move over, but Sebastian leaned away and gave me as much space as he could.

Their control layout wasn't too dissimilar to what I had gotten to know on the *Hope*, so it only took me a second to look over things, and then I tried activating the center panel screen. It gave me a double-kludge error sound, and text blinked across the screen, "Access Denied!"

Sebastian laughed lightly, said, "Sorry, sorry, shoulda thought about that," and he quickly unlocked the console for me with deft fingers. Just like on the *Sirius*, the shuttle's computer was usually keyed to only allow specific users with registered D.N.A. to operate them. At least that system was functioning, though I didn't know about much else.

Once open access was ready, I brought up the appropriate diagnostics display and activated a pre-built subroutine. The shuttle jerked to the side, and I grabbed Sebastian's shoulder to steady myself. "Sorry," I said, and pushed off of him.

"I'm used to it," he remarked with a grin.

I rolled my eyes.

The diagnostic came back and told me what was wrong, and I set to work programming the realignment. It was awkward and uncomfortable, leaning over the center console like I was, and every time the shuttle jostled, I tried really hard not to bump into Sebastian.

Finally, I activated the adjustment, and the alignment started.

The shaking noticeably diminished by the second, until, just as we ascended over the mountain, it was virtually gone. The only time the shuttle shook now was when one of the engines phase-shifted, but that happened far less frequently.

"Well I'll be damned," the pilot spoke with his growly voice and looked at me appreciatively. "You did it."

I beamed at him. "Told ya." I looked ahead to see what lay before us, and then stopped cold. The skies were clearing, beams of sunlight casting down onto a relatively flat surface opposite the mountain. There were still countless trees, but off to port a good distance was a massive lake.

Ahead, and the destination we started descending towards, was the starship *Alpha*.

Or what was left of it.

It was half-buried in the ground, though relatively level as far as I could tell, but the edge of the ship morphed seamlessly into the surrounding forest, as if it had become overgrown. The dome was shattered, shards jutting into the sky. Parts of the superstructure, particularly towards engineering, had collapsed, and at least one sublight engine was wholly missing.

But there was no mistaking the design. It had once looked like the *Sirius*.

It was like looking at my worst nightmare come true.

Sebastian followed my gaze, and said, "Ah, yes. Home, dilapidated sweet home."

"What happened?" I breathed.

With a shrug of one shoulder, Sebastian replied, "We crashed."

I huffed. "Obviously, genius. I mean…why? What caused the crash?"

He shrugged again. "Dunno. It was long before I was born."

The pilot glanced at Sebastian and shook his head. "Yeah, and anything before you were born doesn't matter, huh, kid?"

Sebastian turned his head slowly towards the pilot, and he asked with all the snark I'd expect to hear from myself, "Well then enlighten us, oh wise elder."

The pilot looked ahead and was silent for a moment. "Alright, fine. I admit, I don't know exactly either. All I know is it happened only twenty-one years after the *Alpha* launched. They had to make an emergency landing. Casualties were high, both in the dome and outside. Only a handful of reactors were still intact, so power was a huge issue. Someone was smart enough to eject antimatter storage before we hit atmo-"

"Wait, did you say inside *and* outside the dome?" I interrupted.

The pilot looked back at me and his mouth quirked awkwardly. "Uh, yeah. Why would that surprise you?"

I clamped my mouth shut.

The pieces clicked in my head. The *Sirius* was unmanned outside of the dome, but the *Alpha* had been fully manned.

"Gods," I whispered. "How many casualties in that crash?"

The pilot shrugged and resumed looking forward. "No one knows for sure anymore, but suffice it to say, *most.*"

I blinked at his words. "Most? As in…most people?"

"Yup," he nodded. "If I had to guess, between the dome and the rest of the ship, probably less than a thousand survived."

I stared blankly as we fast-approached the ship, its monolithic size overshadowed by the soil pushed up by its crash and the flora that had overgrown it. I noticed there were patches of green actually on top of the hull now. It was a mess.

It was horrific.

If the *Alpha* had been like the *Sirius,* and manned, then there had probably been at least six thousand people aboard at launch.

I eased back into my seat, my mouth dry, and just sat there, not even bothering to strap in. Rai, Leif and the others must have overheard the conversation, because they too had a solemn, disturbed look.

This could happen to us, I thought. *If I don't get the ship the supplies it needs, we could end up just like them. And most everyone I've ever known will die.*

I clenched my jaw.

I would not let that happen.

I couldn't.

THIRTY-THREE

I didn't pay much attention as the shuttle docked in the landing bay. I was too busy trying to figure out just how we were going to get out of our current predicament and get the supplies we needed. I wished Viden was there to advise me. Granted Leif and Rai were with me, both older than I was, but they were blacksmiths. They hammered all day on recycled iron or other metals, they weren't used to looking for unusual patterns.

Still, they were all I had. That and my own wits and training. I hoped it would be enough.

I did glance up once, and saw we were heading for the port landing bay. Vines hung down from the top of the ship and threatened to get in the way, and a flock of birds scattered from the rusty-looking bay door overhang.

Maybe that was a light of hope. The *Alpha* was obviously in shambles, and if the shuttle was any indication, all of their support craft were in shambles. Maybe all I had to do was cleverly sabotage their missile launchers.

Clever, I thought, and nearly snorted at myself in derision. I didn't feel particularly clever right now.

One of the shuttle's engines phased just as we came into a hover, and we dropped three meters instantly, nearly crashing on the deck. The pilot hissed and cursed while gripping the controls, while Sebastian tried to compensate power levels.

With that last adrenaline surge out of the way, the pilot did his best to land the craft, surprisingly gently, and then I saw his shoulders visibly relax. He called touchdown into his headset, and started spooling the engines down.

Sebastian took his helmet off, showing his short, messy black hair for the first time, and he looked back at me with gray-blue eyes. I was shocked to find a nasty scar on his face, running from the top right of his crown down to stop just shy of his left eyebrow.

"Listen," he started, giving me an awkward grin, "if you're not busy later, maybe you could show me how you fixed the dampers."

Gracing him with a scowl, I asked, "What, you weren't watching?"

He shrugged casually. "I was watching you, not what you were doing."

I felt a blush and a sick feeling fighting for dominance, and I didn't know how to react. He was…flirting with me? And he was doing a horrific job of it, at that. Still, it was unexpected. I was probably the first new person he'd met in his entire life, and his first reaction was to flirt?

My mouth ran away from me and spoke on its own, "Pity you weren't watching my hands. They're rather talented."

Now the blush won out, and the moment I realized what I'd said, I turned away, though not quite fast enough that I just barely saw the smile plastered on his face.

Scowling, I stood up to stalk away, only to bang my head on the low ceiling. I cursed it and its mother, and then turned completely away from him. Annar was smiling, and I rubbed where I'd banged my head. "Not one word, Annar," I snarled.

He covered up a laugh pretending to cough, and then he and everyone else punched out of their seatbelts.

The hatch hadn't opened yet, but just when I was about to grace Sebastian with another scowl, he must have hit the controls, and it jerked and stuttered open.

Leif gave me a narrow-eyed look. I scowled at him and demanded, "What?"

He shook his head and finished extracting himself from the straps.

Once the ramp was down, we all filed out onto the launch deck of the *Alpha*.

To call the sight eerie was an understatement. It was just like the *Sirius's,* but only if the *Sirius* had been allowed to turn to rust. Even after the disaster that nearly ripped her apart, my ship was in far better shape than the *Alpha*. Wall panels and ceiling tiles were missing or were torn to shreds, deck plating rattled under our feet, and I saw no active lights – the bay relied entirely on natural light. *Maybe they're just conserving power*, I thought.

The bay wasn't as full as ours was – I only saw two maintenance shuttles, and one was missing an arm. There were two defense fighters, and Claudia's personal transport was the only one of its kind.

What *was* there was their mining and cargo ship, and I had to give it a double-take – it was in surprisingly good shape. I didn't see any missing pieces, any visible damage, and there was a rather mousy-looking bald girl moving about it, as if performing a maintenance inspection.

Halfway across the bay, I couldn't see all of her features, but when she glanced at me, she graced me with a small smile, and then continued on with her work.

The troops from the other shuttle marched down with military precision, though I wondered how they were able to march so well when they had to stoop out. But then they lined up along the length of their shuttle, weapons at rest, and then turned towards us. The centurion marched over from Claudia's shuttle, and he looked…well, flustered. He inspected the line, barked angrily at a few of his troops, and then clasped his hands behind his back and faced our shuttle, waiting.

We all gathered in a loose assembly, but I noticed that with the exception of Rai and Hector, everyone kept me between them and the troops. Rai and Hector stood side-by-side with me, and I silently thanked them, because I was afraid I'd fall apart without *someone* by my side.

Claudia sauntered over, her hips swaying, and for a brief second, I was hit with her spell again. But she looked at me, and suddenly it was gone. I heard the two men beside me suddenly suck in breaths.

Now they knew. Now *everyone* knew.

Whatever she was doing, she could clearly 'turn it off' whenever she wanted. And back on again.

Had she been trying to seduce the centurion on the flight over?

"Well now," Claudia graced us with her smile. "If you will all follow me." Her smile turned to a harder look, and she added, "And do not deviate from the group."

I nodded, and turned to the rest. "Don't wander, stay close." Looking around at the shambled bay, I added, "Who knows what's safe and what isn't."

When I looked back to Claudia, she regarded me cooly, and I felt a chill run down my spine – I don't think she liked what I'd just said.

Turning to Tiberius, Claudia's voice maintained its liquid smoothness as she commanded, "Centurion, if you would provide us with a small escort."

Snapping his heels together, he nodded, turned, and pointed at four of his troops, and gave the order. "The rest of you are dismissed!"

The four, along with Tiberius, approached and bracketed us, and Claudia led us out of the bay.

After we left the flight deck, the corridors felt slightly claustrophobic, but like the launch bay, these corridors were in rough shape. I half expected the lifts to be non-functional, but then one opened and someone stepped out.

The occupant was a girl, and she wore simple gray cloth for her tunic and pants, and of all things, sandals on her feet. When she saw Claudia coming down the hall, her eyes widened, and she jumped to the side and pressed against the wall, as if terrified of the medici. Granted, Claudia was *very* tall, but the girl's reaction seemed unusually frightened.

Claudia didn't even so much as glance at the girl.

But she glanced up, if only for a moment, at Tiberius.

This was all information that I tried to piece together in my head, to paint a picture of what this…*survivor* society was like. At first, I presumed the hierarchy of Claudia compared to the troops was a command one, but that girl's reaction had me thinking and wondering if it went deeper than that.

Even the wizard Vell didn't command that kind of fear just by being around others. He wasn't a wrathful person in most cases. People respected Vell. Here, people feared Claudia. Except for Tiberius.

Beyond the surface, I wasn't sure what that meant.

Yet.

I eyed the lift and the girl as we passed by, and I wondered why we weren't taking it up to deck two, where I knew the medical bay was. But then I realized that we couldn't all fit on the lift. I also knew that, unlike the aft end of the ship, the fore had a few sets of stairs between decks. I never really understood why, but that's where Claudia took us, and we climbed up several flights to get to deck two.

The medici was quiet the entire way, not even directing us verbally, just leading us. Normally I wasn't one to stay quiet, but I used this opportunity to observe everything. The state of the *Alpha*, the reaction of people we passed – that in and of itself was a new experience to me. I was used to the corridors of the *Sirius* being empty. I was used to being alone. Here, there were *people*. Albeit, not many, but we passed at least two others before we made the stairs.

Throughout the march, I heard nervous whispers behind me, but I couldn't tell who was speaking or what they were saying. All I knew was that everyone, *everyone* in my troupe was afraid, and I wanted to reassure them. But how could I? If I wasn't sure we were safe, how could I make them believe it?

When we reached deck two and stepped out into the corridor, it felt like we had moved into a whole other world.

It was pristine. It was flawless.

The corridors were immaculate and well-maintained. Every light functioned at full power. Everything was *clean*, not a speck of dust. And, stranger still, the corridors were *decorated*, with gold and copper colored draperies and tulle. It was lavish, and given the survival situation, it seemed like an utter waste of material.

Hector murmured, "Did we step through a portal to another world or something?"

I grinned at the irony of his question, but then realized the underlying thought behind it. This wasn't another world, but it was meant to feel like one.

The first person we passed looked nothing like the others we had seen on the lower deck. They had all worn plain, unassuming clothes and looked normal, if disheveled and tired. But the man we passed up here wore a silk gold shirt with elaborate embroidery. He had diamond-studded earrings on, and his pale, milky-white skin was flawless. He was also a few inches taller than Claudia, which was to say, he was very, *very* tall.

Stranger still? His eyes.

They were purple.

I gaped at him, and when he noticed our group, he came to a jarring stop and stared right back at us. "Why, Medici," he spoke, his voice soft and smooth. "You have brought…a group of pets aboard?"

Pets?!

Granting him a placating smile, she replied, "Visitors from another Renovare vessel, Consul Marcus."

"O-oh?" He frowned at us.

Something in Claudia's pleasant smile soured just a bit, her expression becoming…well, *predatory*. "Yes. If you wish, you may accompany us to the medical bay to see test results as they come in."

The Consul keyed on 'test results.' "Oh," he said, and then smiled. "I see. Well I am on my way to the garden to meet with Consul Augustus, but I do look forward to reading the results. As I am sure Caesar shall."

"Indeed," she bowed her head lightly to him. "Good day, Consul."

Claudia continued to lead the way, and I swear Marcus leered at us as we walked by, and all the hairs on my body rose up with a prickle.

Oh, something was very, *very* wrong here. What the hellfire had I gotten us into?

I looked at Hector, and then Leif. They, too, looked extremely uncomfortable. I tried to feel reassured that I was still armed, but I didn't dare touch my weapon, for fear of the escort getting the wrong idea.

I was legitimately scared, in a way I'd never felt before, and for the first time in my life, I swear I felt the cloud of *doom* hovering over us.

Too dramatic?

We'll see…

Finally, after what felt like twice as long as it should have taken, we entered the medical bay.

Like the rest of deck two, it was immaculate, but it was also *sterile*, without any of the extra decorations the rest of the corridors favored. A strange scent stung at my nostrils, similar to alcohol but pure, like something I might use to degrease a moving part on the *Sirius*.

Just like the *Sirius's* main medical bay, the central ward was a giant circle of a room containing countless medical beds lining the wall head-first, and there were several doors that led into other wards. It was clearly meant to service a large crew, and in this instance, it meant that every single one of us had our own beds.

Turning to us, Claudia motioned around and said, "Welcome to my parlor." Oh that didn't help abate the feeling of being trapped by a spider, not at all. "If you would be so kind, I would like every one of you to lie upon a bed, and I shall begin detailed scans immediately, so that I may tailor your vaccines."

I swallowed and nodded to Leif and Hector.

I could tell that *everyone* present felt as uncomfortable as I did, but if Claudia noticed, she didn't say anything. She walked over to the central desk and sat down at a console, immediately logging in and tapping in a flurry of commands that turned on the beds' sensor suites.

"The beds are safe," I assured everyone. Unsurprisingly, Annar looked particularly uncomfortable, but he still also had that dazed look on his face, and he kept sneaking glances at Claudia. "They'll just scan us."

"Um, what does 'scan' mean, exactly?" Hector nervously asked me, even while he moved towards a bed. I walked over to him and chose the bed next to his.

Right. With everything happening so fast, I hadn't bothered to really explain much of what was going on.

How do you explain non-invasive medical scanning technology to pre-industrial people?

They *were* getting more used to technology and the terms associated with it, so I ventured saying, "Basically using advanced systems, it'll record a detailed picture of your body, inside and out."

Hector's eyes widened to great, big saucers, and his face paled considerably. "Uh, w-will it hurt?"

I chuckled and shook my head while climbing onto my chosen bed. "No, you literally will not feel a thing."

"Oh," his shoulders deflated. "Oh, good."

"What's the matter, Hector?" I spoke through another series of giggles, "Afraid of a little pain?"

He didn't shoot me a glare or a withering look. He just swallowed hard. That's when I realized it.

Hector Lee *was* afraid of pain. In a big, big way.

My grin vanished, my giggles died, and I stayed up on my elbows while he climbed onto his bed. "I'm sorry," I said. He didn't say anything, he just glanced at me with forlorn eyes.

Color me surprised – Hector Lee, one of the most popular boys around Rhea, known and adored by all, but especially other boys his age, had a problem with even the prospect of pain.

Gods, I just couldn't figure him out.

And despite wanting to hate him, I really couldn't anymore.

Dammit.

"Please lie down fully to engage all sensors to their full resolution," Claudia impatiently stated. I blushed and looked around, but then noticed I wasn't the only one still leaning up on my elbows – most everyone else was, too, watching Claudia either warily or, more concerning, adoringly.

I tried not to scowl at that. I leaned back against the bed, and waited.

The sensors didn't even so much as hum. The technology must have been performing flawlessly, and I considered that for a moment. Down on the lower decks, things were falling apart. People wore simple, rag-like clothing. They were terrified of her.

Up here, she spoke to that other guy, Consul Marcus, as an equal, and he likewise did to her. He wore immaculate clothing, had unusual eyes.

The picture was growing clearer and clearer, and I wasn't sure I liked it. There was a definite division in the society that had evolved here. I guess in a way, deck two, and probably deck one, was the castle of this society. The rest of the decks were probably all of the 'regular' townsfolk, so to speak.

What bothered me was the fear in that one girl's eyes down by the lift. The way she cowered away from Claudia. The way Claudia didn't even so much as acknowledge her existence.

I didn't always agree with the king and queen, and I hated the idea of having to act 'prim and proper,' but at least they didn't look down upon the people of Rhea, nor did they rule them with an iron fist.

And unlike Rhea, the *Alpha* had what seemed to be a well-trained military.

What did you need a well-trained military for when you're the only humans on a planet? Possibly the only sentient life? Who did they need the military to fight against?

The answer seemed obvious – they were there to keep the peasants in line.

More than ever, I felt like I'd led my people into a trap.

THIRTY-FOUR

The minutes ticked by silently. I didn't know how long these scans usually took, all I knew how to do was fix the beds if something broke on them, so I waited impatiently. I looked over at Hector, whose expression was tight, his eyes clenched shut. His lips moved ever-so-slightly, muttering a prayer or something.

At length, I heard Claudia say, "Oh, yes. Yes, that is promising."

I lifted my head, but couldn't really see her, so I hefted up onto my elbows again. "What's promising?" I asked.

She looked at me with, I kid you not, *hungry* eyes. "You D.N.A., my little pup."

I frowned. "Huh?"

Closing her eyes, Claudia drew in a deep, slow breath and replied, "In due time." She opened her eyes, the smile never leaving her expression, the hunger never wavering. "Once I have vaccinated you all, we may converse." She stood and floated from the room, as if walking on air. "I shall return with your injections shortly." And then she disappeared into what I knew to be one of the labs.

Leaving us in the company of four guards and Tiberius.

The centurion, I noticed, scowled after Claudia.

Hector sat up. "What, um…what do you suppose that was about?"

I frowned and shook my head. "I don't know." Tiberius looked at me, and his expression softened. I had a little trouble reading him, but I swore I saw pity on his face. "But maybe it's time to find out."

I scooted off of the bed and approached Tiberius. The other soldiers tensed, but to their credit, they didn't point weapons at me. Yet. I raised my hands disarmingly, and said, "I just wanted to talk."

The centurion eyed my pistol conspicuously, and he said, "So long. as you keep your hand away from your weapon, you can come closer."

I nodded and closed the distance, though I still gave him a respectful couple meters of space.

After a moment of looking at each other, Tiberius frowned. "Something on your mind, girly?"

My jaw clenched. "For starters, could you not call me that? It brings up some…unpleasant memories."

Giving me a casual shrug, he said, "Sure, whatever."

I wasn't sure how to start the conversation. He didn't seem particularly friendly, or forthcoming, but unless I could get Sebastian into the room at some point, Tiberius was my only point of contact. My only hope of figuring this place out.

I started connecting the dots in my head some more, and I said, "So now that I know the readings we had was the *Alpha's* supplies…I don't suppose there's a way we can negotiate for some of that? Especially deuterium and tritium."

A frown drew deep lines into what I realized was a face that carried a *lot* of worries with it. Laughing a little, he asked, "And just what do you think you have that we might need?"

I shrugged and glanced towards the lab. "I'm not sure yet." I looked him directly in the eye, and asked, "What do you need?"

Tiberius gave me a doubtful, almost comical expression. "More than you can give, probably."

"What's that mean?"

Again, he shrugged. "Well, it depends on who you ask."

"I'm asking you," I pressed.

The humor drained from his face. He looked at one of the other soldiers, who exchanged the look with obvious dubiousness.

"What we want or need," Tiberius said to me, "doesn't matter too much. We do as we're told."

"Because you're soldiers."

"Yeah," he nodded. "And Omegas."

I quirked my head to one side. "Omegas?"

"The end," he nodded. "Or rather, in context, 'those who end.'"

I shook my head. "I don't understand."

He peered at me and said, "You seem to be a lot smarter than I originally thought. Well, sort of," he shrugged yet again, and I figured it was his favorite motion. I tried not to take insult from his words. "I saw you looking around while we came up here. I saw you take extreme notice of a lot of little details."

"You saw a lot," I pointed out.

"It's my job," he once again…yup, you guessed it. Shrugged. "But it ain't yours, is it?"

"Depends on who you ask," I flashed him a smile. "I *am* an engineer now, but before that, I was our town chronicler. My master taught me to look for patterns."

"Chronicler?" he looked at me with sudden curiosity. "Wait, wait, you mean…you're from your ship's dome?"

Eying him, I said, "I thought you already figured that out, given your words over by my shuttle."

Gracing me with an ironic grin, Tiberius nodded. "Yeah, I guess I did figure it out. Ya know, you're kinda hard to pin down, gir…uh, young lady."

"Thanks," I flashed him my teeth again. "So, you were referring to yourself as an Omega, and pointing out my observation skills."

"Yeah. Surely you've noticed there's a hierarchy around here?"

"I noticed," I nodded. "Kinda hard not to notice."

"That's the point," he shrugged, *again*. "The Alphas and the Omegas. Though honestly, those words don't necessarily mean what they used to anymore. Alphas are the beginning, Omegas are the end, or 'least, that's what they used to mean, I've been told. But they were made to mean something else."

Narrowing my eyes, I said, "By the Alphas."

"You catch on quick," he smirked. Was that a compliment or a sarcastic insult? "Now, Alphas are the first in *everything*. They get leadership. They get technology. They get little draperies and fluffy pillows to decorate. They get whatever the hell they want."

Following the train of logic, I said, "And Omega's get…nothing?"

"Just enough," he clarified. "To ensure we can serve them. I say we," he gave his buddy another knowing look, "but frankly, the soldier class doesn't get the short end of the stick as bad as the rest. They know how vital we are. They know that without us, there's no order on this little moon."

I tried not to let the grimace spread across my face, but I'm sure I failed. It was exactly what I'd been thinking.

But to be fair, the ship had been through a lot. "I take it that hierarchy was established after the crash, to try to keep order amongst the ruins."

It hadn't been a question, but he replied as if it were one, "Nope."

I frowned. "Nope?"

"Pretty sure that's what I said."

Huffing a frustrated breath, I said, "What do you mean, 'nope'?"

"It's always been that way, as far as I've been told."

When he didn't elaborate, I clenched my fists. It was worse than talking to Naia. "You mean, before the crash?"

"I mean, before the launch," he replied. "Or so I've-"

"Been told," I finished for him. "Yeah, got that much. Do you believe everything you're told?"

He hesitated. Only for a second, but it was enough to be noticeable. "If I'm told it by an Alpha, yeah," he nodded. "We serve them. They preside over us and give us the best life we deserve." That last part he said with a lot less energy. A lot less gumption. As if he were reciting some memorized code, or something similar. "We are born to serve them. We die serving them. Our children will carry on for us, providing for our eternal masters so that they may advance human society." *Definitely* recitation.

I opened my mouth to ask another question, but was interrupted by the ship's intercom, through which Claudia spoke, *"Centurion, come see me at once, and bring the young princess with you."*

Looking up, Tiberius sighed and replied, "As you command, Medici." Looking at me, he motioned towards the lab, and said, "After you, Your Highness."

I narrowed my eyes, but didn't ask him to stop calling me that. I'd learned a lot about this ship in a short amount of time, and I needed every moment to digest it. Without preamble, I crossed the ward, with Tiberius two steps behind me. The doors parted and permitted me into the lab.

It looked a lot like the medical bay near engineering, a lot smaller than the main ward, with a lot of desks, and two med-beds at the back, both of which could retract into the wall for additional deep scans. On the *Sirius,* those beds didn't have I.A.'s in them, but I had no idea if that held true here.

Claudia stood beside a chair and desk to the left as I entered, and she held in her hands a tray with four dispensers, the blunted-ended ones that somehow just pushed against a carotid artery to infuse medicine into people. I'd used one just like them to wake my friends up after Naia had gassed them.

Ah, good times, good memories…

She waited for us to approach her, and then she handed the tray to Tiberius. "Be a good centurion and have your guards dispense these. I trust you know how to read the scripts, so the correct patient gets the correct injection and dose?"

He scowled at her, "Yeah, yeah, I know how." I could see what he meant about the soldiers being treated better – he wasn't afraid of her in the least. Tiberius grabbed the tray from her, and then, just as he was about to turn to leave, he gave me a look that chilled me to the bone – caution. He wanted me to be careful.

I wasn't sure that was possible.

Once he left and the doors slid closed, I was left alone with Claudia, who gave me the most pleasant smile that she could. "Well, then, young pup. I have examined your scans a little closer, and I have passed the results on to Caesar."

I don't know why exactly, but that made me feel…*violated*. It was one thing to have her scan us to prepare a vaccine, but clearly she had done more than just inspect our immune system, *and* she had passed those results on to someone else without even asking me for permission.

My unease towards her was starting to turn into something a little more hostile.

Her smile grew broader, and my hostility turned back to unease – that sense of being prey returned.

Finally, she finished, "Caesar would like to speak to you."

THIRTY-FIVE

Before we left, Claudia picked up a medicine dispenser like the four she had given the centurion, and she approached me.

I reflexively backed away and held up my hands, fear surging in my chest. "Uh, hold up, just a second," I backpedaled. "You keep using the word vaccine, but what exactly is it?"

She paused and regarded me with narrowed eyes. Had she realized yet that I was from the dome of the *Sirius,* and not a crewmember like her forebearers had been?

After a moment of thoughtful silence, she said, "It is a concoction specially designed to train your body to fight off illnesses common among the Omegas."

I quirked an eyebrow at her, and she searched my expression. I asked, "What about the Alphas?"

A slight, satisfied smile crossed her lips. "We do not experience illness," she said plaintively. "Our immune systems are perfect." Oh, the sheer *arrogance* in her tone...

Looking again at the dispenser, I asked, "But it won't hurt?"

"No," she said with a light laugh. "No, dear pup, it is perfectly safe. Our medical computer is in tip-top shape and has mapped your D.N.A. It was able to tailor the broad-spectrum vaccine to give it the maximum effectiveness with minimal side effects."

I keyed in on what she said, but knew that she wanted to get the injection over with. I lowered my hands and stood up straight, stomping my fear down into the deck plating. While she approached and I arched my head to better expose my neck, I asked, "You said medical computer, but what about your ship's A.I.?"

The cold, blunted end pressed against my neck, and I heard a slight hiss. There was a very slight burn and tingling sensation, but it vanished quickly.

As Claudia backed away and I rubbed at my neck, she replied, "Oh, our A.I. didn't survive the crash."

I nodded, having figured as much. If the *Alpha's* A.I. was constructed like Naia, the sheer damage to this ship would have induced what equated to brain death.

Placing the dispenser on another tray, Claudia turned to me with that wicked smile again, and I felt a prickle crawl up my spine. Gods, she was creepy... "Now, then, young pup. Caesar has taken a great interest in you and your crew."

I blinked in surprise. "Uh, why?"

"You are the first humans to find us in over two hundred years," she replied. "And the results of your D.N.A. scans are quite promising."

I frowned. "Uh, promising in what way?"

"Oh, we'll discuss that soon." Yup. Creepy. "If you would be so kind as to reassure your crew, you and I can be on our way."

She headed for the door, and while I followed, I asked, "Why can't they come with?"

"Caesar only wishes to see you, young pup."

I was starting to get really annoyed at being called a pup. At what point would it no longer be improper to tell her to stop calling me that? For that matter, did I even care if it was proper?

No, not really.

Except...she scared me. In a way no one else ever had.

We walked into the bay just as the soldiers finished distributing the vaccines. Everyone was still sitting up on their respective beds. Tiberius held the empty tray patiently, and one by one, the soldiers placed the dispensers back onto it. Tiberius turned as we approached and offered it to Claudia.

"Medici," he bowed his head. "Vaccines have been distributed."

I looked around at my people, searching for any hint of mistreatment, although I'd begun to suspect they would receive none from the soldiers. Not yet, anyway. Not unless commanded to by the medici, and I suspected she didn't want to alienate us.

Something about our D.N.A.

Something she wanted.

Claudia looked down her nose at the tray, and then at Tiberius, and then sniffed. After a moment of awkward silence, Tiberius sighed and placed the tray on one of the central desks. Then, Claudia looked to me intently.

I walked over to Leif and Hector, and I gave them a quick rundown of the brief conversation I'd just had, before telling them to keep everyone calm and to keep them here, I'd be back soon.

Then, the medici and I left.

A thousand questions burned in my head, and I wanted to ask them all, but I wasn't sure if I'd get a straight answer out of Claudia. Sure, I didn't think she'd lied to me, but any questions she didn't want to directly answer, she evaded skillfully.

It was annoying. It also reminded me of some of the worst qualities that Naia possessed.

I watched her walk, her gait steady, almost rhythmic. Her skirt flowed with hypnotic regularity. Her arms swayed perfectly.

She was the epitome of perfection, and I began to suspect that's what the Alphas were all about. But how much of it was an illusion?

How much of it was engineered?

The idea struck me like a shock, and my pace stuttered when the implications hit me. I knew a *lot* about engineering machines, artificial intelligence, anything mechanical or electronic. I'd already begun to figure out that machines had limits, but those limits could be overcome by advancing technology. In my time alone with Naia, I'd learned that many of the technological wonders aboard the *Sirius* had only just been invented during her construction, or just before, making an otherwise impossibly-large ship possible.

What had *never* occurred to me before was that humans could be engineered, too. I'm not talking cybernetics, like Jonnec's arm, but actual biological engineering. No way that the consul we'd met earlier had naturally purple eyes. No way it was a fluke that he and Claudia, and for that matter, the other occasional Alpha I saw in the corridor now, was naturally a foot or more taller than everyone else I'd ever known, except for Thelon and Marek.

Flawless skin. Flawless hair. Flawless body.

It wasn't natural.

And I wondered something else. Tiberius had said that Omegas, in this context, weren't the end, but instead simply ended. A play on words.

Did that mean that the Alphas somehow…didn't end?

Could you engineer immortality?

We stepped up to a lift, and the doors parted almost immediately. As we stepped on, I asked, "Mind if I ask a rather…improper question?"

"Deck one," Claudia ordered, and then she gave me a curious look. The lift doors closed, and the lift ascended. "Go ahead, young pup."

I ignored the pet name and considered the most polite way to find out what I wanted to know. So, just as the doors opened, I asked, "Were you alive when this ship crashed here?"

Oh, the wicked smile that crossed her face.

She led me out, and I felt my stomach twist. Claudia was old. At least two-hundred forty years old.

And she looked no older than thirty.

What the ever-living hellfire was this house of horrors?

"All of the Alphas were," she finally said, while leading me towards the bow of the ship. Were we headed for the bridge? I wondered what use the bridge was on an immobile ship.

We passed two more alphas. Not a single one bore a scar of any kind, and if they'd all been aboard for the crash, that wasn't possible. Unless their medical tech was capable of healing any wound without leaving a scar.

I thought of Sebastian's scar.

Alphas got the best care.

Omegas got just enough to get by.

Alphas were, apparently, immortal, or otherwise kept alive through medical technology, kept young and healthy. Omegas ended. Omegas died.

The picture of the starship *Alpha* grew ever clearer.

We approached the bridge doors, but then we turned left, towards the port side of the ship. So, not the bridge.

As we continued along, another thought finally occurred to me. Another *startling* thought.

I mused out loud, "Someone told me that, between the dome residents and the ship's crew, less than a thousand survived the crash." Claudia turned her head towards me and smiled, nodding in affirmation. She looked at me as if she were waiting for me to connect the dots, hoping I could figure it out on my own. "Let's say even if a majority of the survivors were dome residents…that's still less than a thousand. And I'm guessing all of the dome residents were Omegas."

We came to a stop before the doors to the captain's quarters, and it dawned on me that of *course* Caesar would live there.

"Indeed," she said. "When I completed inventory, there were less than six hundred Omegas."

Inventory. As if the Omegas were commodities. That soured my stomach a bit.

But that wasn't the point of my line of thought. Claudia turned to me fully and said, "Go on, young pup. You're almost there."

I frowned. "Well, I'm not a doctor or a medic or anything like that, but something about…genetic diversity. That's not enough people."

She gave me a light, breathy chuckle. "No, it is not."

"So, how have the Omegas survived? I guess…well, I don't know what happens when you can't maintain diversity within a population," I admitted. "But shouldn't something bad have happened?" I hated talking about them like they were cattle or something, but I didn't know how else to ask the question.

"Under normal circumstances, yes," she nodded, her tone eager. "However, as you no doubt have figured out by now, we have considerable medical advances at our disposal. Far more advances than you could ever imagine, and never could bargain for."

Again, I was startled by the implication and realization that this woman, this centuries-old woman, hadn't just been with her ship when it crashed, but she'd been around during the ship's construction. She could answer all of the questions I'd had after reading Duncan's journal.

She knew more about the Renovare program.

But more important was the subject of the Omegas and genetic diversity.

Claudia continued, "I have worked tirelessly over the past two centuries to ensure all children born to the Omegas do not suffer from the genetic anomalies inherent to inbreeding, to say nothing about preventing stillbirths or worse. At first, it was rather a simple matter of using biochemical and bioengineering methods to scan and correct such anomalies in unborn fetuses during their earliest stages of development." My brain swirled in confusion, only half of what she was saying making sense to me. "However, I knew that the supplies required to continue to perform such modifications were limited, and needed to be rationed. Which I have done for two centuries. As a result of that rationing, the Omega population has…dwindled, rather than grown."

I nodded in semi-understanding. It wasn't much different from Naia having to ration our raw materials and fuel on the *Sirius*.

But then…

Oh.

Oh gods.

"You said running out."

That wicked, unsettling smile returned to Claudia's face. "Yes," she whispered.

"Which means you can't correct the anomalies for much longer."

She leaned in closer to me, her eyes wide. "Exactly."

"S-so," I started, and my throat caught. I swallowed the lump back, cleared my throat, and asked, "W-what do you need from us?"

Tilting her head to one side, she said very slowly, "You're a clever little pup. You'll figure it out."

Oh, I already had. And I didn't like where this was going, not one bit.

She turned to the doors before us and pressed the button to ring the chime.

A deep voice called out from within, "You may enter."

The doors hissed apart.

And I went deeper into the spider's web.

THIRTY-SIX

Caesar's quarters were dark.

The rest of decks one and two were brightly lit, with gaudy decorative cloth draped *everywhere*, making it a bright, light environment for something so closed off from nature.

But not here.

The lights were dimmed to maybe a quarter of normal, and the drapes and tulle and everything were muted colors, black and greys. It made the over-large room feel small, closed in.

The layout was pretty much identical to what was on the *Sirius*, but it didn't feel like it. There should have been ample sunlight, too, but the polarization on the massive forward-facing window was set to almost maximum, allowing almost no light in, and creating a muted vista of the natural world beyond.

I scanned the quarters, my eyes adjusting to the dimness slowly. I must have passed over Caesar twice, but finally I saw him standing in the living area, directly between me and the window. No, maybe he hadn't been standing there – he must have been sitting on the couch until just now, when I noticed his shoulders and head against the backdrop of the dimmed exterior.

"Hello, Mika Kai," the deep, reverberating voice said.

My eyes continued to adjust, my pupils no doubt opening wide to take in as much light as possible. I was starting to make out details on him.

Blonde hair, tousled in such a way that screamed artificial, fake. He wanted it to look mussed up, but I wagered if I tried to mess it up even more, it wouldn't move, or would go back to the way it was. It was short, too, not long like I'd seen most of the other Alphas wearing.

He had strong, muscled features. His jaw line was sharp and his chin protruded with a dimple. It kinda looked weird, but it also reminded me of some of the illustrations I'd seen in mythology books of 'perfect men' or even portrayals of old-world gods.

His form was strong too, and as he sauntered around the couch to approach us, I realized just how big he was. Taller than Claudia. Taller than anyone I had ever seen. Thelon would have had to look up at him. In fact the only being I'd seen so far that matched his height was the alien's exosuit on the *Sirius*.

He wore a toga. I kid you not, a freaking toga, just like the illustrations in the books. A silver brooch held it in place, but it showed off his chiseled, overly-perfect muscles that flowed and rippled with his movements.

And then, after the doors closed behind us and my eyes fully adjusted, I saw the color of his eyes.

Gold.

Those golden eyes honed in on me, never wavering, not even acknowledging Claudia's presence.

I didn't know what to do. I couldn't think. All I could do was stare at him, enamored and terrified at the same time. He was so much *more* than Claudia, than the consul I'd seen earlier.

He was, for all intents and purposes, a god personified.

Which only made me fear him more. Not because I thought he had a god-like power, I wasn't that gullible. Not anymore.

I was afraid because I knew his attempt to look like a god was intentional. I was afraid because I knew *others* feared him as a god. I knew what that kind of fear could do. I thought of Annar and the Truthspeakers, the violence, the impudence even in the face of a wizard.

If Caesar had ever shown himself to the Omegas, I had absolutely no doubt that they would do anything he ordered them to do without question, if only because of fear.

Suddenly Claudia's hand was on my shoulder, and she pushed me down with incredible force. "Kneel!"

I had no choice but to comply, and I painfully fell to one knee.

"Hey!" I shouted, and batted her hand away.

She made to strike me.

Caesar closed the distance in one giant stride and stopped her hand cold, as solidly as if Claudia had smacked a brick wall.

"Now, now," he shook his head slowly. "There is no need for that yet. Mika does not know better." His deep, thrumming voice sent chills down my spine. I looked up at him, his massive form overshadowing me. I didn't even want to *think* about what was behind the toga in front of my face.

Oh gods, I hoped he would respect my age as much as Claudia had...

Terror gripped my heart when I feared he might not care.

Oh gods, oh gods, oh gods...

I heard Claudia whimper. I looked at Caesar's grip on her, saw her hand darkening. "Y-yes, Caesar," she struggled. "P-please accept my sincerest...apologies."

He held on a moment longer, and then finally let go, leaving behind discolored skin that I knew would turn into a bruise for anyone else. Somehow, I suspected the medici wouldn't let that happen to her skin.

But then Caesar turned his attention down to me. His golden eyes gazed upon me discerningly. Finally, he took two steps back, placed one hand behind the small of his back, and made a lifting motion with his other. "Rise."

My whole body shook, but I did as he asked, fearful that if I pissed him off, he'd just snap my neck in one swift motion and be done with me. So I pushed back onto my feet.

"Mika Kai," he said, slowly, as if testing my name on his tongue, seeing if he liked the flavor or not. Oh, *that* sent a shudder down my body. "I have a proposition for you and your people."

"O-oh?" I asked nervously.

He smiled lightly, but it felt fake, artificial. "Yes. We have a growing problem on the horizon." When he said 'horizon,' he glanced back out the window, as if he meant literal horizon. Looking to me again, he added, "You, and your people, may be the solution."

I knew it was too much to hope for, because I understood what these people were like now, but I said it anyway. "M-maybe we could arrange a trade?"

His fake smile turned genuine, and he bellowed out a laugh. "Perhaps, young one, perhaps." Oh, thank gods he didn't call me pup. "Do you know yet what we need?"

I swallowed back the lump in my throat and glanced at Claudia. She cradled her arm and kept her eyes downturned. I nodded to Caesar.

"You need fresh D.N.A. for your Omegas." I managed to say that instead of calling them what they were – slaves.

"In a manner of speaking, yes," he nodded.

"Maybe in exchange," I ventured, "you could give us what we need?"

The kind of patient expression I'd seen my mother give Phoebus crossed his face. "Oh? And what do you need, young one?"

"Fuel," I said. "Deuterium and tritium."

He tilted his head to one side, his expression changing to one of genuine curiosity. "For what reason?"

I tried to keep the lies and the half-truths straight in my head – what had I already told Claudia? What had I told Tiberius? Had I told them that the *Sirius* was in-system? Gods, I couldn't keep it straight. But then again, this was the time to lay all of the cards on the table. So I told him, "The starship *Sirius* needs fuel."

Caesar's golden eyes narrowed to slits. "You came here in your colony ship? Not another vessel that your colony built?"

My jaw clenched. Crap. I hadn't though of that. It would have been the perfect ruse, but it never occurred to me that, if we had ever been left on a world like we were supposed to, we might have eventually built our own starships to further explore.

But it was too late. The cat was out of the proverbial bag.

I nodded. "Yes."

Realization slowly dawned upon his face, and he folded his arms. "That is unexpected." He glanced towards his living area, towards the couch. I looked over there, but couldn't see what he looked at. "I have read through all registered contestant information for Renovare, and I must confess this has confounded me. The starship *Sirius* was to be uncrewed, run only by artificial intelligence. And," he glanced at Claudia, "your ship was to be one whose dome residents were to be left unaware of the truth. Mika Kai. Descendant of Duncan Kai, I would wager."

Crap. How did he know? Did Duncan's journals contain information about all of the other entries into the Renovare contest?

Or…or was that info stored in the ship's computer?

And Naia had kept it from me?

This wasn't the time or place for such revelations, and I despised my own ignorance.

Claudia drew in a surprised breath. Caesar's eyes flashed towards her. "What is it?"

I glanced at her, and her expression of surprise morphed into one of understanding. "Oh, dear. So *that* was the anomaly I detected. Your session in the Intellectus Apparatus...you received a *massive* amount of information. You did not know the truth before."

"Hmm," Caesar regarded me. I watched him carefully, hoping, wishing he didn't figure it out, but knowing that of *course* he would figure it out.

Except...there was something off about his eyes.

I couldn't see him thinking. I couldn't see the gears turning behind them.

I shuddered at the eerie feeling it gave me.

Nevertheless, he came to the correct conclusion. "You have only recently learned the truth."

I said nothing. I confirmed nothing.

"The starship *Sirius* has been in space for two-hundred forty years," he deduced. "And now, after rationing supplies, your vessel is on the brink of failure. Which prompted your artificial intelligence to force relevant information into your mind, so that you might prevent your own impending doom."

I didn't dare confirm anything he said. I didn't dare let him know just how desperate we were. Instead, I forged on with my original thought. "So? You get our genetic material to help introduce diversity into your Omegas, we get some fuel to help us on our way?"

A light, airy laugh escaped him. "You are a bold one," he mused.

I smirked. "You haven't seen half of my boldness yet."

His eyebrows lifted, and he seemed to find amusement in my statement. Except...those gods damned eyes still looked dead! Like there was nothing behind them.

What. The. Hellfire?

Slowly, in a way that sent an arctic chill down my back, he leaned down towards me, until he was almost nose-to-nose with me. I stared at him, willing him to accept my trade offer. When he didn't speak, I nervously added, "We both win. We both get what we want. Then we part ways and, well...never speak to or see each other again."

Come on. You know it's a good deal!

Then, he stood up and looked to Claudia. "Medici?"

"Samples of D.N.A. are not sufficient," she replied. "We need them to breed with as many other Omegas as possible."

I felt my chest constrict, and my limbs all went numb.

"Ex*cuse* me?!" I whirled on her.

"That is the only way to begin to offset the current predicament," she continued.

Caesar nodded. "I see."

"No!" I screamed. "We are not gods-damned cattle for you to breed!"

Her hand moved faster than I could see. I felt the blow land on my face, and I was down on the deck, my face flashing pain, stars sparkling in my vision.

"Now, now, Medici," Caesar lectured. "You do not want to damage your stock."

I sneered.

"Perhaps not," she agreed, but then she looked at me. "However, if we should wound them too badly, then we will simply have to fly up to their ship and retrieve more breeding stock. I imagine we have at least a few years to exercise that option."

And color drained from my face.

No.

No way.

They couldn't do that! Naia wouldn't let them.

Except…the *Sirius* was in rough shape. Her power reserves low. And if we were held here, then we couldn't refuel her. I knew that plasma generated by fusion reactors was required to power the particle weapons. Power was also required to launch missiles. Power was needed to raise shields and withstand attacks.

Power the *Sirius* didn't have to spare.

The threat was clear, and it was effective.

Myself and the other survivors from the *Hope* were prisoners.

Except…

Except!

Karina, Marek, and maybe Jonnec.

The Alphas didn't know about them yet.

So maybe, just maybe, there was a chance.

"Get up," Claudia demanded.

I swallowed. I wanted to say no. I wanted to defy her. But it would be stupid. She could hurt me, and her threat to attack the *Sirius* was a genuine concern. She and Caesar could easily subdue me in a heartbeat. Hell, if I tried to run, Caesar could catch me in one stride and do who knew what sort of horrific things to me.

We were trapped. We were surrounded.

But I wasn't about to take it lying down. I had to get a signal to Karina. Which meant I had to play along, for now.

So I stood up, and I puffed out my chest and stuck out my chin, and I glared up at Claudia.

She only smiled and looked at Caesar. "With your permission, Caesar."

He nodded. "How long before you can begin?"

"The vaccines will take time to be effective," she replied. "I recommend waiting at least three days before we introduce them to the general population."

"Very well. Quarantine them."

Claudia bowed, and then in an unbelievable blur, she grabbed my wrist and yanked me along, her grip tight enough that I knew it *would* leave a bruise.

"No, NO!" I screamed. "You can't do this!"

"Oh, but we can, darling pup," Claudia sang. "We can and we will." Just as the double-doors parted, she yanked me up, suspending me from my feet by one arm, and she brought me nose-to-nose. "You're *mine* now, darling. And you will do everything I tell you. Or we'll take what we need from your starship, and then *destroy* it."

I shuddered, tears streaming from my eyes.

Phoebus. My parents.

I couldn't let that happen.

She shoved me back down, my legs nearly buckling beneath me, and my whole body shook.

I looked back at Caesar, saw his golden eyes watch me leave. His golden, *dead* eyes.

And with the extra light casting into his quarters from the corridor, I saw something else that made my heart skip a beat, killing my fear for just a moment, shocking me to the core, more than anything else had so far.

Pseudomotion, visible only in the bright light of the corridor.

Blurring features.

Illusion, trying to keep up and cover reality.

I gawked, but if Caesar knew what I saw, he made no show of it.

I recognized that tech. I recognized what it looked like in full lighting, and now, I knew why Caesar kept his quarters so dark.

To hide what he really was.
Caesar wasn't human.

- PART 3 -
REVOLUTION

THIRTY-SEVEN

I drew my pistol and fired at Caesar.

But Claudia was faster! She yanked my gun arm aside at the last possible second. The rust-red beam lanced into the window, a spiderweb of cracks exploding into it, destroying the polarization mechanism. Sunlight pierced the cabin, chasing the shadows away.

Then she broke my elbow.

Pain flashed, I screamed in rage and fury, and my pistol clattered to the deck uselessly. Agony surged through my body, but I lunged at Caesar! Claudia was faster still, and she literally picked me up and slammed me onto the deck, banging my head so hard that I blacked out.

When light again pierced my darkness, I was being dragged through the corridors by my ankle, Claudia lugging me along as if I weighed no more than a sack of potatoes.

I couldn't really move. My arms dragged above my head, my fractured elbow twisting and sending fresh surges of agony, but my body couldn't quite register that pain as anything more than an annoyance. The deck seemed to heave beneath me, and I blacked out again.

Then I was crumpled in a heap on solid, cold carbonate deck plating, and as reality reasserted itself, I heard a distinct, low humming noise.

Pain barreled to the forefront of my consciousness, never absent but suddenly more *real*. I managed to untangle my limbs with a groan, and while I tenderly cradled my arm, I took in my surroundings.

I was in the brig of one of the security offices. Based on the tattered conditions of the walls in the office, I figured I was back on one of the lower decks.

I was back with the Omegas.

A soldier sat on a tall stool at the guard console, idly staring at a data pad. He whistled an unfamiliar tune, and through the noise of pain, that sound grated at me. I tried to stand, but jostled my elbow, and I cried out. His whistling stopped, and he glanced back at me.

I couldn't read his expression, except to see only the slightest sympathy in his eyes, before he resumed reading and whistling.

I managed to get myself up onto the bench at the back of the cell, and I huffed out a breath while leaning heavily against my back. Tears brimmed, mixing with sweat and dirt and burning my eyes. This wasn't right. This *couldn't* be right!

Caesar wasn't human. Caesar *wasn't human,* not even an Alpha. I recognized the shimmer in his movements, the pseudomotion of an illusion trying to keep up with his limbs. There was only one place I had ever seen that before, and it just didn't make sense!

An alien exosuit. How was an alien here, masquerading as the leader of the Alphas? How could they have been duped? Especially Claudia and any other Alphas who had survived the crash, surely they knew!

They had to know!

Right?

Or…

Maybe she was completely ignorant. Gods knew she was *arrogant,* but could she be so arrogant as to miss the most obvious facts in front of her pretentious, perfect nose?

I didn't know. I didn't have all of the facts. It felt like every few minutes, some new Universe-shattering reality was presented to me, and I was *tired.* So gods-damned tired of being behind in the game, of being led around, of struggling against ever-stacked odds.

But if there was an alien here, posing as their Caesar, and they all worshipped him as such…

Oh gods, we were in bigger trouble than I ever imagined.

I looked at the guard, still reading, still untroubled. Ignorant of the truth.

Just like I was for so long.

Gritting my teeth, I pushed onto my feet. The world threatened to flip upside down on me, but I managed to steady myself against the wall, and I approached the humming forcefield separating my cell from the rest of the world.

"Hey," I called for the guard, my voice coarse and harsh.

He stopped whistling, but he didn't look at me.

"Hey, you need to listen to me!"

Slowly, the guard turned to me and quirked an eyebrow.

"You're all in danger, terrible danger," I said, and then stopped. Were they?

Suddenly my claim sounded entirely flat. They'd been here for over two hundred years, and I had to guess that the alien had been here for that long, too.

Right? Or was he a recent arrival? Had he or she or *it* only recently taken the place of Caesar?

I didn't know, which scared me. The Alphas and Omegas probably didn't know, which frightened me even more.

Heaving a sigh, the guard slapped his pad down, stood up, and approached the cell. "Danger of what?" he asked wearily. His voice was deep, and bored.

I tried to figure out how to tell him the truth without sounding crazy. "Your Caesar. He…*it* isn't what you think it is. It's not even human."

Rolling his eyes, the guard remarked, "Yeah, Alphas come off that way all the time. You and your people will get used to it."

My people! "Where are my people?"

"In quarantine," he replied, motioning his head upwards, no doubt towards deck two. "A little nicer place than where you are now."

He turned to leave, and I slammed my fist into the forcefield, frustration boiling within, and the impact sent a static shock through my body, making my arm hairs stand up on end. "Listen to me! Your Caesar is an imposter! He's been replaced!"

The guard snorted a laugh, and he turned back to me. "Right, right, replaced. Like someone could possibly measure up to the Caesar! Tell me, how would an imposter accomplish such a feat?"

"Illusion tech," I said, "and stealth tech. He's not even *human!*"

Barking out more laughter, the guard shook his head and walked away from me, muttering, "We ought to get your head checked out. The medici must have hit you harder than she thought."

"LISTEN!" I screamed, banging my fist on the forcefield again.

But he ignored me and sat back down. Without giving me so much as a second glance, he resumed whistling, and picked up his pad.

"Gods damn, you people are idiots!"

His whistling stopped just long enough for him to glare at me, and then he reached over and pressed something on his console.

A surge of energy pulsed through the forcefield and my whole body convulsed. I gasped, stumbling back and falling onto my butt, while the world seemed to vibrate around me for a second. My broken arm, thank the gods, stopped hurting for a second, as my body registered every nerve ending in exchange.

And then the vibrating faded. The pain returned. The whistling resumed.

He wasn't going to listen to me.

Probably none of them would.

But I *had to try.* I had to figure out something. Claudia had easily subdued me, prevented me from revealing Caesar's true form to her. If only I'd managed to shoot him, it would have disrupted his illusion for just a second! Then she would have seen.

Maybe I could find a way to do it.

I looked down at myself, but my vest had been taken off, along with all of my tools, leaving just my overalls, shirt, and boots. Naturally, they'd taken my shield bracer, too.

I shoved myself back onto my feet and glared at the guard's back. I limped over to the bench and sat down. I tried to think, tried to take stock of my situation, but it was really hard to when the world spun on me and my elbow throbbed. I felt nausea creeping into my stomach, up my esophagus, and grimaced. I feared another concussion, and worried what so many in a matter of months, especially after an I.A. upload, would do to me.

I *had* to think. I had figure this out.

I had to save my people.

I had to save Karina…

Karina!

I looked at the guard. He was oblivious, his eyes fixed on his pad, his incessant whistling still annoying.

Out of habit, I tried to reach my right ear with my wounded arm, and I drew in a quick, pained breath. Then I reached across with my good arm and felt in my ear, and thank the gods, thank the *Oracle,* my earpiece was still in. They'd overlooked that.

At first I was only concerned about the guard, but then I realized there were probably cameras in the cell, and who knew who was watching, or who might review them later.

So I acted like I was scratching my face, and then I tapped my earpiece before I let my hand fall back down. Then, as quietly as I

his pad.

The forcefield was down.

Maybe I could knock him out and escape.

Yeah, right. I tried to stand and got less than an inch up before the world inverted on me again. So I stayed put, and I waited.

For now, I was helpless, and help would have to come to me.

THIRTY-EIGHT

I never heard the guard speak, so when Tiberius walked into the office, I assumed the guard had used his pad to notify the centurion.

They spoke quietly for a moment, and then Tiberius walked into my cell and knelt in front of me. I tried to focus on him, tried to focus on the uniform he had changed into. It was pretty spartan, but the lines were neat and rigid, the fabric stiff and gray, with buttons forming a line down his front. He asked me to follow his finger around, but I couldn't really do it.

Sighing, he nodded. "Yeah, you've got a concussion."

I tried to smile at him, but it felt like it came off weird. "Hey, second one today," I muttered.

Eyebrows shooting up, he asked, "Second? Are you being serious?"

I nodded. "Yeah."

His expression took on a grave look. "The medici should have known that. You're more likely to have complications then. Come on," he reached for my right arm, and the moment he touched it, pain seared through my whole right side and I cried out, louder than I normally would have, but I had to sell it, right?

"Broken elbow," the guard helpfully supplied.

Tiberius winced. "For fuck's sake, she did a number on you."

I shrugged my good shoulder, and said, "I may have earned it."

He didn't laugh. This wasn't a joking matter for him. To be fair, I think I understood. His whole life, his whole *existence* was probably predicated around serving the Alphas, especially the Caesar that I'd tried to kill.

"Stay here," he ordered me and the guard, and he vanished.

Minutes felt like hours, with the pain, the spinning, and the nausea competing for my attention. It all blurred into miserable noise, incessant and unyielding. But when he finally returned, it was with the girl I'd seen earlier in the corridor, the one who had shied away from

Claudia as we walked by, only to risk a look at Tiberius.

While she laid out what I recognized to be an emergency medical kit next to me, Tiberius explained, "Concussion and head trauma. Fractured right elbow."

I nodded, and swallowed back bile. "And, um." I almost threw up, acid burning my throat, but I forced it back down. "Um, my whole body. Slammed to the deck."

Tiberius winced.

The guard went back to his station.

I looked up at Tiberius, and then over at the girl. She met my eyes, and hers were light brown. Dark, curly hair spilled over her shoulders, and I recalled just how short she was, even compared to me, let alone compared to Claudia.

Her eyes, though, I stared at them, and for a moment was lost in them. She felt sympathy for me, and it was so obvious in her expression. Sympathy, concern. Gods, her eyes conveyed so much without her ever speaking a word.

"Hello," she spoke, her voice light. "I'm Livia."

I swallowed more bile back. "Mika Kai."

"Mikakai?"

She'd said it like one word, and I frowned at that. "No, just Mika. Kai is my last name, my family name."

Quirking her head to one side, she asked, "Family name?"

So they didn't have familial last names in this culture. That explained why everyone was only ever one name. Claudia. Tiberius. Sebastian.

Part of me was curious about that, about how they differentiated people with the same first name, but my spinning head didn't really let me dwell on it.

Livia withdrew a pill I recognized from her kit and placed it in my hand, before she handed me a canteen of water. "Swallow this, it'll help with the concussion."

I followed the routine I'd done on the *Hope* before, and swallowed the pill while Livia used a hand scanner to check my body.

Grimacing, she asked, "Are you having trouble breathing?"

I shook my head, but then tested taking a deep breath, and felt pain that stole my breath away from me. "Yes! Yeah, I, oh it hurts. What's wrong?"

"You've got some cracked ribs," she explained, and handed me another pill. "This'll initiate rapid bone healing." I nodded and swallowed it down with another swig of water. "Which," Livia nodded to my right arm, "will help that, too. Once we, um, set it."

Oh. Oh no, I did *not* want to do that…

"Assuming it can be set," she added quietly.

Ice filled my veins. Could my arm be permanently damaged? Oh gods, I hoped not, that was my dominant arm! How could I shoot again without it? Or hold a wrench? Or write?

Livia very, very gently extended my arm out, and I grit my teeth against the sharp pain. Then she asked Tiberius to support my arm while she ran her scanner over my elbow. She held tension in her shoulders while she scanned, but then the tension eased, and I saw her relax just a little. Gods, she couldn't hide her thoughts or emotions if she wanted to, could she?

"Okay, I've seen worse," she gave me an encouraging smile. "This'll heal, but we can't set it by hand. I'll have to use subdermal traction. We should be doing this in the med bay, but I'm guessing the medici doesn't want you in there."

I regarded her carefully, and said, "You know she won't be happy you healed me without her permission."

The girl looked down, and I saw the specter of fear grip her. But Tiberius placed a hand on her shoulder and assured her, "I'll make sure she knows I made you do it."

Livia smiled at him, but it wasn't a pleasant smile. It was a placating one, as if she weren't exactly happy about him taking the blame, either.

"So, um," I glanced at her kit nervously. "Subdermal traction?"

"Another wonder of medical practice," she beamed at me, this time her smile absolutely genuine. But then it faltered, and she said, "But it's gonna hurt."

"Yeah, well," I shrugged, and winced.

Nodding, the girl set her scanner down and picked up a tool I'd never seen in use before. It didn't look all that different from the scanner, and wasn't one I knew how to fix, but that didn't mean much. Most of my engineering knowledge dealt with ship systems, not medical tools.

Tiberius moved around to my other side and took my left hand. "Grip," he said, and I clasped is hand tightly. "Do we have a bit?" he asked Livia.

She grimaced and shook her head. "Nothing that wouldn't hurt her teeth."

He nodded, and then he gave me a serious look. "Don't bite your tongue."

Oh hell. That didn't bode well. "Um, alright," I nodded.

Livia pressed the device into the crook of my elbow, and she looked at me and explained, "This will move your joint into place and partially regenerate the bone and ligaments to secure it. The pill I just gave you will make it heal on its own after that, in about twenty-four hours."

I nodded.

"Ready?"

"No," I shook my head.

"Look at me," Tiberius said. I did, and I stared into his cool, grey eyes. "You wanted me here for more than just this, didn't you?" I swallowed and nodded. "Why?"

"I wanted to ask you about the crash," I said. "I mean, when the *Alpha* crashed."

"What about it?" he asked.

"Do you know why the ship crashed?"

He sighed and looked down, considering the question carefully. "There's a lot of rumors, but nothing concrete on record. Omegas have passed down stories from generation to generation, but they differ somewhat wildly. One account says we were hit with a meteor storm, but I know this ship had sensors and shields, so that makes no sense to me."

I nodded. "Do any of the stories mention an attack?"

His eyes flashed, and he looked up at me.

"Yes," he said.

Something hummed.

My elbow popped, and oh my *gods* the pain and motion startled me and sent fresh jolts of pain up my arm. I think I screamed and cried.

"There we go," Livia said, and set the tool down.

I glared at her, but the sympathetic look she gave me doused my dour attitude. "I'm sorry," she meekly said.

Sighing, I leaned back and said, "It's okay. Thank you." Then I turned my glare on Tiberius. "You were distracting me."

He grunted. "It worked."

I laughed, while Livia gently manipulated my elbow. It hurt to move, but not *nearly* as badly as before. "How's that?"

"Better," I breathed, and winced at my cracked ribs. "But still not perfect."

"Yeah, it'll be hard to move for a while," she said, and started closing up her medkit. "It isn't just the bone, your tendons and muscles are injured, too. They'll all need time to heal."

I flashed a look at Tiberius. "I don't have time to heal."

Narrowing his eyes, he asked, "What do you mean?"

I glanced at the guard, who was busy reading his pad again, and then at Livia, before I looked at Tiberius.

Instead of answering his question directly, I continued our previous conversation by asking, "Tell me about the stories. The ones that mention an attack."

Sighing, he stood up and let go of my hand, while Livia backed away and stood in the corner by the deactivated forcefield. "There's not much to say. We'd been in this star system for nearly a year when we were approached by an unknown ship. It opened fire without warning or provocation. We fought back. We defeated it, but not before it inflicted massive damage. We lost main power, backups were on the verge of failing. The Alphas decided our only hope was to either abandon ship or try to land. The ship's computer determined that the best odds for survival were to stay with the ship and try to crash-land, and that's how we ended up here."

"I see," I nodded, and looked down thoughtfully. "That beginning part sounds familiar."

Frowning, he asked, "What do you mean?"

Meeting his gaze, I told him what happened to us, about the alien ship, and then the alien intruder that we fought, and his illusion technology. Finally, I told him about how I barely defeated the alien by trapping it in our engine core.

Tiberius listened with surprising patience, though I could see a hint of dubiousness on his face.

When all was said and done, he drew in a deep breath and leaned against the wall, crossing his arms. "That's a wild story," he said after a minute of contemplation.

"It's been a wild year," I shrugged. Oh hey, that didn't hurt so badly! And the world wasn't spinning anymore. Thank the gods for small favors.

"So, what?" Tiberius gave me one of his own shrugs. "You think we were attacked by an alien two hundred years ago?"

I met his gaze. "Yes," I whispered.

He didn't laugh. He didn't scowl or give me a scornful look or anything. Tiberius simply stared thoughtfully at me.

"Well, at least we defeated them," he replied, and gave yet another shrug. Gods, he did that a lot. "I imagine if we hadn't, we'd have seen one of them by now."

"Would you know if you had?" I asked.

Gracing me with a smirk, he glanced at Livia and said to me, "I think we would have noticed a mythical creature by now."

"But it can change its illusion," I pointed out. "One of my ship's sarus recorded it as a more human-looking entity, before it engaged stealth tech to counter visual sensors. Then we saw it as a minotaur. Then when the radiation forced it to turn its tech onto a shield setting, I saw its exosuit as it was, a humanoid, metallic suit that was four times the size of the little alien inside. I mean that suit was *huge!* At least seven feet tall, and broad and tough."

"There's nothing we've seen that matches that description," Tiberius frowned down at me. "Not in two hundred years."

"No?" I asked.

"I think my soldiers and I would have noticed and reported it," he growled down at me, his patience clearly waning.

"Oh," I looked down and nodded solemnly. Then I looked again and asked, "How tall is Caesar?"

His and Livia's eyes grew to ultra-wide saucers. He coughed, and managed to sputter out, "Excuse me?"

"How tall is Caesar?" I repeated.

"How the hell should I know?"

"You've never seen him?"

"No," he shook his head. "All of his orders come down to us through our pads and consoles, or through a consul."

"Interesting…" I looked down. "Almost as if he didn't want anyone to see him."

Laughing incredulously, he asked, "I know what you're suggesting, but it's ridiculous! And why would he need to hide?"

"Because in full light, the illusion tech isn't perfect," I replied. "Like a weird shadow effect or blurring of his features when he moves."

Livia gasped.

We both looked at her, and I saw her face slacken. "I…I've seen him," she told Tiberius. "I've accompanied the medici to his quarters a few times, to deliver reports on the Omega population."

So that's why she knew how to treat my wounds, she worked under Claudia in the medbay.

"Tibe, he's…Caesar is huge, *massive!*"

…Did she just call him 'Tibe'?

That's a weird one.

But I could see on Tiberius's face that he wasn't quite convinced. Shaking his head and standing up straight, he planted his fists on his hips and said, "So what? All the Alpha's are big."

"He's bigger," I said. Livia nodded in agreement. I looked at her, and asked, "When you visited, were the lights in his quarters dim?"

"Yeah," she replied. "And his window's were dimmed so much that hardly any light came through."

"I don't think it's because he hates light," I explained. "On my ship, when the alien first attacked, we couldn't tell at all that it was an illusion, because only our emergency lights were on. But the first time I saw it in full light, even from a distance, I could see the blur. Tiberius…when was the last time Caesar made a public appearance?"

His mouth drew into a grimace. He didn't have to answer.

"I think you were attacked by an alien of the same species that attacked my ship," I said. "I think the *Alpha* defeated its ship but didn't destroy it. It survived, and either crashed into this ship, or followed you down to this moon. I think at some point, it replaced your real Caesar. And I think it's been manipulating your people ever since."

Giving me a doubtful look, Tiberius asked, "To what end?"

Now it was my turn to give him a shrug. "To survive. To thrive. To rule over. If I had to guess, your long-range comm systems were destroyed in the crash."

"Obviously," Tiberius said. "Or we would have been rescued long, long ago."

"So why haven't you been?" I asked.

"What?"

"Why haven't you been rescued?" I pressed. "Why haven't your Alphas repaired the comm antenna or built new ones? Why did you immediately try to shoot our shuttles down the instant we made orbit?"

"Well," he hesitated, glancing at Livia, who offered him no help. "W-we've made a life for ourselves here." It was the first time I heard him hesitate, and I felt triumph build in my chest. Maybe I was getting through to him! "We may not be a successful colony, but we've survived despite the hardships."

"You've survived," I nodded. "But I wouldn't say you've thrived. Claudia explained that they're running out of the materials needed to keep anomalies from cropping up in newborns, to prevent miscarriages. And they seem pretty damn intent on keeping the status quo. Keeping Omegas subservient to the Alphas, and if I had to guess, keeping the Alphas subservient to Caesar."

His expression hardened back into doubt. "Why would that matter? That is the way of things. That's how it is back in Alpha Centauri."

I quirked my head to one side. "Alpha Centauri?"

"The star system we launched from," he explained. "That's what it was called."

I had no idea where that was in relation to Sirius, but that didn't matter so much. I'd just questioned their way of life, and he rejected that questioning.

For now.

But I could tell that he was thinking. I could tell that he felt doubt. Maybe I could capitalize on that. "Tiberius, listen. I think you're all being held here against your will, by an alien that doesn't want humans to come rescue you."

"Okay, but why not have his own people come and rescue him?" he asked doubtfully, folding his arms.

"I don't know," I admitted. "That's a piece of the puzzle I haven't found yet. But I saw Caesar. I saw the false-motion, the blur, when light from the corridor spilled onto him. Tiberius, Caesar isn't human! No human would have a need for that kind of tech!"

Gritting his teeth, he shook his head. "Look, you've made some interesting connections, kid, and you've got one hell of an imagination. But you're wrong."

"Tiberius," Livia pressed a hand against his bicep.

"No!" He glared down at her, then back at me. "No, this is just you trying to get under my skin to save your own ass. I sympathize with your situation, kid, but I'm not buying your wild story."

"But…"

"Enough!" he roared. "I shouldn't be listening to you. I let Livia heal you to make sure you survived, now we're done." He spun around and stomped out of the cell.

Livia stared at me and hesitated, and I thought she might try to convince Tiberius that I was right. But she must have doubted me, too, and who could blame them?

I was the stranger. I was the outsider.

"Have the guard contact me if you have any more medical issues," she said, and then she followed Tiberius out. The forcefield sprang to life a second later.

Tiberius looked at me one last time, and then left, with Livia trailing after him.

I slumped on my bench and shook my head.

Sure, it was a start, but how could you convince a civilization that it's been duped for two centuries? Hellfire, I lived that reality and still sometimes had to work to wrap my head around it!

For that matter, we were still tackling that very issue in Rhea. I wondered if there was even an answer to such a puzzle.

But I knew it was the only hope we had, so I stopped thinking about the doom-and-gloom of it, and I considered my options. I mean, not like I had anything better to do. But I figured that the only hope we had was to get someone here, an Omega or even an Alpha, to side with us. To realize the truth. Someone to be an advocate for the truth, like I had tried to be for Rhea.

Maybe it had to be someone a little more even-tempered than me.

Tiberius had been my best hope, and maybe I'd sown the seeds of doubt, but we didn't have an unlimited time. I was *not* going to let Claudia and Caesar…*breed* us.

No way was my first time going to be forced on me!

I was so intent on my thoughts that I was startled when I heard a voice whisper in my ear, *"Mika!"*

I jumped and eeped, and the guard gave me a weird look. I smiled nervously, mind racing for a way to throw him off. So I waved with my right arm, wincing at a twinge of pain, and I said, "Feeling much better now, thanks!"

He grumbled something and went back to reading.

"Mika, are you there?" Karina whispered through the comm.

I reached across again and pretended to scratch, and then tapped my earpiece. "Karina?" I whispered.

"Oh, thank the gods, you're alright!" I could hear the relief heavy in her voice.

"I was about to say the same thing," I said, wishing so much I could hold my girl right then and there. "Gods, Karina, so much as happened since you left the *Hope.*"

"Yeah, same here," she replied. *"Sorry about earlier, but we were being tracked. I think they know we're out here."*

I tensed at that. If that was true, then it was only a matter of time before she was caught. "How'd you evade their sensors?"

"By doing something clever with my own scanner," she said, and I could practically see the prideful grin on her face. *"I don't think it's supposed to do what I've got it doing, but it works. And by the way, we found Jonnec, and he's okay!"*

I practically screamed in happiness and had to clamp my hands over my mouth. The guard must have thought the noises I'd made were stupid attempts to distract him, and he studiously ignored me.

"Thank the gods," I whispered. "How did he survive the crash?"

"Because whoever designed our ships are a lot smarter than we are," she replied, half-laughing as she spoke. *"They have emergency forcefields on the pilot and copilot's chairs. Did you know that?"*

I blinked in surprise, and tried to remember everything the I.A. had downloaded into my brain about the cargo ships. "Um," I started. "Maybe?" Honestly, no, I didn't remember anything about those forcefields.

Weird.

"Anyway, Jonnec's awake and glaring daggers at me," Karina continued, a bit of playfulness in her voice, *"but he took a beating. I've got him patched up as well as I can, but he's hardly in any condition to fight."* There was a moment of pause, and I heard a muffled voice before Karina sighed. *"No, it's not your fault, Princely. I'm just glad you're alive."*

So was I. I hadn't thought it possible for anyone to survive that crash, but clearly something had been missed by the I.A. download. Or I had forgotten it, which was an even more disturbing thought.

Still, it was a huge relief. *Thank you, whoever designed that ship*, I thought.

"Mika, What's your status?" Karina asked.

I grimaced. "This…is going to take a while to explain."

THIRTY-NINE

I spent the next several minutes explaining everything to Karina. She listened patiently and quietly, though I imagined she was only quiet because they were hiding and running from search parties.

At one point, my guard let out a frustrated sigh and turned to face me, and I clamped my mouth shut. "What the *hell* are you muttering on about?" he groaned.

I gave him the stink-eye. "I'm talking to myself, alright?"

"To yourself." He looked at me like I was crazy.

"Yeah, it helps me think," I said with only moderate venom in my voice.

"Well think a little quieter, would you?" He shook his head and turned back to his console and his pad. I heard him mutter, "Gods, why did I get stuck with this nutjob?"

I watched him for a moment longer, and then turned around so he couldn't see my face.

"Sorry," I whispered, and then I finished telling Karina everything.

After a long moment of silence, she asked, *"And you're absolutely sure it's another alien intelligence?"*

I shrugged one shoulder, even though she couldn't see. "Well, pretty sure, but not positive. I mean, it's possible this is still the original Caesar, and he got the illusion tech from the alien they defeated two hundred years ago. But then why cast an illusion on himself?"

"Yeah, that doesn't sound very likely, does it?" I heard her sigh. *"Well, what do we do about it?"*

I thought about it some more. And frankly, I wasn't lying to the guard – I think better when I think out loud. "Well, I had thought about trying to steal one of their cargo ships, after loading it up with deuterium and tritium."

"Yeah, 'cause that's an easy thing to accomplish," Karina snarked at me.

"Hey, leave the snark to me," I said through a chuckle. But then I shook my head, "But you're right, that's not exactly an easy thing. Even if I managed to get out of my cell and find the rest of the crew, loading up a shuttle with supplies from their own fuel reserves would *probably* draw a lot of attention. Not to mention taking off and avoiding missiles."

"Sounds like suicide to me," she grumbled. *"You'd probably have an easier time convincing them to join us."*

I didn't say anything. I let the silence do my talking, a lesson I'd learned from the queen.

The silence lasted a moment. Then a minute. Then I heard a groan on the other side. *"Mika. What are you thinking?"*

"That we do exactly what you just said," I whispered back. "We turn the Omegas, and maybe even the Alphas, against Caesar."

"That's crazy, Mika," Karina lectured. *"You just told me they revere him with almost god-like reverence, why would they turn on him?"*

"He's a lie," I pointed out. "He's not really their Caesar, why would they continue to follow him after the truth comes out?"

There was a distinct pause. Then, with only a hint of sarcasm, she asked, *"Yes, why would a people choose to follow a lie even after the truth came out?"*

I clamped my mouth shut. She had a fair point. Rhea was the perfect example of that. The Truthspeakers rejected all statements that contradicted the reality we'd known for two centuries, no matter what. Though I imagined Annar would have a hard time refuting the truth now.

Annar. Oh, he still hated me, that much was clear from the looks he kept giving me, but as far as I could tell, he'd come to accept reality since we'd landed on Ravenna. How *could* someone ignore the truth when you boarded a shuttle, flew to another planet, crashed on that planet, and then met people from another world? Not to mention the technology he'd been exposed to almost continuously for the past twenty-four hours.

That's when I realized what we needed.

"We give them hard evidence," I murmured.

"Like what?"

"Well, if worse comes to worse, a body," I said, and felt the burn of bile rising again. I didn't like the idea of killing anyone or any*thing*, but I couldn't imagine this alien had the best of intentions in mind.

Then again, maybe he did.

I considered that possibility for a heartbeat, but rejected it a moment later. He'd hidden himself, lied to everyone, and used the Alphas and Omegas as slaves to cater to his whims. At least, that was the impression I had of him. I couldn't believe that he had good intentions when I considered all of those factors.

"That's pretty dark," Karina spoke, worry in her voice. *"Especially for you."*

I swallowed back the bile. "Yeah. Well, let's hope it doesn't come to that, but if this alien is *anything* like the one on the *Sirius-"*

"Mika, they're from two different centuries," she pointed out. *"And even if that wasn't the case, you can't assume they're the same just because they're from the same species."*

I wanted to refute her words, and I started to, but then stopped. No, she was right. I hated to admit it, but she really was right. I couldn't judge this alien based on the actions of another of its species.

For that matter, I was assuming they were the same species.

"Dammit," I hissed. "I just don't have enough information."

"So get some more information," she said. *"Observe. Watch. Listen."*

"We don't have time! For now I'm stuck in here, but come the end of quarantine, they're gonna force us to…" I swallowed back more acid. "To…to *breed.* I'm not going to let them do that to me *or* anyone else, Karina. Period."

"No," she sounded defeated. *"You're right. We can't let them do that. Who knows how they would coerce or force the issue."*

I shuddered to think what methods they had at their disposal. Sure, the starship *Alpha* was in bad shape, but clearly a lot of their technology had either survived or been repaired. With each passing hour, I found new technology to admire, stuff that was either buried in the back of my I.A. download, or wasn't even a part of it. Especially the medical tech.

"It really comes down to one fact," I finally said. "One fact that neither of us can refute. They deserve to know the truth." Karina didn't say anything to that, so I pressed on, "They deserve the truth, and they deserve the *choice* of what to do with the truth."

Again, another sigh. *"Yeah, I agree. It's just gonna cause a lot of conflict and chaos."*

"And if we have to, we escape during the chaos." But then I thought of Livia. Of Tiberius, and Sebastian. Then I thought of Claudia, how she treated them. If they took down Caesar, chances were high that the status quo might otherwise remain the same.

The Alphas would still rule over the Omegas, treating them like slaves.

Leaving them to that fate didn't sit well with me.

Blame all of the novels I'd read, blame all of the mythologies that included political discourse and proclaimed freedom and equality as being necessary and worthy goals. Blame whatever you wanted to, but I *hated* the idea of leaving anyone to such a fate.

I wanted to tear this place's system down bulkhead by bulkhead almost as badly as I wanted to tear down Rhea's system.

Karina would talk me down from that cliff, so I didn't mention it. I just said, "I'm going to see if I can't talk to Claudia tomorrow. She'll probably want to check up on me after letting me suffer overnight."

"You hope."

I shrugged against the stiffness in my arm. "It's all I've got for now. In the meantime, I've already sown doubt into the centurion's heart. Maybe he'll come help."

"That's a big maybe, Mika. But…" I could imagine her nodding. *"I think it's a good idea."*

"What about you? What will you three do?"

"For now, we need to get as far away from the crash site as we can and then rest. We'll start off heading in your direction, but we can't climb that mountain, we'll have to go around. Even if Jonnec heals fast, I imagine it'll be at least a day before we can make it to your position."

"Alright," I nodded. "And maybe we'll be in contact with Naia by then."

"Yeah, maybe. I'll update you as we go."

"Maybe best not to," I said, hating my words even as I spoke them. "Let's keep contact limited for now, in case they can track our comms. Don't want to lead them to you."

"Yeah…good point." The disappointment in her voice was palpable.

I let the comm hang silent for a minute, and then I swallowed and said, "Be careful, Karina."

"You too, Mika."

I hesitated, and then, after pretending to itch my ear again, I clicked the channel closed.

FORTY

Maybe it was all of the concussions. Or maybe it had just been a really, really, *really* long day, but I fell asleep sitting up, and I must have slept for hours.

When I awoke, it was to a great big mass hovering over me. I jerked and eeped, and that elicited a smile from Claudia, who had apparently entered my cell without waking me.

Gods, she was tall.

And creepy.

"Hello, pup," she cooed. "Sleep well?"

Not thinking straight yet, I spat back, "Only until I smelled your breath."

Her smile vanished. I regretted my words a second later, remembering that I needed her on my side. Or at least, not against me. Backpedaling, I wiped sleep from my eyes and said, "Sorry. Sarcasm is an automatic reaction to being held prisoner."

Her smile didn't return. "Well you did try to kill my Caesar."

"It wouldn't have killed him," I remarked.

"Oh?" she asked. "I examined your weapon afterwards, young pup. It was set high enough to kill anyone."

"Except for him," I remarked. "I mean, unless if you're talking about the *real* Caesar. He's already dead." I thought about it, and amended, "Probably."

That made Claudia pause, and she looked up at my forehead. "I must have hit you harder than even I realized. Come, let us examine you for injuries."

I looked up at her defiantly, and then stretched out my right arm, showing her that my elbow was just fine. It was still stiff, but that long sleep had done wonders to help it heal, along with my cracked ribs. That second pill was working wonders!

She stared at my elbow with a frown, but then realization softened her features. "Who healed you?"

I said nothing.

Huffing out a sigh, she said, "Very well, I shall check the entry logs."

Claudia turned to leave, and I said, "You were alive when this ship was attacked, weren't you?"

She stopped at the threshold of my cell, but kept her back to me. She wore different clothes today, a gold and silver blouse and flowing, loose-fitting trousers, an extremely casual look for her that none-the-less managed to make her look gorgeous. Especially from behind.

I blinked away that thought, and then waited for her to say something else. To acknowledge my question.

Slowly, as if wary of a trap, she turned her head, though she didn't fully look at me. "How do you know of the attack?"

"A little bird told me," I said, showing her my teeth. "So tell me, who was the attacker?"

I wanted to hear her answer, wanted to hear her first-hand account. She owed me nothing, and probably thought me dangerous and unstable, but maybe, just maybe, if I could start to sow the seeds of doubt within her as well, I could get my people out of here safely.

When she didn't speak or move, I decided to take the initiative some more. "We were attacked a few months ago. A ship whose hull was black as night and damn-near invincible. It did some weird things to our sensors, too, we couldn't really get a fix on its size or shape. And despite being a fraction of the size of the *Sirius*, it inflicted considerable damage against us."

Now Claudia turned to face me fully, a curious frown on her face. I had her attention. Time to capitalize on it.

Something both the queen and Viden had taught me was to lead people on the journey to discovery, rather than just give them the answers. So I continued my story. "It took out our long-range comms, probably because the attackers didn't know we weren't anywhere near reinforcements. It attacked our weapons next, but our A.I. managed to damage it enough to stop its attack. Then it rammed into our hull at ten-thousand kilometers per hour."

She quirked an eyebrow at me. "Yet your ship remains intact?" Then realization dawned upon her face. "That is why you seek supplies and fuel."

"Partly," I nodded. "And partly because one of the attackers survived that impact and started sabotaging our ship."

That realization startled her. "A survivor? Impossible."

"Improbable," I corrected, lifting an index finger like the queen sometimes did during her lectures. "It helped that the occupant wasn't human."

Claudia's expression darkened, but she didn't refute that claim as impossible.

"It was an intelligent alien," I continued. "In an exosuit with technology far more sophisticated than anything aboard the *Sirius*. It was able to disguise itself with illusion tech while simultaneously hiding itself from all sensors. It looked like a giant minotaur. You know, seven feet tall, broad and muscular. Its eyes glowed now and again, but the real telltale that it was just an illusion? In full light, I saw its movements blur, as if the tech couldn't keep up with the unexpected motion."

Now her eyes narrowed at me. "Why are you telling me this?"

I grunted as I pushed onto my feet, and though I was a *lot* shorter, I stood up to her and said, "Because I think the ship that brought the *Alpha* down was from the same species." I looked around at the prison cell, and said, "Given that your ship is as powerful and advanced as ours, I'm guessing the one that attacked you was bigger. Or more heavily armed, who knows. Or maybe our A.I. just got a lucky shot in. Either way, I fought that survivor, several times." My voice wavered when I added, "It killed one of my friends. I shot it, Claudia. I shot it with a particle weapon and all it did was disrupt its illusion for a second. It didn't hurt it. Didn't kill it." Drawing in a deep breath through my nose, I folded my arms in front of me and said, "That's why I said I wouldn't have killed your Caesar."

I saw her mind work at lightning speed. She wasn't stupid, and surely after two centuries, she would have had her own suspicions. And I saw the moment she came to the conclusion I was hoping for.

Narrowing her eyes, she spun around and stalked from my cell, passing by the guard station without a word. The guard, different from yesterday's, gaped as she went, then looked back at me with a frown. I recognized him from the second transport that had escorted us in. In fact, he was one of the soldiers who had helped dispense the vaccines to my people.

I wondered how much he had overheard.

I also wondered if he would reactivate my cell. The medici hadn't told him to.

But, dutiful as he was, he finally remembered his job, and he tapped the command in his console, snapping the blue-white forcefield on.

I stepped closer to it and stared at him. He stared right back, perplexed and even a little scared.

Good. Scared was good.

Because if I was right, if Caesar was really what I thought he was, then I had just kicked the bee's nest. No, scratch that, it was worse than that.

But I couldn't count on just the medici. So I said to the guard, "I'd like to see Centurion Tiberius, please."

***

It didn't take much convincing before the guard agreed to summon Tiberius. Unfortunately, Tiberius must not have felt a need to acquiesce, because after at least an hour had passed, he still hadn't shown up.

I started pacing my cell nervously. Every hour in this damned cell was an hour closer to the end of our quarantine, and I had a lot of work to do if I was going to save us all. As long as I was trapped in here, my hands were more-or-less tied.

I kept reaching for my ear, wanting to hear a familiar voice, needing to know that Karina was safe, but I resisted that temptation. A stray signal could give away her position, or if someone watching a security feed noticed, they might realize their mistake and take the earpiece away.

How long since I'd last talked to Karina? How long had I slept? I assumed it was morning, due to the change of guard and the medici's presence earlier, but how far into morning? How long since we'd launched from the *Sirius*?

In Rhea, it had always been so easy to know how much time passed, just by watching the sun or the shadows, or the movement of the stars. In the corridors of the *Sirius*, it was harder, but a lot of rooms, and especially all of the computer systems I worked with regularly, had chronometers on them, always showing 'ship time,' which was always synched with the day cycle in Rhea.

Now, to be stuck in a cell with no windows, no chronometer, no *nothing*, it was driving me insane.

My stomach started to grumble really, really loudly. There was what equated to a drinking fountain over the toilet in my cell (which, let me tell you, having to go to the bathroom in full view of the guard was *not* comfortable, but at least he kept his back to me at all times), but I'd not eaten anything since yesterday, and a lot of that had ended up coming back up the wrong way after my…first concussion? Second? First of the day, second overall? Gods, I was starting to lose track of my injuries.

So, when Tiberius arrived with a tray of food, I practically leapt at the forcefield in hungry anticipation.

"Lower the forcefield," he nodded to the guard. And then he looked very intently at me and spoke with a hard edge, "Back up."

It was hard to command my body to follow that order, but I did. And then, with a buzz of grounding energy, the forcefield vanished. He stepped inside slowly and offered me the tray.

The scent of grilled vegetables wafted into my nostrils, and I instantly felt saliva pooling in my mouth. There were scrambled eggs, too. No meat, though, but I didn't care, it was *food*. So I took the tray without preamble, sat on the bench and, ignoring the fact that he hadn't provided me any utensils, I set to eating by hand. Everything was warm at best, and the eggs in particular were ice-cold, but that really didn't matter to me.

I'd scarfed down half of my plate by the time I looked up at Tiberius, who leaned against the wall with his arms folded, an amused expression on his face.

"Oh, do you like seeing half-starved prisoners eating like animals?" I growled at him.

"No," he shrugged. Gods, I kinda wished he'd stop doing that now. "Just you."

I glowered, and then kept eating.

"I heard you wanted to see me."

Gulping down a broccoli stalk, I nodded. But then I frowned at the plate and asked, "Where do you get the vegetables from?"

Frowning at the question, he replied, "Gardens outside of the ship."

I quirked my head to one side. "Not from the dome?"

Shaking his head, he replied, "There was a radiation leak from engineering that washed over the dome after we crashed. It's still too dangerous to go in there."

That sounded weird. Weirder still was that these were all vegetables I was familiar with, so I asked, "Where'd you get the seed for these?"

"I dunno," he said. You can guess how he moved his body when he said that. "Probably cold storage backups. Same with the eggs that hatched the chickens our farmers tend to."

"Cold storage?" I asked doubtfully. "I'm not familiar with any cold storage on the *Sirius.*"

Tiberius shifted uncomfortably. "Well, this isn't the *Sirius,* is it?"

He had a fair point, but so far, everything I'd seen on the *Alpha* was pretty much identical to the *Sirius,* critical damage notwithstanding.

But if there was radiation, then that basically meant that the dome was off limits to Omegas. What about the Alphas?

"Why did you want to see me?" Tiberius pressed.

"Have you thought about what I said yesterday?"

"Which part?" he asked. I gaped up at him, but he quickly added, "Oh, you mean the insane part where you said my people's leader had been replaced by an alien?" He shook his head. "I did, but then I realized you'd hit your head pretty hard, *and* you're an outsider, so I stopped thinking about it and had the most sound sleep imaginable."

At first I was annoyed. But then I frowned and thought about it. Shaking my head, I said, "Nnnnoooo. No, I don't buy it. You're not that stupid." He gave me a dark look. "Enough of what I said was verifiable. And when I pointed it out to your medici this morning, it gave her pause too."

That stopped any smart ass remark he had on the tip of his tongue. Tiberius gaped at me and said, "Claudia was here?"

I took another big bite and nodded.

"And you told her what you told me?"

Shrugging one shoulder, I said, "Not in so many words. I let her figure it out. And she did." At least, I think she did.

Through narrowed eyes, he said, "You're lying."

"Ask your guard."

Tiberius craned his neck around, and I saw the guard give him a pale, ghostly expression. Tiberius turned and watched me eat the last bit of cold eggs. Then he turned to leave. "Hey!" I stopped him. "I want to see my people."

"They're in quarantine," he replied.

"So am I."

He looked at me, and then sighed before he stalked off.

Gods, people liked doing that around here.

FORTY-ONE

By the time anything else happened, I was hungry again. After I'd finished my breakfast, I'd paced more often than not, and I pestered the guard incessantly, but he was good at ignoring me.

Except for the pale looks he kept giving me. His eyes were haunted, and he looked genuinely worried over my conversation with the medici. I also noticed him furiously tapping on his pad now and again, and I wondered if he was chatting with friends. I hoped so. I hoped fear and suspicion spread amongst the soldiers, and maybe even the rest of the Omegas.

Finally, the first guard from yesterday entered the security office, and he urgently said, "We're to escort the prisoner, now." He handed the current guard a data pad, who regarded it with a cursory glance before lowering the forcefield. "Come with me!"

Adrenaline surged in my system, and I practically leapt out of my cell, glad to *finally* be free of that timeless prison. "What's going on?" I asked.

Naturally, the soldier ignored me, but the current guard slapped a pair of electromagnetic shackles around my wrist. I glared at him, but he wasn't playing along – he took his job seriously, and he took me even more seriously.

Good.

The two of them escorted me through the dilapidated corridors of deck three, eventually bringing us to a lift and riding up to deck two. Eventually we came to the medical bay, but not into the primary ward. We went down to another area, and then, after typing in an unlock key onto a panel, the doors parted, and I got to see my people again.

I guessed it was a quarantine room, with bunk beds and a small bathroom at the back. It looked like everyone was there, but I immediately did a quick headcount of those I could see. There seemed to be one missing, but at least six of them were hovering around a single bed, Hector among them. When I came in, Hector turned, saw me, and the hard expression on his face lightened. "Mika!"

At the prodding of the guards, I entered the room, and Hector crossed the distance in a rush.

When he moved away from the bed, I saw Livia sitting on a chair next to it, waving her medical scanner over the one missing person.

Leif. Karina's father lay in bed, and his skin was pale and clammy. I felt my heart skip a beat.

Hector grabbed my shackled arms and yanked me closer. "It's Leif," he said. "He's sick, been sick all day."

I yanked back against Hector's grip, sudden fear gripping me. Illness was more or less unheard of in Rhea, and now I knew why — the closed environment combined with the nanites flowing through our blood. But I'd read about illness, I'd read about *plagues.* Fiction or no, getting sick and dying from severe illness was a real fear that most people had.

"What's wrong with him?" I asked.

Livia saw me and stopped scanning long enough to examine the readings more closely on her device. "It looks like he has a variant of the flu," she said. Looking into my eyes with a deep, consoling expression, she said, "but his body doesn't know how to fight it, and his nanites are shutting down faster than they can fight the virus."

She stood up and approached me, and I instinctively backed away from her. "Woh, aren't you contagious now or something?"

Giving me a plaintive smile, she backpedaled to the bunk, and then reached towards Leif. A forcefield sprang to life the instant she touched it, but unlike my cell, it let her hand through. "Medical quarantine field," she said. "Keeps the two areas separate, and scrubs my hand when I pull it back out," which she did as she spoke. "And lets me scan through it."

I tried to relax. I knew about medical quarantine fields, but I hadn't expected them on the bunkbeds. I tried to think if we had a quarantine room in the *Sirius,* but that knowledge eluded me for the moment.

While Livia approached, Hector looked at my shackled hands, and then he glared at the soldiers. "You can take these off," he lifted my hands up.

Today's cell guard shook his head. "They stay on until she's back in her cell."

I rolled my eyes at him. "This is the medical quarantine, boys, what could I possibly do?"

"Attack us," yesterday's guard said. "Like you did Caesar." The other guy eyed him curiously.

I gave them both a wicked smile. "I'd only do that if you deserved it. Now you boys aren't going to do anything horrific to me, are you?"

"Wait, so they weren't lying?" Hector gaped at me. "You really did try to kill their leader?"

Hesitant, I amended, "It's a little more complicated than that." Livia came up next to us.

I asked her, "Is Leif going to be okay?"

I'd hoped for an instant reassurance, but she didn't give it. Instead, she slowly sighed and regarded her scanning tool again. "I don't know. He was infected too soon, the vaccine hasn't had a chance to fully take effect. Frankly, we should have never let any of you interact with the soldiers so freely. And you," she nodded at me, "are at the greatest risk now. I'm surprised he got sick and you didn't."

Looking between her and Hector, I said, "I feel fine."

"I know," she nodded. "May I scan you?"

"Sure, of course," I said with a shrug, and then second-guessed that action. Dammit, now thanks to Tiberius, I was going to criticize myself every time I shrugged.

Livia reactivated her scanner and walked a slow circle around me, methodically running the device up and down my body, down to my knees, back up to my head. I didn't feel nearly as violated as I had when Claudia scanned me.

When she was in front of me again, Livia examined the readings on the device and frowned. "Huh. You *do* have the pathogen in your system, but your nanites are fighting it off. Why would yours be more effective?"

"Um," I glanced at Hector. "I, uh, I don't know. Honestly I don't really know much about the nanites. All I know is that they're programmed by Naia."

Livia quirked her eyebrow at me. "Naia?"

"Sorry," I shook my head. "Our ship's artificial intelligence."

Eyes widening, she asked excitedly, "Your A.I. still functions?"

"Yeah," I nodded. "I talked to her all the time on the ship."

I kid you not, her eyes lit up upon hearing that. "Oh, how I'd love to meet her!" She stared off into nothing for a second, and then blinked her eyes, and her cheeks turned dark colors. "I'm sorry. I've read records in our archives about this ship's A.I., and I've just always found the idea fascinating. Our surviving computers have rudimentary intelligence at best, so…I've always wondered what an A.I. would be like."

"She's a bit of a prude," I remarked. Both Livia and Hector's eyebrows shot up in surprise, and I suddenly felt self-conscious. I quickly amended, "But when you get her going, she's a real conversationalist." Shaking my head, I said, "But never mind that. What can we do about Leif?"

Realizing she'd let the topic wander, too, Livia cleared her throat, and again looked at her scanner. "Well, there's not much I can do. I've given him all of the medicine I can, and I'm keeping his temperature down for now."

"Can't you extract my nanites and use them on him?"

The moment I said it, knowledge inserted itself into my conscious thoughts that told me no, and Livia confirmed those thoughts. "No, they aren't programmed to operate in his body. They'd shut down. But obviously nanites can help. So unless his body figures out how to augment and fight back too, which could happen…" She sighed and shook her head, looking back at Leif. "His best hope is to get back to your ship, so that he can get fresh nanites infused into his system."

Get back to the *Sirius*.

Which was already the plan, and for which we had to hurry already. But… "How long does he have?"

"I have no way of knowing," she looked at me, her dark eyes piercing mine, haunting me. "I'm sorry."

Clenching my fists, and my jaw, I closed my eyes and tried to control the rising fury inside of me. I didn't care much for Leif, but he was Karina's father. How would she take it if he died? How would her mother take it?

I opened my eyes and looked at Annar, who stood vigil at his father's bedside. Would he blame me?

I'd not had a chance to ask Karina about her family and the Truthspeakers. Annar had stood separate from them during the gathering in town square the other day, but had he forsaken his familial bonds? If so, why did he look like he was about to lose his mind over his father's illness?

"Then again," Livia said quietly. "It may be that it isn't just him that needs to get back to your ship."

I frowned at her. "How do you mean?"

"Well," she hesitated, and looked again at her device. "I've been scanning everyone here all morning, ever since…Leif, is his name?" I nodded. "Ever since he started experiencing symptoms. No one else appeared to be infected, surprisingly, but everyone's nanites are still functional. It's possible their nanites already fully eliminated any infection. The fact that there's any hint of the flu in your system may be an indication that your nanites are already starting to fail."

Continuing on, despite the increasingly confused expression I felt on my face, she said, "It's possible that your bodies, *all* of your bodies, don't have any chance at developing immunity, even with the vaccines. You've become far too dependent on your nanites and your isolated environment."

I tried to understand what she meant, but I sighed and shook my head. I started to say something snarky about being an engineer, not a doctor, but then it clicked, and I understood. "Wait, wait. Are you saying that because we haven't been exposed to illness for generations, we can't develop immunities to them at all?"

"Basically, yes," she nodded. "Not naturally, anyway, which is what vaccines depend on, your natural immune system figuring out how to fight off the illnesses. If that immune system is weak, none of you may be fine for much longer."

I grimaced at that. It wasn't just Leif who had a limited time, it was all of us. The longer we stayed, the worse off we would all get.

But then something occurred to me, a positive spin on it. "Does Claudia know this yet?"

"No, but I'll be going to tell her as soon as I leave here," Livia closed up her device and stowed it on a clip on her belt. "I don't know if she'll listen to me, but if she really wants your people to stay, she'll need to devise a way to kick-start your immune systems."

I couldn't help but grin. "Or…"

"Or?" Livia frowned.

"Or she lets us go."

Lifting her eyebrows, Livia gaped at me and slowly shook her head. "You know why she can't do that."

"Because she needs us to help with genetic diversity here?" I asked. Livia nodded. "Yeah. We can't really do that if we're dead."

Livia considered my words for a second, and then lifted her eyebrows. "True," she hesitantly replied. "But…well…"

I stepped aside and motioned for the door. "Go tell her. See what she says." I glanced at Hector. "Maybe, just maybe, this is our ticket out of here."

Livia didn't look so certain, but she drew in a breath, and then marched out the doors. Just as she left, she bumped into Centurion Tiberius coming to find us. I caught sight of him lightly touching her hand before they went their separate ways, and Tiberius came into quarantine.

Interesting. I'd wondered if there was something going on between those two.

Tiberius stopped by the guards, and said, "Thank you, boys. I'll take it from here." They gave him a quizzical look, so he added more sternly, "Dismissed!"

"Sir," they said in unison, snapping to attention before filing out.

Turning to me, Tiberius spoke with the most serious tone, "Come with me."

FORTY-TWO

I was getting really tired of being led around and forced to go where I didn't want to.

Tiberius stalked along the corridor next to me, and while I didn't know him well, I could see a sharpness to his walk, and frustration in his eyes.

"You've made a lot of waves in your short time here," he finally spoke, his voice surprisingly quiet, maybe even menacing.

"Uh," I replied.

Lifting an eyebrow, he looked at me and said, "Sebastian."

I blinked. "The…pilot? Um, copilot?"

Tiberius nodded. "Seems you managed to fix his ship's inertial dampers."

"Well, yeah," I replied, and studiously prevented myself from shrugging. "It wasn't that hard."

"Maybe not to you," he narrowed his eyes, "but our one and only flight engineer hadn't ever fixed it. You did it in a few minutes."

We came upon the lift, and after a brief wait, stepped onto it when the doors opened. I replied, "Those ships all have self-correcting alignments, you just have to know how to program and activate the diagnostics."

"Which apparently you do," he nodded, his movements jerky. After a moment of staring me down, he ordered the lift down to the lowest deck.

"Yeah, I was given all the knowledge related to that kind of thing," I frowned. "Why are we talking about this? And what's with the attitude?"

I noticed his hands curl into fists. Turning to me, Tiberius grabbed my shackles and lifted them up. He stared at me for a long moment, and then entered the code to disengage the shackles, freeing my hands. I gawked at my free hands, then at him.

At first, he didn't reply. He waited, as if daring me to run, or fight, or grab for his sidearm. Instead, all I did was rub my wrists.

I saw his jaw flex before he attached the shackles to his belt. Once they were secure, he said, "I want you to do something for me." I waited, letting him drive the conversation forward. But he hesitated and looked up, over my left shoulder.

I frowned, and started to look, but then stopped. I knew that over my left shoulder was a camera.

One through which anyone could possibly see and hear us. Including Caesar.

"Our engineer, Zoe," he said, emphasizing his words in an unusual manner, "has requested your help repairing some of our shuttles."

Zoe. I think I saw her when we first landed on the *Alpha*, working on the cargo shuttle. Mousy-looking, bald, tan skin, and wearing a jumpsuit like mine.

She had requested me?

No…there had to be more to it than that. The way he kept emphasizing his words oddly. The strange attitude coupled with dissonant actions. The fact that he pointed out a camera, knowing I'd know where it was. They were very well hidden, if they were anything like the *Sirius's* cameras. Not to be subversive, as I understood it, but just to be innocuous. It was meant to be a safety feature, not something to be used to surreptitiously spy on people.

At least, that was the ethical guidelines by which Naia claimed to operate. I doubted that Caesar had any such ethics.

So what was the real reason for this diversion?

We got out on the bottom deck and, as I expected, we headed for the port launch bay. Tiberius continued to explain, possibly for the benefit of the cameras, "By order of Caesar, we engage in mining operations on a near-daily basis. There's a lot of mines around here we frequent, depending on what we're ordered to obtain and in what quantities. So, as you imagine, our mining and cargo shuttle is the most important vessel in our repertoire."

I followed along beside him. Venturing a guess, I said, "That's why we detected tritium and deuterium down here."

Tiberius frowned, and amended, "Tritium, yes," but he gave me an intent look before continuing to watch where he was going, having to avoid a missing deck plate at one point.

Granted, for those specific materials, they didn't have to mine, but they still needed that cargo shuttle. I imagined that they would fly out to a nearby salt-water ocean or lake to get heavy water, and convert it to one of those two isotopes of hydrogen, either deuterium or tritium.

Maybe it was all the concussions. Maybe it was a lack of quality rest over the past several days, or the disasters and the constant adrenaline surges, I don't know. But it hit me like a blacksmith's hammer the instant my mind focused in on that.

Tritium and deuterium. Obtaining and hording tritium made sense – the *Alpha,* or what was left of her, still probably ran on fusion reactors, and they used tritium as fuel.

But deuterium? Sure, you could use that for fusion reactors, too, but at least on the *Sirius,* that's not what it was used for. Actually, for a fusion reactor to work on deuterium, several adjustments had to be made, you couldn't just interchange them on the fly. On the other hand, deuterium was *the* best normal-matter fuel component for a matter/antimatter reaction.

Except, the plasma generated from a matter/antimatter reaction wasn't generally used to power ship's systems. That would be like setting off a bomb to power a turbine, it just wasn't practical.

In the right conditions, say in the middle of a stardrive reactor core, the plasma produced could be used to energize F.T.L. engines, warping space/time around a ship and flinging it through an artificial wormhole.

So now I had to wonder – why would they be making and accumulating deuterium here? The *Alpha* wasn't going to fly anytime soon, and none of the shuttles had stardrives.

The mystery only deepened when I realized that Tiberius had corrected me and said *only* Tritium. But our probe's sensors had clearly detected deuterium in the area. Did he not know about that?

We emerged into the yawning launch bay, strangely empty compared to the *Sirius's.* I wondered what had happened to their missing shuttles, but didn't voice my question, and instead tried to focus on divining Tiberius's true purpose for bringing me here.

But, true to his word, he led me to the far side, where the cargo shuttle was, and where tiny little Zoe was.

I'd assumed she was just small. But no, she was a damned *kid!*

She looked no older than twelve, and was short and stocky, a surprising amount of muscle on her frame for someone who should have been playing games rather than working on spaceships.

Tiberius spoke first, "Zoe, this is Mika Kai from the starship *Sirius*."

I wasn't sure what I expected from her, but she gave me a withering glare. "So you're the genius," she grumbled, yesterday's patient smile long-gone. "I thought you'd be one of the older ones."

Regarding her with mild amusement, I glanced at Tiberius. The irony wasn't lost on him, either.

"Well, likewise," I smiled at Zoe. "How old are you, kid?"

Oh, the glare she gave me was enough to chill me. "Don't call me kid, lady! I'm smarter than most of the oldies around here."

Oldies? I covered my smile with my hand and coughed.

"Come on, lady," she waved a hand and started trouncing grumpily up the ramp into the cargo shuttle. "I've got a problem, and Sebastian says you can probably fix it."

Gods damn, she was a hothead!

I liked her already.

We followed her up, and like the exterior of the ship, the interior was very well-maintained. I imagined Zoe spent more time on this shuttle than any other craft, and her skill showed in the cargo ship's pristine condition.

She took pride in her work, I realized. But she was only one person. One *kid*. And that's why none of the other ships were in good shape.

They *made* her focus on this ship, and she did exactly that.

It also made me realize for the first time that there were no sarus! At least, none that I had seen so far, and there was a lot of damage to the *Alpha* that they should have tended to.

I wondered what happened to them.

But for Zoe to be the sole mechanic amongst the Alphas and Omegas, and to have kept the mining shuttle is such pristine condition, suggested that she was a lot smarter than she should have been. So what could she possibly need my help with?

Zoe led us into the aft engine compartment, and as we went, she said, "Sebastian told me you fixed the inertial dampers on his shuttle, and that you claimed you could fix the engines. Two of this thing's engines are phasing and I can't get 'em to correct. Thought you could take a look before the next mining group heads out tomorrow, 'cause they bitch and moan so god damned much."

I blinked at her language – even as a teenager, if I'd ever talked that way, I'd have been slapped senseless!

The aft compartment was as cramped as the *Hope's,* so it was a tight fit for us all. It was nearly identical to ours, with the main power reactor in the center, and the four engine reactors on the aft wall. "Uh, which engines are phasing?" I asked.

"One and two," Zoe said, and she trudged over to a console near the main reactor and started tapping in commands. "Here, I'll show you." She tapped some more, and suddenly an electric arch lanced between two components on the main reactor, and she shouted, "Shit, son of a bitch!"

The lights all died for a second, before emergency lights kicked on. Backup power cells took over, and I found myself wondering if Zoe was as talented as I thought. An arc like that could only have resulted from her making a stupid mistake.

Except, when main lights came back up, she turned to Tiberius and beamed at him.

The centurion rolled his eyes, and then he looked at me. "We can talk freely now."

I blinked in confusion. "Huh?"

"I simulated an overload," Zoe giggled. "Cameras are out. If anyone was watching, they'll think it's one of my infamous, and always ever-so-convenient mistakes."

I still didn't get it, and I made sure my expression conveyed that.

"Zoe doesn't make mistakes," Tiberius said. "Not unless I ask her to."

"Come on, lady," Zoe smirked at me. "You're not that dense, are ya?"

I wanted to be mad at her for that remark, but she just reminded me too much of myself, and I laughed. "Only on some days," I rolled my eyes at her. "Okay, so you blinded the cameras in here. So we can talk." My expression slackened. "And you've done this before. You already suspected something was up?"

Tiberius exchanged glances with Zoe, and then shook his head. "No. Well, not consciously." He gave us a shrug. "That's not why we have this routine."

I frowned. "Then why?" Zoe opened her mouth, but I put up a halting hand and said, "I know, I know, I'm not that dense. Give me a second to think."

First I looked at the console, then I looked up at what had arced. It was just the reactor's grounding rod, and all it meant was that she had redirected more power to somewhere it shouldn't have, and the grounding rod had dissipated the charge into the ship's hull, which normally could hold the charge and bleed it off into space, or in this case, into the atmosphere. It was relatively harmless, I realized.

Score one for the brilliant twelve-year-old engineer.

But if they regularly needed to talk without being monitored, and it wasn't because they suspected that Caesar was an alien…then why?

Hmm, let's think, Mika, I lectured myself sarcastically. *You live under the rule of an oppressive regime, the Alphas. What could you possibly be up to that would require they not know what you're doing or saying?*

"You're an underground movement," I gaped at them. "Against the Alphas."

"Heyyyy, there it is," Zoe grinned at Tiberius. "You're right, she's not an idiot."

I turned my gape at Tiberius. "You said that?"

He rolled his eyes. "Not in so many words. Zoe has a knack for embellishment."

I gave him one of my best smirks. "So I'm gathering." I cleared my throat and reminded myself of the seriousness of my situation. "So why am I here?"

"So we can talk in private," Tiberius replied.

"I know that," I gave Zoe an annoyed look, and she giggled. "But we could have talked anywhere. Why *here.*"

"Less chance of someone walking in," he replied. "Plus, I thought you might want to take a look at this ship's sensors."

"Sensors?" I frowned. "Why?"

"Because you're an engineer," Zoe said. "And when Tibes here told me what you told him, I started thinking."

"And when Zoe thinks, you pay attention," Tiberius winked at her.

Beaming, she replied, "If you're smart! So, I started scanning the *Alpha* again, thinking I could find evidence that 'ol Caesar was what you say he is. This shuttle has the most advanced sensors of any of our support ships." She turned to the console and tapped in commands, switching the layout to the sensor controls, and she initiated a scan, directing it upward. "Here's what I found."

I bent over the console next to her and watched the sensor readouts. The raw data streamed through a window on one side, and Zoe tapped in commands to initiate a subroutine to translate the data.

In the lower right, a layout of the captain's quarters appeared.

And nothing appeared inside of those quarters.

"Nothing," I pointed out the obvious.

"Exactly," Zoe said.

"At first, I thought it meant he just wasn't in there," Tiberius said. "But Zoe-"

"Caesar's always in there," she said. "He never comes out. Or so I thought. There's, *conveniently,* no security cameras active in the corridors up by his quarters. Which is kinda odd, isn't it?"

I nodded. "On the *Sirius,* all corridors have active cameras and internal sensors in them."

"Yeah," she nodded. "I wanted to see if he'd left, so I tried to find cameras that could see him if he left and went down one corridor or another. And I found something…well, freaking *weird.*"

The map zoomed out to show a general layout of deck one's entire forward section. Orange dots appeared to show where all of the cameras were, and let me tell you, there were a *lot.* I knew that already, but to actually see hundreds of them represented on a map boggled my mind.

As I'd expected, none of the personnel quarters had cameras in them, and I remembered the privacy law that Naia mentioned. Obviously wherever the Alphas and Omegas were from, they had similar laws. But the corridors were full of them, as were a lot of other common areas.

Except…for one extremely obvious gap.

Not only were there no cameras within view of the captain's quarters, there weren't any cameras along a very obvious and specific route leading away from those quarters.

All the way towards the aft end of the forward section.

Towards the dome.

"I think Caesar does leave sometimes," Zoe said. "I think he goes to the dome. But that doesn't make sense, does it?"

"You're right, it doesn't," I nodded. "Isn't the dome irradiated?"

"So we've been told," Tiberius nodded. He was more suspicious than I had previously given him credit for, and suddenly I had to rethink my entire opinion about him. Hellfire, not only was he smarter than I thought, he was good at hiding his intellect!

"And check this out," Zoe keyed the sensors over to scan the dome. Sure enough, high levels of ionizing radiation were present in the center of the dome. "Pretty potent, huh? If anyone went in the dome, they'd die in a matter of days."

I nodded. "Yeah. I'm not a doctor, but the I.A. download told me enough to be very afraid of radiation."

"And I've read enough about it to know how scary it is," Zoe said. "But here's the thing. The radiation's intensity profile."

A new chart appeared next to the map, showing the radiation levels from the center of the dome all the way out to the edge. The falloff of intensity followed a logical curve. Right up until it hit the edge of the dome. Then it vanished entirely.

I frowned. "That's weird."

"Duh," Zoe said. I gave her a withering look.

"No one's ever run a profile like this," Tiberius said. "Hell, we don't even usually bother scanning the dome, we're more concerned with other things when we're leaving or approaching the *Alpha*. So it's entirely possible that no one has ever noticed this unusual profile."

"In two centuries?" I asked Tiberius doubtfully. "No one's monitored the radiation levels?"

He gave me the utmost serious look and said, "For the most part, we've all followed what the Alphas told us. We had no reason to doubt them. And even when I figured out they *couldn't* be trusted, and then when I was brought into the underground, no one still thought to doubt the idea that there was dangerous radiation in the dome and the aft end of the ship. There was no reason to risk testing that theory."

"But now we're seeing it," Zoe said, "and I *know* it has to be false readings." Grimacing, she added, "But I don't know how to scan through those readings to see what's really going on."

"Which is why I brought you here," Tiberius said. "I thought maybe if you two worked together, you could find a way to…I dunno, fix the scans or something."

I stared at the sensor readout thoughtfully. "Well. I'm an engineer, yes, but only because of an I.A. download. I've learned, sometimes the hard way, that just because I know about something doesn't mean I understand it enough to intuitively go beyond that base knowledge. Still," I frowned. "Worth a shot. But what about Caesar?"

Zoe looked at my quizzically. "What about him?"

"You still don't detect him?"

"No," she shook her head slowly. "I assume he's in the dome."

I grinned. "Not necessarily."

She frowned. "He's not in his quarters, though."

I shook my head. "The alien that infiltrated the *Sirius* could hide from all sensors. For all we know, Caesar is in his quarters, and we just can't detect him. Although…" I trailed off as another thought occurred to me. "That one didn't have to disable cameras. It could mask itself from visual sensors somehow."

Zoe slumped and frowned. "Huh. Why would Caesar need to disable cameras, then?"

I scratched my nose and thought out loud, "Maybe because he's working with technology two centuries old, while the one that attacked my ship had newer tech."

Tiberius's eyes lit up. "Or what if he had to move things either to or from the dome? Let's say Caesar really is an alien, and has the same tech and can hide itself from visual sensors. Would anything, say a cargo container, also be hidden if Caesar touched it?"

"Not likely," I replied. "Good point. *Tibes.*"

With a growl, he said, "Don't call me that."

I damn near laughed. It's good to know that some reactions were Universal.

But then I realized what he'd been saying, and I gave him a skeptical look. "Wait. So does this mean you believe me? About Caesar?"

He hesitated and glanced at Zoe. She shrugged. "It means," he started. "Well. It means there's too much here that just doesn't make sense. Too much we've uncovered that could corroborate your claim, but it's all still only circumstantial. None of this is conclusive evidence of anything more than a paranoid Alpha who likes his privacy. Maybe *that's* why those cameras are disabled, because he doesn't want to be seen at all, and not because he's an alien."

I nodded. Unfortunately, Tiberius wasn't wrong. I hadn't given him any proof yet.

But if we could figure out how to scan through the false readings in the dome, maybe I could find something to prove it.

Another thought occurred to me, then. "What about the deuterium?"

Tiberius and Zoe blinked at me. "What deuterium?" she asked.

I explained my earlier revelation about the deuterium we'd detected, and what it was used for. I wondered out loud, "Can we scan for it?"

Zoe quirked an eyebrow, and she asked, "Just your probe detected it, or your cargo shuttle too?"

I couldn't remember if we'd scanned the planet or not from the shuttle, so I frowned and thought back. I remembered bringing up the location of the deuterium and other ores on the shuttle after our crash-landing, but hadn't that just been the records from the probe?

"I don't think we scanned it with the shuttle," I admitted. I looked at Tiberius and added, "We were a little too busy dodging missiles."

He held up his hands disarmingly, "Hey, I didn't have anything to do with that. All weapons are controlled from the bridge, which means they're controlled by the Alphas."

Part of me didn't want to believe him. For all I knew, he'd sent them up himself.

Unfortunately, I also had no real reason not to believe him, not after everything he'd revealed to me.

Zoe looked back and forth between us, and then rolled her eyes and tapped in some commands on the scanners.

"Nothing," she sighed.

"And you're sure it's only used for these…stardrives you mentioned?" Tiberius asked.

I nodded, "Yeah. I mean, you can use it in fusion reactors, but tritium works better."

"She's right about that," Zoe nodded. "And I've never seen deuterium in our cargo bays. Look," she pointed at the screen, moving the map back over to the forward section of the *Alpha*, "No deuterium."

That made me think about something else. "Okay, but if our probe was right about deuterium, then it stands to reason that there's probably antimatter somewhere down here, too. Maybe we can detect antimatter through the false readings. Tell you what, Zoe, I'll calibrate and scan for that, if you'll do me a favor and look at all of the other decks for more conspicuous gaps in security camera coverage."

She gave me a surprised look, but it was Tiberius who asked, "You think Caesar is going somewhere else, too?"

"Well, maybe," I said. "If he's moving tritium from wherever you all store it to the dome, or converting it to deuterium and then moving it, he'd need a path to lug it without being seen."

"Ooh, good point!" Zoe exclaimed. Beaming at Tiberius, she said, "You really were right! She's not an idiot at all!"

FORTY-THREE

Zoe's job ended up being a lot easier than mine – she found two more glaring and obvious paths in a matter of seconds.

Adjacent to each launch bay were two primary cargo bays, though by no means the only cargo bays. And each of those primary bays had distinct pathways without cameras leading back towards the dome, using outer corridors that, according to Tiberius, almost no one ever used.

Yet despite that obvious sign saying 'look in the dome,' my scans kept coming back negative for antimatter. I guess that shouldn't have surprised me, otherwise our probe would've detected it. And I had no doubt that antimatter stores would have been ejected by the *Alpha's* A.I. before the crash, so that it didn't detonate after the crash and level the entire area.

Finally, I scanned for any other substances that might be conspicuous, but all I found was material indicative of ruined buildings, and flora and fauna.

I almost closed out the scan when I abruptly stopped, and I must have made an eep noise, because the others jumped. Zoe asked through a giggle, "What was that?"

"Uh," I blinked at her, and then back at the screen. "Look," I said, pointing at the scans. "Sensors are picking up life in the dome."

Even Tiberius leaned in over our shoulders, staring down at the results. "That shouldn't be possible," he remarked, and quizzically added, "should it?"

"Not unless everything on this planet is somehow immune to three forms of ionizing radiation," I remarked. "Then again," I sighed and narrowed my eyes, "I'm not exactly an expert. Livia or Claudia could tell you for sure, but what little I know about the dangers of radiation tells me everything living would die from short-term exposure, let alone centuries of it."

I felt more than saw Tiberius lean back away from us, and I heard him grumble a drawn-out, "Hmmmm."

I looked at him, watched as he folded his arms and scrunched his nose up in thought. "Hmm?" I asked. "What's 'hmm'?"

The centurion exhaled breathily. "It's suspicious. But it isn't conclusive evidence to support your accusation."

I blinked at him. "You're joking."

Motioning to the screen, he said, "All we've found is evidence of fake sensor readings, that we've been lied to about the radiation, *maybe*."

"Maybe?!" I interrupted, my voice an octave higher than normal.

"Yes, *maybe*," he grumpily emphasized. "For all we know, the same thing masking sensor readings is creating false plant readings."

"To what end?" I asked.

Very slowly, enunciating very carefully, he said, "I don't know. That's the point. We have no conclusive evidence of anything other than the fact that something is being hidden."

"And the gaps in camera coverage that *clearly* show paths that include Caesar's quarters?" I planted my hands on my hips. "That's not conclusive?"

"That's circumstantial," he narrowed his eyes at me. "Nothing more than an indication that Caesar is hiding *something*, but we don't know what."

I started to utter an argument, but then stopped and let out a frustrated sigh, running my hand through my hair. It was slick from two days without a shower, and felt clumpy.

Two days? Had it been two days since my last shower aboard the *Sirius*? It felt like a lot longer than that.

Gods, how much could happen in just two days?

Or had it even only been one?

Dammit, focus, Mika! That wasn't a good sign — if my mind was wandering, I was fatigued.

"Alright, so we need conclusive evidence," I finally said. "Clearly something's going on in the dome. We need someone to check it out."

"I'm not letting anyone *near* that place," Tiberius said. "No one goes near it, understood?"

"Then how do you propose we prove anything?" I asked.

"We?" he asked. "You mean 'you,' don't you?"

Letting out a frustrated noise, I waved around us and said, "I can't really do it on my own, can I? Unless you're gonna let me roam the *Alpha* freely."

"You're supposed to be smart," he leaned closer. "Can you scan through the false signals or not?"

My voice caught, and after a second, I huffed out a breath and looked back at the console. Zoe was working on it now, tapping in various algorithms into the sensors herself. Nothing seemed to work for her, either.

I wasn't that smart. I knew how the sensors were built, I knew how to fix them if they broke, I even knew how to realign their components to ensure they operated to specifications. But I didn't have a clue how to manipulate them or their data any more than the basics, and my brain hadn't become any more intuitive about it.

But then I remembered that Karina said something about 'doing something clever' with her scanner to send *out* false readings.

She might be able to help me figure it out.

Crap, I thought, and grimaced at Tiberius. I didn't want him to know she was out there, not yet. I didn't trust him anymore than he trusted me. So I had to stall and figure out a way to isolate myself, even if only for a minute.

Where could I go that had no cameras, and that he wouldn't follow?

The idea struck me, it was so simple and obvious!

"Look, I gotta think about it," I finally said. But then, blinking my eyes as innocently as I could at him, I said, "But I'm kind of distracted right now. I need a bathroom, or restroom, or whatever you call them."

Sighing, he said, "Fine, use the one right here," he jerked a thumb to the right, where the shuttle's bathroom was.

I started towards it, but Zoe objected, "Hey! I just finished emptying that this morning. I don't wanna have to do it again before the ship launches tomorrow."

"I'm not gonna…" I started and stopped, feeling my cheeks flush. "I'm just…the ship will filter the liquid out. That's all." I blushed even more, if that was possible.

"Oh," she said. "Well if that's all you're doing, then fine."

I rolled my eyes at the kid, and then stalked out into the cargo bay, with Tiberius following behind me as far as that door. I did a hard left, and entered the tiny little bathroom, which was a small rectangle of a room that consisted of nothing more than a toilet and a sink.

I closed the door behind me, locked it, and then immediately tapped my ear and whispered, "Karina!"

I gave it a few moments, knowing that she might not be in a position to answer right away. Then, *"Go ahead, Mika."*

Tension I hadn't noticed building in my shoulders eased up, and I closed the lid and sat on the toilet, deflating. "Gods, it's good to hear your voice."

"Yours, too," she said. She wasn't whispering, so she must not have been in any immediate danger, which further helped me relax. *"Just checking in?"*

"Well, that, and I needed to ask you something else. But I only have a minute at most."

"Then ask," she curtly replied.

As much as I wanted to ask or talk about more, I jumped right in. "If you wanted to hide something from sensors, how would you do it?"

There was a distinct pause before she answered. *"Uh, well, if that's all you're asking."* Great, sarcasm. *"Not exactly an easy thing to answer, Mika. Could you be more specific?"*

Rolling my eyes, both at her and at my own vague question, I told her about the false radiation signature in the *Alpha's* dome, and the suspicion that it was hiding something else.

"That sounds a lot more complicated than what I'm doing," she said. *"A lot more complicated. Gods, Mika, I don't know."*

I felt my spirits sink. But I also knew I had to get moving. "Well, think about it, and if you come up with anything…"

"I can see the dome from here," she said.

I blinked. "You're over the ridge?"

"Yeah. Did you see it when they brought you in?"

I thought back to it. "Yeah, but all I could see was the shattered dome. And some trees inside." I blinked. "Which means the sensor readings of the trees are real. Which means the radiation *can't* be real!"

My voice had gotten louder, and I clamped my hands over my mouth. I waited for a second. Tiberius didn't come knocking yet.

"Tell you what. I think we'll be there by tomorrow morning. We'll sneak into the dome and see what we can see."

It was half of a day away. And I hadn't told her about her father yet, or the fact that none of us were safe. But there was a pounding at the door, and Tiberius shouted, "Mika. Come out."

I eeped. "One second, just finishing up!"

"Finishing up?" Karina asked.

"I'll explain later," I said. "Gotta go. Stay safe, love!" I tapped my earpiece, and then realized what I'd said at the end and felt my cheeks grow even warmer.

Tiberius pounded again.

"Alright, *alright,*" I shouted, and then for show, I stood up and flushed the toilet. I did a quick rinse of my hands, wishing so much that I could find a shower, and then I opened the door.

Tiberius had a serious look on his face. Had he heard me talking?

"Come on," he growled, and started for the ramp down.

"Uh, where?" I asked, hurrying to catch up to him.

"The medici wishes to see you," he said. "Now."

My stomach dropped out. But I hurried, and just as he started to descend the ramp, I halted him with my hand. He was big and strong enough that he could have pulled away, but he stopped and looked at me. I whispered to him, "I just remembered. When we flew in, I could see trees in the dome." I looked around at the bay, which was empty, but I knew there were cameras. I emphasized, "*Living* trees, Tiberius, of the same species in my dome."

He blinked at me, and then nodded understanding. And then he led me down the ramp, and we headed away from the cargo ship, away from Zoe.

There was no denying it. Even if, somehow, the flora of this moon was immune to radiation, I knew that the trees native to Rhea weren't. And when I closed my eyes and pictured our approach, I saw what looked like huge, ancient oaks intermixed with tall evergreens peaking out of the dome. That meant that not only were they thriving amongst supposed high levels of radiation, but they had to have been a couple centuries old.

The radiation was *definitely* a lie, and had been all along.

FORTY-FOUR

Did I mention that I was tired of being led around?

I needed to take more action, and I felt like I was finally gaining Tiberius's trust. Maybe. Sort of.

But it wasn't enough. Not with my people on the line.

So while we traveled back up to deck two, I tried to think of how I could gain a bit more freedom. But to be frank, with the quarantine that was *supposed* to be imposed, and the fact that I was *supposed* to be a prisoner, I couldn't see a way out yet.

All I could do was push and nudge others in the right direction, and hope to the gods that they actually did the right thing.

When we walked into the medical ward, however, I was immediately put on guard – someone I hadn't met yet was there. And based on his height, he was an Alpha. He was at least a couple inches taller than Claudia, and wore legitimate armor. But not armor like you might find in Rhea, not made of leather or even steel. This was advanced armor, consisting of hardened ablative pads and heat-resistant weave, colored grey and black.

And despite looking no older than thirty, he had a hardened look to his face, and I wasn't even talking about his chiseled jaw. Fiery orange eyes completed his strange, terrifying look.

If Tiberius was surprised, he didn't show it. "General," he nodded to the older man.

I tried not to gape at the rank. Tiberius's commanding officer was an Alpha.

In a way, that made sense, but it might have just made the situation a *lot* more complicated.

There was another Alpha present, too, one that I recognized from earlier. A consul, I think was his title, but for the life of me I couldn't remember his name. For that matter, I barely recognized him, but the purple eyes were kind of hard to forget.

"Hello, pup," Claudia spoke to me from behind her console. Livia stood behind her, meekly staring at the deck while clasping her hands behind her back.

Oh, I didn't think I was going to like where this was going.

The general barely acknowledged Tiberius, his eyes laser-focused on me, as were the consul's. I shuddered, and once again felt like prey caught in a web.

At least this time, I have one foot on solid ground, I thought, resisting the urge to look for reassurance from Tiberius.

Claudia walked around her console to stand between it and me, and she smiled down at me. Glancing at my wrists, she looked at Tiberius and lifted her eyebrows. "No cuffs?"

"My apologies, Medici," Tiberius bowed. "The outsider was helping repair our cargo shuttle, by request of Zoe."

"Ah, I see," she looked to me, and I could see the hint of suspicion in her eyes. "Well, no matter. I trust, young pup, that you learned your lesson the last time you acted out?"

I didn't answer, but I did force down a lump in my throat. Then I asked, "What do you want?"

She placed her hands on her waist and considered me for a second, before she said, "I must ask you some questions, and it would be in your best interest to answer honestly."

Glancing at the general, I nodded to Claudia. "You can ask. I make no promises."

Chuckling in mild amusement, Claudia replied, "Hmm, I would expect no less snark from you. So, tell me, young pup, how fully stocked is your starship's medical facility?"

I blinked at her. I hadn't expected *that* question. "Um. Huh?"

"Your medical bay aboard the *Sirius,*" she said. "Was it fully stocked when you launched?"

Flustered, I glanced at everyone present. When my eyes fell on Livia, she looked at me wide-eyed, and I saw warning in her expression. *Uh oh...*

"Um, I don't...I don't know," I shook my head. "I didn't look."

"Surely some of your people have been injured," she began a slow, predatory pace around me and Tiberius. I followed her movement carefully, fear crawling its way into my gut. "Was your artificial intelligence able to heal those wounds?"

I glanced again at the general and the consul.

"Well," I started and stopped. "W-well yes." Did she know about Jonnec and Karina? Was this somehow a bizarre test? "I, um, one of my friends was wounded fighting the alien I told you about."

I watched for a reaction from the others, and I got one. "Alien?" the general asked. His voice was baritone, and powerful, as if he could speak to an open room of thousands and be heard without the aid of technology. "What alien?"

"As I said," Claudia covered, "she has been prone to telling wild stories to us to distract us. Hopefully, none of us have fallen prey to it," she came around and looked directly at Tiberius. He swallowed.

"An alien," I pressed, looking directly at the general, "like the one that attacked this ship." I don't know why, but I expected Claudia to try to stop me, to hit me, something violent. But no, she let me talk. So I kept going, "A black ship like the one that nearly destroyed the *Sirius*. And just like our encounter, a survivor from that ship made it onto your ship."

I felt like glitching program repeating itself, but clearly, Claudia hadn't told the general or the consul any of this.

"I remember that battle," the general said. "We assumed the black ship was an advanced design from one of the rival colonies. I do not recall an alien intruder aboard our vessel."

"There was none," Claudia agreed, stopping her prowl in front of me. She looked down her nose at me. "The claim of an alien was just a not-so-clever ploy to distract us."

I narrowed my eyes at her. "I saw the look you gave me when I told you," I growled. "You know I'm not lying." I looked at the general. "Your Caesar has been replaced by an imposter."

The consul burst out laughing.

The general did not. He regarded me cooly, his expression unwavering. It was maddening how calm he looked, how undisturbed my claim made him.

"Really, extra-terrestrials, little pup?" the consul snorted in laughter. I didn't recognize the term, 'extra-terrestrial,' but I figured it meant 'alien.' "By God, you must be joking! There has never been evidence of extra-terrestrial intelligence! Not in all of human history!"

"Well there is now," I spoke through a sneer. "I know, I *fought* the bastard!"

"Did you, now?" the general appraised me. It wasn't a doubtful appraisal, either, and that gave me some small amount of hope. "I imagine it was not a difficult adversary for you to have survived."

I glowered at him. "I outsmarted it. Barely."

The consul snorted in laughter again.

But not the general. He met my gaze, peered into my eyes, as if trying to appraise my soul. As if trying to determine the strength of my will and character.

I shuddered, but I didn't look away. I *wouldn't* look away.

Something flickered in his expression then.

"And once again, you've distracted us from the topic at hand," Claudia sighed. "Bravo, young pup. You are clearly a skillful master of distraction."

"Then what is the topic at hand?" I asked. "If not the threat to everyone here?"

"The threat to everyone here is precisely what I speak of," she peered down at me. "Especially the threat of your people."

I felt my insides twist again. "What do you mean?"

"It has come to my attention," she spoke louder, "that your immune system, and that of all of your companions, is compromised." I glanced at Livia, and she looked down and away. I didn't blame her, but now I knew why she had the look of guilt on her face – whatever was coming next, she blamed herself.

I nodded up at Claudia. "Yeah, that's what I understand too. So you see, you should let us go, because we're going to die otherwise, and we can't help you if we're dead."

"Oh, I could kick start your immune systems quite easily," she gave me a predatory smile, and I once again felt like a fly in the spider's trap. "The problem is that I am already short on raw material needed for the proper medication. And to use it on you would deprive us. I thought this a horrific problem, and I was unsure how to reconcile it. However, you then told me about your exploits aboard your ship."

Oh gods. I felt my stomach drop out and a horrific void opened in my chest. Color must have drained from my face.

I knew *exactly* where she was going with this now.

"After further consideration, I realized that twenty people added to our gene pool would hardly overcome centuries of inbreeding, not without additional medical supplies. We need a *much* larger pool." She looked at the general. "So we are already planning a raid."

"NO!" I shouted, lurching towards Claudia on instinct alone. Tiberius grasped my arm in a vice grip and yanked me back.

"Oh, yes, young pup," she leered back at me. "Yes. We need your supplies, and we need *some* of your people. Not all, just some. And you have implied through conversation that your ship is unmanned, controlled only by an A.I. No soldiers to defend, only residents of your dome."

"No, you can't!" I shouted, panic firing all of my nerves and scrambling my brain. "You can't! They're innocent, they're all innocent!"

"Dear pup, this has nothing to do with innocence or guilt," she frowned. "This has to do with survival. We are on the cusp of failure as a society, and we cannot have that. We need our Omegas, you see," she regarded Tiberius, and then Livia, before turning back to me. "And we cannot allow them to die off. So you see, the choice is obvious – we harvest your vessel of what we need, and together our societies will *thrive* as one."

"No, don't you DARE!" I screamed. "Stay away from my people!"

"They are no longer *your* people, pup," she narrowed her eyes at me. "They are *ours*."

I surged against Tiberius's grip, but he was a *lot* stronger than me, and I couldn't break away. My right elbow fired fresh pain into my body, and that only incensed me further.

Claudia looked to the general, who stepped closer. He asked, "What is the status of your ship's defenses?"

"Strong enough to kick your ass," I spat at him.

Pulling a data pad from his belt, he activated and regarded it. "The starship *Sirius* was set to launch only a few days after the *Alpha*, so it is unlikely she holds superior technology. You say you fought an alien spacecraft-"

"Fought and beat," I snarled. "Which is a lot more than I can say about your piece of shit ship!"

His eyes flicked at me, and he tapped in some notes on his pad. "So you took damage from the conflict. How long ago was that?"

"Fuck you!"

Claudia answered for me, "Mika said it happened recently."

"Bitch!"

They both ignored my curses. The general regarded his pad for a moment longer. "If the attacking vessel was similar to what we encountered two centuries ago, it is likely that your vessel's defenses are severely compromised."

"Are you suggesting a direct assault, General?" the consul asked, coming closer to him, but staying well away from me.

"Hmm, no, I think not," the general shook his head, and then looked at me. "Not when we have an alternative at our disposal." His eyes drilled into me, and suddenly I wished he *wasn't* so intelligent.

"NO!"

He didn't smile. He didn't take any satisfaction in my reaction. All he did was turn to the consul, and then to Claudia. "We will take their surviving shuttle, hosting as many soldiers as it can fit. We will land in their bay. I think Consul Janus would be ideal to come along, as he knows how to manipulate computer systems better than any. Perhaps he could remotely take control of the A.I. once aboard."

"Naia will stop you!" I shouted.

"The A.I. cannot directly harm humans," he casually remarked. "It is core to their programming."

"Not if you threaten the ship!" I snarled. "She answers only to me and my people!"

"It is programmed to *protect* you," he said. "All of you. So threat of harm to *you,* Mika Kai, should be enough to ensure its cooperation."

"Naia will *never* cooperate with you!" I lunged at him again, but Tiberius held firmly.

"We shall see," he tapped something else on his pad. "Yes, I think we can begin planning now." He tapped his earpiece, and said, "General Lucious to Consul Janus, please meet me in my office in one hour." He tapped it again and smiled to Claudia. "I think by tomorrow we will be ready to launch." Then he turned to Tiberius and said, "Take her to her cell and keep her there, Centurion."

"Yes, sir," Tiberius snapped, and he dragged me away. I fought as much as I could, tried to tear away, but nothing I did so much as slowed him down.

Finally, when we were about to pass through the door, I thought of one other thing to try to save us all. "General, who do you serve?"

All of my words, all of my actions, nothing had really made him react, until I said that. I gripped the doorframe and managed to stop Tiberius from dragging me out, while the general looked at me curiously. "I beg your pardon?"

"Who do you serve?" I insisted, and cursed at Tiberius. "Let me go, dammit!"

The general lifted a hand with two fingers raised, and Tiberius stopped pulling on me. "I serve my people, young one."

"And your Caesar?" I snarled.

He nodded. "I serve him above all others."

Gritting my teeth, I said the only thing I could think of to make a difference. "That *thing* murdered your Caesar."

The general didn't react, not outwardly. He stared at me, cool and calculating, his eyes blazing fire into mine. I stared back, met his gaze, didn't flinch or dare look away. Maybe it was because he had centuries to learn how to reel in his emotions, but I couldn't tell what he thought or felt. I couldn't tell if I'd made an impression, except for the fact that he had given me a chance to say what I had to say.

But at length, he flicked his fingers, an unspoken command to Tiberius who finally dragged me out of the medical ward.

FORTY-FIVE

When it became clear that I wasn't getting back into the medbay, I stopped fighting Tiberius, and I walked along with him. He held my arm firmly, and I tried to yank out of his grip, but he wouldn't let go.

They won't succeed. They can't succeed!

Can they?

The *Sirius* had a lot of defenses, powerful shields and weapons, and just like the starship *Alpha,* she had missile batteries.

But if they got the *Hope* flying, if their Consul Janus was able to break into the ship's systems to get Naia to let them in, then there wouldn't be any way to stop them. Especially if Naia hadn't restored the *Sirius's* external comms before then, she'd have no way of verifying who was aboard the *Hope* or why the shuttle was returning early and alone.

They could slip in and take the *Sirius* from within.

Naia could defend internally, with forcefields, but the *Sirius* didn't have anything like security drones. And these were well-trained soldiers. I had no doubt that anything Naia could throw at them, they could counter, including depressurization. For all I knew, they'd go in with some sort of armored space suits.

Plus I think General Lucious was right - as soon as she realized the crew of the *Hope* was being held hostage, Naia would cooperate, whether she wanted to or not.

They really could take the *Sirius*, and there wasn't a damn thing I could do to stop them.

Unless I got the Omegas on my side. Unless I got the rebellion on my side. I looked at Tiberius, who kept his eyes forward, his face stoic.

"If you're wondering when the time to rebel is," I said, modulating my voice, trying to keep it calm and collected, but my terror and my anger definitely came through. "Now's the time."

He sighed heavily, but he didn't look at me.

"Obviously you're planning something," I pressed. He squeezed my arm, warning me to be silent, but I didn't care about the cameras anymore. I didn't care if an Alpha monitored us or if Caesar did. All I cared about was my people. I repeated, "Now's the time! Why not fight back now? You outnumber them, don't you?"

"Shut it," he growled at me. "Not here, not now."

"Then when?!" I screamed in his face, all reason lost on me. "When's the time, when's the place?!"

Suddenly he yanked me in an unexpected direction, and the next thing I knew, he shoved me into a bathroom. He closed the door behind us and sealed it with his security code. Then he spun on me and shouted so vehemently that he spat in my face, "Are you really that stupid?!"

I blinked, and then wiped spittle off my face. Infusing cold fury into my voice, I hissed, "Excuse me?"

"Think about it, Mika!" he waved his hands in frustration. "Just think about it for one second! Yes, you're right, I've been working against the Alphas, and we outnumber them at least thirty-to-one, but that's not the issue! Nor is it that they are literally bigger and stronger than us, and *smarter*, and superior in every way. Do you know what *is* the issue?" I stuck my chin out at him, defiant and unwilling to let him lead me on. I waited for him to finish his piece. "There is only *one* person on this entire goddamn moon who knows how to correct the genetic defects in new fetuses. Only one who can prevent the stillbirths and miscarriages."

My fury died, his words a splash of ice-cold water, leaving only smoldering ruins in its wake.

"Livia has been trying to break into the medici's files and figure out how to do it herself," Tiberius continued, rubbing the bridge of his nose and closing his eyes. Defeat was in his voice when he continued, "But so far, no dice. So that's a card the medici holds over all of us Omegas." He opened his eyes and stared into mine, pausing just enough to let me know how important this was. "My people cannot survive without her."

I narrowed my eyes. "But the medici has admitted that she won't be able to do that for much longer. She's running out of supplies."

"Yes," he replied, exasperated, "but until now, she's been the most likely one to find another solution."

I scrunched up my face. "Yeah, well, she *has* found a solution." My voice shook when I finished with, "My people."

He nodded. "That's probably the only reason she admitted to the rest of us that she was running out of options. She has a way out, now."

Pieces clicked together in my head, the puzzle becoming clearer. The fire returned and I glared at him. "And if she forces *all* of my people to come here, she won't need medical intervention to maintain genetic diversity. The Alphas won't be able to hold that over your head anymore."

His lips drew into a razor thin line. "Yes," he whispered.

"That's when you'll make your move."

Tiberius nodded.

I shook with anger, and my hands curled into fists.

"You know," my voice trembled. "You know that they won't be kind about it. They won't treat my people well, and they *aren't* going to bring them all back. And they'll destroy the *Sirius* when they're done ransacking her."

"Yes," he said, slowly. "*We* will."

We. As in, the soldiers. Tiberius included.

Because soldiers followed orders.

I wanted to scream. I wanted to claw his eyes out. I wanted to cry.

"I can't let you do that," I said through clenched teeth.

"I know," he nodded solemnly. "And I'm sorry."

His hands moved quick as lightning. His pistol was pointed at my gut. I only just saw it long enough to see that it was on the absolute lowest setting when he fired, and darkness followed.

***

I woke up slowly at first, until I realized where I was and rage surged through my body. I bolted upright on the bench at the back of my cell, and against the noise in my head, I heard the forcefield buzzing. A single guard manned the station, the one that had helped with injections and had been my guard before. He glanced at me as I sat glaring at him, my breathing rapid.

Climbing to my feet, I stalked towards the forcefield and spoke with venom in my voice, "Let. Me. Out."

The soldier frowned at me, but said nothing.

"LET ME OUT!" I smashed the forcefield with my fists. The buzz of static electricity raised the hairs on my arm.

The guard merely moved to press a button on his console.

"Don't you dare press that fucking button!"

He did.

I was smart enough not to pound the forcefield again, the hum of it growing louder. I screamed in frustration. I railed, wanting to pound the forcefield, wanting to wring his neck, wanting to wring *Tiberius's* gods-damned neck!

I was helpless, it was hopeless. I pounded the bulkhead next to the forcefield, feeling absolutely useless and helpless, the past two days catching up fast and burning in my chest. I'd failed so horrifically, endangered so many people. Those who died on the *Pride* were my responsibility! Those who were about to die would only die by my failures.

I had brought this down on all of us.

Me.

Mika Kai, princess of Rhea, responsible for the well-being of everyone, was helpless to save them all.

"Hey, enough of that, already!" the guard shouted.

I faced him, fury blazing, my entire body *shaking*. He gripped the handle of his pistol, the threat clear. If I didn't calm down, if I didn't stop pounding and screaming, he'd shoot me.

A part of me wanted him to try. He had to bring down that forcefield to shoot me, so maybe I could somehow bolt past his blasts and tear the weapon from his grip. Tear it from him and…and…

And what? It was keyed to his palm print and D.N.A. I didn't have any means of reprogramming it, no A.I. on my side, no tools to pry it open and reset it.

Even if I managed to beat him, there'd be more. I'd be defenseless. Who knew where my own pistol was now, and I doubted it was still keyed to me.

I had to try, didn't I?

Don't I?

I did, I knew that, but I'd already bungled up this whole situation. Sure, I'd sowed the seeds of doubt amongst their ranks, made both the Alphas and Omegas suspicious of their Caesar. But they were too focused on their own survival, there was nothing they were willing to do. And if I spurred the revolution to begin now, all I'd do is make an enemy out of Tiberius, and my crew would get caught in the crossfire.

So I backed down. I backed down because the one and only option I had now required me to be awake. I lifted my hands disarmingly, and I slowly backed away and sat on my bench.

The guard eyed me wearily, and he didn't let his guard down for another solid minute. But finally, when he grew bored, he sat back on his stool, spun it around to face his console, and started playing what looked like a simple game on his data pad.

I was tense and anxious, and I wanted to contact Karina now, but I waited a bit longer for him to grow more engrossed in his game. The minutes stretched on, seemingly unending.

Finally, when I felt like enough time had passed, I turned my head, made to scratch my ear, and tapped the earpiece, thankful that no one had found it yet. "Karina?" I whispered.

She replied a second later, out of breath. *"Mika!"*

Panic swirled inside of my gut again. "Are you okay?"

"For now," she huffed. *"Yeah. Just had to run away from a predator. It was. It was."*

"Giant," I heard Jonnec's voice. He must have been right next to her to come through clear enough for me to hear him. *"Never seen the like of such a dog before!"*

"It wasn't a dog," Karina huffed. *"That was like a gods-damned dire wolf!"*

The panic settled, but only just a little. If there were dire wolf-like creatures on the moon, chances were good that a pack was after Karina. "Watch your flanks," I whispered, probably louder than I should have. "It probably has friends."

"Yeah, we got that," Karina huffed. *"Already had to shoot one."*

"I believe I shot it, not you," Marek's voice, unperturbed by their running, intoned. *"You missed."*

"Yeah, yeah, I'm a terrible shot, what else is new," Karina replied grumpily, then huffed audibly. *"I'm sorry, Mika. Did you need something?"*

I lowered my head and felt a grimace draw down my features. The panic had subsided almost fully now, leaving only the empty darkness and the burn of failure. But I had to tell her. She was our only hope now.

"You have to get here faster," I said. "I know you're all probably tired, gods know that Jonnec probably needs the rest to heal faster, but…" I shuddered. "Karina, it's all falling apart. These people are desperate, and growing more desperate by the day. And I can't convince them not to go through with it, and I don't know what to do,

Karina!"

"Hey, hey, slow down," she cooed. Then, *"Not us! Keep moving, Princely!"* I almost laughed into my quiet sobs, but I glanced at the guard. He was still ever-so-engrossed in the game. *"Mika, slow down. Tell me everything."*

I drew in a deep, calming breath, and I explained. Everything. Including about Leif's illness and the fact that we all were in danger, too. In fact, as I talked, I thought I felt a scratchiness in the back of my throat, and I feared that my time was running out, too.

When I finished explaining the plans to attack the *Sirius* tomorrow, I sat quietly. From the sounds of it, Karina and the others had finally slowed down, and their audible breathing disappeared into the noise suppression filter on the comm channel.

I let the information soak into my friends quietly, and I tried to control my own breathing. Telling the story had calmed me down some, and as I worked through the details, my brain re-engaged. I started thinking again.

Even if I somehow let the soldiers launch tomorrow, they could only approach the *Sirius* with the *Hope*, and that could only hold so many people. Plus with how fast the *Sirius* was travelling, it probably would actually take a full 24 hours to reach her, probably more. By the time they caught up to the ship, Naia will have repaired the external comms antenna, and would try to contact the shuttle during their approach.

Unfortunately, if they were close enough and the signal delay was low enough, that might be just enough for that consul…what was his name? Something weird. Yan-something-or-other?

Janus! Yeah, I remembered, there was an ancient god named Janus.

So he could probably remotely hack into Naia's systems and subvert control. Stop her from raising shields and firing weapons. Force the launch bay doors open. Or even just tell Naia to open the doors or they'd kill me and everyone else from the *Hope*.

Gods, it hadn't occurred to me before now, but open comms would only make things easier for them, not harder.

But then what? How would they proceed? They couldn't load all the people of Rhea onto transports, and the Rhea guard force wouldn't let them just come in and walk all over them. They all still had the shields I'd provided them, but no particle weapons.

There'd be a fight, I had no doubt of that. But Rhea would lose.

And there would be casualties, on both sides.

I wanted to hate Tiberius and his soldiers, but I couldn't, not after seeing how the Alphas controlled them. And they had more freedoms than the rest of the Omegas? Gods, I didn't want to imagine what life was like for the rest.

It occurred to me then that I didn't have a clue what things were like down in the farms or in the mines. These people were just trying to survive. And how many were there, anyway? Less than a thousand had survived, that's all I knew. Less than a thousand total, between the Alphas and the Omegas, and it sounded like the Omega population had dwindled, not grown.

But then something else occurred to me, and I jerked in surprise when an outrageous and desperate idea hit me.

Six hundred Omegas or less was far less than a thousand, and that meant…!

The wheels in my head spun, and I let the idea percolate, but then I chastised myself to slow down. I was making a *lot* of assumptions. I needed more information.

Tiberius probably would ignore me, but I knew one person, whose compassion and heart would never let anyone suffer needlessly. "Hold on, Karina, I've an idea." I stood up, but I left the comm channel open when I spoke to the guard. "Hey!" He ignored me at first, so I asked, "Enjoying your game?"

With deliberate slowness, the guard turned his head and glowered at me. "What do you want now?"

I cradled my right arm, as if hurt, and I grimaced. "I think I re-broke my elbow. Can you have Livia come up and take a look?"

The doubt in his eyes was almost comical, it was so over-the-top. "Try to be a little more convincing next time, kid." He turned away from me.

Dammit. I guess I wasn't a good liar. Maybe the only way to get her in here was to actually be hurt.

I sucked in a breath and grimaced. Oh, this was gonna hurt. But I had to talk to her. I had to talk to *someone* on my side. Or at least, someone who wasn't against me.

So I opened my fists and hovered my hands near the forcefield. I counted in my head… *One. Two. Three…*

I grit my teeth.

Four!

I *pushed,* hard as I could. Electricity jolted through me, tried to throw me back. My muscles spasmed, my jaw clamped down uncontrollably, but I tried to push through it, tried to maintain contact, tried to ignore the pain and oh *gods,* it hurt!

And then I blacked out.

FORTY-SIX

"I can't believe you did this to yourself," Livia's sweet voice sang to me.

I sucked in air, and the world spun around me. But I almost laughed out loud at *how* it felt. It wasn't spinning like when I had a concussion, and I didn't feel nearly as nauseous.

Thank the gods for little favors.

Something pressed against my chest, slightly left of center. I reached up to touch whatever it was, but it *hurt*, my hands stung in a way I'd only ever once experienced – they were burned. I gaped at them, red and raw, but not yet blistering, though I figured that was only minutes away.

"Lie back," Livia pushed my head down. She knelt over me in my cell, while the guard stood sentinel by the deactivated forcefield, pistol in hand. "Let me treat you." Her light brown eyes stared into mine, set in determination. "You know you just died."

It took a second for her words to truly register. "Uh, what?"

"Mika?" Karina's panicked voice screeched in my ear.

Reaching under the collar of my shirt, she pulled a device free and withdrew it, showing it to me. "Your heart stopped, you stopped breathing. I just brought you back with this."

I blinked in shock. "Uh, th-that's…never happened to me before." My mouth felt dry, and I tried to work saliva back into it before saying, "Thanks." I looked intently into her gaze. "Thank you," I repeated.

Karina shrieked, *"Wait, did she say you* died*?!"* I grimaced, but gave no other indication that there was anything amiss. Inwardly, I celebrated the fact that the device Livia had used to revive me hadn't somehow disabled the earpiece. *"What the hellfire did you do to yourself, Mika?"*

Livia gave me a plaintive smile for only half a second, and then put the device away in her med kit before pulling out another. "Let me see your hands."

I'd never heard her be so short with anyone, and I felt like a kid being scolded. Given that I was still only sixteen, I guess I *was* a kid being scolded.

I sure didn't feel sixteen anymore…

Laying my hands out flat, I let her wave the device over them. Suddenly the burns stung where she worked, and I flinched despite my best efforts. Livia didn't stop or even apologize.

I glanced at the guard, who watched with detached interest as she worked. I wondered if I should ask for patient privacy before I spoke to her. *No. No, he deserves to hear all of this, too. And maybe it'll work to everyone's advantage.*

Clearing my throat, I tried to speak, but my voice croaked in dryness. I cleared it again, started to say something, but Livia lectured, "Don't speak. Rest."

"I can't," I instantly replied. "Not with what they're planning to do."

Livia pressed her lips into a thin line, and she nodded. "Yeah," she muttered.

I studied her expression a moment, and hoped I was reading her right. "You don't agree with it."

She drew in a breath through her nose, glanced at me, and sighed. "It doesn't matter what I think."

"Hellfire, of course it matters," I grumbled. "Am I right in assuming that you're the Omegas' only medic?" She nodded. "Then there's a lot of responsibilities on your shoulder. How many Omegas are there, anyway?"

She finished my left hand, which was now pain-free, and she moved over to my right hand. "Just over five hundred," she remarked.

I blinked in mild surprise, then hissed at renewed pain in my right hand while she worked. "Huh," I said through clenched teeth. I forced my jaw to loosen, and added, "A lot less than I expected."

Livia shook her head. "The medici wouldn't allow our population to grow. In hindsight, she *couldn't* allow it. If the supplies she needed to keep our newborns healthy have always been limited, then she had to control our population."

I pursed my lips, glad to hear that my earlier deductions had been spot-on. "Yeah. I know what that's like." Livia flashed questioning eyes at me. "We've been in space for two-hundred forty years," I explained. "And while we haven't needed medical intervention, we *do* have a limited population size that cannot grow larger. So our A.I. has controlled who we marry, and when we have children, and how many."

"Ah," she nodded, and looked back to her work. "Makes sense." Then she frowned and asked, "How many people on your ship?"

"Five thousand," I replied. I looked intently at her. "Over one thousand of them are children." Her face softened in surprise, but then kept working. I pushed on, "And when those soldiers attack, some of those children will be among the casualties."

I saw her eyes dip. I looked up at the guard, and was pleased to see that he also looked down and away from me. I noticed that adults did that a lot when there was something they didn't like admitting to. Hell, kids probably did, too. I probably did. It was an unconscious reaction.

It was easy to look away. You didn't have to face reality that way, you didn't have to face your guilt. So I lifted my left hand, slowly so as not to alarm the guard, and I touched Livia's chin and drew her gaze back to me. "How many children have to die, Livia? How many *people*? And it won't be just on my people's side, either. They'll fight back. How many of your friends might not make it back?" I narrowed my eyes and took another leap of faith. "What if Tiberius doesn't come back?"

Moisture gathered in her eyes, and she held the device above my hand, no longer running it along the burns. I saw her lip tremble a moment, but then a hardened expression replaced her fear. "You want him to rebel against the Alphas. Against Caesar. He could die doing that, too."

"Maybe," I said. "Most likely he'd be wounded," I admitted. "But at least here, you can treat him. If he's hurt on the *Sirius,* who will treat his wounds? And if you all have been planning this coup as long as I think you have, then the odds of casualties are probably lighter here."

I glanced at the guard, hoping I was right that he, too, was part of the plan. I imagined a lot of Omegas were. Maybe even most. How long could you repress a people before they united against you? How long could they stand to live under tyranny?

"W-we don't have a choice, Mika," she shook her head. "My people will die a slow, agonizing death over generations if we don't do something."

I nodded. This next part was the key. This next part was why I had wanted to talk to Livia. "Yeah. If you stay here."

She sniffed back tears and frowned. "What?"

"If the Omegas stay here," I said, "then yes, you're right. Your people will slowly succumb, over the course of centuries. But you don't have to stay here."

I wanted to say more, but I let that offer sink in. For both her *and* Karina.

It was Karina who asked, *"Are you offering them what I think you're offering? Mika, that's…that's crazy. We don't have the room, we don't have the supplies."*

I replied to her, but meant it to be heard by Livia, "Our ship is uncrewed, and it was meant to hold a compliment of a thousand. So there's plenty of room for five or six hundred more people. And if we bring supplies from here, we can supplement the food and water source we already have on the *Sirius*." Livia and the guard both watched me carefully as I spoke, and I could practically hear the gears turning in their heads. "I'm not saying it would be easy, but if all of the Omegas work as hard as you all do, I have no doubt you would contribute to everyone's survival."

Livia's eyes darted around in thought. While her and the guard thought about it, Karina mused, *"Mika, this is crazy! This would completely upend everything in Rhea, on the* Sirius. *Nothing would ever be the same again."*

Again, I ran with it. "Everything *is* changing, Livia. One way or another."

"You're asking us to leave our home behind," she spoke tersely, fear giving her voice an edge. "Leave everything we know behind."

"Claudia wants us to do the same," I said. "Except she isn't asking. The Alphas are *forcing* us to. They're gonna make that choice for us. Much like they make your choices for you. I can't let them hurt my people, but I sure as hell won't leave your people for dead, either. I couldn't live with myself if I did that. And," I added for both the Omegas and for Karina's sake, "I *am* technically the princess of Rhea. This is unprecedented, but I imagine that this offer is well within my rights to make." Livia blinked in surprise at me.

I heard Karina repeat what I'd just said, and then I overheard Jonnec say, *"She…she is right."* Well that was a shocker. I didn't expect him to side with me, a *lowly* woman. Maybe his rough edges were being smoothed out from all of our experiences.

Maybe people could change.

And I was suggesting the biggest change of all.

Livia looked up at the guard, and he met her gaze. I don't know how well they knew each other, but I imagined a lot of unspoken words were exchanged between them. Then she looked at me. "I…I can't make any promises," she said. "But you might be on to something. I can go talk to Tiberius and the others. I can spread the word, try to get a consensus."

I nodded. "I hope you understand, though. We need to know sooner rather than later." I frowned and glanced around, then asked the guard, "What time is it, planet-side?"

He glanced at a wristwatch. "Six hours until sunset, if that's what you're asking. Fifteen hours until the next sunrise."

I lifted my eyebrows. "Short nights."

"You get used to it," Livia remarked. Frowning, she asked, "How long do days last on the *Sirius*?"

I smiled. She was curious about her new potential home, and that was something. "A little over twenty-four hours."

She smiled. "That's only an hour longer than this moon's days."

I frowned at that statement, but the guard clarified, "The nights are short right now because of the axial tilt of the moon. Long days, short nights."

"Ah," I said. I should have known that from our sensor records from the probe, but I hadn't really paid attention to that part. "Well…" I looked at Livia. "I hope you'll decide fast. Because if there's going to be a fight," I lifted my chin. "I intend to help."

Livia nodded. Then she blinked and looked at my hand. "Let me finish. Almost done…" She set back to waving the device over my palm. Thirty seconds later, and my right hand was as good as new. She closed up her medical kit, and then we helped each other stand.

Livia stared down at the deck. I saw her jaw working around for a second, and then she looked at me and repeated, "I can't promise anything. They may not listen." After another second of consideration, she added, "But I think your idea is the best one we've come across so far. So I'll try my hardest to convince them."

I returned the nod. "That's all I can ask of you." It really wasn't, but I was afraid that if I pushed harder, they'd resist out of sheer stubbornness. Maybe that was something only I would do, but I wasn't going to risk it.

They left my cell, and the guard reactivated the forcefield, sealing me in.

I sighed, and then slumped back on my bench. The guard didn't resume his game, but he did seem to stare off into nothingness, possibly considering my proposal.

I whispered, "I'm alone again. Sort of. What do you think?"

There was a pause, and then I heard a click. Karina must have muted her connection somehow, but she restored it and said, *"We were just discussing it. Jonnec is worried about the Truthspeakers, but we could maybe make it work. Especially if the Omegas stayed away from Rhea at first."*

I nodded and whispered, "We'd have to enforce a quarantine anyway. Find out if they can get nanite infusions like us to help prevent illness. It'd be a slow integration."

"Marek pointed out," Karina added, *"that we'd still need to bring supplies up. Not just food and extra water, but the supplies we came here for."*

"Yeah," I nodded. "It'd be a long slog, getting both people and material up. A lot of back-and-forth travel." I shrugged and added, "But at least we'd have some of their ships to help with it."

The longer I thought about it, the crazier it all sounded. At the same time, it was the only way out that I could see.

They just *had* to agree to it.

There was no telling what would happen, no telling if they would be onboard with the idea. And I still wasn't sure about the Alphas, what their plans were. Had I succeeded in sowing doubt in their minds about Caesar? How would that all play into this? I didn't imagine Caesar would let us just waltz on out of here.

I had a really bad feeling about that damned imposter.

"Karina," I whispered. "I know you guys are evading predators and all, but I need you here. Are you willing to walk through the night?"

"Sure," she said. *"Jonnec was already suggesting it, anyway. Why, what do you need us to do?"*

I narrowed my eyes. "I need to know what's in that dome."

FORTY-SEVEN

I wish I could say that I spent the rest of the day in stoic silence, patiently waiting for the seeds I had planted to grow and bear fruit.

Yeah, that's not me. I hate waiting. I hate having nothing to do. The only time I sit quietly is if I'm reading a good book. So I practically wore a path into the deck plating in my cell, pacing back and forth like a caged animal, walking off the aftereffects of electric shock.

They fed me, thankfully. More fruits and veggies for lunch, though this time, the guard didn't drop the forcefield to give it to me. He must have thought I was crazy after my last stunt, because he warily put it in a slot next to the forcefield that then pushed the food into a slot on my end. I grinned at him and set to ravenously eating.

For dinner, someone either took pity on me, or someone was starting to care more about me. Either way didn't matter, because it was cooked meat! Chicken, specifically, and it was a deliciously-spiced grilled chicken breast with potatoes on the side, and oh my gods, whoever cooked this could give my mother a run for her money!

Shortly after dinner, Karina checked in with me, telling me that they were only a few hundred meters from the *Alpha*'s hull, having covered a lot more ground than I expected. She informed me that they'd infiltrate the dome within ten minutes, assuming they could find an easy way in. Light was failing outside, according to Karina, so if they had to do any climbing, they had to do it fast.

My impatient pacing grew more frenzied.

The guard eyed me wearily.

And then, *finally,* something came from all of my efforts over the past two days.

Tiberius walked in, and he laser-focused on me, ignoring the guard that had jumped up from his stool and stood at attention. Tiberius eyed the guard, and said, "You're dismissed."

The guard saluted with one fist over the heart, and then grabbed his data pad and rushed from the room.

I was glad for something to happen, but his timing couldn't have been worse. Somehow everything felt a thousand times more dangerous with Karina's life more directly on the line. I wanted to be able to answer any questions she had without worrying about someone realizing I had an active comm device.

Once the guard was gone, Tiberius set his eyes on me again. Strong, patient eyes, seemingly peering into my soul. I stood next to the humming forcefield and stared at him through the blue-white shimmer, studying his expression while suppressing the urge to bounce up and down impatiently. Every time I thought I'd had a read on him over the past couple days, he'd proven me wrong, and now I just couldn't figure out what he was doing or thinking. In fact, the longer he stared, the more uncomfortable I felt.

An image flashed in my memory, the blast of his pistol going off into my stomach. I surged towards him, only just barely resisting the urge to hit the forcefield. "You shot me," I snarled at him.

He lifted his chin. "I did what I thought I had to."

"And now come to gloat?"

He answered with his own question, "Are you really offering to take my people with you?"

It hadn't been the question I'd expected, and it derailed my fury and train of thought. Once I recovered, I said, "Yes!" I nodded intently. "I am. There's more than enough room on the *Sirius*."

He sighed and walked around to stand between the console and the forcefield, but he faced me, not the console. "You're talking about taking my people away from their home."

A familiar argument, but I'd had time to think about it. This time, I had a better response, a less accusatory one. "I'm talking about you leading them into a better life. To a place where they aren't controlled by an Alpha, and where they'll be free to intermingle with five thousand other people. We can help solve one another's problems. I'm talking about a mutually beneficial arrangement."

A small smirk quirked up the corner of his mouth. "There it is. I knew there was more than one angle to your proposal."

I quirked my head sideways. "What do you mean?"

His gaze met mine, and he said, "If it was just about escape, I'd not trust you on it. But there's something about you. About the way you care so much for your people. About the way you care about *people*, in general."

I pursed my lips. "Well. I know what it's like to have every aspect of your life controlled. I know what it's like to be forced to live in a lie. Your people deserve the chance to be more, same as my people."

Nodding, he said, "I couldn't agree more." He drew in a deep, hesitant breath, and then turned and tapped commands into the console. The forcefield died with a snap of released energy. He looked at me and folded his arms. "So this next part's gonna be tricky. I wanted to think on this some more, I wanted to figure Caesar into our original plans more, but…turns out there's no time. And yes," he glanced over his shoulder, towards what I suspected was a camera, "Zoe disabled the camera in here just before I came in, so we can speak freely."

I honestly hadn't thought about that this time, but I nodded like I understood and expected as much.

He continued, "But Caesar is forcing our hand."

When he didn't keep talking, I frowned and cautiously stepped out of my cell. "What do you mean?"

Still hesitant, Tiberius said, "Caesar has demanded to see you. Now."

I titled my head up. "Oh," I managed to say, fear building inside of me. "W-what about?"

"No idea," he said. "I'm to escort you to his quarters, and you're to go in alone."

I swallowed back a lump in my throat. "That doesn't sound like a good idea."

"Perhaps not, but I intend to take advantage of it." He hesitated again, and then stepped closer to me. "If you're willing to help us."

"Ah," I grimaced. "You need proof."

"Yeah," he shrugged. "I need proof, to show everyone, but especially the Alphas."

"To sow doubt and chaos into their ranks," I surmised.

Surprisingly, Tiberius shook his head. "No. To give them a chance." I frowned at him. "They've oppressed us, they've used us, but they're still part of our home. They're still *our people*. I've served them all of my life, and at least some of them deserve a chance to repent and make up for their," he hesitated. "Sins."

"That's a joke!" I snorted. He didn't laugh, and my stomach dropped. "Right?"

With his serious expression never wavering, he shook his head. "No, I'm serious."

"If you give them a chance…"

"I have a plan," he growled at me, over-enunciating each word. "One which will ensure that they will fall, *tonight*." I blinked in surprise. "Even if every single one of them rejects my overture of peace."

"Your overture," I frowned at him. "Hellfire, I thought you were just a top-ranking guy at most, but you're the leader of the…resistance? Movement? Whatever you call yourselves?"

He nodded. "I'm *a* leader," he clarified, "but I'm the one who planned the action that has already been put into motion tonight."

"Aaand what exactly is that plan?"

"Better if you don't know," he shook his head. "But you're part of it, and if you're telling the truth about Caesar, then this meeting will give us the opportunity we need."

I peered at him, and cautiously asked, "What did you have in mind?"

He pulled something from a pouch on his belt and presented it to me open-palmed. It was a communicator earpiece. "I trust you know what this is?"

My face flushed, and I became ever so self-conscious about my own earpiece. "Uh, yeah," I nodded.

"Good." He came closer. "Wear this. I'll monitor and record your conversation with Caesar. The moment he says something to prove what he is, I'll transmit it across the entire ship, to all Alphas, and to all of the Omegas sneaking aboard from our village right now."

I blinked at him. So *that* was his plan. Or part of it. Every single Omega that was in on this underground movement was going to board the ship in the night and surround the Alphas.

Sheer numbers, that's how they planned to win.

It was bold. It was risky. It might just work, but it might just fall flat on its face, too.

But if the Alphas suddenly had proof that their revered leader had been a lie for two centuries, maybe that would be enough to distract them long enough for the Omegas to take them at gunpoint.

There was one big problem with it. "Aren't you afraid that General Lucious will see through your plan?"

Tiberius gave me a wicked smile. "General Lucious is under the impression that our coup will take place on the shuttle tomorrow. My soldiers have let slip that fact to him, by whispering around his overly-acute hearing, acting like they hoped he couldn't hear them. He won't expect anything tonight."

I gave him a frown. "Wouldn't it have been better not to let him know *anything* was planned?"

Gracing me with another shrug, Tiberius replied, "Like you seem to have figured out, he's brilliant. He's been our general for two centuries, so he was bound to suspect something. Better to throw him off than to expect him to hold zero suspicion over us."

I nodded. "I see. Still, won't he put measures into place here, now?"

Again, he graced me with a wicked smile. "And just who do you think he'll need to put safety measures in place?"

I quirked an eyebrow up quizzically. Then it dawned on me. "Soldiers. Soldiers he thinks are loyal to him."

Tiberius's smile grew wider. "Indeed. And, point of fact, there *are* soldiers who are not part of our movement. They'll be dealt with, too." He thrust the comm device towards me. "Now, are you in, or not?"

I looked at the proffered earpiece, and then I looked at him. "What happens when Caesar decides to kill me?"

As if anticipating that question, Tiberius pulled something else from behind him – my pistol! He offered it to me with his other hand. "I trust you know how to use this, too?"

I favored him with my own wicked smile.

And I took both items.

All or nothing tonight.

I holstered my gun, and then pressed the earpiece into my left ear. "When do we start?"

"Well as I said," Tiberius gave me another shrug. "Caesar wants to see you *now*, so no time like the present."

I nodded.

Finally! After being led around, after being held captive and made to sit idle, it was time to take action!

FORTY-EIGHT

When Tiberius led me out of the security office, I was shocked to find another familiar face – Sebastian leaned against the opposite wall in the corridor, his arms folded while he tapped his foot impatiently.

He stirred when we stepped out, and he quickly brushed off and straightened the front of his clothes, a far cry different from the flight suit I'd last seen him in. Sebastian wore olive-green clothes of refined fabric, another sign that he lived in a world far different from Rhea where textiles were either hand-made or manufactured from primitive looms. He likewise wore an olive-green jacket made of a more reflective and noisy material.

"Hey there," he said, flashing me a smile.

I frowned and looked at Tiberius, who nodded, "I have to go to a control room to monitor, record, and transmit. The lieutenant will escort you and provide backup."

I blinked. "Lieutenant?"

"My rank," Sebastian flashed me another smile. With a canned haughtiness, he added, "I'm an officer."

"I recognize that rank, but not from Roman history," I said, my frown deepening. "Why's your rank different?"

"Uh, well," he faltered and scratched at his head, further mussing up his messy black hair. "T-that's a good question."

"The Alpha space navy never converted to ancient Roman ranks," Tiberius explained with a surprisingly helpful shrug. "And as I understand it, they likewise refused the commands to convert to ancient Greek ranks."

Sebastian gave his own, innocent shrug. "What can I say?"

"That you're arrogant," Tiberius quipped coldly. "Self-involved."

Taking the insult as a compliment, Sebastian polished what I guessed was rank insignia on his jacket's collar, and bashfully said, "Well, ya know."

"Aaaaand you want *him* watching my back?" I doubtfully inquired.

"Hey!" the copilot protested.

"There's no better marksman," Tiberius explained. The centurion turned to me fully and grasped my shoulder, and to be honest, I tensed, half-expecting him to shoot me again. "Mika Kai. I risk much for my people in doing this." He looked intently into my eyes, and I returned his gaze steadfastly. I didn't *feel* steadfast, but something inside told me I had to project confidence, so I did my best. "But so do you. So be careful. Your people do not know of the bargain we have struck, so I need you as much as you need me."

I drew in a slow breath, debating if I should tell him that I wasn't the only one who knew. How would Karina, Jonnec, and Marek factor into his plan? Would he stop trusting me if he knew I had companions breaking into the dome as we spoke?

But I had to assure him, I had to set him at ease. "That's not true," I admitted, and swallowed. I turned my head and pointed at my right ear, even though the earpiece was probably impossible to see in this lighting. "I've been in contact with three others. They know the deal."

Tiberius tensed, and I felt his hand cinch on my arm. "So my troops were right," he murmured. "There were survivors from the other ship."

I didn't correct him, his assertion was close enough. I just looked at him and nodded.

"Will they help fight?"

"They're already working on finding proof of their own about Caesar," I said. After only another moment of hesitation, I added, "They're going for the dome."

Narrowing his eyes, Tiberius asked, "Then you are confident that the radiation readings are, indeed, false?"

"I don't know," I replied. "But their hand scanners should be able to tell them. And if it's clear, they'll be able to look around."

Tiberius nodded, and then pursed his lips. "You should have told me about them."

I gave him a sour look. "You shouldn't have shot me."

"Wait, he *shot* you?!" Sebastian blurted.

Tiberius gave him a withering glare, and then regarded me. "You know, if our two peoples are to coexist, we must learn to trust one another."

I lifted my eyebrows. "Well, I *am* going into Caesar's quarters with a pistol and a cocky pilot for backup on your word that he'll actually *back me up.*"

"Hey!" Sebastian protested. "I resent that."

Ignoring the pilot, Tiberius grinned and nodded, patting me on the shoulder. "Good luck, Mika Kai."

"Same to you," I nodded.

He squeezed, and then let go and turned away, stalking down the corridor.

I turned to Sebastian, and then without waiting for him, I headed for the lift, my feet moving rapidly as anxious energy built up inside. "H-hey, wait up!" Sebastian called, hurrying after me.

I didn't glance at him, knowing exactly where I was headed. But I did want to know how Karina was doing, so I tapped my right ear. "Karina."

"Karina?" Sebastian asked just as he fell into step beside me.

"Go ahead," her sweet voice came back.

"All hell is about to break loose over here," I advised. "And I'm about to face off against Caesar."

"Wait, you what?!" she squeaked.

"It's a long story," I shook my head. "And I can't go into details just yet, but just be aware, and make sure your weapons are ready. What's your status?"

"Wait, wait, why are you going to see-"

"We don't have *time,* Karina," I said, a little more sharply than I meant to. We came up to a lift, and I pressed the summon button. "Where are you guys?"

I could hear the annoyance in her voice when she replied, *"We just got through a hull breach in the port-side transit tunnel. It's definitely abandoned, Mika, no one's been in here in a long, long time. There's some spider-like things that are the size of fists, and Jonnec's learning he doesn't like spiders."* I almost growled that there wasn't time for *that* kind of commentary, but just as the lift opened before us, I laughed. I couldn't help it, the image of Jonnec screaming in terror around an arachnid entered my head and played on repeat. Karina giggled as she finished, *"Anyway, we're about to enter the radiation field. At the levels it jumps up to, we'll only have a few seconds to confirm if it's real or fake."*

I nodded, leading Sebastian onto the lift. "Deck one," I ordered it.

"Huh?"

"Nothing," I told her, while the lift closed and started moving. "I won't be able to reply to you after this, but definitely let me know if you're okay."

"Will do. Let's keep this channel open. You know, since you're going into the lion's den and all."

Now *that* was a mythology we hadn't read in a long time. I grinned. "At least I'm going in with teeth of my own," I slapped my pistol.

The lift opened, and I walked us out onto deck one, and turned to walk past the bridge to the ship's port side.

After a few paces in silence, Sebastian said, "Oh, finally done chatting with your invisible friends?"

I gave him a tired look. "Jealousy? Really?"

He smirked. "What can I say? I'm a lady's man, you know?"

"Not this lady," I rolled my eyes at him. "No offense, but I don't go for your type."

"What, confident sharpshooting pilots?"

I glanced at him. "Men."

He blinked in surprise. "Men?"

I gave him an annoyed glare and said, "Yeah. You know, what you are."

He didn't take the bait this time. Instead, Sebastian scrunched his brow and stared ahead, suddenly silent. I reveled in the blissful quiet for a second. He wasn't a loudmouth, per-se, but when he did talk, I found it...*grating*.

But then he asked, "They let you be with women on your ship?"

It hadn't been a sarcastic or playful question. In fact, I heard a certain earnestness in his voice, and I regarded him carefully. "Well, no, actually." I wondered if Karina could hear his side of our conversation. I decided she probably could. "But I don't care if they 'let me' or not."

"Hm," he said quietly, and clammed up.

Interesting.

But then we were in front of Caesar's doors.

The captain's quarters.

It made me miss home. It made me miss my quarters on the *Sirius*.

It made me miss Naia.

"Mika, the readings are definitely false," Karina reported. *"We're heading into the dome."*

I nodded, then felt foolish. She couldn't see me. But I felt like she could. I felt like she could always see me, like she was always with me.

I *needed* her with me, now, because all of a sudden, my courage faltered, and I was terrified to step through those doors.

I remembered facing the alien on the *Sirius*. I remembered watching it emerge from the fog in the stardrive core, intent on killing me, on killing everyone I knew.

It had been intelligent *and* ruthless. A monster with brains, the most terrifying kind. Knights and wizards in my books had never faced such creatures, and I almost envied them. What I wouldn't give for a quest against a formless, shapeless, but dumb monster.

Now here I was, about to face another intelligent and ruthless being. Gods, I was scared.

Sebastian stared at me, waiting patiently.

Then, I was surprised when I heard a voice in my left ear, Tiberius. *"I'm right here with you, Mika Kai. You're not alone."*

I smiled and tapped my left earpiece. "Good to hear," I said.

Sebastian tapped what I presumed was an earpiece in his right ear, and said, "We're at the door."

"Troops are in position," Tiberius said. *"Do it."*

I drew in a shuddering breath and looked at Sebastian. He returned my gaze, and all arrogance and joking was gone from him. I don't know how long we stared, but finally, he said, "Don't take this the wrong way, now that I know what I know about you, but..." He took hold of my hand, and squeezed it gently.

I took comfort in that friendly gesture. There was no romantic interest, there was no inky and ulterior motive like I often felt from Jonnec. It was really and truly just a friendly act.

Smiling, I squeezed back. With all of the surprises I'd had over the past two days, it was nice to finally have a *pleasant* surprise.

Then Sebastian pressed a button on the door's control panel.

"Yes," Caesar's deep, resonating voice spoke through the panel.

"Good evening, sir," Sebastian said, his voice surprisingly confident. "I have Mika Kai here, as ordered."

Caesar didn't reply. The doors hissed apart, and the shadows of Caesar's quarters opened before me. Sebastian took two steps back. He couldn't come in with me, but he did whisper, "I'll be right out here."

I nodded absently.

And then I stepped into the lion's den.

FORTY-NINE

Caesar's window still hadn't been repaired, and the setting sun off in the distance blinded me.

The door hissed closed behind me.

A combination of deep, dark shadows cast from furniture and the light in my face made it impossible to see anything, so I stepped further into the room and shielded my eyes. The room was much as I remembered, a dark and foreboding place with muted colors for decorations.

And there was Caesar. Standing in the kitchen, hovering over the counter, his hands splayed out menacingly on the granite top. When I lived in the *Sirius's* captain's quarters, I had thought the tall ceilings a waste of space and gaudy. Now, it gave Caesar room to be intimidating without even coming close to touching that ceiling.

"Welcome, Mika Kai," he spoke in that bone-shaking deep voice. His gold eyes flared, bright enough that I knew it wasn't just a reflection. Bright enough that I knew it was his exosuit's optical sensors, or the illusion, or both.

I remembered the minotaur's red eyes flashing at me.

Desperate to cover my fear, I unclenched my jaw and said as casually as I could muster, "You wanted to see me?"

While my eyes adjusted to the darkness, hard as that was in twilight, Caesar gave me a sneer. "You have been busy since you're arrival, young one."

I keyed in on those last words. "Interesting that you call me young one, not young pup." The sneer faltered, his expression uncertain for a moment, but he didn't reply. Taking that as an open question, I added, "Claudia always calls me 'young pup.' Same with one of the consuls. But not you."

Caesar's uncertainty vanished. "The medici has many unusual quirks."

"But it has something to do with me being from Sirius, doesn't it?" I asked, finally putting the pieces together. "In mythology, Sirius was a dog. And I feel like there's even more to it than that. Why does she insist on calling me a young pup, just because my home is named after a hunting dog?"

Pushing up to his full height, Caesar stalked around the kitchen island, coming closer to me. His footsteps reverberated on the deck plating, even through the carpet.

"So this ship," I said, letting my mouth run to hide my anxiety. I looked around, an idea clicking into place. "The *Alpha*. Is it somehow named after the star system she's from? What's it called again?" I hoped he took the bait.

Caesar didn't stop coming closer, but he did answer, "This ship came from Alpha Centauri."

"Oh, right," I nodded. He was past the island now, but I tried not to let my nerves control me. Tried really, *really* hard. "What about you? What star system do you come from?"

He stopped mid-stride.

I waited for Caesar to deny it. To say, "Alpha Centauri, of course." But he didn't.

Instead, a broad, wicked-looking smile crept up the edges of his lips, his perfect teeth glimmering in a beam of sunlight.

Very slow, his voice inducing goosebumps on my arms, he said, "I come from a world far from here."

I blinked, surprised. That had been easier than I expected. Except...

"We need more than that," Tiberius's voice whispered in my ear. *"Keep him talking!"*

Dammit.

I shoved my fear down as best as I could, and I stood as tall as my petite frame would allow. "How far?"

"I was forged over three thousand lightyears from his place," he said, as if that had any meaning to me other than the fact that I knew it was a long distance. I frowned at the use of the word 'forged' rather than born. "I have lived longer than you can imagine."

"Uh huh," I nodded sagely and planted my hands on my hips, ever-so-conscious of the pistol on my right thigh. "And now you're here. Posing as a human. As an Alpha."

Caesar's smile only broadened. "This surprises you?"

I shrugged, in the best spirit of Tiberius. "Well, yeah. The last of your kind I met was more interested in *killing* my people, not ruling over them."

Now Caesar's expression faltered. In fact, it drew out into an almost comical expression of absolute shock.

I lifted my eyebrows mockingly. "Oh, you didn't know? Claudia didn't tell you? After I spent the past two days convincing the Alphas and Omegas that I'd met and *killed* an intelligent alien entity, you didn't know?" I pursed my lips and said, "I thought you were listening in to *all* of my conversations, but clearly you have your limits, *Caesar.*" I scornfully spat out the name.

"You know," my mouth kept running now, and I couldn't stop it if I tried, "if I've learned anything about these people, it's that you don't deserve that name. You don't deserve that *title.* Say what you will about the Alphas, at least they aren't stupid like you." His glowing eyes narrowed to slits. "Honestly, if the real Caesar was alive, he'd have gotten his people out of here safe and sound by now. But that wasn't your plan, was it?"

He was closing in on me, but I hardly noticed, my brain and my mouth running at lightspeed. "The long-range comms could have been repaired by now, right? But you stopped them from repairing or rebuilding the antenna. You wanted them cowing before you, serving you. What I can't figure out is why?" He was so close now that I had to crane my neck to look up at him. "Why would you need humans to serve you? Why haven't you called your-*Hrk!*"

Caesar lunged forward and wrapped his hands around my throat, cinching off my breath and my voice. "Do you *ever* shut *up?!*" he snarled.

My pistol was already in my hand, and I fired into his chest. A rust-red light flashed, and his grip vanished, dropping me to the deck, where I crumpled onto my knees. Caesar staggered backwards.

And the illusion died. It didn't fluctuate, like I expected, it completely died. Leaving before me an eight-foot-tall mechanism. The exosuit was similar to the one I'd faced on the *Sirius,* metallic, mechanical, knees bent backwards, and two glowing eyes.

But that was where the similarities ended. The eyes glowed orange, not red. The surface of the suit wasn't covered in complex patterns, it was perfectly smooth.

Most importantly, I noted a distinct lack of any weapons embedded in its arm. Plus my weapon, which had barely phased the one on the *Sirius,* had left a smoldering dent in the exosuit's stomach. Sparks sputtered from cracks in that dent, but it was less than an inch deep.

Still, it was damage.

My weapon wasn't useless against it.

I pushed up onto my feet, and I kept my weapon trained on it. "So," I croaked through my aching throat. "You're not invincible." A hissing noise that sounded strangely mechanical emanated from Caesar. "Funny, the last alien I fought, his suit was impervious to my weapon." I grimaced as the memory of Thelon's death played through my head again. "Frustratingly so."

It clutched the hole in its stomach, and I kept my weapon trained on its chest, not its face, where I knew the little being inside was centered.

And that's when I realized why my weapon was a threat to it. Hell, I'd already guessed it earlier, but this was proof of it. "Because your technology is two centuries out of date. The one I faced on my ship had more advanced technology. But you? You're vulnerable. To me. To my weapons. To the Alphas and the Omegas. You're at risk, being amongst them. But then, why?" I frowned. "Why risk it? Why, for two centuries, have you pretended to be Caesar?"

The illusion flickered back into place for a second, but then died again. "These humans were eager for leadership," it said, its voice still Caesar's, but with an electric quality to it. "I gave it to them."

"But you could have called your people," I said. "You could've been rescued. Abducted these people to serve you off-world, in your own territory, on your own ship. So why the hellfire have you felt the need to trick and oppress them for so long?"

The exosuit was eerily still, now, the illusion of breathing absent. When it held still, it was unnatural stillness, and it sent shivers down my spine. I jumped when another spark escaped from the cracks, searing between the metallic fingers covering the damage.

And then its head jerked to the side, as if the alien had just been startled by something.

It was Karina who answered for it. *I think I know why, Mika. The dome…it's filled with crates and crates of material. Heavy metals. Deuterium. Tritium. Literal tons of valuable cargo in storage containers.*

My eyes widened, and I gaped at the monstrosity before me.

"Greed?!" I whispered incredulously. "The mines. You had them mining heavy metals and converting ocean water into fuel, so that you could stockpile it!"

Caesar growled, "You humans are surprisingly effective beasts of labor." It stood up to its full height, dropping its hand from its wounded stomach. "But I knew that eventually you would outlive your usefulness. That time has come."

"Mika, something's happening out here!" Karina shouted. When the audiofeed picked up her voice, I heard a high-pitched whining drawing up in the background. *"There's a ship! Holy hellfire, it's a black ship!"*

I heard Jonnec's voice, *"It appears to be similar to the black ship we diverted from crashing into the* Sirius*!"*

A black ship. Caesar's ship. The one he'd used to attack the *Alpha*. Which he's had two centuries to repair and refuel.

"But," I shook my head. "If it's anything like…no way, your ship isn't big enough to haul all of that cargo."

He slowly lowered into a crouch, and I gripped my pistol with both hands. "It is like you said, *human*." I blinked questioningly at him. "It is time to call my own people in. And the wealth I will be granted for all of the material here will give me the power I have always desired!"

Caesar lunged at me.

I fired, the rust-red light blinding.

But Caesar hadn't aimed for me. He sailed over me, my blast missing and blowing a hole into a bulkhead by the kitchen.

Sebastian was through the door then, and to his credit, he didn't gape at the exosuit barreling down on him, he just aimed and fired.

But he didn't know where to aim. His blast hit the exosuit square between the glowing eyes, but there wasn't a brain in there, there wasn't an *alien* in there, so all he did was damage the exosuit. Caesar batted Sebastian aside, flinging him twenty feet, and I heard him cry out in pain.

And Caesar was out the door.

"The ship's taking off," Karina shouted. *"It must be controlled remotely!"*

While I rushed to Sebastian's side, I said, "Tiberius! Alien ship taking off from the dome!"

"We're a little busy with the Alphas," Tiberius snarled over comms. *"I've just transmitted a cut of everything that was said."*

I helped Sebastian up. He winced when I grabbed his right arm, but he didn't scream. "You okay?" I asked him.

"Yeah, fine, just dandy," he grumbled. "Didn't break clean

through, but I'm pretty sure my arm's fractured." He wheezed a little and added, "And maybe some cracked ribs."

"Well, come on, we have to stop it!" I shouted, bolting for the door and careening into the corridor. I looked both ways, but wherever Caesar had run to, he was long gone. "Dammit," I hissed.

Sebastian caught up, his face screwed in pain, and he likewise looked both ways. "Where'd he go?"

I blinked and shook my head. "Um, well. It, uh…needs to get away. Its ship is coming for it. Where could it get aboard its ship?"

We looked at one another, and echoed each other, "The launch bay!"

Together, we ran as fast as we could down the corridor for the lift we'd just come from.

That's when we came across the first bodies. Two Omega soldiers, one with his head facing an unnatural angle, the other with an obvious dent in his chest.

And their weapons were gone.

"Oh shit," Sebastian hissed. He pressed his earpiece and said, "Tiberius! The damn thing killed Ajax and Eros and took their weapons!"

I heard Tiberius curse over comms. *They were meant to apprehend the medici!*

"Well, she's not here," Sebastian said. He bent down and checked for pulses, even though they stared back at him with lifeless eyes.

Tiberius didn't reply, and I presumed he was organizing another group to come after Claudia. "Come on, Sebastian," I tugged his sleeve. "Before that thing kills anyone else!"

Cursing, Sebastian joined me, and we ran after Caesar.

Ahead, we heard the barking of compressed particle weapons firing, and a lot of shouting. When we came around the bend, we found four more bodies, three Omegas and the purple-eyed Consul, all with smoking holes in their chests.

More shouting.

More shooting. But this time behind us.

Be aware, you two, some of the loyalist Omegas are fighting back!

There wasn't time to question him, we just had to hope that the fighting stayed behind us. We had to keep after Caesar.

We careened around a corner just in time to see the exosuit disappear into the lift. The doors slid closed before I could get a bead on him. "Dammit," I hissed, and practically slammed into the wall and punched the controls to summon another lift.

Except that just then, all of the lights died, all of the *power* died. Emergency lights came on a second later, every fourth ceiling panel glowing a little dimmer than normal.

The fight for the starship *Alpha* must have escalated rapidly.

Tiberius's plan hadn't succeeded after all, not fully.

I glanced at Sebastian. "That's not gonna stop Caesar," I said.

He nodded. "Maintenance ladder?"

I nodded behind him, "That way," and I pushed past him to sprint for a hatch I knew to be only three sections away.

"How do you know all of this?" he wheezed.

"Magic," I quipped over heavy breathing.

Sebastian didn't have a comeback for that.

While we ran, Karina spoke over comms, *"Mika, we're just about out of the dome, heading your way!"*

"Meet us in the port-side launch bay," I huffed. I glanced at Sebastian, "Port-side, right? Starboard's out of commission?"

"Okay, how did you know *that?*" he breathed.

"Lucky guess," I said. "And I saw that the ship was half-buried on the starboard side when you brought us here."

As we drew up to the door into a maintenance junction, Sebastian remarked wryly, "Well aren't you the observant one."

The door, of course, didn't open, so I pried open the panel to get to the release lever, and I yanked it down. Then Sebastian and I worked to pull the door open. A second later, we made it to the ladder. I started to climb down, but as I descended to the next deck, Sebastian asked, "What the hell are you doing?"

I looked up at him as he stooped over the hole above me. "What?" I impatiently shouted.

"Get out of the way and watch how it's done!"

I didn't have a clue what he was on about, but I stepped down onto the next deck, clearing the ladder. I watched as he grabbed the sides of the ladder, planted his feet on either side *outside* of the rungs, and then he slid down past me, rapidly gaining speed.

Oh. Well, that's a neat trick!

So I emulated him as best as I could, and I slid down after him, noting that this could come in handy in future emergencies.

We got to the bottom deck, and I slammed down a little harder than

I meant to, and then…

And then we noticed that Caesar had come this way. He hadn't bothered with the emergency release on the door, he'd blasted and shoved his way through. And left more bodies behind.

"Son of a bitch," Sebastian cursed when we passed by more fallen Omegas, but these weren't soldiers. They were armed, but they looked thinner, bonier, and wore clothes that looked muddied and harrowed. These had been ordinary people, taking up arms to rebel against the Alphas and their false god.

My blood boiled, but I knew it was nothing compared to what Sebastian must have felt.

My heart thudded in my chest, my breathing came harder and harder, but we had to catch that *thing* before he got on that ship. I knew that if he managed to contact others from his species, they could come with more ships, with *larger* ships. They could come with the advanced exosuits that I'd faced on the *Sirius*. They'd take the *Alpha* in minutes, and worse, they'd take the *Sirius*.

None of us would stand a chance.

They might take minutes, days, or weeks to come, but I had no doubt they'd come, and there was no way we'd have the *Sirius* ready to leave before then.

I'd hoped the bulkhead doors leading into the launch bay would have slowed Caesar down, but he was already through when we arrived, the door melted to slag and shoved and pried apart. I leapt through the hole first, Sebastian hot on my heels, keeping up with me despite his injuries.

The bay was mostly empty, but Caesar, halfway between the door and the open launch bay doors, was already blasting holes through the Omega soldiers. And outside, its engines howling, was the black ship, difficult to see against the darkening night behind it.

He was getting away!

I skid to a stop and took aim, but before I could pull the trigger, Sebastian said, "I've got this!"

Rust-red lanced out, and true to Tiberius's word, the pilot's aim was perfect, and he tagged Caesar's right leg, sending the exosuit stumbling into a crash two-thirds of the way across the flight deck.

I gaped. "Nice shot!"

Sebastian grinned.

Then Caesar pointed a weapon at us. "Look out!" I shouted,

shoving Sebastian aside just as a rust-red pulse-blast rocketed past where we'd been a split second ago.

"Go for cover!" he shouted, and we scrambled towards one of the maintenance shuttles. More blasts bolted past us, reverberating explosions echoing in the massive bay as chunks of bulkheads and walls and framing were blown out.

Those were gods-damned military grade weapons, level four! The highest available on the *Sirius* were level three weapons, civilian-grade.

Caesar managed to get up onto his feet, though he listed heavily to one side, and he kept shooting at us. The maintenance shuttle took damage, but it kept us protected for now. I glanced around the side to see Caesar limping towards his ship, which hovered closer now, its pointed front-end piercing into the bay.

I tried to aim and fire, but Caesar kept shooting at us and I had to duck back into cover, my own shots missing Caesar by a wide margin. Sebastian moved to the other side of the shuttle and tried to get in a shot, but Caesar apparently wielded two weapons, and he kept us both covered.

Thinking that a larger target would be easier to hit, I fired at Caesar's black ship, but my blast was simply absorbed by its hull, leaving no visible damage.

"He's getting away!" I shouted, frustration boiling into my voice.

"No shit!" Sebastian roared. He tried to move from cover to head over to one of the fighters, but a flurry of blasts pushed him back. "Dammit, we need to get him into a crossfire!"

"Karina, where are you?" I screeched between blind-firing at Caesar.

"Almost there!" her harried, breathless voice came back. I knew it was literally kilometers between where she'd started and the launch bay, but I was still annoyed at how long it took her. We couldn't let him escape!

"Tiberius, do you have any more troops near the port launch bay?" I asked.

"None that are responding," the centurion replied, frustratingly calm.

"Gods DAMMIT!" I screamed, and sent out a flurry of blind fire. I wish I'd still had my shield bracer on, at least then I could duck out for longer than a second!

The alien's ship had further penetrated into the bay. I saw a ramp suddenly *appear*, extending down from the core of the ship as if it had always been there, no visible mechanical parts to it, and a red light illuminated the way up for Caesar. The vessel drew lower, only a dozen meters up now.

So close. We were so close, but couldn't do a thing to save ourselves!

Until an explosion lit up the night, and shoved the alien ship downwards, crumpling the ramp on the deck with a strange, mechanical screech. The blast wave blew Caesar back into the bay, and he slid across the deck a hundred meters.

I blinked in shock.

And then General Lucious's voice echoed over the launch bay speakers, *"Attention, false Caesar. I have missiles and defense cannons targeting your vessel. Stand down at once and surrender!"*

I blinked upwards in shock, my mind taking a long time to process the sudden turn of events.

Finally, I realized what had happened, and what it had meant.

I'd convinced Lucious of the truth! He must have been on the bridge of the *Alpha,* controlling the same weapons that had tried to shoot the *Hope* down!

"Yeah!" I shouted, breaking from cover to jeer at the alien. "Yeah, that's how it feels!" I pointed at his ship as it slowly eased up off the deck, its ramp a crumpled mess. "Not so nice when they're shooting at you, huh?"

But Caesar wasn't done.

The ship rapidly reversed out of the bay, turned, and bolted into the night.

I blinked in surprise, and looked down at Caesar as he watched it go. He must have still been capable of remotely controlling it. But where was he sending it?

I saw the *Alpha's* A.D.S. light up the night sky, tracking the alien ship. They missed most of the time, but even when they hit, it didn't stop the ship. Missiles launched out towards it, missing but still detonating and illuminating the black hull, as the ship veered around and headed back towards the *Alpha.*

"No," Sebastian said. "NO!" And he aimed and fired at Caesar, destroying one shoulder.

The alien ship fired. Golden light arched above.

The *Alpha* rocked.

And I knew without having to see. The ship's bridge was gone.

General Lucious was dead.

FIFTY

I opened fire, but I wasn't nearly the crack shot that Sebastian was, and my rust-red blast drilled into the deck plating.

Sebastian fired again, but Caesar rolled, dodging the blast while picking up one of its dropped rifles. I dodged back behind the shuttle just in time, a pulse-blast singeing past my trailing hair.

We were back to square one, and it was only a matter of time before Caesar brought its ship back into the bay.

I glared at the weapon in my hand, saw its power cells were nearly drained. It wasn't a bow and arrow, and that would have been even more useless in this situation, but damn if I couldn't aim this as well as my bow!

I heard Caesar's exosuit clomping around noisily on the deck.

The *Alpha* rocked again, no doubt from Caesar's ship firing, though why he kept shooting, I couldn't fathom. Maybe he was just making sure the bridge was truly obliterated. Maybe he was taking his frustrations out on all of us.

This wasn't working. We couldn't stop him, we couldn't defeat him! His exosuit was damaged, but obviously he wasn't out of the fight yet, and until his military-grade weapon ran out of power, we were pinned!

If only we had an exosuit of our own, or a shield, or a…

I blinked, and looked at the shuttle we used for cover.

"Hey," I shouted at Sebastian. "Does this thing still fly?"

He blinked back at me, and then at the closed shuttle door that we bracketed.

Grinning, Sebastian palmed the control, and the door split in the middle to open, the bottom half turning into a ramp.

"Mika, we're here!" I heard Karina call.

I looked over at the starboard-side entrance, and was beyond relieved to see carrot-red hair through the hole that Caesar had made.

"We'll cover you, flank the bastard!" I shouted, and then looked at Sebastian. "Power the shuttle up, I'll provide cover fire!"

He clambered in without a second thought, and I moved into his position to get a better angle on Caesar. I knew I'd never hit him, so I adjusted my power levels to a low stun, hoping to conserve enough power to keep firing and hold Caesar's attention, and then after glancing around to see Caesar heading for the port-side, I started blinding firing blast after blast after blast.

"Go, Karina!" I shouted. "Flank him, flank him!"

I didn't stop to look, I just kept firing.

The whine of the shuttle's engines spooling up grew to an ear-splitting crescendo, and the smell of ozone bit the air.

I glanced around to make sure I was still shooting towards Caesar, and he discarded his spent weapon and scooped up another one from a fallen Omega. I blinked in surprise, the safety light on it visibly turning green the moment he had it in-hand. How was he bypassing the personnel lockout?

He fired at me, at the ship, but even though those things could do damage to unarmored hulls, it wasn't so strong as to destroy the shuttle, and the engines ramped up fast.

Then rust-red blasts lanced across the bay at Caesar from near the massive bay door's starboard-side. Karina and Marek had added their own weapons fire to the mix, with Jonnec weaponless and taking cover behind a crate. One of them struck Caesar's already-damaged leg, and sent him to the deck for half a second before he recovered, and he returned fire.

"Come on, Princess, get that cute ass aboard!" Sebastian shouted.

He didn't have to tell me twice. While holstering my weapon, I flew in, slapping the control to close the door behind me, and I quickly sidled into the copilot's seat.

"Sensors show his ship coming around," Sebastian said, just as he lifted the shuttle off of the deck. I felt the engines thrum and everything started rattling. "Shit, don't give out on me now!" he grit his teeth, clenching the flight controls. "Her engines have been phasing badly for months!"

There wasn't time for me to align them, so I said, "We just need a few seconds!"

I activated the arms, taking the controls in a familiar grip, though I was ever-so-grateful for a more experienced pilot next to me this time.

Sebastian turned the shuttle towards Caesar, who was limping towards one of the fighter's now, trying to find cover. The alien fired at our viewport, cracking the glass. Fired again, and this time its blast punched a hole through the transparent metallic viewport.

"Go!" I shouted.

And Sebastian did, engaging aft thrusters at full. We rocketed at Caesar, and I tensed. The exosuit predictably used its good leg to try to dodge back to its left, our right, and as we flew past at blinding speed, I smacked it with one of the shuttle's arms with a satisfying *CLANK!*

My stomach twisted and tingled as Sebastian banked us out to starboard, leaving the bay and trying his best to bleed off the speed we'd just gained, and we barely missed smashing into the port-side wall of the launch bay, careening out into the dark of night, campfires visible below us from the Omega camps.

He banked us back to look into the bay, easy to see into with nothing but blackness surrounding us.

We both searched the flight deck for Caesar. But there was no sign of him. "Karina, where is he?"

I looked left, saw Karina, Jonnec, and Marek hiding behind a crate, but they emerged and looked around. *"I don't see him,"* she said. She looked over at us, and even from hundreds of meters away, I saw her baby-blues go wide. *"He's on your arm!"*

I looked right, saw that he must have latched on when I hit him, and he pointed a weapon straight at me. At this range, he'd punch through the glass and kill me instantly!

"Hold on!" Sebastian shouted, and he pitched the ship into a roll.

Caesar fired, lighting up the cockpit but missing me. Something exploded inside, alarms screamed across all consoles. My stomach flipped, I tumbled out of my seat and banged my head, and the maintenance shuttle fell from the sky.

We'd only been about fifty meters up, but when we crashed, we crashed *hard*, and rolled along with what little forward momentum we'd picked up, the shuttle tumbling. Something snapped in my left leg, then the breath was knocked from my lungs, and for a second, blackness engulfed my vision.

When my senses returned, I could smell smoke and the ozone scent of burning electronics, and I felt heat. My lungs protested against smoke and my chest seized in a coughing fit. I was upside down, slumped against part of the shuttle, and it took me a moment to realize that we'd settled *upside down,* at an angle, so orientation was hard. I was behind my seat, while Sebastian was still strapped into his. Behind him, in what would have been the ceiling, an electrical fire burned, fire-suppression systems no doubt offline.

Through my coughs, I yelled, "Sebastian!"

I looked out of the viewport, shattered now, and saw another flickering fire ahead of us, a campfire, and behind it, a hut made from local wood.

I tried to move, but my left leg, broken somewhere below the knee, screamed in protest, and I screamed back at it.

That stirred Sebastian, and he blurted, "Bwah, what?"

All I could do was whimper back, and I gritted my teeth against the pain, righting myself and pushing back from the fire. Another fit of coughing hit me. I crawled back to the aft end of the shuttle, and tried to unscramble my brain to recall if there was a way to open the back without ship's power.

There was. I just had to reach it.

"Sebastian," I coughed. "Get out. Get out now!"

While he worked to release his harness and get away from the fire, I had to pull myself up into the smoke. I found the safety cover on the emergency release, fumbled with the protective cover, and finally punched it. The door released with a pop, but it only opened an inch.

"Oh, for fuck's sake!" I spat.

Something sparked in the fire, and it suddenly grew twice the size in a matter of seconds.

Screaming against the pain, I shoved the door, and the top half fell down, letting me tumble out onto gouged-out muddy grass.

While another coughing fit clenched my torso, I looked around at my surroundings, at huts and at a handful of faces.

Children's faces.

They gaped from the shadows near wooden huts.

Right. Most of the adults were on the *Alpha,* fighting in Tiberius's coup.

"Mika!" I heard Karina. *"Are you alright?"*

I looked up towards the *Alpha,* but we were beneath a tree, and I couldn't see her or the launch bay as anything more than a vague glow behind a blanket of leaves.

"I'm alright," I breathed. "I'm okay, I just…"

A wrenching noise startled me, and I looked towards the right side of the shuttle. The entire *shuttle* shifted, and the wrenching turned into a screech of something metal tearing.

There was a gust of wind, and a loud hum filled the air. The Omega children scattered, the few frail, older adults amongst them calling them into the huts.

The alien's ship came to a hover overhead, and a bright red beam of light illuminated the area.

If its ship was still responding to its control, then that meant…

A metallic hand reached out from around the ship, clung to the muddy ground, and pulled the exosuit into view, mud sluicing through its metal fingers. It struggled to find purchase in the muck, but it came, centimeter by centimeter. Aside from the hole blasted into its forehead, a chunk of its face was actually missing, and its left arm was likewise missing. One golden eye gleamed out, and it fixed on me like a mechanical nightmare.

It crawled closer.

Its legs were gone, just below what would have been a pelvis on a living being. Microelectronics and wires and hydraulic lines trailed behind it, and I thought I saw shredded flesh and bone trailing along, leaving a blue-gray trail.

And it kept coming for me. It was only two meters from me when I remembered my gun, so I scrambled to pull it out, panic making my fingers fumble, but finally, I had it, and I sat up, aimed, and fired.

The blast glanced off harmlessly. I cursed, remembering that I'd set it to low stun. The exosuit came closer, almost within reach.

I fumbled with the controls, setting it to the highest level. The power cell was almost completely empty, but all I needed was one or two shots…

The alien grasped my left ankle, and *squeezed!* Something popped. I screamed. I took aim. And I fired into its damaged head.

Rust-red light flashed. My blast penetrated into the exosuit like I'd hoped. The exosuit jerked, clenched harder on my ankle…

And then stopped. It didn't release, but it stopped. The golden light of its remaining eye died.

It died.

Sebastian stumbled around the other side of the shuttle, his hair singed, his face blackened, and his weapon in hand. He stared at the scene, pointed his gun at the exosuit, but then paused. "Is…is it dead?" he breathed.

I looked at it, then at my weapon. It beeped a warning at me. I ensured it was set as high as it could still go. Then I took aim at the mangled head, and I fired again, illuminating the hulk one more time. Fresh ozone singed my nostrils.

That exhausted my power cell, but it was good enough for me.

With a groan, I collapsed onto my back, and I stared up at the tree and the black ship hovering above us.

It was over.

Except that the Omega rebellion was still in full swing. And Tiberius's voice came to me, *"Mika, Sebastian. Get up to what's left of deck two, now!"*

I sighed and coughed up more crud. "Gods dammit."

FIFTY-ONE

My body protested every inch as I sat up and looked at the dead, metallic hand gripping my ankle. Between the ankle and the fracture in the same leg, the prospect of climbing multiple decks of ladders didn't sound appealing.

"Tiberius, I'm kind of indisposed at the moment," I grumbled, while Sebastian holstered his weapon and knelt next to my leg. He gripped the metallic hand and tried to peel the fingers away, and surprisingly, they gave, if just a little. The hydraulics, or whatever functioned as the exosuit's actuators, must have been damaged enough to release.

Even still, the motion sent fresh surges of pain into my body.

"It's the quarantine ward," he replied solemnly.

My heart skipped a beat, and the bottom of my stomach fell out. "My people?" I asked.

He was silent for a second, and then said, *"We have a hostage situation."*

Sebastian and I exchanged looks, and gritting against the pain I imagined he felt in his fractured arm, he quickly finished prying the exosuit's thumb away, freeing my ankle. "Help me up," I demanded, and he did so without protest.

The children and their supervising, elderly adults slowly emerged, curious now that the battle was over. But then the fire in the cockpit sparked brighter, and Sebastian waved them away, "Keep clear of the shuttle, her power cells could blow at any second."

But not everyone did. A young boy rushed forward, awkwardly carrying something as tall as he was – a wooden cane. "Here," he thrust it out to me, his voice dark and mute in the red light. "Gramps wanted you to have this."

I blinked down at the boy, his face disheveled with dirt and grime, as if he'd been playing in the mud and hadn't washed up yet. I looked up at the elder man corralling the group of children that the boy had come from, and the poor guy had his hands full as the kids kept pointing up at the alien ship in a mixture of awe and fear, scarcely paying attention to anything else.

Smiling down at the boy, I took the proffered cane and nodded. "Thank you. Both of-"

The instant I had the cane in hand, the boy bolted away. When he ducked behind a taller friend, he peaked around at me, and then smiled shyly.

I grinned, and then tried the cane. It was a little too tall for me, but it worked well enough, and between it and Sebastian, I was able to keep most of my weight off of my wounded leg.

"Karina, you still on?"

"Impatiently waiting for you to acknowledge my existence again, yeah," she grumbled. *"Sounds like everything's okay?"*

I shook my head. "Down here, yes, but…the crew of the *Hope* are in a bind. We're headed back up now…somehow?" I frowned at Sebastian.

He pointed through the brush ahead, though I couldn't quite see the hull of the *Alpha* through a cluster of trees yet. "There's a ramp up to an open maintenance hatch," he explained. "It comes out right next to the launch bay."

"Did you hear that?" I asked.

"Yeah. I think I know which one, too, I'll meet you there."

I wanted to run, but that was impossible, so we hobbled along as fast as my leg would allow, leaving the ominous, red light behind. My other leg wanted to give out, but I wouldn't let it stop me, not when twenty-two people were still depending on me. I could rest later.

We came upon the ramp, which was wide enough and sloped low enough as to allow easy carrying of supplies back and forth, and I was ever so grateful for that. The ramp looked old, with two-by-fours obviously having been replaced at regular intervals, and I wondered if it could hold our combined weight.

When we emerged from beneath the last tree, I craned my neck to look up at the hull of the *Alpha*. Even in the darkening night, I could see black smoke billowing up into the starry sky, an eerie orange glow illuminating the underside.

Fires. The ship was on fire.

When we ascended the ramp, it held surprisingly well, with only a little creaking and groaning, and not a bit of sway. Say what you will about these folks, they knew how to build a solid structure.

The moment we made it to the hatch, carrot-red hair appeared, and Karina practically knocked me down the ramp when she lunged into my arms, squeezing the air from me.

I didn't care. I laughed and I cried and I held my girl with all of my might, relief flooding me! Tears stung my eyes, mixing with sweat and smoke particles and who knew what else. When I opened my eyes again, through teary vision, I saw Jonnec and Marek. Both looked the worse for wear, but none so much as Jonnec. His tunic was torn across his chest and there was a bandage beneath it, with a bit of dark red staining the center, and I grimaced when I saw another bandage covering his right ear, plus he had a nasty-looking black eye on that same side.

Marek just looked tired, but I frowned when she inched closer to Jonnec and grasped his hand.

I pulled out of the hug and took in Karina's visage finally. Her clothes were grimy, her face dirty, her hair matted, but she was still the most beautiful girl I'd ever known.

Karina glanced beside me and lifted her eyebrows.

"Sebastian," the pilot said, thrusting his hand out. "Nice to meet you!"

"Right," I shook my head, "Sorry. Sebastian, this is Karina. Marek. And Prince Jonnec of Rhea."

"*More* royalty?" he asked. "Uh, do I bow to you, or…?"

Jonnec took Sebastian's proffered hand and shook it wearily. "As you are not one of my vassals, a firm handshake will do."

I motioned at Jonnec's wounds and asked, "You good, Princely?"

He smiled weakly at me and nodded. "As well as can be. Karina is quite the healer, now. Though two days on the run has exhausted-"

"Good," I interrupted, "come on. We've gotta get up to deck two."

He gave me a sour look, but didn't protest.

The maintenance hatch we'd entered was only for an airlock, it didn't have any ladders heading up. Karina took over helping me, freeing Sebastian to lead the way out into the corridors, and we headed further into the *Alpha*.

"I have so much to tell you," Karina said, half-excited, half-weary. "The things we saw out there, you wouldn't believe!"

I nodded. "Yeah. I've got some things to tell you, too."

But neither of us were ready for those conversations. We just had to survive the next ten minutes. And make sure everyone else survived.

We came across the nearest maintenance junction, and I glared at the ladder leading up. We had a lot of decks to climb, and I'd have to hop up one-legged. I wondered if power could be restored soon, but who knew what kind of damage the alien ship had done. And I had no doubt that Zoe was busy elsewhere.

So, one grueling deck at a time, we made our way up, with Tiberius asking about our progress frequently. I finally snapped at him, "One more gods-damned deck, alright? I'm going as fast as I can!"

When we finally made it to deck two, my arms burned, my right leg burned, and my left leg and ankle throbbed painfully. I swallowed, but it felt like sand in my throat, and I knew I was dehydrated, too.

But I kept going. I had to.

Again with Karina's help, we hobbled out of the maintenance hatch…and came across a wall of debris, and a hole in the ceiling. I could see bits of starry skies amidst burning flames and billowing smoke.

The section of deck one above us was gone. Just *gone*.

"Oh gods," I whispered. It wasn't just the general who was dead…anyone who had been on that part of deck one, and the sections of decks two and three below it, were dead.

I wondered if any Alphas were left alive. I wondered how many Omegas had perished.

"This way," Sebastian said, clicking on a flashlight he pulled from one of his pockets. "We'll have to go around."

I updated Tiberius, and we hobbled as fast as we could, the pain in my legs growing stronger, demanding my attention, and my breathing came a little harder, worse than Sebastian's wheezing, pain-induced breaths.

Well at least we were headed for the medical bay. Assuming there was much left of it.

After far too long, we finally made it…to what was left of the corridor. It wasn't open to the night sky, and the emergency lights still worked, but the walls were crumpled all around us, the ceiling broken in more places than not, and debris littered the deck.

Tiberius and four others huddled outside of the doors into the quarantine ward, and when he saw us, he walked over to us. "Status report," he ordered Sebastian.

The pilot planted one hand on his hip and cocked it out slightly, a very casual stance next to someone who probably outranked him, even if they were, apparently, from different branches of service. "Caesar's dead." The four soldiers gaped at him. "Mika did something clever, and then shot the bastard in the head."

Karina's mouth fell open, and she looked at me. "Is that true?"

"Long story, but yeah," I nodded, and swallowed more roughness back. I could use some water, but I imagined that Karina and the others were worse off. We all needed water, food, and a long rest.

"What's going on?" I asked Tiberius.

He nodded towards the door, and said with more than a little disdain in his voice, "Claudia. The coward is threatening to kill your people. Considering you and I have an arrangement, I did not think it would be wise to let her kill them."

"Has she asked for anything?" Jonnec asked.

The centurion stared at me. "Yeah. She wants you."

"Me?" I frowned. "Why me?"

"If I had to guess," Tiberius glanced over his shoulder. "She blames you for everything that's happened tonight."

I clenched my eyes closed. That wasn't exactly a sane position to take, and I didn't feel like dealing with insanity.

But I was going to anyway.

"Alright," I nodded and looked at Tiberius. "I'll talk to her."

Karina helped me hobble over to the door. It was opened just a crack, enough that when I got to it, I was able to peek inside. I couldn't see much in the emergency lighting, but Claudia stood facing the door. And I swore there were forms surrounding her, but I couldn't quite tell in the moment I had to look.

"Claudia," I called. "It's Mika."

"Are you alone?" she asked, a frantic quality in her voice.

"No," I said. "I'm wounded, I can't move on my own."

The medici didn't reply for several seconds, but finally said, "Fine. One person may accompany you. You may enter, but I had better not see any weapons in-hand."

I sighed and glared at the door. I murmured, "Come on, Zoe, now'd be a good time to get power back up."

But I knew that wasn't going to happen. So Karina and I worked together to pry the doors open. Then, with her help, we hobbled into the medical bay.

And it was worse than I expected. Claudia stood in the center of the ward, and the *entire crew* of the *Hope* surrounded her. Or most of them, anyway, because Leif still lay on his quarantine bed.

Front-and-center, between Claudia and us, was someone else…

"Annar!" Karina surged forward, but I hissed in pain when she jolted my leg. She winced in sympathy and stopped, though she glared fury past Annar, at Claudia.

But Annar didn't look so good. Despite holding a weapon, and despite *pointing* it at me, he looked pale, and weak. They all did. Every single member of the expedition looked on the cusp of death. Someone coughed. Another followed suit. The nanites had clearly failed in all of them.

They were all clearly sick. One towards the back fell to a knee.

But they all shared one other trait – a blind devotion, an intense need.

And I felt it then, too. It competed with the pain in my leg, but the surge of lust, of *need* hit my like a hammer. They needed Claudia, just like I needed her…

Her hair was covered in ash, perfection ruined. Her clothes dirty, but still somehow so very lovely, and…

"Hey!" Karina shook me. My broken leg *screamed,* and I hissed and glared at her.

Except…the spell was broken. At least, enough to let my brain re-engage. The pain broke Claudia's hold over me! I don't know how, but the pain just killed my unnatural desire, and I gazed into Karina's baby blues.

"Stay with me," she said, staring back, eyes darting back and forth between each of mine.

She wasn't affected.

Karina…wasn't affected?

How?

I don't know what my expression must have looked like, but Karina grew visibly uncomfortable, her eyes darting away.

Then she focused on Claudia, who watched our exchange from between *Hope* crewmembers, a frown creasing her brow.

I looked at Annar. The lust was ever-present in his fervent glare. His hand shook, and I worried he'd fire the pistol.

I thought of the only thing I could to yank him back, just as Karina had done for me – I found his pain, and I pressed. "How's your dad?"

He didn't reply directly, but instead said, "Keep your hands where

I can see them."

I narrowed my eyes, but motioned my head towards his sister, "Kinda hard to do, I'm relying on her to hold me up."

Annar shifted his attention to Karina, and she locked eyes with him. "Annar. Dad's in trouble." He still didn't flinch. She lifted her eyebrows. "We don't have time for this."

"We have all the time in the Universe," Annar's hand stopped shaking, if only for a moment. "The whole Universe, all of our days, ahead of us."

What…the hellfire was he spouting?

Karina took it in stride, "But Dad doesn't. Mom's waiting for him." His grip loosened, and his hand fell half an inch. "For us."

"That's enough from you," Claudia snarled.

"Annar," I tried to speak with confidence, and with volume, but I struggled to do anything over the pain and lust. "She's manipulating you."

His grip tightened again, and he pointed the pistol right at my head. "I've had *enough* poison from your lips!"

I felt Karina tense. "Annar," she shouted.

"I said ENOUGH!" Claudia roared. "Annar, if the red-haired one speaks again, *shoot her!*"

The gun shifted back towards Karina. Annar's eyes softened, hardened, softened again. But I knew how strong Claudia's gifts were, and he didn't have pain to wake him up.

I realized it was a losing battle.

Claudia shifted to one side, revealing a weapon in her hand, too. *Hellfire,* I thought.

The medici's eyes were venomous, but when she fully looked at me, eyes wandering down and then back up, she tutted. "My oh my, young pup, but you do look rather…*disheveled.*"

I shrugged one shoulder. "I've been worse." Karina eyed me doubtfully, but didn't say anything. "Stop, um," I frowned and scratched my nose. "Hexing? Stop hexing my team."

"Stop seducing them," Karina clarified, defying Claudia's control over Annar. I felt my breath catch, and I looked at Annar.

He didn't fire. His hands shook, and he looked frustrated, but he didn't fire.

Claudia's pretentious, perfect attitude faltered. "And why should I?" she asked, her voice low and surprisingly menacing.

I could have told her that she'd already lost. All the Alphas had. She had nowhere to go.

But I remembered reading about the dangers of backing a predator into a corner.

So instead, I played on her logical brain. She was a doctor, right? A woman of science. So I banked on reason, and I recalled her shock when she discovered how young I was. "Because some of them are as young as fifteen," I said simply, pointing to one particular, sickly-looking girl to Claudia's right. I thought I remembered that girl's name was Dana. Despite the lust in her eyes, her shoulders slouched, and she looked ready to collapse, or throw up. Or both.

Claudia narrowed her eyes, and somehow that made the predator analogy felt more appropriate than ever. *She's a spider,* I reminded myself. *And I've just mangled her web.*

That's when I realized what was really going on. She wasn't afraid. She was *furious.*

So much for reason.

I raced for an answer, a reason to make her let Annar and Dana and all the others go free. What would Claudia want? What would overcome her fury?

She gave me an opening when she pointed the pistol at me and growled, "You ruined everything."

Ah *hah!* Gotcha!

"You did that yourself," I shook my head, splaying my left arm out disarmingly, while gripping Karina with my right. Karina shifted uncomfortably under my weight, but she held her ground. "This uprising?" I looked around the ship. "The destruction of the *Alpha* by Caesar? This wasn't my fault."

I saw her tense when I mentioned Caesar, and the first bit of uncertainty played across her features.

She recovered a moment later and snarled, "Everything was fine before you came along." I saw her finger move from outside of the trigger guard to the inside.

"You know that's not true," I insisted. "You hid it from the Omegas, but you've admitted to everyone now that your time was running out. And what do you think that creature you called Caesar was going to do if we hadn't come along and your Omega population plummeted? Caesar was stockpiling supplies in the dome, a lot of it. More than his ship could possibly carry on its own."

Her fury faltered, and she looked around with further uncertainty.

Claudia's 'whammy' still clamored against my better reasoning, so I leaned a little more on my leg, sending fresh, lust-clearing pain into my brain.

Gritting my teeth, I infused as much calm as I could muster into my voice. "Claudia. Caesar is dead."

Further doubt creased the edges of her eyes. Carefully, enunciating her words, she asked, "Which Caesar?"

I nodded.

The weapon in her hand lowered.

I knew I had to push the matter further, so I explained, "Caesar revealed himself to be…not human. He was a small alien inside of an exosuit, and he intended to bring his people down upon you all to take you as slaves, or worse. He wanted the supplies the Omegas mined and refined to fund a better life for himself. He was just…" I shrugged. "Greedy."

Anger flashed in her eyes. "And you think I am, too?"

"I didn't say that," I shook my head, resisting the sudden lustful urge. Did her anger enhance her ability? "Nor did I mean to imply it," I hastily added.

Her grip on the pistol tightened again, and I tensed.

I thought about what to say. I looked around at the quarantine ward. I thought about her console in the main ward, and her lab.

Well, what the hell, might as well try reason again. "You're a scientist," I said. "Not a hoarder." She blinked in surprise. I didn't know if what I was saying was actually true, but I pressed on, appealing to her vanity. "You've been alive for centuries, but you never stopped questioning, never stopped looking for answers. I mean, look at what you've done here," I motioned around us. "You kept everyone healthy against the odds, with limited supplies, for *centuries*. That's incredible, Medici!"

I waited. I wanted to say more, but I remembered my lessons from the queen, and I let silence do its work, allowing Claudia to think. I *had* to believe that reason could actually win out! Maybe I was flailing, shooting out thought after thought, idea after idea, but in the end, I wanted to believe in intelligence winning out.

Knowledge. Knowledge set people free, didn't it?

Wouldn't it?

Has it set me free?

How many stories worked out that way? How often did the hero of a story reason with a villain rather than destroy or defeat them?

Except, I realized that she wasn't the villain. Oh, she wasn't a good person, not by any stretch. She used people, like all of the Alphas did. She was willing to kill or hurt everyone on the *Sirius* to get her way, and in that same vein, she held Annar and the crew of the *Hope* virtually hostage, no doubt ready to kill him, and me and Karina, to get her way.

But she was still intelligent, breathtakingly so. And I hoped, practically *prayed* to whatever gods existed, that after centuries of living, Claudia had *some* level of self-awareness.

If an A.I. could develop a conscience, couldn't Claudia could, too?

She didn't lower her gun further, but her finger pulled out of the trigger guard. "What do you want?" she asked, her voice morose. Not defeated, I couldn't imagine a powerful woman like her ever giving up. No.

She was *thinking* again.

The fury was dead. The predator soothed.

"To take my people home," I said, nodding at Annar. "To save *all* of my people. To keep them all safe."

She stared at the deck for a moment, but then looked at me with just her eyes, her face still lowered. "And me?" Now she lifted her chin, that streak of haughty pretention returning. "What would you do with me, if I lowered this weapon?"

I looked at Karina, and I could see the genuine fear in her eyes.

"That might not be up to me," I finally said. "The Omegas will decide-"

"No!" Claudia hissed. "Not them! You."

I blinked. "What?"

"You decide," she insisted, nodding at me. "You make a deal with *me*. Right here, right now."

I tilted my head to one side. "And what deal would you have me make?"

"Take me with you," she instantly replied.

Take her with us? But that was already the plan, her and any other survivors.

But then I realized what she meant. Whatever Alphas survived, they were now prisoners of the Omegas. It was entirely conceivable that the Omegas intended to exile the Alphas here, alone. Without their slaves to do their bidding.

Honestly, I wouldn't blame them if they did.

Claudia wanted a guarantee that she wouldn't be left behind.

I drew in a breath and considered her demand. It wasn't my place to determine her fate, or the fate of any other Alphas. Not to mention that having even one Alpha on the *Sirius* would present a danger to us all, in ways I probably couldn't even guess. They were powerful people, physically and mentally, and while Claudia might not be a computer genius like the consul they'd mentioned before, Janus, I imagined she could hack Naia's systems if given enough time and leeway.

But when I looked at the expedition members surrounding her, standing steadfast against me despite their illness, I realized that I might not have a choice in the matter.

More than that, I realized the value of having a legitimate medical expert on the *Sirius,* especially if we were going to intermingle with the Omegas, who could possibly bring untold diseases to the *Sirius.* Hopefully diseases that the nanites could fight off, but what if they couldn't? What if the system that controlled the nanites failed, or some other unforeseen disaster fell upon us? We hadn't exactly had the best of luck lately.

Tilting my head up, I finally said, "Alright. As Princess of Rhea, I am willing to grant you your request and allow you to come with us." I thought of the terms I'd read in fiction, and I said, "I will provisionally grant you asylum, with restrictions."

She narrowed her eyes. "What restrictions?"

"Restricted access to the *Sirius.* No direct access to Naia or any primary systems. And while you're there, you will provide medical care for both my people *and* the Omegas, if they will allow it."

"The Omegas?" she queried, confusion in her tone. Then realization dawned upon her. "They're going with you."

Oh. She must have thought the Omegas were going to stay here, and *that* was her fear - she had no desire to remain with either them or the Alphas. But now she would be surrounded by Omegas.

"Yes," I nodded. "They cannot survive here any longer." I swallowed, and said, "Everything must change. For your people," I glanced at Karina, "and mine." She didn't meet my gaze, but I saw her eyes sink downward for a moment.

I looked at the medici, and she stared back at me. Her grip on the pistol was firm, but her finger moved further and further away from the trigger guard. And, I noticed finally, I no longer felt the intense desire to rip her clothes off. Even some of the other expedition members looked weaker, sleepier, as if her hold over them had been the only thing keeping them on their feet.

Finally, she nodded and lowered her weapon.

"Drop it," I commanded.

She hesitated, but then she complied. The safety on it turned red automatically as it clattered on the deck.

And then she let go of the others. Half of them collapsed, including Annar, and Karina rushed forward, leaving me to my cane. I winced and nearly fell, but I let her go.

"Annar!" Karina cried, tumbling down to the deck with him, but managing to cradle his head..

I glanced behind me, and said, "Alright, Tiberius. We're clear."

Soldiers rushed in, shouting for Claudia to raise her hands, and to get on her knees. They arrested her, while Karina helped Annar to an empty bed.

Those of my team still standing seemed to slowly remember what it was to *think*, and I sympathized with them. Then, when they saw their comrades fallen on the deck, they finally fully came around, and knelt to help the fallen.

Tiberius, Jonnec, and Marek came up beside me, and Jonnec offered me his arm. I gratefully took it, leaning against him for support. I looked at his artificial arm, the glove that he normally covered it with missing. Then I glanced at my leg. I wondered if my leg could be saved, or if they would have to replace it, too.

I looked at the medici as a guard moved to shackle her, and I said, "Wait."

Tiberius frowned at me. "Mika?"

I said, "I need her help."

FIFTY-TWO

I love advanced medical tech!

Despite only emergency backup power in the ward, Claudia, with Livia's help, was able to heal the bones in my left leg and ankle, and drastically reduced the swelling and pain.

A procedure that, according to the medici, should have taken only minutes ended up taking almost an hour, but all I cared about was that it worked, and I felt immense relief. After the procedure, I still limped heavily, but Livia told me that I'd be walking just fine within two days.

She also gave me a better cane, a poly-composite one that she adjusted to my height perfectly, and she spent a few minutes showing me how to use it properly. I felt bad, since the wooden cane had been a gift, but I mentally promised to find whomever it belonged to, and give it back.

Tiberius disappeared while I was in surgery, apparently to help break through some final Alpha and Omega holdouts. Thankfully, the few surviving Alphas had surrendered, stricken and shocked to learn that the last two centuries had been lived under a terrible lie.

I sympathized.

Once my surgery was completed, soldiers escorted Claudia away. She glared at me, but I just nodded, hoping she trusted me to speak on her behalf. If she tried to break free, she could hurt a lot more people, herself included.

Karina stayed with her family throughout my surgery, but Jonnec and Marek kept watch over me, and I couldn't help but notice that they kept standing closer to one another, and found any excuse to touch. I reasoned that a lot had happened between them over the past two days, and I wondered if maybe, just maybe, I wouldn't have to deal with Jonnec's romantic advances anymore.

And, as we waited for Tiberius to finish up and return to the medical ward, I decided to ask Jonnec and Marek, "What happened out there?"

I meant between them, but I knew that they'd probably not directly address their sudden closeness. Instead, Marek told me about the long, arduous search for Jonnec, and how they found him, still strapped into his seat, surprisingly sporting only mild wounds.

Karina had spent two hours working on healing him, but eventually the Omega troops honed in on them. They had to carry Jonnec away sooner than Karina had wanted to. The troops hounded them constantly, until Karina figured out they were using scanners to track them, and she figured out how to 'scramble' the scanners, whatever that meant. Shortly after that, Jonnec had finally woken up.

Marek shook her head, "I honestly have no idea what any of that means, but Karina kept us going, and she kept us alive."

Jonnec nodded. "Karina is quite ingenious. But it was Marek who kept *me* going," he gave her a smile, and I saw something then, his expression unlike anything I'd seen in him before.

Genuine caring.

He wasn't being a lady's man, he wasn't treating her like he owned her. The caring look he gave her was real.

Marek still had that one-handed axe strapped to her belt, and for some reason, I interrupted their lovey gazing with the question of, "Is that Thelon's?"

Marek's cheeks flushed, and she consciously covered the axe-head with her hand. "Yes," she nodded.

"It was Thelon's wish that I gift it to Marek," Jonnec explained, "If the worst should happen. They were…friends." Suddenly the lovey, adoring looks turned to guilt, and now *I* felt guilty for bringing it up.

"Oh," was all I managed to say.

So. Things were complicated between them.

I looked towards the quarantine ward, towards Karina, and Hector, and I thought, *That seems to be going around.*

And that also meant some…*complications* between Jonnec and me. If he and Marek were growing close, then what did that mean about our arranged marriage?

I started upon realizing that I was actually unsure how I felt about it. I still had zero desire to marry Jonnec, but the idea of losing my status as Princess of Rhea suddenly scared me. Not because I'd lose power, I never wanted any of that power or status. I still didn't.

But…the people of Rhea, the crew of the *Hope*, I'd come to think of them as…

As 'my people.' I'd said it a lot over the past two days, and I felt responsible for them. *All* of them. I didn't like the idea of reneging on that responsibility.

When had that happened?

Livia came back in a minute later, and reported, "I've done what I can for your people, but they're going to need a lot more medical intervention than I can provide."

I nodded and looked at Jonnec. "We need to get them back to the *Sirius,* as soon as possible."

"The fighting has ended," Livia said. "I must help treat some wounded, but I thought you all should know."

"Thank you, Livia," I smiled at her. "For everything."

She blushed and smiled, and then after grabbing some additional medical supplies, she scurried off.

About another hour passed, and finally the centurion returned. Tiberius strode in with two soldiers flanking him, but they were mere guards, and I felt zero threat from him now.

Realizing I'd not made introductions yet, I said, "Centurion Tiberius, this is Prince Jonnec Impavido of Rhea, and guard Marek Harun."

Tiberius lifted his eyebrows. "So one of the ones evading my guards was royalty?" He bowed his head slightly. "On behalf of the liberated Omegas, I'd like to apologize for hounding you so, Prince…Jonnec? Prince Impavido?"

"Just Jonnec is fine," the prince smiled lightly. I blinked at him, shocked by his willingness to be so informal. Gods, how much had he changed in just two days?

"Well then," Tiberius hesitated, eyes darting between the two of us. "Did Princess Mika indeed have the authority to invite the Omegas to come aboard your vessel?"

I glanced at Jonnec and wondered that myself. When I told Tiberius that, I'd been desperate to resolve a, well, *desperate* situation, and I hadn't given it much thought. But now, it was time to follow through on those promises.

Jonnec glanced at me, and then nodded. "She does, indeed, have that authority. However, you must understand that my…*our* people have been resistant to change, and have suffered much in recent months. The general reception may not be amicable at first."

"But," I interjected, "for the time being, we can, and for medical reasons *should* segregate our two populations. The Omegas, and any Alphas that come with, should remain outside of the dome for now."

Tiberius's eyes flashed. "The Alphas," he started hotly, but then stopped and clenched his fists, as if chastising himself and reigning in his first instinct. "The Alphas," he tried again with more calm, "may not be coming."

"That is for you to decide," I nodded, and swallowed. "However. There is one that I have to insist comes along."

Tiberius narrowed his eyes at me. "I heard your conversation with the medici. I cannot promise that the rest of my people will allow it."

"They must," I pressed. "I won't let them force my hand and renege a promise I made, even if that promise was under duress."

The centurion ground his teeth, and his jaw muscles flexed visibly. "I will…take that under consideration."

"I know it's not perfect," I continued hurriedly, "but she can be of value to us all."

Tiberius drew in a breath and let it out in a slow, thoughtful sigh. "I guess that's true." Nodding, he said, "I'll present it to the other Omega leaders, and try my best to convince them it'll be for the best. Any other…*conditions* to our joining your crew?"

Jonnec jerked his head towards the quarantine ward. "We must get my people home immediately. The journey will already take nearly a day, if not longer, and their time is running short."

Tiberius folded his arms and hesitantly said, "Yeah. About that. The alien craft is still hovering right in front of the launch bay. Getting anything larger than a small shuttle in and out of there will be difficult."

Jonnec almost immediately looked at me, and I frowned at him. "What?" I asked.

He smiled. "Perhaps you and I can assist in that regard."

***

We came up with a fast plan to use the only remaining maintenance shuttle to move the alien ship, and meanwhile, Karina and Sebastian were asked to take a shuttle back to the *Hope* and get it back to the *Alpha*.

When we all entered the port-side launch bay, we couldn't see the alien ship from here, it was so dark outside now. The forest was dimly lit from the crescent gas giant, but that ship's hull absorbed all the light, and just knowing it was only one- or two-hundred meters beyond the wide-open bay made me shudder.

Hopefully Caesar hadn't programmed a self-destruct protocol into it, but if he had, all the more reason to move it away from the *Alpha* and the village below.

Karina and Sebastian left first, taking one of those tiny shuttles next to the defense fighters out, easily able to navigate around Caesar's ship. Zoe met Jonnec and I at the maintenance shuttle, and she was bent over the pilot's console tapping in commands. We stopped just outside of the shuttle, and I cleared my throat.

She turned around, and her eyes affixed on Jonnec. "O-oh," she stammered, her face turning a distinct shade of pink. "Um. Hi."

I grinned, remembering that she was younger than I was. Still, Jonnec seemed to have that effect on a lot of girls, and the fact that she stared at him even when he was so dirty and grungy made me roll my eyes.

"Zoe, this is Prince Jonnec Impavido."

Her eyes grew to wide saucers. "Prince? Uh. Shit. I mean! Dammit. Err, that is…"

I covered my growing smile with a hand, and forced myself not to laugh. It wouldn't be nice to tease her about her instant crush on the Prince of Rhea.

Nodding at the console behind her, I cleared my throat and asked, "Whatcha doing?"

She blinked at me. "Hm? Oh! I was programming the computer to allow a new pilot access to her controls. Only qualified pilots are allowed to fly, so we lock the controls down most of the time. But it'll work for you now," she nodded at Jonnec, and then blushed harder.

"Thank you very much for your help," Jonnec gave her a flourished bow. "Your assistance is *greatly* appreciated, Miss Zoe."

She giggled, covering her mouth. "Just…just Zoe is fine, Sir Prince."

"Please, call me Jonnec," he said thoughtfully.

I tried not to roll my eyes. "We should hurry," I nudged Jonnec.

"Yes," he nodded. We stepped aside and let Zoe out, who kept glancing at Jonnec with puppy-dog eyes.

"Go on," I shooed her, giving her a good-natured push.

She giggled and ran off to do who-knew-what. And, much to my pleasant surprise, Jonnec didn't watch her go. He climbed ahead of me into the ship, and got situated in his chair. I followed, closing the door behind me. Then I paused before getting into my seat, and looked around, a sudden sick, anxious feeling roiling up in my gut.

"Don't take this the wrong way," I whispered to him, clenching my eyes shut. "But please don't crash."

I felt his hand take mine, and when I opened my eyes, he looked into mine intently. Something was different, then, but I wasn't sure if it was with him, with me, or even both of us. I didn't feel sick when he touched me, and I didn't feel like he was trying to make me swoon with his eyes.

Instead, he looked like he was genuinely trying to comfort me.

"I promise," he said. "Believe me, I have no intention of reliving that experience."

My stomach eased up a bit, and I sat in my seat and strapped in. Jonnec started the engines, and I immediately detected a power fluctuation in the inertial dampers. I ran through a quick maintenance cycle to clear them up, and then was pleasantly surprised to find the engines operating far better than the other shuttle's had been.

I gave Jonnec the OK, and we lifted off relatively smoothly.

Another pleasant surprise, the alien ship didn't resist our nudging it along. I used the upper arms to cinch onto its sharp-edged hull, having learned my lesson from the other alien vessel, and we pushed it along. Without input from its owner, it simply maintained its altitude and let us move it. I wondered how long it would stay aloft before running out of fuel.

A short time later, we were back on the flight deck, helping Zoe move other craft aside to make room for the *Hope* to land right next to the *Alpha's* cargo shuttle. We barely finished moving everything to the starboard side, clearing the middle for Karina to land, when her voice surprised me in my right ear, telling me they were on final approach. I watched her green, red, and white position lights as she brought the shuttle in for a landing, and I noted that the *Hope's* engines sounded a little off. I'd never gotten around to those repairs on her.

We met Karina at the ramp, and the first thing I asked was, "What repairs does she need?"

Karina rolled her eyes at me. "Honestly, it was fine, Mika, just a little shaking on takeoff and landing."

"Well, I wanna do a once-over before we take off again, anyway," I looked up at her. Then I remembered the bypass I had on the inertial dampers, and I decided I needed to bypass the backup line, too, just in case. "Zoe, do you have an auto-bypass kit I could use?"

"Only if I can install it for you!" she quipped and smiled at me.

It took us less than a minute to get it installed, and then she helped me run diagnostics and fix some of the minor damage we'd incurred in the attack and subsequent crash landing. Zoe was a wizard when it came to mechanics and electronics, and I was excited to get her help on the *Sirius!* Maybe she could help me restore more sarus, especially if we had the raw supplies to fabricate replacement parts.

While we adjusted the alignment on one of the main thrusters, she shyly glanced over at me and asked, "So, uh. Prince Jonnec."

I eyed her and said, "Don't even think about it, kid."

"Oh!" she blushed again. "So…if he's the prince. And you're the princess. Oh shit, I didn't even think about that! I'm so sorry!"

"Don't be," I shook my head and focused on what I was doing. "It's not exactly what you think, but just…trust me. Don't even go there."

Out of the corner of my eye, I saw her features slacken, and she slouched away from her work for a minute. I felt my heart ache for her, and in a way, I knew how she felt. I knew how *I* felt.

I'd told Claudia that everything must change, for her people and mine.

I wondered if that meant giving up on Karina.

I wondered if I could do that.

And…I wondered how Karina had resisted Claudia's abilities.

A sick feeling crept into my chest, and I shook my head and got back to work, ignoring those thoughts.

By the time we finished performing a quick maintenance check and a handful of repairs, the crew of the *Hope* worked their way down to the launch bay. They looked even worse than I felt, and I was grateful that, despite everything, I wasn't feeling anything worse than a scratchy throat.

Yet.

Most of them could at least walk, but a few of them, especially Leif, had to be carried in on anti-grav gurneys. Leif had a portable respirator attached to his chest, forcing his lungs to breathe. I was scared he wasn't going to make it.

I noticed Zoe bustling about out of the corner of my eye on the other side of the *Hope,* and while I wanted to help load my crew up, I was curious and went over to check. She'd attached a fuel line to a storage tank, and was in the process of transferring fuel over to us!

I thanked her profusely, and offered to help finish up, but she shooed me away to go help my crew.

A few minutes later, Claudia, escorted by Tiberius and a few others, came along. Jonnec, Karina and I met them at the bottom of the ramp, and he said, "We would like to accompany you. And the medici has said-"

"I can speak for myself," she growled down at him. He gave her a withering glare, and I shot her a warning look. But she powered on. "Your people are sick, and while I have no doubt that your artificial intelligence is capable, they might need my help. You will *definitely* require my assistance while en-route. The one red-headed man," she nodded up towards Leif, "may not survive without my intervention."

I thought about it for a second, and then looked at Karina. "What do you think?"

"I only have basic field medic knowledge," she said, shaking her head with a grimace that yanked on my heart. "If he were to crash, I might not be able to bring him back."

I winced at the word 'crash,' but figured it was meant in a medical context this time.

"Alright," I nodded, and turned back to Tiberius. "And you want to come, too?"

"Yes. I feel it would be appropriate to begin negotiations with your people in earnest."

It was a good point. "Alright, then. It'll be a tight fit, but life support should manage fine. Welcome aboard the *Hope of Rhea.*"

We climbed up the ramp, and our new passengers secured themselves in seats closest to the cockpit. The harness *barely* fit Claudia's larger-than-normal frame, but she managed.

Then Karina and Jonnec climbed up to the cockpit, and I watched them go. I wanted to go up there, but Jonnec was a pilot, too, and it made more sense for him to be there in case he had to take over flight controls.

I was about to close the ramp when I caught sight of Zoe staring up at me, a longing in her eyes. She wanted to come with, though whether because of Jonnec or for other reasons, I didn't know. But now wasn't the time. I nodded to her, and as the *Hope's* engines spooled up, I said, "Next time, kid. I promise."

She smiled meekly, and then forlornly shuffled away. I felt bad for her, but frankly, they needed her here, now. Sure, the Omegas were abandoning the *Alpha,* but until then, they needed her gifts to fix whatever she could.

I hit the button, and the ramp lifted and formed back into the hull, sealing us off from the moon that had nearly destroyed us in a matter of days.

Once the pressure seals checked, I called up to let the pilots know.

When I turned, I looked across the faces of all of those strapped in, down at those lying on gurneys, and I felt…alone. I didn't want to be around them, or anyone. So I started my way towards the aft end, while the deck plates rumbled from main power and the engines spooling up.

Just when I reached the back, from the corner of my eye, I saw rapid motion, and tried to stumble away, terrified of another attack.

When I realized it was Annar, and when his hand latched onto mine, I panicked further, and ripped free of his grip. "Don't touch me!"

He held stock-still, his hand hovering in the air, reaching for me. And…and he wasn't angry. He wasn't hostile.

Instead, he had the look of someone struggling. Annar's eyes darted around for a second, but then he looked at my chest. Then my neck. And finally, he met my eyes. His jaw flexed before he spoke, "Thank you." I gawked at him, and he added, "For saving us."

He glanced at the deck, and that's when I realized that Leif was right by him, and was the last person I'd carefully stepped around. I'd been so intent on brooding that I hadn't even noticed.

"Whatever happens," he added, and met my eyes for one more second. "I…I'm glad you didn't kill me. Or let me die."

He turned away then, and sat back in his harness. I felt the deck shift beneath my feet, and the *Hope* lifted off, while I stared across the chasm between Karina's brother and me.

I didn't know what to say. I wanted to tell him he was a fool, an idiot, easily manipulated, easily led astray by hatred.

But who was I kidding? I wasn't much better.

And then he said, "I'm…I'm sorry I wasn't strong enough."

I furrowed my brow. "Strong enough?"

He swallowed, but couldn't meet my eyes again. Sullenly, he finished, "I wasn't strong enough to resist her. Like you."

My throat cinched shut, and I felt my breath catch.

I hadn't. Not exactly.

But Karina had, and she'd broken me free of Claudia. I shifted so I could look over my shoulder towards the bow of the cargo hold, towards the medici, and the centurion next to her.

What could I say to that? How could I reply, when I was just as guilty as Annar was? When I was just as weak as he was?

Then the answer became obvious, and I managed to smile at him. I held my gaze upon him until he looked up at me with uncertainty. I said, "Our strength lies in each other."

Wise words, right? I'll admit, they weren't mine – I'd stolen them from a book I'd read long ago, with his sister.

I don't know if there was a moment of understanding that passed between us, but for the first time since we'd left the *Sirius,* I felt like there might be a sliver of hope.

For all of us.

I turned and headed into the aft compartment.

The engines thrummed louder, letting me know we'd cleared the *Alpha* and were accelerating towards space. The fact that I barely felt any change in motion let me know that our inertial dampers were working, that the patches Zoe and I had installed were holding.

I put my arm up on the bulkhead, and rested my eyes against my sleeve, and for the first time in what felt like ages, I felt tension in my shoulders bleed away, if only a little.

We were going home!

FIFTY-THREE

We left the atmosphere behind us, and shortly after entering orbit, Karina called down to me and asked if we were set for our first burn. I did a cursory check of systems, strapped into a bucket seat in engineering, and gave her the go-ahead.

The burn went without a hitch, and after an hour of listening to the engine rumble and watching diagnostic readouts, I was satisfied that, with Zoe's help, we'd gotten the *Hope* into better shape than ever.

You know, aside from all the scuff and scorch marks on the hull.

Once the burn was done, I checked our course and was pleasantly surprised to see that Karina, Jonnec, and the flight computer had come together to plot a slingshot trajectory that would put us at the *Sirius's* expected position in only twenty hours, only two hours longer than our initial flight down.

Still, it occurred to me that we hadn't brought any provisions aboard. All we had was whatever our onboard water supply still retained.

However, while I'd forgotten about the supplies stashed here before the soldiers had come for us, Karina hadn't, and shortly after the first burn ended, Karina appeared in my little den, holding two wooden, covered bowls that I knew contained soup.

My stomach growled.

"Join me for dinner?" she asked.

I wanted to say yes. I wanted to say no. I wanted to know why Claudia hadn't managed to control her.

Hellfire, who was I kidding, I didn't know *what* I wanted.

We were right back to where we'd started this crazy journey together, and I suddenly felt incredibly awkward.

But I couldn't spend the entire flight cooped up in engineering. So we sat on the deck across from each other and dug into our cold but delicious stews.

It made me long for Rhea. It made me long for my mother's cooking and my brother's laughter and, yes, even my father's sometimes-obnoxious voice. It didn't matter how much of a lie it had been, Rhea was still home.

Which made tomorrow's meeting with Naia even harder.

Pushing that future out of my mind, I turned to a different future.

I watched Karina eat for a moment, waiting patiently until her eyes met mine. When they did, I asked, "Did you feel anything towards Claudia?"

I wanted to clamp my hands over my mouth – had I *really* just asked that?

With a weird frown, she asked, "What?"

I tensed, my jaw tight. "Um. When she put the…whammy on me. On all of us in there. Even some of the other girls were under her spell." I narrowed my eyes. "So why weren't you?"

Eyes wide, Karina looked around the engine room. "Hellfire, Mika, I don't know! I mean, I felt *something,* but nothing strong enough to make me do anything I didn't want to do."

I thought about that for a moment. Claudia was insanely beautiful to begin with, unnaturally so. Coupled with her gifts, or abilities, or whatever the hellfire you called it, anyone and *everyone* should have fallen head over heels for her.

Except…

Except Tiberius hadn't been affected by it earlier. Had he?

I realized I wasn't sure how the medici's abilities worked.

Swallowing my pride, I cleared my throat and changed topics, "Hector's a good man." Saying it sent a rushing sensation through my stomach, but I did my best to ignore it.

Karina coughed over her stew, swallowed, and looked at me with utter shock. "Um. You think so?"

I swallowed bile back and nodded.

"Did you two get to know one another better or something?" she asked with a half-amused frown, and I was grateful that she didn't press me more about Claudia and my outburst.

"Not so much," I shrugged, and then was glad that Tiberius couldn't see me now. "But he did defy my orders to save my life on the flight down. And he was a pretty steadfast member of the crew during everything. Him and…and Leif."

Karina's expressions shifted throughout my speech, but ended on worry with my final words. She looked down at the deck, her wooden spoon hovering over her half-finished meal.

"How's he doing?" I asked.

"Claudia says he's close to critical condition," she murmured, "but he should pull through enough to get home." She laughed ironically and rolled her eyes. "Home. Can't even take him to Rhea. He'll probably spend the next week in the *Sirius's* medbay."

I nodded. "True. Buuuuut," I drew out the word and thought about it. "There's no reason your mother can't come visit."

She eyed me. "I thought we'd have to keep the two crews separate."

"It's a good idea to," I said. "But not necessary, as long as the nanites do their job. We'll ask Naia once we get him into the medbay. Then again," I grinned, "I doubt we could keep your mother away."

Laughing nervously, she nodded, "Yeah. My mother is a *force of nature.*"

Silence fell for a minute after that, and we resumed eating again.

Until Karina glanced back towards the cargo hold. She sighed and looked at me, her baby-blues delving into my very soul. "Everything's going to change now, isn't it?"

I met her gaze, held it as long as I could. And then kept holding it even after I thought it'd tear me apart. I remembered feeling this way only a few months ago, in that cold-but-warming winter landscape, when I was headed back into the corridors of the *Sirius* to repair our vessel. Hopeful for her affection. Hopeful for her love.

I still wanted it. I still wanted *her.*

So I said, quietly, "Yes."

She looked down, breaking our gaze, and I felt my heart mourn.

Until Karina said, "Let's take it one day at a time, yeah?" Her eyes met mine. "Because...I still love you, Mika." I felt a lump swell up in my throat, and hope welled in my chest. "But if I have to choose between doing what I want, and doing what's right, well..." She pursued her lips. "I have to do what's right."

Even as recent as three days ago, I would have rejected that. But now?

"I get it," I nodded. "And at this point, I, um," I swallowed, *hard*, "I think, maybe I might, um...do the same in your position."

She gave me a playful smirk. "Oh? When did you get to be so wise?"

I thought about it before answering seriously, "Maybe when I thought we'd be trapped on that moon forever. Maybe when I thought they'd come and destroy our home."

Her playful look vanished, and her face slackened. "Yeah," she nodded. "That'd just about do it, huh?"

We fell silent for a moment. Then I rolled my eyes. "Gods, it's just like in those stories, isn't it?" She quirked an eyebrow at me. "All those ones we've read, but especially when it's just kids or teenagers, thrust into conflict and action and adventure. Next thing you know, we'll hear some adult say, 'you kids shouldn't have to bear these burdens,' or something."

She snorted a chuckle and nodded. "Yeah, or 'I lament the loss of your childhood.' What was that line from?"

"Hell if I remember," I shook my head, joining in her laughter. "But how long before someone says anything like that? Half an hour? An hour?"

"Two at least," she said. "I'll betcha."

"I'll take that bet," I grinned.

And with the mood finally lightened, we finished our meals.

***

Shortly after our reverse burn, I was up in the cockpit, leaning between Jonnec and Karina, looking for the first glimpse of home. I was refreshed from having slept between burns, but now I strained my eyes searching for the *Sirius*. We came up on her fast, having waited until the last possible second for a calculated safe slow-down so that we could get everyone into the medbay as fast as possible.

The three of us searched the stars, trying desperately to find that one glint of light that wasn't a stoic, ancient, burning gas ball lightyears away.

We hadn't heard from Naia yet, but I had a hunch that, if her estimate had been accurate, she'd be calling us moments before we landed. Surely the instant she detected our approach, Naia would have redirected all of the sarus to hurry repairs on the near-field comms.

I thought I saw something, and I pointed ahead, "There!"

The others tried to follow my finger. Jonnec squinted, shook his head. "I don't see it..."

"I do!" Karina practically shouted in excitement. "There she is!"

"Where?" Jonnec gaped, shaking his head. And then the *Sirius* caught the sun just right and glinted brightly. "Oh, I see it!"

I turned back and shouted down into the hold, "We see it! We're almost home!"

Almost everyone from our expedition was achingly sick, but a general wave of relief visibly washed over those seated, while those lying on secured gurneys were, at this point, unconscious.

I looked back into the void and watched the ship rapidly grow from just a tiny dot to a much larger dot. We'd be there in ten minutes, according to sensors, but actually *seeing* her made my heart soar.

And then, just as I predicted, the comm system beeped.

Practically jumping out of her seat in excitement, Karina flipped the channel open. "This is the *Hope of Rhea*, go ahead, Naia!"

"Hope of Rhea?" Naia asked.

She and Jonnec exchanged grins, and I laughed and said, "We decided to name the shuttles, Naia."

"Mika Kai!" Was that excitement in her voice? I think it was! *"I am relieved to hear your voice. And you as well, Karina. Although I did not expect you to come back so soon."*

My smile faltered just a little. "Yeah, well…things didn't exactly go to plan down on that moon."

Naia didn't reply right away, and I let her process my remark. *"What happened?"*

"It's a long story that I fully intend to tell you," I said. "Not to mention it's gonna make one hell of an update in the town chronicles. But we're gonna have to make a few more trips down there. And…" I hesitated. "Well, do you have anything in your databanks about any other Renovare starships?"

"Of course," she replied.

"Good," I nodded. "Refresh your active memory with info about Alpha Centauri's ship."

"In the meantime," Jonnec interrupted. "Please prep the medical facility for incoming. We have twenty-two very sick people."

Karina added, "Some of whom are in critical condition."

Again, we let her process that information. And then, *"Understood. You are cleared to land in the port-side docking bay."*

"Acknowledged," Karina said, and she glanced at Jonnec. "May I?"

He was in the copilot's seat, and he motioned across to her controls, "By all means."

By now I could make out the *Sirius's* shape, and I grew more and more anxious to be home. Even if we weren't quite yet at the end of this leg of the journey.

Karina turned the *Hope* to port, and I lamented as I watched the *Sirius* fall away from our view. Karina fired the engines for one last, short burn, exactly when the flight computer told her to, and then turned us forward again. I had to looked down, the spinning starfield still making my stomach twist and turn uncomfortably.

We were coming up alongside the ship's port side, and I was able to look at some of the damage to the hull and superstructure from the earlier disaster. Thankfully, nothing appeared to be leaking, but then again, there wasn't much left to leak out, except atmosphere.

And then…*home!* We slowly passed by the dome, and Rhea was illuminated in full daylight. I could see people moving about inside like tiny little bugs, scurrying from one point to the other. I wondered if they could see us, but figured that the dome illusion kept us hidden from their eyes. Still, I hoped that Naia had let them know that we were home.

At least, some of us were.

Twenty-two people hadn't made it, the twenty-two that had been aboard the *Pride*. Twenty-two families were about to learn that a loved one was never coming home again.

Karina used a combination of manipulating inertial dampers and firing thrusters to ease us back, and we came around the front of the *Sirius*. The port-side bay doors were already open, the atmospheric forcefield shimmering blue-white. With incredible grace for only having done this once before on the *Alpha*, Karina landed us liquid-smoothly on the flight deck.

The instant we touched down, the dread of the coming conversation melted into relief.

I looked out into the bay, at our full complement of shuttles and transports. Once we retrieved a few more Omega pilots, things would go a lot faster with a combination of our shuttles and theirs.

Then movement caught my eye, and a dozen sarus entered the launch bay, pulling or pushing anti-grav gurneys with them. Naia had assembled the troops fast.

I thought I saw a familiar shape amongst the various sarus, and a broad smile spread over my face. I went down the ladder fast, using Sebastian's trick to slide down, and I flew past the closest passengers to slap the controls on the cargo doors. Pressure equalized, and the doors yawned open, the bottom one lowering into a ramp.

I flew down the ramp and, as I'd hoped, my Saru met me at the bottom, his segmented tail whipping back and forth excitedly. "Saru!" I cried and slid to my knees on the flight deck, throwing my arms around him.

"Wuff!" he replied, his body gyrating in excitement.

And that was when I first felt it. First felt the relief, and the sense of belonging.

Naia's voice echoed in the massive bay, "Welcome home, Mika Kai."

***

Those that couldn't walk were loaded onto anti-grav gurneys, and with Tiberius and Claudia's help, we got everyone to the medical bay.

While en-route, Naia said, "I am detecting two unknown human life forms with you."

While we rushed through the launch bay, I said, "Naia, this is Medici Claudia and Centurion Tiberius of the Renovare starship *Alpha.*"

They didn't acknowledge the introduction to the ship's computer, but Naia replied, "I see. So you found their colony?"

"Not exactly," I said, and while we traversed the corridors of the *Sirius,* I explained.

There was a *lot* to explain, but if there was one thing I was good at, it was telling stories. Naia listened patiently and didn't interrupt even once to ask questions. I didn't know if that was because I was doing so well, or if she was just patient and saving her questions for last.

The medbay was fully powered, and we loaded everyone onto beds, each of them humming to life. I continued my explanation, while Jonnec, Karina and I watched over the crew.

Claudia sauntered over to the central desk and tried to activate a console, but was met with a double-kludge error tone. "Access denied," Naia interrupted me to tell her.

The medici glared up at the ceiling and said, "I am a doctor, computer. Let me help."

Tiberius edged closer to her, his hand on his pistol, but I lifted a halting hand and approached the central station. "Are you really going to help? Or are you going to hold my people hostage again?"

The medici stared down her nose at me. "I am a *doctor*," she said, emphasizing the title, as if that answered my question. When I didn't respond, she explained, "It is my duty to help the sick."

"Like you helped my people?" Tiberius spat out.

"Yes," she reeled on him, eyes flaring with frustrated rage. "Exactly like I helped your people!"

"You enslaved-"

"Stop!" I shouted, stepping between them and pushing my hands out to keep them apart, particularly to keep Tiberius from getting closer to her. "Stop it, both of you." When Tiberius started to object again, I glared at him and interrupted, "Unless you intend to let my people die while you bicker?"

He directed his irate glare at me.

I lifted my eyebrows, and I kid you not, I channeled the queen's voice into my head when I thought about what to say. "You're on my ship, now. You follow my rules, my command. You are a *guest* aboard the *Sirius,* and I expect you to act accordingly." I turned and said to Claudia, "Both of you."

And I'll never admit this to the queen, but it worked! Neither objected this time. Tiberius backed away, though he didn't take his hand off of his weapon. Claudia folded her arms and looked down at me imperiously. But neither objected.

"Good," I nodded. "Naia, please provide medical access to the medbay's computers for Medici Claudia. No other access, and absolutely no privileged user access."

"Understood, Mika Kai," Naia replied dispassionately. "Please stand by..." A beat later, "Access granted."

The console in front of Claudia illuminated, and she set to work immediately.

Between her and the automated systems on the *Sirius,* a sort of tedious work set into motion, so I finished telling my story about our adventure on the moon. When I got to the part about Karina finding fuel tanks and cargo containers of raw material, Naia interjected and asked how much Karina saw. She tried to give her best estimate to the A.I.

Then, when I got to the part about shooting Caesar, twice, after he'd crushed my ankle, I realized two things.

First, my ankle didn't hurt anymore, and when we'd arrived on the *Sirius,* I didn't even bother with the cane anymore.

Second, I never verified that Caesar was, in fact, dead.

I shuddered.

I vowed to make sure he was dead when we went back down there. Plus, I had the feeling that Claudia and Naia both wanted to examine the alien's body.

I let Naia process my story, and I watched Claudia work. Tiberius never took his eyes off of the medici.

At one point, Jonnec sauntered over to me and leaned in to whisper, "We must talk about you calling this *your* ship, Mika." I skewered him with my best glower.

Finally, Naia said, "Mika Kai." Then she said nothing.

That was weird. "Naia?"

After another momentary pause, Naia continued. "I have estimated the amount of fuel and raw material that you and Karina Ticho have said was present in the *Alpha's* dome, and concluded that it could actually fuel both our fusion reactors and our stardrive for another century."

I lifted my eyebrows. "Damn. That little alien was industrious."

"You mean greedy," Karina rolled her eyes.

I thought about that for a second, and marveled at the idea that greed could be such a universal concept, even outside of the human species.

"However," Naia broke through my thoughts. "Even with the added raw material and supplies, and even with the added food and water reserves, seeds, and animals that the Omegas would bring with them, I do not believe that the *Sirius* can facilitate such a high influx of new occupants."

Tiberius looked specifically at me, surprise on his face. I lifted a halting hand – I had anticipated this conversation. Still, I asked Naia, "Why not?"

"Primarily due to the excessive damage incurred over the past six months, but also due to the sheer logistical challenge in bringing those individuals aboard."

"You promised," Tiberius growled at me.

"Hold on, Tibes," I said, and tried not to smile when he glowered at the nickname. "Trust me."

"Mika Kai…" Naia started.

"Naia," I interrupted. "I've thought a lot about this. First and foremost, this ship was designed to have one thousand crew members.

We're talking less than five hundred. Especially…" I hesitated and looked again at Tiberius. "Especially after the casualties they suffered yesterday."

"If they were actual crew members who could help maintain the ship's systems, then perhaps it would be viable," Naia said. "However, they are not."

"They're intelligent and resourceful people," I countered. "Some of them are pilots, some are mechanics, some are miners, some are cooks, some are farmers. They can contribute to every single aspect of our lives, Naia. And I made a promise, as Tiberius just pointed out." I looked at him intently. "I intend to fulfill that promise. We can enhance one another's cultures, teach each other new things, and learn to live with one another."

"Be that as it may," Naia said, "the dome was not designed for the additional strain the extra farming would place upon its soil, nor the strain that would be placed on the technology used to keep crops and animals healthy. Over time, we would over-farm the soil. You are right that the ship was designed for a crew of one thousand, but that crew was not meant to live off of the land of the dome. Food provisions would have been brought aboard, provisions designed to last decades, but not much longer. Even the *Sirius's* emergency food rations have expired and are no longer safe to consume."

"I might be able to help you with keeping crops and animals healthy and viable," Claudia interjected while hovering over Leif with a medical instrument. "I have some specialty in genetic modifications, and we had to alter our own crops and animals to survive and thrive on Ravenna."

I nodded at her, and then gave Tiberius an 'I told you she'd be useful' look.

Naia was silent for a full minute after that, and once again, I let that silence do the talking.

"Mika Kai," Naia's voice lamented, "this is not wise."

"Maybe, maybe not," I shrugged. "But in the long run, it doesn't matter."

Everyone stared at me. This was the moment. The big moment I had been waiting for. The one I had both looked forward to and dreaded. This was the conversation I'd rehearsed in my head repeatedly over the past twenty hours aboard the *Hope*.

"How does it not matter?" Jonnec asked.

I looked at him. At Karina. At Tiberius and Claudia, and at those lying upon medical beds surrounding us.

Then I looked up at the ceiling to address Naia. "Because this mission is over," I said. "Project Sirius has failed. The original social experiment that Duncan Kai forced on all of us lost its integrity, and things have spiraled *way* out of control." I lifted my eyebrows. "Am I wrong, Naia?"

There was only a slight pause before, "You are correct, Mika Kai."

I nodded. "There's also the fact that even if we use all of the raw mined metals and materials the Omegas bring to the table, it's unlikely we'll be able to repair the *Sirius* enough to drop the dome on a planet or moon, correct?"

"Again, you are correct, Mika Kai," Naia concurred. "We require a drydock facility to fully repair the *Sirius*."

"So the mission is a bust," I folded my arms. "Project Sirius is a bust. And we can't just keep floating through space, drifting by stars every four years until we run out of fuel again. Hellfire, not just can't, but I *won't* let us do that. So that really leaves only one other option."

Naia didn't reply at first. I waited patiently. The others, not so much. "What other option?" Karina asked. Laughing nervously, she said, "Mika, it sounds like there *are* no good options left!"

I shook my head, and then asked, "Naia, do you know what I'm suggesting?"

"I do," she said. "It is, in fact, a failsafe protocol in my programming. Unfortunately, I believe you are correct. There is no other alternative."

"What?" Jonnec asked impatiently. "What failsafe protocol, what option do we have left?"

I explained, "We get everyone and everything aboard. We refuel and repair the ship, enough that she can jump to F.T.L. again." I stepped closer to him, to Karina, and I unfolded my arms, and reached out a hand for both of theirs.

Karina uncertainly took my right hand. Jonnec looked at mine suspiciously, but then took my left hand with his prosthetic. I looked back and forth between them and willed my courage to say what needed to be said.

And my courage finally won out.

"It's time for the *Sirius* to return home."

DID YOU LIKE THIS BOOK?

Reader reviews play an important role in a book's success by helping other readers discover stories they might enjoy. Please consider taking a moment to leave a review for *The Alpha Expedition – Project Sirius Book 2* on Amazon! You'll be making this author's day :D

ABOUT THE AUTHOR

Jon Wasik has been telling stories since he was a little boy, usually with a cookie and milk at his Great Grandma's kitchen table. It wasn't until 5th grade that he finally put pen to paper, and from that moment on, writing has been his greatest passion.

When he isn't writing, Jon likes to read, play video games, and watch insanely geeky movies with his wife. His Gollum voice impressions are eerie, he quotes Doctor Who like others quote the bible, and he can leap terabytes of data in a single bound!

Want to find out more about Jon, or keep up on the latest news about his books? Check out his website, and while you're there, subscribe to his mailing list! Just go to the following website and click "Join Mailing List" at the top!
http://jonwasik.com/